With thanks to Steve Bullman for his help in kindling this Initiative; to Steve Roberts for expertly fanning the flames with his insight; and to Elizabeth Moseley for keeping the fire burning.

Copyright Dixie Dean 2024

Illustrator Elizabeth Moseley

TYLER'S INITIATIVE

Chapter One

New Year's Eve 1987

England's West country was in grave danger of developing gills.

Weeks of Atlantic rains had left its citizens floundering like bewildered amphibians in an ocean of cloud that had flattened every contour from the river Avon to the Solent. Not even Glastonbury Tor could keep its head above water.

And now, in an attempt to drown party night, a severe storm had struck havoc, leaving roofless buildings and fallen trees in its wake.

Through the dark, rolling hills, a clunking old Range Rover surfed the cascading torrents as it headed towards the market town of Marlsbury, where celebrations were defiantly attempting to keep afloat.

At the wheel, Tilda Bahnlich focused her cuckoo-clock features on the battle with debris and deluge. She was a forty-year-old ex-paramedic, late of Swiss rapid response units dispatched to international emergencies. For her, this was just work.

Beside her sat the fidgeting figure of Stephanie Star, a once stunningly beautiful woman. *The* face of the seventies some would have said. But alas, no more. Booze and other temptations frequenting the rich and famous had seen to that.

Right now, she was in a panic. Not from the driving conditions, although they weren't helping, but from the conditions her life had thrown up that were taking her to the edge as witnessed by the tortured face mirrored in the steamed-up windows. She was barely holding on.

Tilda was unfazed by any of it, the weather or her 'rogue' patient. She had been employed for her experience in such matters, many times having had to deal with traumatized people. Experience which ideally suited her character – unemotional and precise; perfect disciplines for nurse-maiding this once glamorous but now sadly drug-dependent supermodel at her side.

As they entered the town's circuitous one-way system, Tilda slowed the heavy vehicle to negotiate the narrow streets searching for a parking space. Losing patience, Stephanie seized her chance and leapt out into the night, leaving the door swinging as a wave goodbye. 'Yah yah,' Tilda muttered, stretching over to grab the door. 'Here we go again. No problem. I find you. Try not to fall over, huh?' she muttered to herself as Stephanie disappeared like an anorexic ghost between the fading Christmas decorations of two half-timbered shops.

This wasn't the first time Tilda had dealt with such situations in her position of nurse, minder, driver, caretaker. The overall aim of these duties being ostensibly to limit the amount of embarrassment Stephanie could heap on the family name of Ludlow. Her antics under the influence of drink and drugs went further than one paragraph in Marlsbury's local paper. Her driving violations had all made national front page tabloid news. Unless she cleaned up her act drastically, there was little hope she would ever be allowed behind a wheel again. That would go the way the catwalk had!

In recent weeks, an additional burden had been laid at Tilda's door; that of 'snitch'. Her employer, Edward Ludlow, Stephanie's husband, now was eager to know of his wife's every move. Who was she talking to? Who was she meeting? Phone calls, contacts, the lot. All of which added quite a load to Tilda's day. Others might have found these 'extras' to be an unreasonable imposition. But from day one, Tilda had seen that she was likely to be on call as with other emergency missions she had tackled, 24/7. She had accepted the conditions of the job with eyes wide open. The size of the fee she was being paid took the sting out of that.

However, she could not be at Stephanie's side every second of the day, as this latest visit to Marlsbury demonstrated. 'Take her wherever she wants to go, give her whatever she wants.' Within reason, of course. 'Keep her sweet. Try not to wind her up, but keep a close eye on her, especially in public.' Ludlow, her master's voice speaking. More resoundingly of late.

It was one of Stephanie's tricks to jump out of the car and disappear as she had just done. It didn't concern Tilda too much, because in Marlsbury, catching up with her was never a problem. The town centre was quite compact, and Stephanie would almost certainly be in one of the pubs, never making herself too difficult to find. She needed a lift home, after all. But why the screaming match to be taken into town tonight? In weather like this? It puzzled Tilda. No way was it to have a cozy drink with the locals and wish them Happy New Year. To score Drugs? Possibly. But Tilda never saw any real evidence of that happening and certain drugs could be found back at the house if in dire need. Yes, but always under a strictly controlled regime, which got up Stephanie's nose for a different reason!

These thoughts teased Tilda as she shunted around the narrow streets seeking a parking spot. It seemed half the county had braved the weather for a night out or had got stranded in town because of it. She decided it would have to be the small car park that had once housed cattle pens on market days. Spaces could usually be found there.

Tilda guessed there must still be a glimmer of ego lurking somewhere within Stephanie, driving a need to be out in public and be recognized; idolized, as she once had been. But these days, she was a mess. A very recognizable mess. Did the mirror ever lie? Well, apparently it did for Stephanie Star. One of the roots of her problems?

For her husband, these trips into Marlsbury, which had become more frequent in recent months, had coincided with other signs of a change in Stephanie's behaviour. And not for the good, he would have gambled. She had become more secretive along with her growing paranoia. Instinct told him she was up to something.

Tilda had also noticed a change. But to her, it was a brooding introspection. There had been fewer hysterical outbursts of late, apart from the one levelled at her husband most recently that really shook the house. She had been hurling all sorts of abuse and threats at him as well as anything she could lay her hands on. Was it because he was to be off on one of his international travels again? Today? New Year's Eve of all days? She doubted it. They had never even sat down together for a meal to Tilda's knowledge. In her experience, Stephanie was only too happy when her husband went away on a trip. Who knew what was behind this latest outburst. And tonight, she seemed even more on edge than usual? The driving conditions had little to do with it, Tilda was sure.

Since taking up the post some months ago, she had spent much more time with Stephanie than had Ludlow himself. Almost exclusively, in fact. She had learned straight off that the pair did not sleep together, not difficult to work out that there was a 'situation' between them.

Apart from introversion, Tilda saw loneliness. On more than one occasion she had found Stephanie in silent tears, deep in thought, as if in a trance. She was one very troubled woman.

Tilda could also see the stress that had infiltrated her employer's usual flamboyant manner in past weeks. His bounce had gone. Bags had appeared under his normally bright eyes. Lack of sleep? Even his wavy hair wouldn't sit up. She knew this latest trip to Kenya was something of a big deal for him. The BBC were covering his visit. That wouldn't be making him edgy. Tilda knew that much about him. He thrived on publicity. No, if it was stress, Stephanie had to be behind it.

At last, she found somewhere to park in the old cattle market, if not perhaps quite legally. It was at the end of a line. But other cars could still get by, just about. Would anyone be out checking at approaching 10pm on New Year's Eve? Surely not. It seemed a fair gamble.

Corfu was two hours ahead of UK time as British Airways flight 055 to Nairobi over-flew the island. 'Good evening, ladies and gentlemen,' the captain announced to his full payload of passengers, 'I trust you all enjoyed your last meal of 1987 and are settling back comfortably with a complimentary drink. For your information, it is almost exactly midnight on the ground below us, so I would like to take the opportunity of wishing you all a happy, healthy, and prosperous New Year on behalf of myself, the crew and British Airways. Happy Year!'

At that, certain sections of the buzzing Boeing 747 broke into spontaneous, if not melodic, strains of Auld Lang Syne.

In the tourist cabin, not only singing rocked the Jumbo. Some be-kilted Scottish holidaymakers out for adventure on safari danced jigs in the aisles like gay Gordons about to do battle with the Masai, kissing every stewardess and game steward up for grabs.

In the first-class cabin, vintage champagne bottles were shedding their corks with equal abandon. As one of the stewardesses made ready to fill the glass of perhaps the most illustrious passenger on board, Edward Ludlow, who tonight looked more than his 45 years as he sat shoulders hunched, which tended to exaggerate his executive paunch.

The captain spoke again. 'There's one more thing I'm delighted to announce while you contemplate your new year's resolutions. We have a very special passenger travelling with us today. I'm sure many of you noticed all the cameras surrounding him at Heathrow earlier today and the television team on board with us. That passenger is of course Mr. Edward Ludlow, and it is my pleasure to reveal that in the New Year's Honours' List today he is to receive a Knighthood. Your good health, Sir! Congratulations. And thank you for choosing British Airways.'

Murmurings circulated the economy section as the captain went on: 'Some of you will perhaps have read in the newspapers that this trip to Kenya marks another special advent for Sir Edward; the launch of the 100th pump donated to Africa by SODA, the charity he founded. 'Stamp Out Drought in Africa', which British Airways strongly supports. So, on behalf of myself and the crew, Sir, I would like to say that British Airways are once again proud to have you with us on this particularly auspicious day.'

A smattering of applause graced the first-class cabin. With heads turning toward Ludlow, he straightened up, pulled his sagging midriff in and bowed his head graciously, feeling more himself to have the polite attention.

The attention Stephanie Star received when she charged into the crowded King's Head public house five minutes after leaping from the Range Rover was not quite the same, apart from heads turning. Conversation lulled. It wasn't so much that a stranger had entered the bar - everyone in Marlsbury along with the whole country knew Stephanie Star - more that until recently she had not taken to showing her celebrated face in town so often, let alone inside the pub that won all the awards for being the seediest in the county. The sort of pub that catered for the great unwashed. Bikers with torn leathers and earrings. The long-haired and scalped alike; the tattooed and toothless. Wayward youth and ageing hippies all came from far and wide to gather at the King's Head, especially at weekends. It had become a Mecca for the downtrodden. A traveller's rest. To have Stephanie Star, one-time sophisticated model and wife of the most notable man this side of Belgravia choose to visit it on New Year's Eve, came as a shock even to spaced-out rock and rollers like this lot. Surely, the murmur went, a woman of her means could find a cozier place to score? Why else would she show up here? She couldn't pick up much more than pills and smoke here. None of the hard stuff she was spoken of being on, if you could believe what you read in the papers.

Seeing her in the flesh, you *could* believe it. She was hardly recognizable as the Stephanie Star the world had known and loved, once seen on every fashion magazine cover from New York to Paris. The nation's sweetheart. Now look at her. Within the space of a year or so, she had become a monument to the worst the eighties had thrown up, greed, famine, over-indulgence and the blind eye.

The blind eye. She had turned that on herself enough times, sometimes with the encouragement of her marriage-weary husband. Early in her rise to fame, the boost to her ego was the only *high* she needed. Inevitably, perhaps, as the shine of being at the top began to dull, she succumbed more and more to the artificial replacements that were always easy to come by in the wild world she had captivated.

Inevitably, the drugs eventually took a grip. In her more lucid moments, she could see what she was doing to herself. 'It's okay, I can manage it,' she would tell herself one moment. The next, 'Got to stop.' And so it went, until she hated the filthy stuff, and loved it; needed it! There was no sense bleating about it. The milk had been spilt. Many times over. Forget treatments. None of them worked. None of the substitutes, controlled like a metronome by the unbending Swiss woman who had been dumped on her in recent months like a torture rack. But through the haze of paranoia and cravings, Stephanie had come to accept that it was either putting up with Tilda Bahnlich, or the real threat of being committed. It was *that* serious. She knew it. She was a no-hoper. A drip-feed case and she had been 'losing it' lately. Her fits of rage came like a blitz of short circuits somewhere in her head and scared her to death. Something new had brought these on. She needed help. Booze didn't do it. That was another mountain to climb. She could drink herself to oblivion, but it would only throw a temporary veil over her real problems. That of losing the plot and with it her youth. Running close, her will to live.

Her youth, her looks and the fame that had gone with them. Nothing could bring them back. The money she had accumulated somewhere down the line had always been secondary, wherever her 'fuck' of a husband had hidden it. Just give her back those years. The good times.

A superstar at 17, washed up at 34. Some show! Was that it? Game over, with the will to live torn from her? No. Not now. Things had changed. After years of looking no further than the mirror, something had jumped out at her and grabbed her by the throat.

Conscience.

Out of her dark past, a monster had risen.

Guilt.

Tilda was feeling a twinge of guilt herself for parking so 'untidily' as she legged it from the car park. But she doubted to be in town very long once she had located Stephanie. That's how it usually went. There were two pubs she usually frequented, albeit briefly. The Turk's Anchor was the nearer from where she had parked. So that first. Then The King's Head.

It was in the latter of these into which Stephanie had staggered and now stood impervious to the silent ripples her unexpected arrival had created. She hovered on the threshold for several moments rubber-necking the motley ensemble like a punch-drunk Judy. As might be expected on New Year's Eve, the place was crowded. Too crowded? Was she having second thoughts about making it to the bar? After more seconds of scrutiny, she seemed to have overcome her doubts. Anxiety drained from her face, and she lurched forward, her rain-soaked hair flat to her head, bouncing unsteadily off people and chairs in her dripping oilskin.

Her rat-trap memory of ensuing events was a jumble of paranoia. She had barely got halfway to the bar when she tripped and fell headlong in spectacular fashion. Was it her own clumsy fault? She didn't think so. A perverse perception of humanity made her think someone had stuck out a foot just for the pleasure of seeing her fall flat on her face. No one laughed, however. Precious drinks had been sent flying.

'Shit!' she grunted, finding herself pressed against a female leg which happened to be completely bare from toe to crutch.

'You alright, Steph?' the owner of the leg asked with genuine concern, using the familiar 'Steph', which reminded Stephanie that she had once belonged to everyone. She didn't know the bare-legged woman, but she appreciated the helping hand.

'I've tried that technique myself, but it doesn't work with this bunch,' Joked Janet Tomlinson, a well-known fixture in the Marlsbury night spots. She wore a gypsy smile beneath her gypsy hair. And tonight, being New Year's Eve and party time, that was about all apart from her flesh-coloured leotard. This was so tight-fitting; she might just as well have wrapped herself in cling film. It was the sort of garment a fun girl might wear as a bet. And if you couldn't have fun on New Year's Eve, when could you?

Stephanie steadied herself, throwing glances like poisoned darts at anyone who might dare to grin at her downfall. All she got in return were a few good-natured raised glasses as if to say: 'Welcome to the club!' It was the sort of pub where falling down was no stranger.

But there was at least one regular visitor present who didn't belong to that club, it could safely be said. Someone who had possibly never even touched a drop of alcohol; a Salvation Army Officer doing her usual collection rounds, armed to her teeth with War Cry's.

Stephanie eventually caught on that she was making a fool of herself. She was used to being looked at, but not like these looks. Her mood seemed to do a somersault. In a profusion of apologies, she fished into her purse and pushed a five-pound note into Janet Tomlinson's hand. 'For the drinks,' she spluttered with a vague wave at the mess she had caused.

Janet pulled a face as if to say: 'Hey! Big spender. That's way too much. But, OK. You can afford it.'

Stephanie now found the diminutive Salvation Army woman facing her sympathetically, as if come to offer a helping hand. To the astonishment of those still watching, another fiver was pulled out and pushed through the purpose-built hole in the collection box. Some penitence, Steph!

The recipient looked Stephanie directly in the eye as if assessing her condition. Seemingly satisfied she wasn't about to keel over again, the caring Salvation Army woman gave a smile and nodded. It was a generous donation. Was this a soul to be saved? The smile seemed to suggest there was always a chance. A folded copy of the 'War Cry' was thrust forward into Stephanie's hand.

At that very moment, all hell broke loose in the pub. Every door flew open and within seconds the place was swarming with police and sniffer dogs.

Chapter Two

'Congratulations, Sir,' a stewardess said, echoing the captain's words, champagne bottle in hand standing over newly Knighted Edward Ludlow.

'Well, thank you,' he replied with a gracious nod.

The 747 hit a pocket of turbulence, making the stewardess crouch deftly to steady herself. It took four of five efforts to fill Ludlow's glass, but despite the awkward balancing act, drinks' tray in hand, she lost not a drop, nor let her smile slip.

If only his wife had the same poise and control, Ludlow was thinking, a nightmarish vision of his domestic situation hitting him momentarily.

When the turbulence had eased, the stewardess stretched her legs again. 'You must get plenty of exercise like that!' Ludlow joked, breaking into a bright but lop-sided grin since his teeth, a sparkling mouthful of them, were conspicuously uneven. This gave him a jaunty look that suggested remnants of his early tearaway years still lurked within him. However, his bushy eyebrows needed constant attention these days to help compliment that image.

He touched glasses with the man sitting beside him, whose accompanying chuckle struck the stewardess as disguising something vaguely obscene.

This was Victor Rose. Charm was not his strongest point; never had been. Something that Ludlow made good use of on occasion. Right hand man perhaps better described where Rose figured in his master's inner circle.

They had known each other a long time.

Almost immediately after the captain had finished his announcements, the BBC film crew arrived from economy with their cumbersome equipment, looking harassed and more than slightly the worst for wear. The director himself, Simon Dickson, was wiry and alert compared to his technicians, but plainly nervous. One look told Ludlow he was a worrier, the nit-picking kind. In his green velvet suit with his sun-tanned face, Dickson looked more like a holidaymaker than a hardy television producer enroute to the heat and dust of Northern Kenya to document the unveiling of a water pump donated by the S.O.D.A. Charity. He somehow didn't fit the bill.

Once his camera crew had set up, a painfully bright light was switched on and a crouching Dickson looked up from his notes to put a rather wordy question to start the interview.

'We'll soon be landing in Kenya, where later in the day you'll be inaugurating the 100th water pump donated by your charity, SODA. To coincide with that, today marks your elevation to knighthood. A big day indeed, Sir Edward. Can you share some of your thoughts right now with us? Describe to us how you feel, what this means to you?'

Ludlow assumed a mildly serious look, chin down, pursed lips, deep-set hazel eyes staring unblinkingly out from under the protective shade he was managing to create with his bushy eyebrows. He was putting to full use his ability to project a sense of benign solidity, an ability he had developed early in his life to help convince influential people they could put their trust in him. The entrepreneurial flamboyancy of his youth had called for it more then, perhaps, but he still drew upon it when a close-up lens was focussed on him. Old habits die hard.

As Ludlow began his reply, his expression lightened. He raised his penetrating eyes and looked about humbly as if searching for the right words to describe his gratitude. 'Oh. Utterly and completely taken aback. Speechless. Elated. Deeply honoured, of course, to be thought worthy of a Knighthood. But at the same time, hopeful that it will serve to bring to more people's notice the continuing desperate fight to Stamp Out Drought in Africa, if I might use the very words of the charity's aims.'

He stopped, lowering his chin again to cut down the glare in his eyes. Dickson, who in the great tradition of television interviewers had been silently encouraging the words out with punctuating nods, seemed hesitant. He took a moment to make his next point.

'Sir Edward,' he began, 'do you see yourself taking more of a back seat now you've received today's recognition?'

Ludlow pursed his lips, frowning as if confused. 'How do you mean *back seat*? Sorry, I'm not with you.'

'Well, sir,' Dickson went on unabashed, thinking it was a straightforward question, wasn't it? 'You have devoted much of your personal time to carrying out your charity's aims, and ....'

'Of course.'

'I think I'm right in saying that you have personally overseen the delivery and installation of practically every pump that's been donated throughout Africa, which, of course, has been very time consuming. Do you not see yourself delegating such tasks to someone else from now on? I mean, always personally attending these events takes up your time, not to mention the expense?'

Ludlow could see where this question might be leading. He forced himself to brighten. 'Tell you why,' he gesticulated with open palms. 'I'm still far too young and selfish to delegate. And I can assure you that I cover all the travel costs myself. I *never* eat into the charity's funds, if that's what you're being so bold to infer?' Dickson made to deny this, but Ludlow went on. 'Yes, it's time consuming and however far it takes me, the excitement of the villagers is more than payment, most rewarding to witness. Worth all the time and effort spent. I wouldn't miss those experiences for the world.'

There was a slightly awkward pause, then Dickson asked: 'So Africa can count on your continuing hands-on leadership of SODA?'

'Naturally. Onward and upward!'

'So you don't see your many business interests syphoning your energy away from SODA?' Dickson had been rehearsing the use of the intended pun.

'Not at all. On the contrary. I have an excellent team around me, quite capable of handling my business affairs without too much interference from me. Probably better, if truth be known.' Ludlow joked, with that uneven smile in evidence.

Another uncomfortable pause ensued before Dickson spoke again. He seemed worried he might be labouring a point and Ludlow could see that he was.

'Do you not think that your, shall I call it, city sense might have had something to do with your being knighted? You have had what could be termed meteoric success in that field in the past few years.'

Ludlow was quick to answer this not-so-subtle change of tack.

'I put some of my success in the city down to luck, but most of it to the inspired judgement of my financial advisors. It's a quaint notion, but I don't suppose anyone has ever been knighted for taking good advice.' He chuckled and shifted in his seat, catching a glimpse of the stewardess's constant smile before settling back into his studied pose.

'Perhaps you're being too modest, sir. After all, your management skills are renowned. Your sensitive handling of the potentially explosive industrial relations situation during the Marlsbury-Higwell merger two years ago did not go unnoticed in government corridors at a time when take-overs and insider dealings were very much under scrutiny.'

Ludlow was wondering whether the next question would be to delve deeper into the reasons his holdings had held up so firmly in the wake of the crippling stock market crash of a few months earlier. But no outsiders would ever be privy to that information, least of all on camera.

'Thank you for the compliment,' Ludlow finally responded, chuckling again. This time more ironically, 'I mean, it was *meant* as a compliment, wasn't it? But I cannot go along with what you are inferring any more than I can completely endorse what you say about the handling of the merger. Sadly, not everyone at the Marlsbury plant looked favourably upon the move, as I'm sure you remember. Jobs had to go. That still haunts me. But I have to say, most of those displaced were properly compensated. But let it not be forgotten the benefit it has brought to the unemployed of Manchester.' He turned for support and got a nod from Victor Rose, who was out of the shot. The cameraman tried to follow Ludlow's glance but missed the moment. Ludlow cannily waited. As soon as the lens was focused on him again, he adopted his look of profound sincerity and went on: 'No, I believe my knighthood is for more enlightened reasons than my being able to talk management sense.' He cleared his throat and for once it appeared Dickson was about to respond without delay, but Ludlow gave him no chance. 'And I must state here and now that I accept this honour on behalf of every SODA stamp holder who ever donated to the Charity. It's theirs as much as mine. So, I would like to give a big 'Thank you' to everyone who sails under the SODA flag.'

He turned his eyes directly into the camera lens for that final remark so there could be no doubt he was calling the interview to an end. The novelty of it had worn off. Dickson was trying to make more out of this than straight background material for a documentary about the plight of a remote African village.

'OK. Cut it there,' Simon Dickson said after a second or two, rising awkwardly. He had wanted to continue, but his uncomfortable position did its bit to stop him. He could tell Ludlow had had enough and he didn't want to rub him up the wrong way so early in the shoot.

'Thank you, Sir Edward,' he said, as sincerely as possible.

'My pleasure,' Ludlow lied congenially, reclaiming his champagne glass before asking suggestively: 'You'll cut out the boring business talk, I hope? You'll have 'em switching channels straight away otherwise.' He chuckled through his jaunty grin.

'It'll add a nice personal touch to the build-up,' the whippet-like Dickson uttered without the slightest hint of enthusiasm. 'I have more questions. Perhaps tomorrow…?'

'Good!' Ludlow butted in, cutting short the imminent request. He turned his gaze to the cameraman and sound recordist: 'Sorry chaps, can't offer you any champagne,' he apologized, raising his glass to them. 'IATA rules, I'm afraid. Cheers!'

The TV trio shuffled off with a reminder from Dickson that they would be on the tarmac in the morning to film his arrival. 'We don't want to miss the reception party, so perhaps you could be sure we get down the steps before you?'

There was no conviction in the nod Ludlow gave him.

With them gone, Ludlow turned to his travelling companion: 'Was I imagining it, or was the man trying to make me say things I didn't want to say?'

Victor Rose was a few years younger than his boss, although his overly short hair had receded further. He was big-boned and athletic looking, with remarkably clear blue eyes even with the copious amounts of champagne he had recently consumed. He dressed with uncompromising neatness, perhaps to offset his untidy facial features, which, reflecting his character, were hard and not quite straight. Rose was one of Ludlow's two personal 'secretaries', the one who was never required to type. He arranged things, smoothed the way protectively, was a very efficient gofer. Ludlow found him indispensable on trips abroad.

'You weren't imagining it,' Rose replied, shaking his hammer thrower's head pensively. 'I looked at his notes. The nosy sod was even going to question you about that wonderful wife of yours!'

At that precise moment, his not so wonderfully disposed wife was being questioned by officers of the county drug squad in The Kings Head, Marlsbury. Angie, one of the three sniffer dogs on duty to do their thing was feeling very pleased with herself after a brief sniff of Stephanie's purse. She let out an excited yelp then sat down obediently, tail a-wag, tongue flapping like The Laughing Policeman before being rewarded with a pat of the head and taken off to sniff elsewhere. Two young police officers were left to deal with the purse owner. When told to hand it over, Stephanie grasped it tightly to her body in rejection of the demand. After a few well-chosen swear words, she concluded her outburst with an oft repeated mantra when finding herself on the defensive: 'Don't you know who I am?' The muttering answer she received was equally familiar: 'No, but we know who you used to be!' which set her off again in a rant of Yorkshire-tinged expletives which even made Angie turn her head. Where the fuck was Tilda? She could usually sought this sort of thing out.

The officers had to do their job, so, being non-compliant with the request to come quietly, Stephanie was man-handled as gently as possible from the pub to the awaiting black maria. She didn't make it easy for them. Gently it wasn't. More chairs and drinks went flying care-of her flaying legs. By comparison, other law-enforcement proceedings underway were going on as smoothly as quiz night.

The situation outside was no better for the young policemen. Stephanie was struggling so much they couldn't get her into the black maria without fear of injuring her. There were too many witnesses to think of forcing the issue. Quite a crowd had gathered to enjoy the show. Fortunately for Stephanie, one of those rushing to find out what was going on was Tilda. Seeing the flashing lights outside the pub, she had quickened her pace to get there. When she saw Stephanie causing the rumpus, she feared the worst. 'What has the *dummkopf* done now?' she asked herself. With that number of police vehicles clogging the streets, it seemed like over-kill. She had no idea a general drug bust was going on until she got closer. Stephanie just happened to be the first person pulled out. Others were about to follow, more compliantly, however.

'Wait!' Tilda shouted, rushing to confront the situation. 'Stop, please.' By the time she had reached the officers restraining Stephanie, she was waving an identity card and an official looking document. A senior officer was clearly impressed when he studied them. 'This woman is my responsibility,' Tilda explained, in near perfect English. 'She is in my care. Please explain to me what she has done.'

The officer turned to the young men struggling with Stephanie, lifting his chin as if hoping for the right answer. 'Resisting arrest, sir,' it came, so perfectly in unison that if it hadn't been for the time and place, it would have sounded comic, something straight out of a Gilbert and Sullivan operetta. Neither of them could have been long out of his teens. New recruits?

One of them added quickly; 'Drug possession, sir.'

'This woman is on a recovery program,' Tilda stated authoritatively. 'She is allowed certain drugs as part of that program, Please to show me which drugs you have found in her possession.'

Stephanie had ceased to struggle now. The offending arms had released her. She now wore a smug but impatient expression. The two officers looked at each other as if not wanting to be the one to answer. 'Angie, the dog, gave a positive response, sir,' one of them explained, looking at the senior officer for support. 'The lady wouldn't hand over her purse, sir.' The other ventured his support.

'And why should she?' Tilda jumped in. 'She had every right to protect her personal possessions not to be searched in public by male officers.'

'But we weren't going....' About to protest, they were not quite in unison this time.

'Please bring a female officer if you should wish to search Mrs. Ludlow's purse,' Tilda demanded. 'We can clear this matter up here and now.' Tilda was quite sure Stephanie had had no chance to score drugs in the short time she could have been in the pub. She guessed what 'Angie' had sniffed was the *lingering* smell of drugs, nothing more. Tilda always made a clean sweep of Stephanie's pockets and bags before taking her out in public as part of the regime put at her door to lessen the chances of bad publicity besmirching the family name.

With no drugs being found, and Tilda officiously in control of her charge with convincing paperwork, Stephanie was released with nothing more than a verbal reprimand for unruly behaviour.

However, the incident made the pages of a number of national tabloids, spiced by a photograph some lucky punter had managed to capture of Stephanie in full fury as she resisted being shoved into the black maria.

Sir Edward Ludlow would not learn of his wife's latest escapade until the news spread around the globe in diminishing copy over the next couple of days. But it added weight to his misgivings about allowing the BBC into his life while so much turmoil surrounded his personal life.

'Better put Dickson straight about the sort of documentary I agreed to make before we go much further,' Ludlow said for Rose's ears only over the hum of the 747. 'I'm beginning to wonder if agreeing to it was a wise move.'

'I second that opinion after listening to that prick. I was just about to call it a wrap, but you beat me to it.' Rose revealed in Queen's English.

Rose was well spoken, despite his coarseness of style. Oxbridge, some would have thought. But he had never seen the inside of a university college, not to study, at least. He had gone to the same public school as Ludlow, for whom he had 'fagged' with few complaints during his first year. That period had laid a solid foundation for their future relationship.

Academically, Victor Rose was a total failure. But in no way was he 'thick', except of limb. The term had not been coined in those days within the cloistered walls of Marlsbury Public School, but Rose was 'street wise' before his day. His final report upon being expelled in the middle of his fourth year described him as 'having animal cunning with criminal tendencies'. He had pulled many stunts at school, most of them at Ludlow' behest, had shown maniacal daring on occasion to the admiration of less adventurous pupils. But his vain attempt to remove the chapel bell without detection had proved his ultimate downfall. And the bell's! It had been far heavier than he had imagined, and it had never rung out so loudly as when landing on the quadrangle flagstones. He left the school in silently revered disgrace eventually to find his vocation in a profession that openly welcomed his talent for tackling the perilous; that of stuntman for action films. And thence, with Ludlow's business interests expanding into certain areas that could use those talents, Rose advanced to his current position of right-hand man, minder.

At school, by far the most demanding tests Master Edward had laid at young Victor's door, not only called for extra limits of guile and daring but introduced the fag to a practice he would come to employ with regularity in later life when he wanted to get his own way; namely, the threat of violence.

And he was always ready to put it to use.

'Impress upon our green BBC man exactly what's what,' Ludlow uttered, running a hand through his wavy brown hair that was showing signs of greying at the temples. 'Mergers and matrimony have got nothing to do with charity! We've agreed to a documentary about drought and pumps, not to a bloody soap opera! Like me, the world must be fed up to the teeth with my dear wife's shenanigans! Tell him she's a no-go area!'

At that moment the stewardess appeared with a damp cloth and towel. Sir Edward had been perspiring under the heat of the television lamp.

'Thank you very much, Veronica,' he said with sincerity, glancing at the name tag on her uniform. 'You're taking extremely good care of me, if I may say so. You wouldn't care to run away with me and make a fresh start, would you?' It was light-hearted flirtation to help take his mind off other things for a moment.

She had noted that he liked attention. Indeed, seemed to expect it. First class travel did that to some people. The flirting, too. She offered him a matronly look to remind him he was a married man even if unhappily so, as gossip columnists were forever suggesting.

'What would your good Lady say, eh?' Veronica joked, showing her sweetest smile. She had received as many such alcohol-induced offers at five miles high as she had served micro-wave dinners.

She was still managing her sweet smile six hours later as the passengers disembarked at Nairobi Airport.

The early morning African air was scented with fruity warmness, a blessing after the controlled atmosphere of the jumbo.

The sun had not yet risen, but a golden glow was lifting the eastern horizon.

As Ludlow walked down from the plane looking fresh and relaxed, he completely missed Veronica's final attentions as flashbulbs and television lights cut holes in the languid dawn.

'Welcome to Kenya, Sir Edward! Congratulations and a Happy New Year!' Mr. Solomon Kirini, the Junior Agricultural Minister beamed, grabbing Ludlow's hand. 'The Minister apologizes for not being here personally. He hopes you will find time in your itinerary to drop by his office.'

'Of course. Of course. All in good time.' Ludlow replied, quite happy to accept the perfunctory offer. He had more often dealt with Kirini than the man above him just mentioned, and things had been working out just fine. 'I'll leave it to you to decide if there's time. And thank you for coming to meet me yourself. It is always good to see an old friend.'

They exchanged warm smiles for the cameras.

'I trust you had a comfortable flight. Got some rest?'

'Absolutely. I was well looked after.'

'As you know, you have quite an exhausting day ahead of you.'

'I would want it no other way.'

Solomon Kirini turned to introduce the rest of the welcoming party to more flashing bulbs. As he did so, Simon Dickson's ragged TV crew barged their way to the front not to miss one word or handshake. Dickson was visibly pissed off. Ludlow had ignored his request to let the film crew get off before him.

Most of the people greeting him were known to Ludlow. The last of these most of all. Ernest McKintosh, S.O.D.A.'s main organizer in Kenya. They greeted each other warmly.

'What would we all do without this man?' Ludlow declared expansively, turning to Solomon Kirini. 'Now I know everything is under control.'

Ernest McKintosh was indeed a reassuring figure. Six feet seven inches of imposing Masai pedigree, with a long handsome face full of compassion, a quality that some people had learned could turn like a cheetah.

Limousines were waiting to take the party to the Norfolk Hotel. A flight to the site of the new pump had been arranged for later that day.

'Sorry, boss,' Ernest apologized. 'You'll only have a few hours' rest before we have to leave. But we don't have to stay too long up there. We'll be back before nightfall.'

'We'll survive, Ernest,' Ludlow replied, swelling his lungs in an unconscious effort to make his five feet eleven measure up to the vast size of his colleague. 'First a shower and a freshen up. Then you must tell me how things have been going in Nairobi.'

Chapter Three

For Peter Tyler things were going much the same as ever as he shuffled to his garden workshop that first morning of 1988. His prospects could have been better, as could the wet weather hanging over Newton Stoat, the small village where he lived.

Selecting one of two keys, he jiggled it into the padlock securing the top half of the split door. Right first time. It sprang open. Bang! Ludlow was dead. An evens chance.

It was a stupid game he had been playing for two years. Ever since losing his job at Marlsbury Pumps. More correctly, ever since being forced onto the dole by Ludlow. He could only guess why the door was in two halves. Had a horse been kept there once upon a time? He released the other lock and went inside. He knew he should mark the keys and let the past go.

It was 6.45 am.

Inside his workshop, he switched on the power. A blow heater hummed into existence from a corner as a single neon strip spat and flickered before liberating its lumens.

Gently at first, he set about his morning session, stretching limbs and spine, touching toes with legs as taut as rods. Nothing too strenuous. Just a general loosening up before starting a more rigorous routine using his personal gymnasium. This was a self-built scaffold-like contraption bolted to the wall with all manner of exercise options built into it. He was proud of that.

At 7.30, in an effusive sweat, he took to deep breathing exercises for five minutes before rattling off forty plank-stiff press-ups.

This exercise mania had started for want of something to do with himself when he had found himself out of work. It had soon become part of his daily life, almost to the point of ritual. Now he was wondering how he could do proper justice to the racing bike he had bought himself in better times.

During the winter months, it hung like a glittering trophy from the central beam of the workshop ceiling, only ever coming down for special occasions, apart from being oiled and cleaned. When out riding it, he often fantasized about entering the 'Tour de France' one day. Just daydreaming.

He wasn't really into competitive racing. Best was when it was just him and his old mountain bike against the clock. But first, it was always his exercise bike, which is what he jumped onto next. He slowly wound it up until his taut leg muscles were gorging on energy like after burners.

When it was over, he collapsed in a panting spasm of satisfaction. Aglow with exhaustion.

It was only just getting light outside.

His workshop was about the size of a double garage. Brick built, cold in summer as well as winter. No-one knew for sure what its original purpose had been. Obviously not for cars. The door wasn't big enough and there was no direct access from the road. There was a solid but shallow glazed sink with dimpled sides and a single tap in one corner, but nothing else suggested the place had been meant for human habitation. Especially the door being in two halves. He had run the electricity supply in himself from the junction box in the house some forty or so yards away, quite safely, if not quite legally. He was good with circuits and wires thanks to his apprenticeship at Marlsbury Pumps.

The workshop was his place. It said a lot about him. He had virtually lived in it from the moment his father had turned it into a 'playroom' for him years ago: 'The perfect place for you to let off steam, my lad.' He had been a mischievous child. A real handful, but so lovable; so inquisitive. 'Stop you pulling the house to bits.'

One day, to give his lad a challenge, his father had brought home a model airplane kit, not really the sort meant for a child, a quite complicated radio-controlled model. A proper flyer once completed. It was pure inspiration. It transformed 'fidget features', as his parents lovingly called him, overnight.

Young Peter had submerged himself in its complexities, finishing it with a few rough edges, but with no fatherly help whatsoever. After that, another one. Then another, even more complicated. It was like magic. They had harnessed the lad's hyper-activity.

His love for constructing kits had never left him. Since then, he had even graduated into designing them. In fact, in the past two years of being out of a proper job, his hobby had turned into a useful side-line. People paid him to build models for them. He had become an expert.

Seven years of advanced engineering study care-of Marlsbury Pumps had added precision to his natural flair, and eventually led him to exploit his aptitude for invention. He was developing something far more ambitious than airframes plain and simple. He didn't have the right word to describe it, yet. It wasn't fixed wing, nor exactly a helicopter. And he didn't see it as being a *toy*. He had bigger ideas for it, although he felt sure it was something that every model aircraft fanatic would want. What he was going to call it was his initiative: 'Tyler's Initiative'. One day it would make his name and he would strike it rich.

Having so much free time did have its compensations, he had come to accept.

At 9.30, after two slices of toast and a mug of tea, other amenities his workshop offered for convenience, he locked up and sloshed his way back up to the house.

The garden was a magnificent mess. Half an acre of organic wilderness. He hadn't touched it in the three years since his father died. It was so overgrown with brambles and ivy, that even in winter his workshop couldn't be seen from the house.

'It's only me, mum,' he shouted as he wiped the mud from his trainers. 'I'll be up in a minute.'

Twenty minutes later, he backed into his mother's bedroom carrying her breakfast on a tray. He lifted her up and surrounded her with pillows and cushions. A television glowed at the foot of the bed with some sort of talking heads show. The sound was off.

'Are you actually watching that, Mum?'

'Keeps me company.'

He put the tray on the bed table and swung it round in front of her. 'Tea up,' he said, perkily.

'Lovely,' she uttered gerbil-like. 'A nice cup of tea.'

She was frail these days. Barely into her sixties but riddled with chronic arthritis. It scared him sometimes. Genetics and all that. One day he could end up like it.

'Dad wouldn't have let you leave the box on if you weren't watching it,' He pretended to reprimand her with a mock swipe about a foot above her head. 'Splat!'

She didn't notice.

'It warms the room up.'

The room didn't need warming up. It was stifling. The heaters had been on all night, and she wouldn't sleep with the windows open. A musty smell of old inactivity and stale sherry pervaded. He hadn't bothered to tidy up after their New Year's celebrations the night before. Two unfinished glasses of Harvey's Bristol Cream marked that occasion, standing beside a half-finished box of Quality Street chocolates on the dressing table.

'I'll just let some fresh air in for a few minutes.'

She didn't argue.

After opening a window, he spread a slice of toast for her, cutting it into convenient sizes to save her the battle. It was struggle enough for her to pick the pieces up. Painful to watch. Marmalade going everywhere.

Sitting down beside her, he picked up the TV remote control and switched to teletext news.

The first thing he saw was like a punch in the stomach. For a second, he was back at the Marlsbury Pump closure demonstrations. On the screen was a rundown of the New Year Honours' List. One name jumped out at him.

'I don't believe it!' he exclaimed, a frown creasing his forehead. Bristling, he ran a hand over his cropped hair.

'See what they've done? They've given Ludlow a bloody Knighthood! What a diabolical joke after what he's done to Marlsbury!' His thin lips disappeared into his pinched mouth for a second. 'For charity work, it says. Good that, isn't it? Who couldn't be charitable with all the money he's made from wheeling and dealing with people's lives?'

His mother was hardly listening. A piece of toast had fallen onto the bedclothes: 'Bugger it!' she croaked, trying vainly to scoop it up.

The sight of her struggling brought him back to reality.

'Here, mum, like this.' He threaded a fork into her crooked fingers before cleaning up the mess with a cloth. 'We make a good pair, don't we?' He grinned with resignation.

Breakfast done, he took a shower, puffing like a leaking boiler as he thought about the Honours' List. One minute putting people out of work, the next getting knighted. Where was the charity in that?

After drying himself, he got into his riding gear. The elasticated material fitted so tightly over his lean frame; the muscles could be counted through it.

Oh well, he was thinking, I suppose it shouldn't have been too much of a surprise. S.O.D.A. did good work around the world. He couldn't argue with that. But most of the donations came from the generosity of the public and from companies buying into its discount stamp scheme. Not a penny came from Ludlow himself, he'd bet. The man's colourful past probably had a lot to do with it. His show-biz years in the public eye. His success as a businessman.

Peter went back to his mother with a bowl of warm water and a flannel.. 'Gwen'll be over later.' he told her. 'She'll give you a proper wash.'

He gathered the spillages in a napkin and wiped her hands.

Gwen had been his mother's home help carer for the past three years. She was like one of the family now. He couldn't possibly have taken proper care of his mother without her.

'I'm off on my ride now, mum.'

'What, on Christmas Day?'

'New Year's Day,' he corrected her silently. 'Tell Gwen to leave the washing up. I'll do that when I get back.'

He left a note downstairs for Gwen to that effect, before wheeling out his trusty mountain bike from the utility room at the back of the house.

At the gate, he slid his cropped head into his crash helmet, so closely cropped it exaggerated how much his ears stuck out. Wriggling his hands into his close-fitting leather gloves, he looked at his wristwatch.10.17. Three minutes earlier than usual. He zeroed the milometer bolted to the handlebars and the race was on.

As soon as his first thrust hit the pedals, he forgot all about charities and knighthoods and got up to speed.

Nairobi was the nerve centre of S.O.D.A.'s operations in Africa, although to look at its modest headquarters, you would not have thought so. Just two rooms in an office block perched above a terrace of open-fronted premises dealing with all manner of automobile needs, from re-molded tyres to panel beating. It was felt that anything more extravagant would suggest the Charity was ill-spending its reserves. Everything necessary for its small band of volunteers was there; telephones, a photocopier, a one ring bottle-gas cooker, and maps galore. After all, the real work in Africa was done in the field.

Nairobi itself was the natural choice for a base, not least for its accessibility within the continent. Kenya had developed into a substantial trading nation since independence. Its communication network throughout Africa was second to none. Apart from this, Kenya still had many commercial and cultural ties with its former colonial ruler. Ludlow helped consolidate this link not only through the pan-African work done by his S.O.D.A. charity, but also through his association with Wilson-Hughes (Kenya), a by-word for plant engineering and petro-chemical exploration all over East Africa.

Wilson-Hughes was a multi-million-dollar group of companies employing over 21,000 people in nineteen different countries. It had swallowed Ludlow's Marlsbury-Higwell company like an oyster. The group had many areas of activity covering a wide range of industries, from massive civil engineering projects to the manufacture of the minutest medical equipment. In Africa, its affiliated spin-off company Wilson-Hughes (Kenya) was conveniently contracted by S.O.D.A. to run its test drilling program in search of suitable sites for its water pump installation program. It made good financial sense to keep transactions within Ludlow's extended business family whenever possible. Where was the crime in scratching one's own back?

As drilling exploration progressed, other commodities were occasionally chanced upon, if not sometimes directly sought. Valuable minerals and ores, for instance. Oil. This could be good news for the government of the country in question should such reserves prove too large to be ignored. Further excavation would proceed to the benefit of all concerned; a case of all parties winning. The fact that a charity had in some way helped to spawn a commercial venture (a small percentage of whose profit would quite rightly filter through into SODA's own coffers) was neither here nor there. The needy country would be the richer for it, and who could argue with that?

It was no wonder the recently honoured Sir Edward Ludlow was regarded as somewhat of a saintly figure in that part of the world, especially to those officials who helped grease the wheels of such fruitful explorations.

As a major shareholder and the newly appointed chairman of the Wilson-Hughes corporation, following the global stock market crash of '87, (from which hair-pulling investors were still reeling), there was much Sir Edward Ludlow could quietly achieve in passing for the group's interests during one of these high-profile charity visits. Simon Dickson, the BBC director, had shown signs of being cynical about this aspect of Ludlow's regular travels to Africa.

Ludlow's international stature as a man of ostensibly great generosity and human concern was not such a hidden asset for one moving in what could often be fiercely competitive trade and business circles.

The company aircraft taking the group to the pump site, a Jetstream 31, was painted in the rather garish corporation colours of pillar-box red and lime green. It's black logo, an acronym of the group's registered name regaled the tail plane; the W of Wilson sitting on the crossbar H of Hughes, which made the whole thing look like a symbolic crown. That was clearly how the designer envisioned it. But to most people it looked more like a Christmas party hat.

Ludlow sat beside the pilot, Richard Whitton, a compact man with dark slicked-back hair and a moustache fashioned like wings, immaculate in his captain's uniform. The couple were well acquainted.

Richard Whitton had owned a small flying school near Marlsbury, where Ludlow had done all his training to become a pilot himself, albeit single engine, daylight only. During the early eighties, the business was slowly going to the wall. Ludlow helped shore it up for a while, but in the end bought it outright. It was in his interest to keep the airstrip operational for his own occasional personal use. He allowed the local model-aircraft club to use it in return for keeping an operational length of the runway free of weeds. It did the club a favour at the same time as saving him money and inconvenience. About the same time, he saw to it that Richard Whitton got a job with Wilson-Hughes Fleet Services in Africa.

It was a magnificently clear day. As they leveled out over the southern finger of the Aberdare Mountain Range, the rift valley gave a flash of its distant lakes.

Ludlow hardly noticed. His mind was elsewhere, eyes fixed on the horizon where a watery image of his wife danced on his nerves.

She was more than an embarrassment these days. She had become a danger. Paranoid beyond belief to the point of ruin. His as much as her own. She had achieved everything she could possibly want from her life in the glamour business; had reached the top of that particular hall of fame.

Having himself lifted her to those giddy heights, he had long let her take her own course. She would have it no other way. His advice was no longer wanted, manager or not. He had no argument with that. He was done with it. She had run her course and could not go any lower. It was too late for therapy. What she needed was treatment, meaningful treatment, not pussy footing around in celebrity spas. Her fame had turned into infamy. She had become hopelessly drug dependent. He couldn't handle her screaming matches anymore.

And now, her threats.

From very early on, their marriage had become a business arrangement. There had been serious misunderstandings in the 'love' department on Edward's part. But he had held the relationship together, his pride helping him cover up the embarrassing condition that had struck him. That of falling 'madly' in love.

How she had played him! He had been head over heels fooled. Absolutely taken in. And the madness had utterly shaken his perspective, undermined his self-confidence. It took him a while to regain any semblance of balance. When he finally did and was able to think reasonably straight again, he made a vow: that old devil called love would never be allowed a place in his life again.

Publicly, that life had every appearance of having been charmed from birth with good fortune and wise counsel. His 'fairy-tail' marriage did nothing to disparage this belief.

Until that day, when their wedding bells rang out on the front pages, Ludlow had been the archetypal bachelor in the field of romance. He had 'put it about a bit' before going 'up' to Oxford, where the world of love opened up to him with no effort. For *love*, read: sex, drugs, and rock and roll. It was the sixties, after all.

He managed to indulge in such diversions without abusing the generous allowance his father had been happy to bestow on him as encouragement to embark upon a course of economics and business management. Those subjects having been seen as the most appropriate for his son and heir to have on board when the time came for him to take over the family business of Marlsbury Pumps.

As a child, Edward had been doted upon and overindulged to the point of wanting for nothing. He wasn't particularly lazy, but as he grew up, he sensed there was no danger that life was going to be a struggle. The idea that he might have to work one day hadn't occurred to him, not *work*, work. He had ideas of what he might want to do in later life, and they all took him in a fun-loving direction. The sex, drugs and rock and roll at Oxford helped him further along that road.

It wasn't so much rock and roll to start with, but jazz. Traditional New Orleans jazz. The blues of the late fifties, early sixties. More Bunk Johnson and Muddy Waters than Bix Beiderbeck and Jelly Roll Morton. Edward had reached a basic level of piano playing at school, enough to be able to thump out a rhythm with basic chords. It didn't take him long at Oxford to team up with five other like-minded would-be musicians. The most proficient of these was a trumpeter called Robin James, who had a whole bunch of rare jazz records he had found in a shop in Soho, London, called Dobell's. The group listened to them tirelessly, shamelessly copying their parts as best they could. They rehearsed assiduously in a derelict pub in St. Ebbs, a run-down part of the city. Before long they were good enough to expect modest payment for playing gigs, starting with a residency at a music venue uptown in the neighbourhood of Jericho. That spurred them on. Before the academic year was out, they had graduated to lucrative spots at college balls.

For his second year, Edward rented a thatched cottage on the southern outreaches of Oxford that had a spacious unkempt garden, mainly consisting of lawn skirted with trees and shrubs. Very privately situated. He rented one of the rooms to Robin, the trumpeter. From then on, all the band's rehearsing was done there.

It was also there that Edward started a one-page guide to all things musical and artistic going on in the city during term times. He called it 'Platform One' and printed it out on an old industrial photocopier that Marlsbury Pumps had finished with.

During his second year Edward began to see new horizons.

The horizon he was currently gazing at through the aircraft cockpit window was shimmering in the heat of the African sun, leaving little to focus on but more recollections from the unusually hot summer of his second year at Oxford.

Platform One cottage, as it became to be called, developed into a venue of its own. More accurately, perhaps, its garden did. All events there 'happened' outside; music, poetry, mime, art; performances, rehearsals, discussions. Word soon got out that it was *the* place to score, somewhere 'cool' to hang out and smoke pot. Plenty of that went on. But not into Edward's lungs. Smoking of any kind made him vomit. However, there was always a barrel of Marlsbury Cider sitting on a purpose-built A-frame in its own cool place for whenever he and other 'straighter' students had a thirst for intoxication.

Platform One Cottage had just as much going for it as did a Californian summer of love.

The one-page guide grew into a more substantial offering, with articles, opinions, ratings and by the end of the year, money from advertising. Soon after came 'Platform Two', a similar publication produced for Cambridge students, Oxford's rival, perhaps, in more ways than the annual boat race. Almost immediately, to avoid possible inter-university discrimination, the 'One' and 'Two' were quickly dropped, and the magazines were simply named, 'Platforms'. Before long, other universities were targeted and joined the party.

With all these 'out of college' activities to occupy him, Edward's official studies began to suffer proportionately. However, he was beginning to hone his talents in the field of business and marketing at grass-root level. His most inspired decision was to give up playing piano for his jazz band and move into managing it. Helped by publicity stunts he was forever dreaming up, the band began to gain recognition on the national gig circuit. The most notable of these 'stunts' was achieved by bribing the porters of the Oxford Union to allow the band to conceal itself in the upper gallery of the Chamber on the day that the Prime Minister had been invited there to make a speech.

As that right honourable gentleman entered the hall with great pomp and dignity, the band burst forth with a rendition of 'When The Saints Go Marching In' to thunderous applause from the surprised gathering, and a wide, uneven grin from the man himself. A photographer from the Oxford Mail had also been smuggled in. The copy, written by Edward himself, flanked by pictures that included one of the band, was syndicated to newspapers up and down the country.

As well as realising he could make more money as a manager-come- agent than by playing, Edward found that the wheeling and dealing it involved was also as much fun. This was the way forward for him. Helped with the success of his 'Platforms' franchise, his profile was on the rise in the public eye. He was someone who could make things happen. Soon, other groups outside the university circuit were seeking his management prowess.

Then came a real bonus. Looking back on it now from his lofty cockpit seat, he saw it as a turning point. The first game changer.

He had been encouraged to go and listen to a young musician perform during the interval at a different jazz pub in the city. This guy stood confidently at the microphone, electric guitar casually strung about his neck, and sang his heart out as if being the only person in the crowded venue. As soon as he hit the first note, all conversation stopped, eyes turning to face him. It wasn't just the quality of his voice that silenced them. The sound coming from his small guitar amplifier was electrifying. At once unusual and hypnotic. Not exactly what was expected to come from a guitar, electric or acoustic. The audience was instantly mesmerized. How was he doing it? This was a new sound. Not blues, jazz, pop, or folk. Weirdly, it came closer to full-on orchestral strings. A big, big engulfing reverberation. Unique to the ear. Edward was intrigued. He wanted a closer look. He moved forward. What he saw fascinated him. The guitar wasn't plugged directly into the amplifier. First it went into a roughly hewn wooden box which had two makeshift pedals connected to it. As the guy played, his foot moved from pedal to petal, sometimes straddling both at the same time, and out came this extraordinary variety of sounds. Intriguing and exciting stuff indeed. Edward had to know more.

When the guy had finished his set, Luke Lake was his name, Edward introduced himself.

'Thanks for coming,' Luke said coolly. He knew who Edward Ludlow was. With a smile, he nodded down at his pedal contraption. A shiver of recognition tweaked Edward's spine. The pedals had been transformed from the type used on car tyre pumps. Still visible on the worn rubber treads were the embossed letters MP, the Marlsbury Pumps logo. 'Hope you don't mind.' Luke added jovially. 'They were the best I could find for the job.'

Of course, Edward didn't mind.

Once Luke had wrapped his gear away, the two of them sat over a beer in the downstairs bar. Edward had a proposition. No, two. Then, three. He was thinking off the top of his head, and not entirely altruistically. He offered his management and agency know-how, the promise of a record deal (the idea of starting his own record label was formulating as he spoke) and a partnership in patenting his unique 'sound' box, the development of which Edward would fund with a view to exploiting it commercially. His wherewithal, Edward stressed, was in place to guarantee a good shot at ample riches. Not only that last enticing possibility, but Edward's unreserved enthusiasm convinced Luke this was the way to go. His time had come.

A deal was done. The icing on the cake was that Luke wrote all his own material! Everything Edward had been listening to that night had come from Luke's pen. Such talent! This was too good to be true. Within weeks, Platforms Publishing and Platforms record label were established and Luke was signed up on all fronts.

Without delay, a four-track sound studio in North Oxford was hired 24/7 for one week. This would allow Luke to go in whenever it suited him to lay down his songs, night or day. With only himself to please, in just two days, he had recorded 11 tracks. Edward was amazed. They could all be hits. For the other five studio days, Edward suggested Luke overdubbed more guitar and voice harmonies to enhance 8 of the tracks. The idea was to compile an album, and have it pressed commercially under his own soon to be operational 'Platforms' label. Then, advertise and plug it mercilessly in all the Platforms' guides, and see how it went down. Only then would he decide if it would be a better move to approach an established record label that could perhaps reach a wider audience.

But the more Edward witnessed Luke's outstanding recording talent, the more he wanted to keep its control in his own hands. His judgement proved to be wise.

The result of the sessions was too good to be true. At least three of the tracks were sure-fire chart material, according to Edward. He chose one of these and released it as a single to test the market. The response he got from plugging it in the Platforms' guides was beyond all hopes. Bingo!

He sent copies to every possible outlet with some publicity photographs and a splurge of background information. The music journals were slow to react, but Pirate radio stations jumped at the prospect of 'discovering' this new sound. Next, with some of his Oxbridge connections now enjoying influential posts in entertainment broadcasting, Edward managed to get the single accepted on the BBC playlist.

From that moment, life went mad.

Chapter Four

Peter Tyler had his head down almost touching the handlebars. The first half mile was straight and flat, a mere minute or so to cover. It landed him plum in the centre of Newton Stoat, his own village, population about half what was necessary to warrant a pub, but enough to boast a church and telephone box, neither of which seemed to work these days. To find the nearest pub, he would have to take a left at the T-junction by the church and travel to the next village about three miles away. Thence, if he picked up the main road and continued for a further seven miles, he would find himself in Marlsbury. That was the quickest way into town. He hardly ever used it since being laid off unless he was in a hurry, which was practically never. It was too short and much of it usually cluttered with traffic. He had devised a more gratifying route; sixteen miles of practically deserted B-roads, footpaths and cross-country tracks where he would encounter few cars and rarely any sign of other human beings apart from cyclists at weekends.

Two miles of narrow high hedged lane and close to six minutes pedaling time from Newton Stoat, the terrain became hilly. Another half mile or so it steepened more drastically, and he was out of his saddle standing on his pedals, pushing down with every ounce of his 9 stone 8 pounds to keep his momentum going. At the crest, blood rushing, he picked up speed again, touching 30 mph as he sprinted through a tunnel of trees toward the gentle rise of Beacon Ridge. From there, he would kiss goodbye to tarmac for an hour or more.

But he nearly kissed goodbye to everything that morning as his concentration lapsed, his thoughts drifting back to Ludlow and his knighthood. To avoid losing momentum, he had pulled out to the middle of the road to make a wide turn onto the ridge track. At that moment, a car came hurtling round the bend ahead and nearly flattened him.

It was his own fault, as the car's blaring horn let him know in no uncertain terms. He was too used to having the road to himself. Close thing!

Beacon Ridge was blanketed with woods dissected by a bridal path that ran more or less North-South along its undulating summit. Over the years, the trees up there on the westward side had been dying off for some reason, earning them the name of Deadwoods. Many of them now lay in disarray, uprooted by the hurricane of a few months earlier that had torn through Southern England and added to by the recent storm.

All the land up there was owned by Ludlow, but there were several tracks with public right of way which Peter put to full use, although he never really kept strictly to them.

The uphill trek to the crest of the ridge was slow whatever the conditions. Quite often he had to get off his bike and either push or carry it if the ground was too slippery. Today was like that with all the recent rain. He had barely got halfway up before his back wheel began to spin. So, it was a push job to the top.

His first check point was a pylon at the crest. He was riding again by the time he came to it but had lost almost nine minutes off a normal run.

Compton Stud, the huge Ludlow residence, being where it was, had introduced him to this cross-country circuit. It happened to be the most direct way of getting to the place from his house as well as being the sort of physical challenge he enjoyed. Soon after the Marlsbury Pump shut down, he rode the route daily to join the other laid-off workers protesting against the way Ludlow had closed down the company with such unwarranted haste and lack of consultation. All within months of Ludlow senior's death. The old man, so long the exemplary employer, must have been raging in his grave. He was a Marlsbury man, born and bred. He would never have agreed to his son's idea of moving the plant to a disused coal mine plot in Greater Manchester even if it *did* make sound financial sense. Although it brought employment to an area that needed regeneration, it was taking it away from its roots.

By the time the demonstrations finally fizzled out, Peter had come to notice a marked improvement in his riding performance. He put it down to the Beacon Ridge run, so he kept it up.

Passing the marker pylon, he began his jaunt through Deadwoods, ducking and weaving through the lifeless jumble of trees like a slalom rider. After a mile or so he picked up a fairly steep downhill track that shot him straight across a bridle path into Goodwoods – the trees east of the ridge. Even with a fair coating of leaves still on their branches, the trees on the leeward side had survived the ravages of the hurricane much better.

As he sped along the deep furrow he had cut into the track over the months, he was jolted from his thoughts by the sound of pounding hooves.

It all happened in seconds.

Through the bushes and buckled tree trunks, he saw the horse charging along the bridle path at a mad gallop on perfect collision course with him!

He slammed on his brakes, but nothing happened! He was going too fast. The wheels locked solid, and he was sent down the slope in a frightening skid.

'Look out!' he yelled, up to his eyes in adrenaline. 'I can't stop!'

Neither could the horse.

As he hit the bridle path, he turned his front wheel sharply in a last-ditch effort to avoid catastrophe. The result was spectacular. The soft soil acted as a buffer, and he was sent flying over the handlebars.

He would never know how the horse missed him. It somehow managed to swerve without losing its rider. But only just. It reared up instantly onto its hind legs, throwing its head from side to side in utter panic.

Stephanie Star was in the saddle! She clung on desperately, as white as a sheet.

'Sorry! Sorry!' she cried with genuine concern, as though it had all been her fault. 'Sorry! I'm so sorry!' She wouldn't stop saying it.

Peter got to his feet as she continued her tirade of apologies. She was in a state of hysteria far beyond the seriousness of the accident.

'I'm OK, I'm OK,' he tried to convince her. But she seemed inconsolable.

She looked dreadful, nearer fifty than her mid-thirties. He couldn't believe his eyes. She was drained of beauty. Haggard. A look of terror on her face. It suddenly struck him that she wasn't dressed for riding out in this weather. No helmet, no boots, no gloves, no protective clothing. Just jeans and a sweater, splattered with mud. She was drenched. White, shaking and drenched!

Her constant stream of apologies suddenly stopped, to be replaced by a bombard of entreaties.

'Help me! Help Me!' she pleaded over and again before evaporating into another gush of hysteria equal to the stamping and pulling of the horse. 'No! No! Sorry. Please. No. No-one must know!' She didn't seem to know *what* she was saying or wanted to say as she struggled to keep the horse under control.

The rein was held with only her left hand. The right seemed to be rigid in her lap. Had she injured it? Torn a muscle?

'Are you OK?' he asked. 'Have you hurt yourself? Can I help?' He stepped closer and took hold of the rein. 'Have you done something to your arm?'

'No-one must know!' she screamed. The horse reared up again with him so close. Shaking the rein free from his grasp, it took off without warning, bucking and kicking violently, trying its utmost to get Stephanie off its back.

She now grabbed the rein with both hands, holding on for dear life. In doing so, something fell to the ground.

'You've dropped something!' He yelled out to her.

She couldn't have responded even if she had heard him. There was no stopping the horse.

He shouted again but it was in vain. She was gone.

He went to pick up what had dropped; a large envelope, the type fastened by a metal catch through a hole. Stuffed. One word was scribbled on it: Major.

He was in a quandary. It was useless thinking of going after her. He'd get nowhere riding along the bridle path.

The episode had shocked him. He was really concerned for her. The horse was going berserk. She could easily be thrown. It was a wonder she hadn't come off already.

The envelope was soaking wet and bulging almost to the point of splitting open.

He went back to his bike. There was no permanent damage. Just twisted handlebars. He slipped the envelope into his saddle bag to save it getting even wetter and started thinking about what he should do.

'When in doubt, do nothing' sprang out from somewhere in his past. He had already decided that it was pointless chasing after her. She could be anywhere by now. The bridle path ran for miles, crisscrossing itself in places. He was sure it ended up back at Compton Stud in a loop.

He decided to stay put for a while. What else could he do? At some point, she would be aware she had dropped the envelope. Once the horse had calmed down, she would probably try to retrace her steps looking for it.

The rain had really started to drop, so he found a nearby fir tree to huddle against, unable to wipe Stephanie's haunted look from his mind. It was a horror story. All semblance of beauty gone.

Years ago, when she had first moved to Marlsbury, he had often gone out of his way to catch a glimpse of her, like most in the town. And not just blokes. She was always being asked to open fetes and bazaars. He had got her autograph on more than one occasion.

But he hadn't seen her up close like this for ages. She looked really sick. As white as a ghost.

Everyone knew she was having problems. All was not cozy at Compton Stud. The tabloids had been having a field day gossiping about it for months now. You'd think they'd give it a rest, cashing in on people's misery.

But Stephanie was more than just miserable. Booze and drugs. Peter didn't know what to think about that side of things. The desperation he had just witnessed suggested something more than withdrawal agony.

And she had almost stretched out her hand to him for help.

Chapter Five

Ernest Mckintosh tapped Ludlow on the shoulder and pointed out of the aircraft window. 'Never seen the Lady looking so brilliant!'

The snow-capped cone of Mount Kenya was resplendent; it seemed close enough to reach out and touch.

'Quite beautiful,' Ludlow agreed.

There were several people aboard the Jetstream 31 apart from the pilot: the two new arrivals to Kenya: four government officials including Mr. Solomon Kirini, three representatives of Hughes (Kenya), one of whom was Howard Pankerton, its jovial PR officer, and two S.O.D.A. volunteers, big Ernest and his son, Hannington, who, in spite all his features being unmistakably African, was as pink as the flamingo rich lake after which he had been named. In contrast, his eyes were deep grey, and as sharp as Scottish granite.

'Pink Magic,' Ernest addressed him, using his son's favourite nickname. 'Are you enjoying it?'

This was the sixteen-year-old's first flight, and he was hypnotized. He sat with his face glued to the window in wide-eyed fascination. 'It is like being an old eagle!' he breathed without turning his head, misting up the window around his squashed nose. 'How high are we, fatha?'

'We are very high,' was all his father was prepared to speculate.

'High enough to start the party!' Howard Pankerton announced instead, with a flick of the hospitality ice-box lid to reveal a crate of champagne. 'The hundredth pump, Sir Edward's Knighthood, and your maiden flight, Hannington. Plenty to celebrate!'

Laying out some dry-looking smoked salmon sandwiches, Pankerton handed round disposable cups, full of apologies. 'Sorry about the plastic, the cups, that is, not the smoked salmon.' He chuckled at his feeble joke. His face had a ruddy, almost scalded look about it, as though it had a constant battle with the climate. But it wasn't just the unforgiving sun that had done it. Some of the rawness came from within. He plainly gave his joyful all to the Hughes (Kenya) hospitality program.

Everyone drank but Hannington, who eyed the bubbling champagne with a look of disapproval. Such extravagance did not seem right when so many people were dying of malnutrition.

Edward Ludlow caught the questioning crease of Hannington's brow. 'Not to worry, old chap. The drinks are on me,' he explained as he raised his glass in a silent toast to the forthcoming event.

He recalled another silent toast he had made years earlier. The day he had won over Sheila Braithewaite, alias, Stephanie Star. An achievement that was now threatening to drain him dry.

Within two years of graduating from Oxford, poorly, it must be said, he had already signed up enough 'clients' under his entertainment wing to be able to open plush offices in Wardour Street, London, which was perhaps the epicentre of that thriving British industry at the time. Not a stone's throw away was Carnaby Street, where he had also established an outlet for his other burgeoning interest, Platforms Designs. It was there that the face and body of newly named Stephanie Star was launched in a blaze of publicity that propelled her into the fast lane of Brit Fashion to become a global icon.

Even before crowning her the National Beauty Queen, 1970, Edward, was smitten. The moment she set foot parading around the lido pool, he knew he would be choosing her as the winner. Sheila Braithewaite stood out from all the other hopefuls in line like a flashing neon sign saying 'Supermodel!'

Also flashing in his sights was the thought of exploiting her captivating beauty at the bank. He wanted agency and management, the works. In and out of bed.

Edward Ludlow had been first choice as the National Beauty Queen judge. By 1970, still only in his late twenties, he had his fingers in some fairly fat managerial pies. Rung by rung, he had climbed the swinging sixty's ladder. His name and face had become part of the 'scene'. Luke Lake's album, a classic in the making, had set the ball rolling. It was No: 1 in the charts, nudging out all the four-man super-groups of the sixties for weeks on end. Another album was on the way promising to be as successful. Other groups anxious to be signed up by Ludlow Enterprises were also making chart moves. The Platforms' guide was no longer simply a university one-pager. It had become a national magazine that every 'with-it' tourist wanted in their Platforms' designed shoulder bags slung over their like-named designer clothes.

The prize for winning the beauty contest was a twelve-month modelling contract with his Platforms' management agency. For Sheila Braithewaite, Edward extended that offer to being of indefinite length, and exclusive. All in.

Very soon, his 'Stephanie Star' franchise was to outshine that of 'Luke Lake'. Edward had seen fit very early on to engage the services of an accountancy firm prominent in the world of show business. Handling his growing wealth was something he would prefer a wise head with years of experience juggled with. Gerald Silver Associates was the company he chose, and, to keep his growing business portfolio nice and tight, a company he now owned.

Edward's multiple interests in Luke Lake were neatly being exposed to best financial effect using tax avoidance ploys, shell companies and offshore tax havens. Luke had made it big in USA and Japan, but no income from those markets had ever touched 'Blighty' for tax purposes.

The same treatment for 'Stephanie Star Ltd' was adopted from day one.

Edward chose to call his first shell company the Cowrie Conglomerate, registered in Zurich. It seemed an appropriate name. That pattern continued as his portfolio expanded.

The company through which he bought Compton Stud was Abalone Property International, registered in Liechtenstein. Compton Stud was a huge estate that had been empty for some time, parts of which had been falling into disrepair. It even incorporated its own chapel, and this was one of the reasons Edward decided to acquire it. Always keen to keep his hands on the controls, he saw the opportunity of converting the chapel's large space into a state-of-the-art sound recording studio, which, now with Stephanie Star aboard could also double as a photographic studio for fashion shoots and tv commercials. Ten of the eighteen bedrooms were available for hire during shoots along with the studio. These were given a complete makeover to compete with any top-end hotel within striking distance. Other accommodation, less fancy but comfortable enough, was created in the large, detached barn situated away from the main building as an overspill for big production crews.

The rest of the property, apart from that which had been originally for the live-in staff, was split into two, comfortable living quarters and office complex.

Edward Ludlow now had so many shell companies jumping through the hoops of tax avoidance that it was a wonder he didn't rattle.

His wife knew little about this network of covert offshore companies that were possibly denying the British taxpayer of millions. Why should she? He had once told her she was 'the pearl' of Abalone, the shell company where the bulk of her wealth was squirrelled away. But he sensed she had not completely understood the ins and outs of what he was trying to tell her, which suited him just fine.

None of these considerations would have worried him unduly had Stephanie not come by a certain floppy disc which could prove his downfall without some very clever footwork. The data on the disc had been encrypted, but in the hands of someone who knew what he was doing, not failsafe. It wasn't shell companies being exposed that overly concerned him, but certain encoded information about S.O.D.A.'s early drug acquisition and distribution program. Unfortunately, there were too many interested parties now to safely wipe that slate clean. His wife knew nothing about these, but his overreaction to the missing disc had opened a can of worms for her to prod.

Human error by a junior member of Gerald Silver's team had brought this on, and forthwith, the immediate loss of his job.

The computing system at Compton Stud was being upgraded. Floppies could hold nothing like the amount of data that compact discs now boasted. Technology in that area was developing fast.

Stephanie had not yet been eaten away by drugs at that time. She still had looks and presence, not to mention a cheeky sense of fun. She was the queen bee, could be quite intimidating to impressionable admirers. One of these was Philip, the young accountant charged with transferring company files from floppy to compact discs using the new computers that had been installed at Compton Stud.

With the run of the house at that time, Stephanie would occasionally sashay about the offices in between photo shoots playing the big 'I am', looking for compliments, or playfully, merely to shock. Philip had never met Stephanie before, and when she waltzed into the computer room wearing nothing but a loose silk dressing gown and panties, he reddened with arousal and embarrassment. There was currently an evening break for the crew members of a photo-shoot that was running late. A famous lingerie company was paying a fortune to use her body to advertise its wares and she was bored. To pass the time, she had wandered off looking for a bit of fun.

'Hello. Haven't seen you here before,' she had said to Philip, enjoying the shock on his face she was looking for. 'I hope you belong here,' she teased, letting her dressing gown hang loose. 'Not nicking stuff, are you? Lots of secret stuff in here.'

He could hardly face her. The dressing gown hid nothing. He guessed she was joking, but still felt he should justify himself.

'Er, no. I'm from Gerald Silver and Partners.'

'Ah! Then you probably *are* nicking stuff. Be my guest.'

She leaned over him, so closely the gown was brushing against his cheek. Her left nipple was inches from him.

'No, well…' he spluttered, embarrassed beyond belief to be so close to that part of this beautiful woman's figure he only knew about in mathematical terms.

Stephanie was enjoying his utter discomfort, especially when he suddenly crossed his legs to hide what was happening to him. She bent over, looking blatantly down at his crutch.

'Steady, tiger,' she said with a smile. 'You need a break. That boss of yours is a slave driver. Come and have a look in on the shoot. You'll see a bit more of me down there.' she continued to tease. 'Not *that* down there, you naughty boy! Down there in the *studio*, I meant. Don't get your hopes up!'

'Well, no…I can't. Not really... er…' Philip was having trouble getting words out. 'I was just...on my way. It's late. Gotta get back to London. I've finished for the day.'

What he didn't realise until later was that he was finished for good, in terms of working for Gerald Silver and Partners.

His downfall: in the flurry of having Stephanie standing over him virtually naked, teasing him, he had forgotten to remove the last floppy disc being transferred and add it to the many others that were about to be destroyed.

Stephanie noticed it sitting there, partially ejected, but wasn't going to draw his attention to it as she shooed him out. 'Off you go, then. You're no fun if you don't want to stay on for the after-shoot party. Give my love to Gerald,' she adding as a gibe. 'Tell him not to spend all my money.'

With Philip gone, she removed the disc with no intended malice. 'Well, well,' she said to herself. 'Very naughty boy. Now Steph will have to look after it.'

It was meant as innocent mischief at the time. She had given no thought to it being of any use to her or that it would be the cause of Philip losing his job. The amount of disruption and upheaval the missing disc caused, however, soon changed that. There was such a furore about its loss, she chose her moment to admit that she had taken it. 'What's all the fucking fuss about? The poor kid copied all the stuff off it, didn't he? Nothing's lost!'

The response she got from her husband told her she had been presented with a useful thorn to stick into him whenever it might prove necessary.

'Are you being naive, Stephanie, or just plain stupid? There's 'stuff' as you call it embedded on the disc that would do neither of us any favours if it got into the wrong hands. And that's putting it very mildly! So, what the fuck have you done with it? It needs to be destroyed!''

The true answer to that desperate question was that she couldn't exactly remember which of the many wastepaper baskets in the studio she had thrown it into. But she decided not to tell him that. Why should she? Too late to do anything about it, anyway. The baskets had long been emptied.

Naïve she might once have been, but hardly very stupid. She could have fun with this!

'I've put it somewhere safe, if you must know,' she had told him. And there was some truth in that, thinking it must now be residing in the municipal tip. But she continued with the lie. 'It's in safe hands just in case you fuck me about, as you've been tending to do of late. Just looking after my own interests.'

It was no news to him that she had noticed a decline in his concern about her career. That decline had matched the increase in her drug dependence and the bad press that came with it. He couldn't be sure if she was bluffing about the disc or not, but one way of trying to find out had been to put phone taps on all the lines at Compton Stud in the hope that she might reveal the truth. Then, if necessary, a course of action could be determined to limit the damage. Her accomplice, her 'safe hands', if she truly had one, could be bought or dealt with. Rose was on hand for such duties.

He hoped she was just bluffing, however.

She was good at that. Her biggest bluff having come at the very beginning.

She was no Cinderella.

Although she had led him on, gently encouraging his advances, she had resolutely refused to sleep with him until the knot of marriage had been tied.

And not until that festive day, in the cozy privacy of their nuptial bed, was the real reason for her 'stand-off' brought home to him. Stephanie Star, alias Sheila Braithewaite, was not the innocent virgin Edward had been led to believe. She was not exactly like a burnt-out volcano turned to marble, but not far off. There was no attachment in evidence, no shy awkwardness one might have expected with a first sexual encounter. It was all business for Stephanie, passively provided with no help nor hindrance, like a tired 'professional'. No consummation, neither real nor fake came from her. 'Sorry,' she had apologized, politely rather than heart-felt. That's how it was with her, she felt she should tell him, given his passion had suddenly stopped at full throttle, actually thinking she had fallen asleep.

'It's not you,' she had tried to reassure him. 'Don't beat yourself up about it. What can I say? Sorry. Just do your thing. Whatever floats your boat.'

He could not believe this. Her coolness. His heart was going hammer and tongs. Hers, hardly a ripple. Suddenly, her northern accent he had always found quaint, jarred.

'I'm not gay, if that's what you're thinking,' she explained.

He had wondered.

For him, it was a rude slap around the groin. He felt deceived and frustrated. Completely taken.

The honeymoon was over even before the front-page pictures had started rolling off the presses. A royal wedding could hardly have been given more coverage. And it was a royal wedding of sorts. Stephanie Star, beauty queen; Edward, the fairy prince. It caught the public's imagination. To many people it signalled the end of an era. The affectionately named sixties were now gone.

But for those who had witnessed them, they would forever live on, having spawned a new enlightenment.

For Edward Ludlow, who for the world to see had never had it so good, their demise was more poignant. His dynamic rock and roll years were behind him. But with his Stephanie Star franchise and off-shoots going global throughout the seventies, he was to become a much higher roller. Up ahead, a change of direction would be blowing in the wind.

Big business.

Ludlow was shaken from his reveries by a pocket of air turbulence. The flight had taken them over the fertile land of the Rift Valley, northwards to the southernmost tip of Lake Rudolf where the air had become choppy. From there on, they would head north-east across increasingly arid terrain towards the Ethiopian border.

The metalled road below them now cut into scrub land. The brackish waters of Lake Rudolf slid away, shimmering in the intense heat haze of the day. The inhospitable monotony of the desert wilderness then prevailed.

At 14.45 the pilot announced they were about to make their descent. Minutes later, he banked the aircraft. In the distance clusters of shacks and tents stretching along a snaking wadi came into view. As the jet bounced lower on the thermals, they saw crowds had gathered for the occasion. Caravans of camels were scattered all around the area.

As the plane leveled out to approach a makeshift airstrip, the crowd on the ground started waving spears and sticks in a riotous greeting.

The Jetstream landed amid clouds of dust and grit, coming rumbling to a stop on the uneven ground close to an older twin-engine aircraft that had brought the press and other officials on ahead.

As the engines cut, the plane was surrounded by a mass of excited tribesmen leaping high into the air seemingly without having to bend their knees. Sonorous chants from deep within their rib cages accompanied each choreographed jump. The women swayed erotically, enhancing the operatic spectacle with piercing wails from their ululating tongues like broody peahens.

Despite the apparent chaos of swirling dust clouds, the greeting had an orderliness about it. The men fanned themselves out around the front of the aircraft while the women formed a chorus behind them. The children ran about wildly, smiles like golden charms, trying to emulate the leaps and shrieks of their elders.

As if being conducted, when Ludlow appeared in the doorway of the aircraft, a mesmerizing hum replaced the chants and wails, the pounding of sticks and spears and the slap of bare feet on the dusty soil adding a hypnotic beat.

Before alighting, Ludlow stood in the open doorway as if in appreciation of the show. This was indeed partly the cause of his hesitation. But not the main reason. He looked about to take in the scene and when he saw what he was looking for, his smile grew bigger, and he started waving.

Simon Dickson and his film crew had just burst untidily through to the front of the display. As the camera rolled, Dickson tried desperately to encourage the men to continue their leaping and chanting by frantically waving his arms not to miss the photo-opportunity, Ludlow gave the cameras time to turn to him as he posed royally, hoping that the logo of Wilson-Hughes could be seen in the shot.

He would later be told by the very happy PR man Pankerton that it had been.

While the chief engineer joined his men on the ground and set about the final preparations for christening the pump, Sir Edward was taken on a brief guided tour of the main medical facility in the village. This was functioning gratis of S.O.D.A. It was no more than a long open-sided shed with a corrugated iron roof. No beds; just rush mats on a concrete floor.

'We house the really sick in here,' the volunteer in charge, a young French doctor, said in near perfect English, letting the photographers and BBC crew push past to the front. 'As you can see, most of them are young mothers and children. Some of these will sadly die soon. There's little we can do for them. It will take time for just one water well to make any real difference to the health of this village. Of course, it is very welcome and will play its part, but more would be good. What we're also in dire need of is more medical supplies and drugs.'

Ludlow nodded gravely. He understood what the doctor was saying. The pump on its own would barely scratch the surface of the problem the people faced in this drought susceptible part of the country. 'Well, we've made a start,' he said, making sure he was out of range of microphones. This was not the time to discuss shortcomings. This was meant to be his day of celebration. He didn't need to be reminded that nothing would hold back the advancing desert in this and other regions of Africa short of vast irrigation programs. It would cost billions, involving dams, desalination plants and industrial pumping stations. The contract for the project was currently in the initial stages of tender and it was the quiet aim of Ludlow during this ostensibly S.O.D.A. visit to convince various governments that the Wilson-Hughes Group were the best people for the job.

Not only was he hoping to secure this huge contract for the company he part-owned, moreover, he wanted to be seen as the main force behind clinching it.

The pumping house he now faced was little more than four poles holding up a sheet of corrugated iron. Underneath, in its limited shade, was the power plant, a diesel engine. This drew the water up to a storage tank just below ground level. The focus of attention was a bright new hand pump set in concrete under its own rickety canopy. This was the business end of the process and as such had a single strip of white tape ceremoniously tied around it. Mounted above, hanging limp in the torpid air, were the Kenyan flag and S.O.D.A.'s own ensign. The latter resembled an imitation postage stamp with the face of a starving child in place of a royal head, franked with the charity's famous initials. This was the same image that graced the discount stamps that raised the funds to make such pumps available.

There was no plaque nor speech to mark the pump's inauguration. With everything ready, the tape was cut by Sir Edward for the sake of the cameras before the diesel engine was cranked into life with a belch of black smoke.

Ludlow posed, gripping the pump's handle for more pictures, then worked it symbolically until the first trickles of water ran free. To avoid delay, the pump had already been primed.

The appearance of the priceless liquid was heralded by the loudest chanting and wildest leaping yet. The crowd was ecstatic. Drums beat, feet pounded, spears clashed, and dust flew in a cacophony of tribal sound. A miracle had just been performed. Water was flowing from the parched earth.

Naked children ran forward completely engulfing Ludlow as they fought to get at the first precious drops.

Sir Edward, the new Knight, saintly father of his flock, stroked their dust-caked heads with gusto, smiling in earnest for the hungry cameras.

'OK. Have you got it?' he asked of Dickson and his crew after a minute of holding the same benign grin. 'You must have enough by now.' He beckoned Mr. Kirini to join him. 'Come, come. We must have some pictures taken together.'

The Junior Minister stepped forward in his well pressed safari outfit. He seemed somewhat reluctant, not totally at ease to have all the snotty-nosed kids rubbing up against him. He kept his manicured hands well above their heads, which meant holding them at shoulder height as if in surrender.

'Smile, Solomon,' Ludlow urged, hardly moving his lips from their renewed grin. 'This will not go unnoticed in Nairobi.'

Solomon Kirini's feigned smile suddenly left him. One of the jostling children had just peed against his trouser leg. Not much, just one little spurt, but it was rich and yellow and stank to high heaven.

The Junior Minister was not amused. Forgetting the cameras, he flicked the erring child across the ear with the feathered fly-swot he was carrying, which only forced another odious squirt from the poor boy's minuscule outlet. This time Mr. Kirini's other leg got the benefit.

'I think a handshake is in order, Solomon, don't you?' Ludlow said, offering his hand, becoming aware of Kirini's discomfort. 'And please smile. Try to think of our mutual agreement should Wilson-Hughes win the irrigation contract.'

Whatever that agreement might have been, the thought of it did the trick. Solomon Kirini forgot about smelling like an open sewer and tried to see the funny side of the incident. They both did. Ludlow more genuinely as they shook hands.

The photograph on the front page of the Kenyan Times the next day read: 'Sir Edward Ludlow and Junior Minister, Mr. Solomon Kirini share a joke at the unveiling of S.O.D.A.'s 100th water pump.'

No-one reading it came close to guessing the exact nature of the 'joke'.

Chapter Six

Peter Tyler was still huddled against the tree like an injured animal wary of going out into the open. He had been there 20 minutes or so with no sign of Stephanie returning. His decision was to hang around for another fifteen or so and if she hadn't shown by then to ride down to Compton Stud stables in case she had gone back by another route.

But he decided to move sooner. He was cold and wet and sensed she wasn't going to appear. While waiting, he'd had time to think about why he was taking this trouble to help Stephanie. It wasn't hard to figure out. If he was to believe all he read in the papers, she hated her husband. 'And that makes two of us,' he mused. 'Partners in crime.'

The tabloids made no bones about declaring the marriage was on the rocks. The pair had not been seen together for months. The copy steered clear of suggesting extra marital affairs were the cause, since, for all their efforts, journalists could not find the slightest hint of one. They pushed the drink and drugs angle to the limit, moralizing about the pitfalls of having too much money. The biggest selling weekly on the planet, The National Enquirer, after weeks of column inches spent probing, decided to sum up the couple's disharmony in a report that could have been summed up in two words: 'Shit happens.'

To revive his circulation and to warm up, Peter Tyler selected a low gear and took to the bridle path. The deep sandy soil was perfect to make his legs work. He had to hammer his pedals like a pile driver to get any movement and keep his balance. It did the trick. He couldn't get up to any speed but by the time he had broken out of the woods ten minutes later, he had built up so much of a sweat, he had to stop momentarily to remove his cape. From where he was now standing, the bridle path curved gently down through ferns and young pines. Beyond, rising out of the trees about a mile distant, sat Compton Stud.

From his elevated viewpoint all focus of attention fell disharmoniously upon two gleaming satellite dishes sitting on its roof. Ludlow was well ahead of the communications game.

'The 'big-bang' of '86 had hit the mansion with the subtlety of an air-raid.

Compton Stud was a stud no more. The stables remained, however, horseshoed around a yard set away from the rear of the house outside the boundary wall. It had twelve stalls, only two of which were occupied these days. A colt and a mare had that honour. Both hers. Ludlow did not ride at all.

The main building was a beautifully proportioned William and Mary Manor House, with an elegantly pillared front portal and all-round dormer windows on the third level. Its classic lines retained the solid charm and permanence the architect had so meticulously created. But seen from any distance, all visual attention was drawn to those two monstrous satellite dishes placed atop like a gas mask on the Mona Lisa.

Peter coasted the downward stretch of the bridle path keeping to the side to avoid the soft stuff. He was wondering what he might do if Stephanie hadn't got back. He couldn't hang around all day. Should he try to get to the main house? That would mean climbing the wall, which he didn't fancy doing. Security cameras were all over the place. Extras had been added during the demonstration days.

Stephanie had been screaming 'no-one must know'. What was that all about? She must have been on some sort of mission. He would have to tread carefully. The bulging envelope had to be given back to her in person. He couldn't just plonk it through the letter box even if he could find one. That was out of the question.

Peter knew all the regular staff were on holiday. Robby Pike, the gardener, better known as the 'Marlsbury Echo' on account of the interest he took in knowing everyone's business was the source of that knowledge. Ludlow was away in Kenya. That left Tilda Bahnlich, Stephanie's personal 'au pair', as old Pikey sarcastically called her. She followed Stephanie around like a shadow, so how come she hadn't been riding out with Stephanie today? That had been curious.

As he got closer to Compton Stud, he would have to be a little bit canny in case he bumped into that woman and not Stephanie. He would invent something. Say he was looking for Robby Pike, the gardener, and hope that satisfied her.

These thoughts suddenly went out of the window!

As the bridle path took a final dip down toward the stables, the back of the house came into view beyond its surrounding wall.

He pulled up. Was he seeing things?

He wasn't.

With its two rear wheels hanging over into the sunken garden, its chassis lying flat on the parapet like a beached whale, a Range Rover was throwing up smoke as if about to burst into flames.

'What the .?' He was trying to work out exactly what must have happened.

For some reason he suddenly thought Stephanie might be in the vehicle. He raced down, circumnavigating the stables. Leaning his bike against the boundary wall, he stood on the saddle ready to jump over if he had to. But one look told him that wouldn't be necessary. No-one was in the car. Neither was there any danger of fire.

The bonnet was so hot, the rain falling on it was turning to steam. The engine must have been running for some time. As if to confirm this, it began to cough and splutter and a few moments later, died. Out of fuel?

Someone must have shoved the car into reverse by mistake, or lost control somehow. Stephanie? Did that explain her hyper-state?

'Stephanie!' he shouted; in case she'd got back and was within earshot in the gardens. No response.

Should he jump over and knock on the door? No. He was already 'out- of-bounds'. Cameras might be focusing on him right now for all he knew. Best leave it.

He checked the stable area just in case she had come back. But she hadn't. There was just a lone horse in its stall.

He retraced his steps to where they had bumped into each other, but there was no sign she might have returned. He didn't bother going further. The envelope would have to stay with him for now.

He headed home.

Compton Stud was by any standards a very big place. And, what with the studio complex, self-contained accommodation, offices and private living quarters, it was expedient to have four different telephone lines, each with its own number. Two of these were for business, two were private, the latter having multiple telephone points spread around the entire property. There was a fifth line, however, only familiar to Ludlow's inner circle, that went directly to his private office care-of one of the satellite dishes on the roof. The other more conventional four lines were manned in normal working hours by a telephonist who sat in front of an exchange point situated in a cubby-hole of a room little more than a closet with only a small window. This alone was good reason enough for the position to often fall vacant. But there were other reasons; boredom, isolation, and most of all, once the thrill of working in close proximity to a famous supermodel had worn thin, the terrible atmosphere in the building. One that could not possibly have been foreseen before taking the job, but which would all too soon became apparent.

Without question, the incumbent telephonist's most satisfying task of the day was to set the system to its automatic relays at going home time.

This Mary Sutton had faithfully done at 5.30 on New Year's Eve, the day her employer, Edward Ludlow, had that morning left on his trip to Africa. It had been the most unpleasant past couple of days she had experienced in three months of holding the post. Some of the wildest abuse and threats that Mary had ever witnessed had echoed around the house daily, even penetrating the thick walls and closed doors of the office suite, an area of the house into which Stephanie was not allowed to venture. If this was for the sake of peace and quiet for the staff, it wasn't working. Mary Sutton had just about had enough of it.

Thus, on that last day of 1987 as she put on her coat against the foul weather and braced herself for the journey home, Mary came to a decision. She would never set foot in the house again. She would get a job in a shop, or something. Compton Stud was beginning to frighten her. She'd had enough of the foul mouthing and violent outbursts, let alone sitting alone in what was little more than a cell.

Everybody in that mad house seemed to be on edge and bad tempered. None of it was directed at Mary herself, mind you. She would have been long gone even sooner if it had been. But it rubbed off. It would have taken someone really thick for it not to have.

Stephanie could be terrifying sometimes. So unpredictable. One minute as calm as anything, as if on another planet. Serene and distant. Then bang! Eruption!

Mr. Ludlow and his cronies had their moments, too. That was usually about business, though. On the phones, generally.

Mary often wondered if it was a hormonal thing with Stephanie. She looked much older than her years, but still young enough to have kids.

Was that something to do with it? Was she hankering after having a baby? She shuddered. The thought of it! In *that* house? 'Do me a favour! If she's left it too late, it was her own bloody fault. You pays your money and makes your choice.' Mary thought. It was pointless wasting sympathy on someone that rich. But even so....

When Mary finally flicked the switches to automatic on that last day, she had not the slightest inkling that every call she had connected on the four lines while she had been in the job (including her own rather lengthy ones to friends to help the days pass quicker) had been automatically recorded on a tape recorder tucked discreetly away in the computer room. The short delay and barely perceptible click each time the receiver was picked up had gone innocently unnoticed.

The only line without these diversions was Ludlow's personal line in the clouds.

It was not this line that Victor Rose called just after 6 pm on Friday, 1st January 1988, UK time. All he got was noise. No connection. The same response came from all four house lines. 'Fuck. Fuck! What's going on?' Finally, he called the Motorola cellphone that Tilda Bahnlich had been told to always keep in her possession.

Same result.

In Nairobi, Rose slammed the receiver down, picking it up again to check the lines weren't dead going out from the hotel. All was well there, he was assured, which wound him up even more. 'What the fuck's going on? Nothing's getting through.'

'We *did* give Bahnlich a brick phone, didn't we?' Ludlow asked. Bricks were what he called the weighty Motorolas. He could already guess the answer. Victor would not have forgotten something like that.

'Tried that number,' came the frustrated answer. 'Over and over! Nothing! The stupid cow probably forgot to charge it or won't carry it because the thing doesn't fit in her fucking handbag!'

Victor Rose knew he was exaggerating. Although the Motorola was built like a brick, so was Tilda. She had no problem carrying it around. Muscle for muscle, she would have given Victor, himself, a fair run for his money. She was not a woman who bothered with a handbag, either. She had a pouch on a belt around her tight midriff for the 'brick', and a backpack strapped to her wide shoulders for other necessary things. Hands free.

Ludlow let the comments pass. He knew Rose didn't get on with Bahnlich, being somehow intimidated by her uncomplaining efficiency. 'Maybe she's out of range.' He suggested.

'She was meant to be sitting on the phone in the office!'

'We did say six, didn't we? UK time?' Ludlow checked, wondering if Victor had got his part of the arrangement wrong. Bahnlich rarely made mistakes. 'Too right, we did!' Rose responded, put out by the question. '*And* she was expressly told to ring us here at the Norfolk if she didn't hear from us!'

'Sounds like our Tilda might have a problem.'

'She'll have an even bigger one if she doesn't call soon,' Rose threatened.

'Give her some space, Victor. Try her again in a few minutes. She can usually handle things. Don't forget who she's dealing with. Try my private number. See if that's got a problem.'

Victor did. This time it rang. So, the house exchange was down. And Tilda's cellphone. But not the satellite line.

Chapter Seven

Ludlow had moved Tilda Bahnlich to London from S.O.D.A.'s international headquarters in Zurich where she had been in charge of health and security. He had seen the worth of employing her talents closer to home where a more poignant local health and security risk had been developing in the form of his wife's both physical and mental deterioration.

Bahnlich had made her presence felt immediately and was initially well received by Rose as well as by Jenny Grant, Ludlow's conventional secretary, both of whom had become increasingly irritated by the growing burden of having to deal with Stephanie's disruptive behaviour. They had enough worries running Ludlow's everyday business affairs without having to iron out the crumpled sheets of his matrimonial bed.

At first, Stephanie thought the Swiss woman might be there to share her husband's bed? Good luck to her if she was. But she soon doubted it. Jenny Grant was more her husband's type, and vice versa. 'It takes one to know one!' was how Stephanie saw Jenny Grant. On the make, slyly angling to get between the sheets with him. Well, good luck to her, too, if that's what she was after.

But the penny soon dropped. Tilda Bahnlich had not been recruited as her husband's bedmate, nor as a productive member of his workforce. She was there to keep an eye on her! Personally, and exclusively! The woman was never out of her sight. She did have her uses, though, as a driver. Stephanie had only avoided a prison sentence by some smart lawyer-talk after being caught drink-drug-driving one time too many. The other good thing about Tilda was that she never complained. Another time, another place, they could have been friends.

Apart from not being allowed to drive, her husband would no longer even allow Stephanie into a car with him, whether he was driving himself or being chauffeured. She was too disruptive. All down to Tilda now and she was doing a good job. But right now, her silence was rubbing Rose up the wrong way as he paced about Ludlow's suite at the Norfolk Hotel in Nairobi.

'If there isn't a good reason for this, I'll give her such a bollocking she'll wish she was back in the fucking army!' Rose promised, hovering over the telephone ready to pounce, willing it to ring so he could do just that. 'Six o'clock, we said. And six it should have been!'

Peter Tyler took it easy on his ride home from the stables at Compton Stud. He forsook his normal run to beat the clock. He needed a gentler pace to allow him to think.

One way or another, to state the obvious, Stephanie had problems. Drugs, yes. Drink, yes. Marriage, oh yes. But what could possibly be the reason for her to go riding out in this weather dressed like that? It had to have been her who had backed the Range Rover onto the parapet. That was the only explanation. She probably hadn't driven for yonks, having the threat of prison hanging over her. What had made her so desperate to take such a chance? It had obviously all gone wrong. So, she jumped on her horse instead! Dressed like that? Lunacy in this weather. Why not go back and put some sensible clothes on?

Plainly something was wrong, and he felt she had been about to reach out to him for help. Beseechingly. And he would have helped. In anyway, if he could. Still would. Who wouldn't? The world had loved Stephanie once, and the world could be a forgiving place. If her husband was the cause of her troubles, Peter Tyler would be first in line to help her. No love lost there.

Her last words kept coming back to him. 'No-one must know!'

Come what may, he would respect her wishes, whatever it was she didn't want people to know. That meant keeping the envelope safe until he could get it back to her.

It was 2.35 pm when he arrived home. He had been hoping for some time to himself when he got back, but as expected, Gwen was there, her bouncy old French car she called The Red Frog parked up in the street outside. On its second rock around the clock at 50 flat-out, it was all noise and no performance, the complete opposite to its owner's quiet efficiency. The only thing the car had in common with her was reliability, and occasionally, colour.

Stephanie's envelope was ringing wet. He had to be careful with it as he removed it from his saddle bag. He didn't want it splitting open. There was already a slight tear in it, revealing newspaper print.

He needed to keep it out of sight of Gwen's prying eyes until he could get it up to his room. With no pockets in his tight bike clothes, he breathed in and slid the thing down into his skin-tight shorts.

As soon as his feet touched the doormat, Gwen jumped out and grabbed him in a bear hug.

'Happy New Year!' she cried, trying to plant a kiss anywhere on his wriggling face that was trying to avoid just that. 'OK. Don't panic!' she bleated, 'I'm not trying to rape you!' She pushed his chin up so he could see the mistletoe hanging from the hall light. 'You *do* know what day it is, don't you?'

She now stood back and looked at him. 'Blimey! You're in a state.' she said frankly, 'and what's that in your shorts?'

She blushed, suddenly thinking she might have aroused him, casting what was intended to be a quick glance down only to get the shock of her life!

There could be no hiding place in those tight shorts. She *had* aroused him! But it was a funny shape. And big! Her face lit up like the Richter Scale.

'What's got into you, Gwen? Are you still pissed from last night,' he gibed, trying to cover up his suspicious cargo with a hand.

'I'm not. But why shouldn't I be?' she reasoned.

A bowl of water balanced on top of a door was more Gwen's idea of a caper. This was the first time she had ever tried to plant a kiss on him, even if it was only meant as a friendly peck. Nothing to be disturbed about. Gwen was like an older sister to him.

One of her great giveaways being fair skinned, was blushing a lot. Which, with her soft Irish looks, was quite becoming. But when she started to redden up, it increased her embarrassment. She knew it and hated it. When she was *really* embarrassed, even the tip of her nose went red. Like now.

'Your nose has gone all froggy on you.' His usual taunt when she blushed.

'So what?' she said, tossing back her long red hair from her green eyes. 'It's a free country.'

'This is not what your smutty mind is thinking,' he teased, pointing to his groin.

She wasn't going to look down again to satisfy him.

'Playboy!' she teased back.

'You *have* been drinking!'

'Only one sherry! With your mum. It *is* New Year's Day after all in case you hadn't noticed. Some people have to work on Bank Holidays. That's why I'm here. One drink won't do me any harm. I'm thinking of staying over tonight, anyway, so I won't have to drive.'

Her expression suddenly changed to one of concern.

'Have you hurt yourself?' she asked, the colour quickly disappearing from her cheeks. There's blood on your neck.'

'Blood? Can't be," he contradicted. Now the compromise was on him. 'Must be mud. I came off my bike in the woods. It's so slippery up there today.'

'You ought to clean it up in case you've cut yourself. Looks like blood to me.' She tried to turn his head to get a better look, but he wouldn't let her. He shook her away. 'It's blood. I know what bloody blood looks like!'

To escape further unwanted scrutiny, he went up to the bathroom to check himself. It *was* blood. Dried. Where had it come from? Maybe he had cut himself after all. It couldn't be much, though. He hadn't felt a thing.

He stripped off completely but couldn't find a scratch anywhere. A few bruises but nothing else.

In his customary manner after one of his muddier rides, he threw all the clothes he had been wearing into the shower tray and trampled on them to get most of the grime and sweat out while he showered. They would go into the washing machine later.

Looking down, he noticed that each time he stood on his gloves, the slight squish of a stain oozed out. Mud or blood? He studied his hands closely, but there wasn't even a pin prick. Mud.

Wrapping himself in towels, he went to his room and dressed. He rested the envelope on top of some tissue paper in the wardrobe. It could dry out there safely enough until he decided on the next move. Gwen would not venture into his room while he was home.

His mother was asleep when he looked in before going downstairs. He didn't disturb her. Those were her happiest moments.

Gwen was in the kitchen, red in the face again, not through embarrassment this time. Through whisking eggs.

'I thought I'd invite myself to supper to save you the bother of inviting me,' she joked. 'I know you meant to. And I expect you've been dying for me to throw away that turkey stew of yours. You've been eating that since Christmas, I bet.'

There was no hint in her voice of where Gwen hailed from. She was originally from Bristol, so she hadn't strayed far. But her red hair, green eyes and soft manner spoke of Ireland.

'Beats me how you keep up all that training stuff on your diet. I know you're as hard as nails, but there's not much of you.'

'Mind over matter,' he grunted, ignoring the dig about his size. She topped him by about an inch. 'It was a good stew, anyway.'

They ate on their laps. Only rarely had the table been cleared for a proper sit-down meal since his father died. With his arthritic mother invariably in bed, the dining area had become an extension of his workshop. 'Tyler's Initiative' had laid claim to it. It looked like the inside of an exploded television set. The nearest wall was stuck with drawings and plans like a wartime operations room.

His food was gone like a Grand Prix pit stop. The principle being precisely the same. The quicker it went down the sooner he could get on with more important things.

'I have work to do,' he white lied, hoping she would change her mind and decide to go home so he could get back to the drying envelope without interference. 'Somewhere on this table there's a fortune to be made. It won't happen by just looking at it."

He picked up a small length of carbon fibre rod and casually measured it.

'What you need is development money,' she advised. 'I can lend you some more, if you like. Not all that much, though.'

He knew her offer was genuine, her generosity always on tap. Quite a few components owed their existence to donations from Gwen. He had promised her company shares one day.

'Why don't you write to Ludlow? He's rich. You used to work for him. He knows you. Or knows of you, at least. You're always saying he owes you 'big time'.'

Peter ignored the remark rather than give Gwen the pleasure of seeing his feathers ruffled. She knew his feelings about the man.

Actually, on the quiet, he had often thought of touching Ludlow for a loan. He was the obvious target for sponsorship once Peter could get a prototype up and running. The man was sure to remember him, but perhaps not all that fondly. Peter's record at Marlsbury Pumps had been exemplary. But his face had been all over the local newspaper during the demonstrations about the firm's closure. He didn't suppose that had gone down too well with Ludlow.

'I suppose you heard what happened today, didn't you?' Gwen went on, toying with Peter's mood. 'He's been knighted.'

'Yeah, I heard,' he replied with calm irritation. 'I suppose it was inevitable. *Sir* bloody Ludlow.'

'Quite amusing, really, though, isn't it? When you think about it. While he's just about to get knighted, his 'Lady' wife is out getting herself arrested.'

'What?' he blurted.

'Oh. You didn't hear about that, then?'

'About what?'

She paused, playing with his sudden interest.

'Come on, Gwen,' he said. 'Out with it. Stop pissing around.'

'The police raided The King's head last night. Looking for *drugs*.' she emphasised the forbidden substance by squinting her green eyes. 'And who did they drag in with their net along with all the other Marlsbury dead-beats? None other than our lady of the manor. There's slumming it for you, even for *her* these days. You could have got high just walking past the place last night, according to Old Pikey.'

Old Pikey *would* know, wouldn't he? But he might also be embellishing the truth. Surely Stephanie couldn't have been in a cell overnight?

'And she got arrested?'

'For a bit.'

Ah. Now the truth.

'How come?'

'Apparently, when the police told everyone to empty their pockets and bags, she refused outright. Started yelling and screaming 'don't touch

64

me!' Didn't they know who she was? All that sort of thing. Having a right old fit, she was, apparently. Well, according to Pikey, one of the coppers said he knew who she *used* to be, and she really went up the wall. Nearly throttled him before two of them grabbed her. They managed to get her out of the pub but not into the black maria. She was making a terrible racket. There were police everywhere. Reinforcements from Septon.'

'Blimey! Serious stuff,' Peter said, then asked. 'What about that 'minder' woman who's always running round her these days? Wasn't she there?'

'Well,' Gwen paused, knowing she had his undivided attention for once. He tended to blink a lot when he was only pretending to be listening. He was virtually staring at her right now, not a blink in sight. 'Apparently, she suddenly appeared from nowhere, had words with a flat-cap, and got 'madam' off the hook yet again with just a warning. It's alright for some, in't it? Being rich and famous.'

Gwen suddenly giggled and her cheeks went pink.

'I shouldn't laugh,' she went on. 'But something really hilarious happened in the middle of all that last night. Someone told Old Pikey that when the cops arrived, that Salvation Army lady who's always in the pubs doing her rounds was caught up in it. And do you know what? One of the sniffer dogs went straight for her collection box! Some of the lay-abouts must have dumped their dope in it as soon as they saw the cops coming. It was full of pills and stuff, apparently. Can you imagine it? The Salvation Army on suspicion of pushing drugs!'

Peter had to admit there was a touch of uplifting irony in the situation.

Chapter Eight

The helicopter taking Sir Edward Ludlow and his aide to the world-famous Treetops Game Lodge rose above Wilson Airport in Nairobi like an angry cicada.

'Needs a bit of grease up its arse!' Victor Rose shouted over the high-pitched rattle without the hint of a smile. 'Just like Bahnlich!'

It was Saturday morning, 2nd January, and there still had been no word from Stephanie's Swiss minder. She had not surfaced from anywhere.

More out of anger and resentment than feelings of duty, Rose had been constantly trying to reach Bahnlich through the night. All the while, doubts had been growing in Ludlow' mind. There could be no question. Something was amiss.

Jenny Grant had been alerted. There was little they could do about the situation but wait for her to report back.

'We should hear from her in a few hours,' Ludlow yelled over the chopper's clattering rotors. Jenny was driving up from her parents' home in Cornwall, having broken her new year's holiday at his urgent request.

'As long as she hasn't lost her precious contact lenses and ended up in a ditch!' Rose muttered under his breath. There was even less love lost between Victor Rose and Jenny Grant than there was with Bahnlich. Grant was neurotic. Too full of her own importance for a jumped-up typist. Rose was convinced she had hidden designs on her boss. 'Thinks she's royalty!' This opinion of Jenny, some might have said, sprang directly from the fact that she had wound him up on more than one occasion by tacitly intimating he should come out of the 'closet'.

'It'll take her all day the way she drives!' he shouted.

'Well, we couldn't have chosen a better place to wait than Treetops,' Ludlow yelled back. 'And far safer than being back in England,' he was thinking.

Treetops was one of those immensely romantic African hotels where an Ernest Hemingway lurked behind every bush and gin and tonic. It was built on stilts overlooking a water-hole flood-lit at night to show off the various creatures dropping in for a nocturnal drink, much the same as the packaged tourists who were also gone by morning. But what better pleasure for thirsty travellers after a long and dusty journey than to sit on the balcony at twilight, favourite tipple in hand, and await the silent call of the wild to drink?

Ludlow and his aide were guests of the Kenyan government for their short stay at this magnificent 'game lodge'. Dr. Daudi Bamdar, the minister under whom Mr. Kirini served had thought Treetops the ideal setting to continue the series of informal discussions about the forthcoming irrigation project. The waterhole below them was symbolic, was it not? If that dried up, not only would the animals die, but so would the tourists and thence, Treetops itself.

No hard bargaining was expected during their brief visit. These meetings usually took the form of a public relations jolly, where views on the underlying principles of partnership were exchanged. There would be a lot of contractors and subcontractors involved, all wondering what was going to be in it for them. This quest started at the top. Various arrangements had to be ironed out first before the joint venture would be assigned to the successful tender. Ludlow was fully aware that other groups were in the race, but he was sure Hughes (Kenya) were best placed in the field. Whatever 'extras' other companies should offer, Hughes (Kenya) under Wilson Hughes large umbrella, could step in and offer more. Knowing what the competitors were offering was where Ludlow's personal relationship with the Junior Minister, Solomon Kirini, paid dividends. It was the sort of knowledge that deserved reward. Substantially more, should Hughes (Kenya) eventually be given the huge contract.

'You're certain they know at the desk where we are, Howard?' Rose questioned the ruddy-faced PR man Pankerton as the newcomers settled down to lunch. 'It doesn't actually feel like we're at the centre of the universe here. I swear the telephonist was asleep when I went to find out why I couldn't get through to him from my room.'

'They're on the ball now, Victor, I promise,' Pankerton assured him, fully geared up for the occasion. 'It's a different pace here, but things do get done.' He turned to Ludlow. 'Is everything else OK? Any requests?'

'How are the other trips jacking up?' Ludlow asked with no real interest.

'All in hand,' Pankerton was happy to report, okaying the wine that was to go with the freshly caught impala on the menu. 'The Trade Fair in Jo'burg at the end of the week. Then Abuja.'

Ludlow nodded distantly, in a way that told Pankerton his supremo was not completely with him. And he was right. If Sir Edward could have been faxed, he would have been flat out to Compton Stud.

The roasted impala appeared at their table by pure coincidence to squeals from outside. A family of baboons had chosen the same moment to arrive at the waterhole. One of them must have committed a social misdemeanour and perhaps the rest were ganging up on it.

Ludlow was brooding inwardly. His acolytes sensed it and left him to himself.

For more than three years now, ever since things had started moving with great force for him in the city, Stephanie had been becoming more and more unbearable. Having a junkie for a wife did him no favours. It had been bad enough from the start after that original shock in the bedroom and her sudden rise to fame with all the demands her growing ego had let loose. There had been a steady decline in her career, but now it had become terminal. The contracts had long dried up along with her skin. Booze and drugs had taken over. It had reached the point now for Ludlow where she had to be controlled, kept sweet and *alive*. And least until he found a way to stop the rot, to nullify the threat posed by the disc and her 'safe hands'.

For a while she had tried to hide her fading youth by smothering her face with the products that had once played their part in her rise to fame. Bad move. She would sometimes end up looking more like the cocked arse of daddy baboon down there at the water hole after plastering herself. Her day had gone. She had become yesterday's news as a supermodel. For more than a year now, she had been hitting the headlines for different reasons.

He had to take some of the blame, he guessed. But making money from his wife's drug addiction had not been his intention, just that it was wiser to control the source of her habit by cutting out the dealers who might become a problem down the line, so to speak. He could protect his enterprise better that way.

He knew only too well that the riches flowing from his creation, Stephanie Star, would not last forever. Other, younger darling things were emerging. Fashions were changing. Stephanie had already had what could be called 'a very good run', but it could have developed into something more lasting had things gone differently. Things took a dive for her when her drug addiction had finally taken a crippling hold about three years since. And now, in recent months, a Frankenstein monster had metamorphosed.

Peter Tyler had a rough night. He was up long before dawn doing his exercises. He crept back into the house just after eight hoping Gwen and his mother were still asleep. They were. He grabbed a yogurt and a bottle of water and was out again with his bike within minutes. Rain was still in the air but at least it wasn't lashing down.

He usually spent time some mornings in the back room of a shop called Hollom's Attic in Marlsbury which sold toys, games, model kits, as well as all things second hand too valuable or cumbersome for a charity shop; tv sets, tape recorders furniture, kitchen appliances and the like.

Peter had his own set of keys so he could come and go as he pleased whenever Martin Hollom, the owner, wasn't there. His main task was putting model kits together, as well as helping out in the shop at busy times. Martin was a bit like an uncle to Peter, having no children of his own.

He took his time pedalling into town, not taking the Beacon Ridge route. That would be even muddier today after another wet night. He thought of taking the road past the front gates of Compton Stud and giving the entry-phone a buzz. But he reckoned it might be too early for that. Maybe on his way back later.

The road he chose took him past the site of the relocated Marlsbury Pump factory. In little more than two years the place had been knocked down and replaced by a 24-hour supermarket. Next to it stood its own multi-story car park and a 'village' complex of box-like town houses you wouldn't have seen Peter dead in.

One word summed up Marlsbury; pigs. In the good old days, some locals would have told you, Marlsbury Market was the biggest and best in the county. The whole range of British livestock once paraded the cobblestoned town square each Wednesday from early till late, spilling over into the side streets with the smell of a ripe profit in the air. Market day was *the* day of the week as far as Marlsbury was concerned. The day when the town exploded into life.

In the ways of the modern world, Marlsbury had been driven to specialise, much to the regret of anyone who had ever witnessed the hard-fought deal for a pedigree bull. Now it was just pigs, and being just pigs, the pens and enclosures had been taken down from the square to make room for yellow lines and vehicles, removed to a far less dignified plot away from the town centre where the old cinema once stood.

Nowadays, the market square was filled by that itinerant band of traders who move from one market town to the next like drunks chasing extended pub hours.

There were two pig processing factories in and around Marlsbury owned by the same company. One specialized in cured bacon products, the other in fresh meat. Also rolling off the conveyor belts of both plants in their thousands, was what many a pundit in the field considered to be their finest creation, the product that had made the town a household name; the Marlsbury Pork Sausage. Eaten with a dip of Marlsbury mustard or the like named sweet pickle, so the advertising went, and a true taste of Olde England was promised on the tongue.

When Marlsbury Pumps Ltd closed, the food processing plants took on a few of the younger laid-off workers, but a certain amount of unemployment had come to stay. This brought a feeling of waste among those affected, which over the months had been exasperated by the gradual influx of people being pushed further and further out of London by escalating house prices. The commuter belt was becoming more and more extended.

It was a picturesque town in its own way even now, with many old buildings listed and protected along the High Street and around the square. The church with its wonderful spire still pulled in coachloads of visitors during the summer season, which helped a handful of souvenir shops to survive.

But the place that perhaps thrived most from the passing trade was the S.O.D.A. charity shop. In fact, it had grown into something of a tourist attraction itself, with its tangible connection to that once national treasure, Stephanie Star, wife of the charity's flamboyant founder. This was the very first S.O.D.A. shop to have been established, which happened to be in one of the older, better-preserved buildings in town. Worth a look at for that reason itself. Half-timbered, with slightly over-hanging upper levels, it immediately drew the eye, evoking unmistakably Dickensian flavours.

As Peter passed the shop that morning, it was even more eye-catching than usual. One of its bow-fronted windows had been smashed in!

He pulled up and looked at the gaping hole. Two workmen were carefully tapping away at the jagged edges.

Whatever had happened, it couldn't possibly have been a smash and grab. There was nothing in the window worth stealing. In the whole shop, come to that. The place was full of jumble like most charity shops, mainly old crockery and once loved clothes and books. SODA stamps didn't come here to be sorted anymore, as they had in the early days. They now ended up at the central S.O.D.A. premises in Slough, West of London, where they arrived in their millions.

This mother shop in Marlsbury was little more than a showpiece now, a place to remind people of the humble beginnings of the Ludlow empire.

There were three people in the shop apart from the workmen. The two women who ran it and the daughter of one of them, Mary Sutton, the young girl who until her recent decision had worked the switchboard at Compton Stud.

Mary had just been telling her mother about quitting the position when she noticed Peter Tyler standing outside.

'Maybe he was the sod who chucked the bottle through the window?' Mary's mother joked. 'He's the one who kept ranting on about being put out of work, isn't he?'

'No. It weren't 'im, mum,' Mary said, turning her head to avoid Peter's eye. She always thought eye-contact meant you were promising someone something. 'It was Lady Muck, alright. You should have heard her goings-on the other day. She's demented, that one. Then all that kerfuffle at The King's Head. They reckon someone saw her throw the bottle from her Range Rover.'

'Poor woman,' her mother said, watching Peter move off. 'Something's going on up there in that big house.'

'You don't have to tell me!' Mary responded knowingly.

Peter's first port of call was Hollom's Attic.

'Morning, Peter. What are you looking so mysterious about?' Martin Hollom asked as soon as Peter walked in. 'Haven't finally pieced that initiative thing of yours together, have you?'

This was an on-going gibe.

'Won't be long now. I'll soon be able to buy you out.'

'By the time you've finished that damn thing, I'll be ready to pop my clogs! You'll be welcome to the place.'

Martin Hollom was a jovial, avuncular middle-aged man with rosy cheeks he authentically called his cyder blossoms, or sometimes simply Hollom's blossoms. The local cyder was a drink to which he was especially partial. Its excellence, he reckoned, rivalled that of the Marlsbury sausage itself. Partaking of the two at the same sitting (with mustard, not pickle, he would stress, because that took away the sweetness of the cyder) was better than champagne and caviar any day of the week.

'What's up? Any rush on?' Peter asked, without real interest.

'Nothing new, m'boy" Martin answered, glancing at the door which had just 'pinged' open. 'Anyway, you've got enough to be getting on with out back, haven't you? With that Sopwith Pup?'

Peter nodded. 'You could say that.'

'How much longer is that going to be taking up space?'

Peter chose to treat that as a rhetorical question.

Two young boys stood patiently in attendance with tight fists around some money they had no doubt been given for Christmas. Hollom's Attic was possibly about to get its first sale of the new year.

Peter left Martin to deal with them and went through to the back room where he helped out assembling kits. It was really just a hobby to stave off the boredom of being unemployed. Martin paid him whatever he thought each particular job was worth rather than hours spent. It was never very much, but it was cash in hand with no questions asked.

Right now, he was constructing a kit for an old man who had years ago piloted a Sopwith Pup. There was an original blueprint that the old guy wanted scaled down by a third. Peter had jumped at the project, which was now taking up quite a bit of space in the already cluttered back room. The wingspan of the model worked out at almost nine feet! Hollom had guessed this might be a problem, but the size of the fee had been too tempting to turn down.

Peter was happy about that. Hollom took the lion's shar of the fee, since he was providing the space and components, but it was still a good little earner for himself. A bonus being it was less of challenge than his Initiative, because he had a detailed plan to work from which made it easier to think of other things whilst working. Today he had been doing a lot more thinking than model building trying to figure out how to handle the situation he found himself in with Stephanie's soggy envelope.

Chapter Nine

'Your doppelganger's been at it again, Sharon.' Kim said from across the formica table in Ches's Cafe as she waited for her bacon sarnie.

'What's she done now?' Sharon wondered, elbows on table, hands wrapped round a mug of weak tea. You had to ask for *weak* tea at Ches's if you didn't want the roof of your mouth taken off. Ches's Cafe was open five days a week at six in the morning to cater for all those early-morning workers who couldn't bother, or didn't have the facilities, to cook breakfast at home. It was a very popular cafe. Sharon and Kim rarely came in before one o'clock and very often only just made it before closing time at three. It was one of those days. The girls had had a late night. Girls? Women, really, with the amount of experience they had under their suspender belts. They were both still only twenty but knew all the ropes of street life in Manchester.

Kim had her nose in a dog-eared copy of The Daily Scan she had picked up as they entered the cafe. Its 'girlie' page had been well thumbed. Mary Whitehouse's cage would have been rattling loudly to learn that just one copy of 'that sinful publication' should have tainted so many eyes.

But Kim was looking at a different page.

'Your Steff seems to have thrown a bottle through her old man's junk shop!' She chortled, offering Sharon the pages she had open. Most of the left one was taken up with a photograph of SODA's smashed window in Marlsbury. The right-hand side had an equally large picture that had captured a raging Stephanie Star, looking very displeased, struggling with two uniformed policemen. A smaller picture of the 'The Kings Head' pub sign was inserted at the foot of it.

The copy-writer's headline: 'Scenes From A Marriage' might have evoked a copyright claim had a pedantic lawyer for the Ingmar Bergman Estate noticed it.

'Gawd,' Sharon said, more interested in the picture of her 'doppelganger' than the one of the smashed shop window. 'Look at the state of her! What would Tony say if I turned up for work looking like that?'

'I doubt he'd see the funny side of it. You never know, though. It would give the punters something else to laugh about,' Kim suggested.

Tony was the owner of the nightclub where Sharon and Kim worked the tables. 'Tony's Ring' it was called, *ring* as in wrestling ring. Tony had found modest fame and fortune in the show-biz version of the sport, the one that was never seen at the Olympics Games. His club was situated in a southern suburb of Manchester where little else in the way of late-night entertainment could be found.

'Tony's Ring' offered more than a small dance floor and expensive drinks. One of its more innocent pleasures was to present the clients with an opportunity to be waited on by the stars of past and present. Not the actual stars themselves, of course, but their lookalikes, their doppelgangers.

All those who worked 'out front' at Tony's had to have the potential of being made up to look like someone famous: anybody famous. Even a 'Hitler' worked at Tony's! That was Andrew Collins, and the more he kept in character, the bigger the tips came his way, often thrown at him like hand-grenades!

When Sharon and Kim had seen the advertisement and rang Tony, Sharon was offered a job without a second thought. She bore such a remarkable likeness to Stephanie Star she would need very little done to astound people with the likeness. Just a wig to match the page-boy look that had helped make Stephanie Star internationally famous, and Bob would be your uncle, as long as it covered Sharon's own wild punk hairstyle and studded ears convincingly enough.

Sharon could tell how enthusiastic Tony was about her, but not so keen on Kim. She didn't exactly say it out loud, but he sensed that if he didn't take Kim, he would not get Sharon. Which was in fact the case. The girls had been doing things together all through their school days and ever since. They had no plans to go their own ways.

Tony could see Sharon was a gem. There was a bit of fun about her too, apart from her good looks. He liked that. He reckoned with a little work, Kim could pass as a reasonable Jane Russell from the neck down, at least. Her big tits more than fitted that bill. He could go along with that, so they were in.

It was exclusively table service at 'Tony's Ring'. Very little food was available. There had to be *some*, for licensing reasons. Most people who frequented the place knew that the menus on the tables were for the sake of appearance. Most of the dishes on it were marked, 'sold out' or 'unavailable tonight'. If you wanted a slice of pizza, however, you were in luck, although the choice of topping never changed. It was either cheese or pepperoni, bought in bulk from Iceland (the store, not the nation, of course), charged out at exorbitant prices to discourage demand. Microwaved into the bargain for expedience.

There was more profit in cocktails than food. Apart from that, plates were messier and took up more room in the dishwashers. So, if a punter's hunger was great enough for a slice of pizza, it would arrive on a cardboard plate with no trimmings and no cutlery, just tissues for wiping hands.

Tony's never got going until after the pubs closed. It was assumed most people would have eaten by then. A punter's appetite was more likely to be for what was on offer 'Upstairs'.

Jenny Grant was feeling quite sorry for herself by the time she was nearing Compton Stud. Why her? Why couldn't someone else check up on Bahnlich? It wasn't Jenny's job. If Edward would only get his wife committed instead of covering up for her all the time, Bahnlich would not have been necessary at all.

The impressive wrought-iron gates to Compton Stud were set back sufficiently from the road for vehicles to pull in out of the way of passing traffic.

When Jenny jolted to a halt in front of them, she delved into her Guchi bag for the gate-opening device and pointed it through the windscreen. One press would have been enough, but in her up-tight mood her patience was non-existent. She kept hitting the button again and again as if it would make the heavy gates open any quicker. Once through them, there was a long winding unpaved single-track driveway bordered on both sides by rhododendron bushes. She drove now with more care. Any sort of speed tended to throw up gravel. Even though the jeep was vaguely meant for recreational 'off-road' use, being custom-sprayed pink changed any idea of that. Jenny was acutely concerned about damaging the paintwork.

As she took the final bend in the drive and the house finally came into full view, her feeling of pique at being asked, no, ordered, to make this journey was joined by one of apprehension. It was obvious something unusual had been going on, and she was the one who had to deal with it. Alone.

She couldn't handle Stephanie at the best of times, especially if she was in one of her cold turkey moods. As for Bahnlich, Jenny had no say in her terms of employment. They had hardly ever spoken to each other. And now, on her boss's instructions as relayed in the words of Victor Rose, Jenny was to give Bahnlich 'a right bollocking' for not answering his calls.

She pulled the car up close to the portico at the main entrance, switched off the engine and took a deep breath. She sat for a moment looking down at the large bunch of keys that lay on the passenger seat. It had been a long drive, and she hadn't been looking forward to this moment. She had to prepare herself. It would be easy enough to tone down verbally reprimanding Bahnlich for whatever she had or had not done. But trying to sort out what was wrong with the telephone connections? What did she know about that stuff? She had been strictly forbidden to call in a technician to help. For security reasons, she was told, while no staff were there.

Jenny got out, cradling the bunch of keys. There were so many of them, she found it difficult with her small hands to turn the things en masse to open the door. Hopefully Bahnlich was out nurse-maiding Stephanie somewhere, so she could take a quick look at the telephone problems in peace and make a rapid exit. The 'bollocking' could then be left in the form of a note, telling Bahnlich to get in touch with Edward immediately. His itinerary had been left for her, with all the numbers she might need to know.

The alarm system was off, which meant someone was in. 'Shit!' Jenny swore as she braced herself. She made directly for the heavy oak stairs. She turned left on the first landing, which led to that part of the house set aside for all things business. There were several offices in this wing, one of which was her own. There was also a storeroom, a basic kitchen, his and her bathrooms, a telephone receptionist's 'cubby hole', a computer room and Ludlow's private office which was always double-locked.

Along from the top of the first flight of stairs, she turned into the corridor leading to the 'office' entrance and stopped dead. 'What the fuck!' she breathed involuntarily. The door was wide open. This was not good. It was never meant to be left open, whether occupied or not. Always locked, going in or out. The reason? Stephanie. For her, it had been a strict no-go area since the incident with the floppy disc. Even more now, because the computer room was where the tape recorder keeping tabs on her telephone calls was kept.

And that door was also wide open!

As Jenny moved toward it, she breathed in a foul odour, adding panic to growing nausea. Then, horror. One of the Motorola brick cellphones lay on the floor in the doorway. Something glistened on it. Blood! Sickeningly, with strands of hair caught in it.

Looking into the room, she had to grab the door frame to stay on her feet.

Sprawled across the floor, head down, face obscured by rivers of congealed blood, lay the stinking corpse of Tilda Bahnlich, a gash so deep in her skull that the blow must have been horrendous.

Jenny dropped to her knees in a whispering faint but recovered enough to prevent complete collapse. The stench was unbearable.

There had been other blows. Bahnlich's hands had been battered mercilessly. The tape recorder lay in tatters beside them. No tape. The petty cash box lay open and empty.

Jenny had to get out of there. As she staggered along the corridor to escape the horror, she somehow held back from vomiting. She was weeping in gushes. What the hell should she do?

She'd been told to ring Edward as soon as she knew anything. But what about the police? Shouldn't she call them first? Her mind was racing. No. Edward first. Let him deal with it.

All the offices had telephones, but she couldn't get a line out. When she looked in at the small reception room, she immediately saw why. The switchboard had been demolished! Tangled wires sprouted everywhere.

Now what?

Her mobile! The slab she called it. She groaned as she switched it on. Did it have enough charge? It did. Just about. But she wasn't going to ring him from here. She was shaking uncontrollably. The missing tape told her it had to be Stephanie's doing. What if she was still lurking somewhere? Jenny didn't want to be around for a repeat performance! She rushed out of the house and drove, trying to keep the details of the horror in her head. Edward would want to know everything. The tape and the petty cash had gone, they were the main things to remember. Petty cash! She knew there had been over twenty grand in the box. That might suggest burglary if anyone knew about it. But the smashed tape recorder and telephone lines? That said, Stephanie, in one of her rages!

Jenny knew she should have checked all the doors and windows at the back of the house. Perhaps it was as well she didn't. Had she seen the stranded Range Rover, even bigger panic would have hit her about Stephanie still being around somewhere. She already had enough without that telling her to get away from the place as quickly as possible.

She felt it would be safer to wait until she was outside the gates before ringing Edward in case she needed a quick getaway. Once through them, she parked, trembling like jelly. Her heart was thumping as she sorted through the contact numbers she'd been given. With the charge on the phone running low, she had to get this right. She noted the time and did a calculation. Edward should be at Treetops Hotel.

It took ages to get through.

Her distressed call came at a bad time for Ludlow. Dr. Bambar had just arrived, and the two parties were being ushered into a private conference room. It was left to Rose to take the call. He went to his room for that pleasure, not wishing to be restricted in his use of language. It was just as well.

'Fucking hell! was his predictable response to the news that Tilda Bahnlich was dead. 'Are you serious?' He guessed she was. Jenny could hardly get words out. 'OK, calm down. Take your time. Give the whole thing to me slowly. Every detail.'

This Jenny managed to do between sobs and brief spells of amnesia. The tears continued to pour, much to her annoyance at having someone as thick and unsympathetic as Rose to witness her tender state. His only response was the occasional 'Fucking Hell!' He showed no concern for her feelings whatsoever.

'That's it?' he barked when he sensed she had dried up. 'You didn't see the bitch anywhere?'

'No.'

'OK. Don't touch anything. Don't do anything. Stay put! Understand? Just make sure you've got a signal on your cellphone and standby for a call back.'

'Make it quick!' she urged. 'The battery's getting low.'

Ludlow knew the tidings were not good as soon as he saw Victor's face.

'Please excuse me, Doctor. I've got some personal international news to attend to,' he explained, managing to stay calm. They went to a quiet corner.

The news was even worse than he had been expecting. Unimaginably worse. His face went grey. There was only one glimmer of respite he could see. He was thinking ahead. It was Saturday night. None of the financial markets would be open.

'What do you want me to tell her, Ted?' Victor asked, with his own sense of helplessness, a condition he would normally have tried to cure with violence. But that wouldn't work here.

No answer came. Ludlow looked doom-laden. He was trying to get his head around the significance of what had happened. This had not been expected. Not this. Nothing remotely like this. Everything had now changed. The proverbial shit would soon be hitting the tabloid fan when this got out! And it could go everywhere.

'Place a call to Silver,' he said, coming to life. He was now thinking fast. 'I'll ring Jenny back myself as soon as I've spoken to him.'

'Got it!' Rose replied like a gun shot.

Ludlow tried to put on a brave face when he went back to Dr. Bambar, but the news was like a scar on his face not to be noticed.

'Trouble, Sir Edward?' the Doctor asked politely. He was a bespectacled man with a shiny, shaven head and inquisitive eyes.

'No, no,' Ludlow lied unconvincingly, trying to conceal his inner turmoil with a weak smile. 'No more than usual when I'm away.' That part was partially true.

But it was trouble indeed. It sounded like Stephanie had finally pulled the plug on her wasted life.

Where did that leave him?

When he finally got through to his financial guru, Gerald Silver, an hour later, it was to tell him to make urgent arrangements to limit possible damage before Stephanie's fit had a chance to send shock waves through certain areas of the Stock Market.

'You've got to find her first, Edward,' was Silver's unambiguous response. 'We need to know the exact position. If we start shifting stuff for no obvious reason before the news is out and the market takes a nosedive, not only questions of insider dealing will start flying.'

Ludlow sensed this, but he wasn't fully focused. 'Just do what you have to, Gerald.' he said lamely.

'Look, Edward! Things really might not be as bad as you think. If Jenny Grant got this right and the petty cash has gone, this could simply be a chance break-in.'

'I wish.'

'The world knows you're out of the country. It could well be a timely burglary.'

'Gerald, Gerald,' Ludlow whined, in mental pain. 'No burglar's going to hang around smashing up tape recorders, telephones and God knows what else. This has to be Stephanie gone berserk. A hundred percent. She's obviously discovered her calls were being recorded. Bahnlich has somehow slipped up big-time. After slaughtering her, what's to stop Stephanie now with the disc?'

'The disc may not be such a problem as you think,' Silver suggested. 'It would take Alan Turing and the rest at Bletchley Park to get inside it.'

Silver was silent for a few moments, before going on: 'It must be at least two days since Bahnlich was murdered and there's been no hint of it in the press. What does that tell us?' Another pause before continuing. 'Stephanie's gone to ground, trying to save her neck. If we can cover up what she's done for a few days, all the better. It'll give us more time to sort something out. The news is sure to break sooner or later. But if we can make it sound like a break-in gone wrong, it shouldn't necessarily affect the irrigation project you're after out there in Africa.'

Edward wished he could be as positive as Silver.

'OK, this is what we'll do. I'll start shifting much of what's not directly attributable to you as soon as the Far Eastern markets open. Nothing that will cause a stir. The longer we can delay the impact of this, the more time it gives us to organize a strategy. Banhlich's body must remain undiscovered for as long as possible. Get Jenny to lock up and get away from the place.'

Ludlow had been listening to Silver's words, but at the same time his mind was racing on a different track, trying to piece together exactly how this mess could have happened.

Bahnlich had somehow screwed up and Stephanie had somehow found out about her calls being recorded. That was the only explanation.

His world could be about to collapse.

'Listen carefully, Jenny,' Ludlow said, when he finally called her back. The urgency in his voice went to the pit of her stomach. 'Are you quite sure there was no tape on the recorder? You didn't see it anywhere?'

'There was just an empty spool.' But Jenny hadn't looked much further than the machine itself.

'OK. What I want you to do is search the whole house from top to bottom for that tape in case Stephanie's thrown it somewhere.'

'God! No!' She screamed inside her head. Not that. She wasn't going back into that place whatever he said.

'I can't, Edward! I can't do it. She might still be in there!' She was shivering with fear. What he was asking her to do made her push open the jeep's door just in time to avoid throwing up over the dashboard. After that, she started sobbing uncontrollably.

Ludlow heard all this and sensed he was chasing a lost cause. She was in no state to handle Stephanie should it come to it. He had to think again. 'OK, OK, Jenny. Calm down! Here's what you do. Lock up and get the hell out of the place. Did anyone see you driving in?' he asked, thinking a pink jeep was hard to miss.

'I don't know. I don't think so. The road was clear as far as I remember.' But she hadn't been paying attention while fiddling with the sensor to open the gates.

'Good. Make sure no-one sees you leave, either.'

She wasn't going to tell him she had already left!

Thank God she hadn't pulled out onto the main road! A few cars had passed, but she was set back. Hopefully they had been going too fast to notice.

Ludlow's mind was racing. 'Once you're safely away, call all the staff and tell them I'm giving everyone an extra two days' holiday in celebration of my Knighthood. Tell them they're not expected back at Compton until midday on the 6th. No make it the 7th. Three days.'

She hadn't the foggiest what he was planning but was happy to say yes to everything now he didn't want her to go back into the house.

'And, Jenny, once you're away, bring Gerald Silver up to date without delay! Then get your arse on the first available flight out here. Tell Silver to sort it. He'll understand.' Insurance, Ludlow was thinking. When the news broke, as it surely would one way or another, it was better to have Jenny safely out of the way.

'Yes!' she whooped, fist-pumping as soon as they hung up. She had been truly pissed-off he hadn't wanted her to go to Kenya with him in the first place. She suddenly felt a whole lot better.

Thinking Africa, she whooped again, beating the steering wheel almost to the point of bending it as she edged the car into the road and went through the gears like a rally driver. 'Yes!' she yelled again. 'Yes!'

Chapter Ten

Peter headed to The King's Head in the hope of getting a clearer insight into Stephanie's antics there on New Year's Eve. Someone who had witnessed it firsthand.

But the pub was closed, a discreet note placed on the door explaining the circumstances. 'That bad, eh?' Peter said to himself, deciding to make it The Turk's Anchor.

He was growing more and more concerned about Stephanie. It was a strange sensation, but he was beginning to see himself as perhaps her only friend. That anguish in her voice! 'Help me!' Well, he would try. He knew he had to. The stuffed envelope was telling him he might be the only person who *could*. He had to get it back to her somehow. He couldn't where she could be going with it dressed like that? OK. It looked like she had planned to take the Range Rover but had screwed up. The question that needed an answer was why had she not gone back for some proper clothes before jumping onto her horse? Why the urgency?

'No-one must know!' He could still see the look on her face, crying out for help.

As he entered the pub, Peter spotted Robby Pike, Compton Stud's head gardener, and local gossip. He was sitting on his regular stool at the end of the L-shaped bar where he could clock all that was happening in the pub. Once sporting three different bars, public, saloon and snug, The Turk's Anchor was now one large space with pretensions of being a restaurant-cum-gastro-pub.

Peter wondered if Pikey could know anything about the Range Rover sitting on the sunken garden wall. He would soon find out, because the old gossip couldn't keep anything to himself. Robby Pike liked people to think he was the font of all knowledge. Come to Pikey if you want to know what's going on in the town. People put up with him, but what most actually thought was he was a boring old sod. Old Pikey made use of his nosiness, though, whenever possible. Certain people of the press had often taken advantage of this, encouraging him with drinks or financial gain to be an interfering pest, knowing he worked at Compton Stud. Over time, he had become the 'local source' of all that was going on at that fashion hot-spot even before rumours of fissures in the fairy-tale marriage had seriously started to line his pocket. If someone farted at Compton Stud these days, he would make it his business to know about it if it could earn him a bob or two, such was the interest in the goings-on there. Whoever offered most got the story. The News of the World and The Daily Scan often called on him on the odd chance something could be made newsworthy, and Pikey would normally oblige with some invention or other. Those two tabloids were his biggest payers, and never asked too many questions about authenticity. In those quarters, he had come to earn the name of The Marlsbury Echo.

But he plainly knew nothing about the beached Range Rover, otherwise that would have been in all the broadsheets as well.

Peter ordered Spring Water and two sausages as Robby Pike sharpened his imaginary pencil ready to make enquiries. Almost everything he came out with was in some form of a question, often rhetorical. And the first one was on its way.

'So, you haven't found yourself a job yet, lad?' The old chinwag knew that perfectly well. 'You ought to've found summat by now, n't you? What's it been? Nearly two years, innit?'

'Not for want of trying, Pikey. Nothing out there for a man of my calibre, is there?' Peter could give Pikey as good as he could take in the banter business. 'Overqualified, that's my trouble.'

'You bin taunting Sir you-know-who lately? Still smartin' about him, ain't you, lad?' Pikey pinched his nose, which was something that might grow underground; a radish more than a beetroot because it wasn't all that big. His hair had a scare-crow look. His clothes not much better.

'Even if I had a job now, it wouldn't change my opinion of that bastard you work for. And you can tell him that from me when you next see him.' Peter knew Pikey was trying to wind him up. But he could handle it these days.

'Well, he'll be smartin' more than you, lad, won't he, when he hears what she done to his shop the other night? Got away with it, too, didn't she?'

Ludlow would be even more peeved when he learns about the Range Rover, Peter was thinking with a smug sense of achievement to be one up on the 'Marlsbury Echo' with that knowledge.

85

'Went potty, didn't she?' Pikey added, finishing his drink.

The barman automatically pulled him another. 'They know it was her for sure, do they?' Peter asked, knowing the answer already.

''Cause they do, don't they?' Pikey answered knowledgeably. 'Weren't none of them druggies old bill nabbed, was it? Only one bugger'd do that, in't it? That's what I told...' He suddenly stopped himself going further before revealing exactly who he had told. Peter smiled. Most people knew Pikey was the 'local source' as named by the tabloids. 'Yeah, t'were her alright. Unless it be you, Peter. But even you ain't that daft, are you, lad?'

Tyler ignored the insinuation as Janet Tomlinson, Stephanie's leg-up friend walked into the pub with more clothes on today.

'I see the bedspring's popped out of its mattress again, then?' Billy Pike said astutely, with a nod toward Janet.

Peter knew Janet's reputation went before her, but it was the first time he had ever heard her called that. It amused him because she *was* like a spring when he came to think of it when he thought back to the one and only time their bodies had clashed. Perhaps, not so much a bedspring, though. More like one of the springs on his weights machine; narrow and compact, and likely to make you sweat when stretched.

His amusement must have shown.

'Do you know, lad, that's the closest I've ever seen you come to smiling lately. And I ain't never seen you laugh. I reckon you spends too much time at home with your old mum, don't you? You ought to get out more. Have a couple o' pints of 5X. That'll soon get you giggling, won't it?'

The pub was getting smoky. Peter was ready to go.

'You know what, lad?' Pikey said, leaning closer, trying to hold on to Peter's company. 'There's something about that Janet girl. Got a lot in common with our druggie lady of the manor, ain't she?' There was some truth in that, Peter thought. They both seemed to have the same manic way of charging into things. Drugs possibly were a common denominator, he supposed. Everyone knew about Stephanie's addiction. With Janet, Peter had often thought she might be on something to get her going. But experience edged him into believing she was built that way naturally.

'*You* tell *me*, Pikey. You're the one with his nose to the ground.'

The old man shifted on his stool and moistened his lips. 'I reckon them two are up to summat. That one over there was at The King's Head the other night, weren't she? And when our Steph pokes her nose in, who's the first person she goes to? You guessed it. Old bedspring over there. Gave her some money, too, didn't she? Sid behind the bar told me. Those two must have stood out like sore thumbs in there with all them long-haired lay-abouts, mustn't they?'

Peter couldn't quite see what Billy Pike was getting at. But he wasn't going to hang about to hear more.

'You could be right,' he said thoughtfully, as he bid farewell. Time to make a move.

Next morning, leaving his mother to her dreams, Peter put the parcel in his saddle bag wrapped in a tea towel. It had nearly dried out now. He was itching to know what was in it. But no, he would get it back to Stephanie in one piece as best he could in the circumstances, to show her he was on her side and that if she still needed help, he was her man.

He had set his sights on riding out to the stables first in case she was there with her horse.

Did he have an ulterior motive for wanting to help her, he asked himself? Was he perhaps thinking she might become interested in sponsoring his Initiative if he could get into her good books? He had to admit something like that had popped up at the back of his mind. It would also be a very neat way of winding Ludlow up if he could swing it.

Pulling out just after seven, there was a hint the sun might show itself. Thankfully, the rain had stopped, so he decided to go via Beacon Ridge just like a normal morning workout.

His trek through the woods was still slippery, as expected, but he was in no hurry. Again, he had to dismount and walk the last section of the climb. Going down the other side, he took it more carefully.

At the point where he had nearly collided with Stephanie, he was caught by an eerie vision which made him stop short. Crossing the muddied path was a fresh set of horseshoe prints. But it was something else that sent a shiver up his spine, making his neck tingle. At first, he thought he was seeing a snake. A long thin snake slithering through the mud alongside the horseshoe marks. But a snake could not possibly be as long and as thin unless Charles Darwin had missed something in his travels. It was more like a piece of cord or string, moving in fits and starts.

Looking in the direction it was moving, he soon realized it was neither. And if he had been unsure that the horse tracks were fresh, the doubt went immediately. Not five paces from where he was standing, the string-like material was sliding through a small pile of steaming horse dung which seemed to be acting as a cleaning agent. As it came out, he saw it was magnetic tape, stretched in places which made it look more like string, but definitely magnetic tape.

'Stephanie?' he shouted. Someone had to be pulling it.

No answer came. 'Without a thought, he laid his bike down and picked his way through the ferns and bushes following it like an African hunter on the trail of a big cat.

After thirty or forty yards, he glanced up and there through the trees looking back at him was not a big cat, but Stephanie's horse, alone, whinnying and stamping.

He moved toward it gingerly. Getting close, he saw the tape was twisted around its rear right fetlock.

'Steady, boy,' Peter murmured, keeping perfectly still. It was as if the horse whisperer himself had spoken, for the colt lowered its head and came right up to him in complete supplication.

'There, boy,' he assumed it was a 'boy'. He hadn't bother to check, but it was. Taking a loose hold on the rein, he gently stroked its neck. 'Easy. Easy. What happened, old fella? Where's your mistress?'

Peter was cooing calmly into the horse's ear, but his mind was in turmoil. Where indeed was Stephanie? It had been two days. It was unlikely she would have run off and left the horse up here in the woods on its own.

He feared the worst. What else? Stephanie must have been thrown. Two days ago! Unthinkable.

The horse started nudging him, holding its entangled hoof off the ground.

'OK, let's have a look, shall we?' Peter whispered, slowly moving round to its hind quarters and reaching down. The animal could not have been more compliant.

He didn't have anything sharp to cut the tape away but there was a loose end to it. Once he got it started, it was quite easy to unwind. But carefully. It had broken the skin, but with the impediment gone the horse nodded as if to show its appreciation.

'Now what?' Peter was asking himself.

He began to wind the magnetic tape loosely around the fingers of his left hand. 'Stay, boy,' he murmured softly. 'Everything is going to be fine.'

Moving slowly away as he gathered the tape, the horse followed, nudging him from time to time like a long-lost friend.

Things changed as soon as Peter drew level with his bike. It was as if a cross had been thrust into the face of a vampire. Flaring its nostrils, the horse pulled back with fear in its eyes. Rearing up, it turned and in a flash charged back in the direction from which they had just come.

'Shit!' Peter muttered, turning to go after it, but stopped before taking a single step. What was he thinking? What could he do with the horse? It was Stephanie he needed to worry about. But if she had come off and injured herself what were the chances of finding her? There were miles of woods. She could be anywhere. And what could he do if he *did* find her? What if she had broken a leg or worse? He'd heard of people being pulled from the rubble of earthquakes after days without food or water. But it was teams of paramedics doing that. It had rained a lot lately, so water might not be a problem. But the exposure? She had hardly been wearing any clothes when he had last seen her. And if she had been thrown? Well. Who knew what that could mean?

Was he being over melodramatic? Misreading the situation?

Whatever it was, he was in no position to do much about it.

The only thing was to alert the police and let them deal with it. They could find her quicker than he ever could if she was still out there and in trouble.

He would keep finding the tape to himself. It looked like it might play back. If it *did* belonged to Stephanie, it would definitely be worth knowing what was on it, given how anxious she had been. 'No-one must know' ringing ion his ear.

Before he had finished winding it, he felt it snagging. Trying not to stretch it any further than it was already, he delved into some coarse bracken and found the cause. The tape's spool was caught up. He carefully removed it and, taking his time, carefully wound the tape back onto it as best he could.

The nearest public call box was in his own village. He preferred to ring from there but when he got to it, as expected, it was out of order, so it would have to be from home.

He rang 999 asking for the police. The response he got made it sound like he would be wasting police time. A loose horse on someone's private property didn't sound like an emergency to the man at the other end of the line.

'And why were you trespassing up there, sir?' the officer wanted to know with undisguised intimidation. Peter explained that there were public right-of-way paths all through Ludlow's woods that he had been using for years without any come-back. The explanation got some acceptance, but he still felt like he was being treated as a criminal. He made no mention of the magnetic tape, nor the envelope, of course. Why should he?

'I saw Mrs. Ludlow out of control on that horse two days ago,' he stressed, pissed off with his reception. 'She could have come off and still be lying injured up there somewhere.'

The police had had no reports of any missing persons, came the reply.

'Are *you* actually reporting Mrs. Ludlow as missing, sir?'

'No, not exactly. I'm just reporting what I've told you. And I'm concerned.'

'What is your relationship with Mrs. Ludlow?'

'No relationship. I'm just telling what I've seen: her horse running wild without her on it!'

He was told the matter would be looked into, and that was that.

It had been a frustrating conversation, but necessary. He had acted like a decent citizen and felt the better for it. They could discover the beached Range Rover for themselves. Telling them about it would indeed be admitting to trespassing.

He kept waking during the night, his mind racing, juggling thoughts. One thing was clear; he had more concern about Stephanie Star's welfare than the police appeared to have. They'd probably had enough of the run-around she'd been giving them in recent months. However, he had done his bit. It was now down to them.

Chapter Eleven

At Treetops, it was becoming obvious to Sir Edward Ludlow exactly what Stephanie must have revealed on the tape to push her to slaughter Bahnlich. The identity of her 'safe hands'. He could not forgive himself for responding the way he had when she told him she had the disc. What a fool he'd been to give her that weapon!

How had he allowed things to come to this? They had been a successful money-making double act. OK, leaning much more in his favour, but she had all she had ever wanted. The marriage was just a fairy-tale side show. A fake. But they had both played their part in making the world believe theirs was a dream partnership.

The more the small print tied him to her fame, the more he had begun to feel stifled by the claustrophobic world of Stephanie Star. A world that he alone had cultivated. He had continued to reap the rewards offered by Luke Lake's talent with his publishing and recording ownership, but he had begun to seek more solid ground than the 'entertainment business' to expand his interests.

He had gradually become a slave to the all-consuming regime he had created that was now top-heavy with an endless variety of companies associated with all things Stephanie Star: Ludlow Management; Star Holdings; Star Enterprises; Star Franchises; Star Merchandising. They had all been flying high back then in Stephanie's Hey-Day.

Her soulful look was everywhere, endorsing cosmetic products and fashion house wares the world over.

How to move on?

An idea that could add a touch of gravitas to his 'showbiz' profile came to him on a day when the two men whose opinions he trusted made similar random recommendations.

The first came from his accountant, Gerald Silver, who Ludlow described as being able to pick out a stray figure in the battlefield of tax avoidance like a sniper with telescopic sights.

Figures for the year in question were extremely good. Overwhelmingly good. There was so much profit, hiding places were running out. That was considered failure. Being outwitted.

'If you can't come up with some bright idea to divert some of this, you might just as well give it to charity.' Silver had suggested.

Food for thought as Edward nursed his Aston Martin across Hammersmith flyover in Friday's rush hour traffic leaving London to the West.

The second reference came from his father.

'You've managed to make quite a name for yourself now, Edward, when all's said and done,' his old man had mused, sitting in his cozy lounge, glass of sherry in hand. 'Although, to start with, I did wonder how this show business obsession of yours would pan out.' Never the complete compliment. 'But now, your high public profile could give Marlsbury Pumps a big leg-up when you come to take over the reins.' That latter prospect had been getting closer by the day. 'I've been thinking. There are tons of spare parts lying about the factory taking up space, as well as quite a few complete units that have reached their sell-by date. We've been keeping ahead of the game making more efficient machines these days.' Edward was particularly pleased to hear that. He would go through the place with a clean brush when his time came.

'You're big in this advertising lark,' his father went on. 'You must know it back to front by now, with all your Platform experience, especially the way you've handled that gorgeous wife of yours.' His father paid little attention to tabloid headlines. 'Put that talent to use when you take over here. Make a big splash by donating all that obsolete stuff to some worthwhile charitable cause. In Africa, for instance? There's an awful lot of drought in Africa, son. They could use a pump or two out there. Put Stephanie's charms to work promoting the idea. Stamp Marlsbury Pumps' name on it. Could be very good publicity.'

There it was again: charity. Not a bad idea, dad! Edward had always thought his adventurous streak of 'give it a go' came from his father's side of the family.

But why half measures? Why not go the whole hog and create his own charity? Something that might lift him onto higher moral ground to counter the fickleness of the glamour world associated with him.

A name for the charity came to Edward spontaneously, no hair-pulling necessary. Three words from his father's initial proposal jumped out: drought, Africa, and stamp.

Marlsbury Pumps would set the ball rolling with the first donation of water pumps. But, for a charity to succeed, it needed the public on board. Funds had to be raised continuously to keep the pumps flowing, keep the charity buoyant and self-supporting.

An idea jumped out at him. One tried and tested that had catapulted Tescos to the top of the supermarket league, thank you very much! Loyalty Stamps! Why not use them to fund a charity? This time not to be redeemed in the form of gifts, but as donations to help Stamp Out Drought in Africa?

Get petrol stations and major retail outlets in on the act. Package holiday companies and hotel chains.

And some of the big ones did jump onboard! With Stephanie up front putting her own stamp of endorsement on it, S.O.D.A. took off big time. Good people across the country were happy to feel they were helping to support the less fortunate in needy African countries whenever they did their weekly shop or filled their petrol tanks.

With the success of SODA, Ludlow started flirting with another 'charitable' idea that could have been launched with the same acronym as his existing charity, just by replacing 'Drought' with 'Disease'. There was an awful lot of malaria in Africa.

Drought, pumps. Disease, drugs.

It was in that area, Ludlow now regretted, that he had begun to lose his bearings. Using SODA's growing charity network, pharmaceuticals could be moved discreetly across borders without too much fuss with the right people in the chain. Most movement originated in Bolivia, serviced by a company called BiloChem. It was what happened to certain drugs after leaving South America that would send alarm bells ringing should the *wrong* people get wise to it.

Ludlow continued his musings in the balmy evening African air. Diverting supplies to feed the giddy worlds of fashion and music swinging around him seemed preferable to having others muscle in.

Even though it was years ago now, Ludlow could still clearly remember the champagne celebration going on in full swing when he had arrived back at Compton Stud that evening after the SODA seed had been planted. A party was in full swing to mark the end of a successful three-day shoot promoting a new jewel be-decked Swiss watch about to be marketed under the name of 'Red Cross'!

Charity was being drummed into him! Red Cross!

Stephanie had leapt on him, offering up her lips for the sake of propriety. Despite there being no real affection between them, keeping up the pretense of perfect harmony in the public arena was something they had both grown to accept as the way to go. It was better for business. And that was all their marriage had long become.

'How did it go?' he had asked, already knowing the answer by the quality and quantity of champagne being uncorked.

'The usual dramas with all the agency hangers-on wanting to justify their existence,' she complained with ethnic undertones. Her elocution lessons proved of dubious worth when topped up with alcohol, no matter how good the quality. 'How about you?' she added more keenly. 'Did you get the….?' her voice tapered off to be replaced by a long 'Ah! Bisto' sniff that wrinkled her famously cute nose. Her nostrils flared when the reply came: 'Victor will oblige you.'

'They're a lively bunch, this lot,' she told him, 'Cleaned us out already.' He could tell by her pin-prick eyes that she had not gone short herself. 'Now where's that ape of yours?' No love lost there.

Within minutes she had found Victor Rose and could be heard singing out: 'Follow me all those in need,' as she swaggered into the privacy of what was called the projection room, where all illicit substances were now meant to be consumed. House rules. Not only could no eyes see in, but the expensive air-conditioning system installed for that reason sucked out tell-tale odours like a blast furnace.

Ludlow exchanged a nod with a sharp looking guy who plainly took care of himself. Dark, angular and without a spare ounce of flesh on him, this was Karl, enlisted as minder-cum-bodyguard for those public occasions when fans might want to get too close to Stephanie. Ludlow put fingers either side of his nose to indicate, 'keep your eyes on her'. Stephanie knew Karl's role well welcomed it, happy to have his discreet presence close to hand for whenever needed.

At Treetops, Ludlow continued his reverie as he awaited further news from Jenny Grant and Gerald Silver.

His thoughts were where he had left them, the very extravagant post-shoot 'Red Cross' party. When Stephanie had reappeared from the projection room, she was more pin-eyed than ever.

'Look what Jonathan has just given me, Edward,' she had gaped, inventing wonderment. 'The demonstration wristwatch! He says he can think of no better charity to donate it to than me. Is he after something, do you think?'

'Indeed, Stephanie. Well spotted.' Edward knew the giving of the watch was no act of charity, even if it did bear a red cross. Jonathan, who was the UK sales manager of the Swiss manufacturer, was on the make, professionally, of course.

Edward wasn't born yesterday. Ludlow Enterprises were being paid handsomely for Stephanie Star's endorsement of this new range of wristwatches. If the ploy was to get her to actually wear one in public, it would cost them much, much more.

'Nice try, Jonathan. How kind of you,' Edward had said with a tight smile as he released the watch from his wife's wrist and valued it. 'About five hundred quid's worth, at a guess. That's if this one's not just a dummy.' It wasn't. The second hand was moving.

As Ludlow sipped his gin and tonic at Treetops, he had the uncomfortable sensation that the watch echoed his current position. Time was ticking away.

'Let's call it quits,' he had told Jonathan, who could be seen to have had ample reimbursement in the projection room for the timepiece that had cost him nothing himself.

By way of compensation, Stephanie led the salesman back into that room, 'He's got you there, Jono,' she quipped merrily as they sped off like a couple of Keystone Cops. 'Come and get your money's worth!'

It was a quiet Sunday night in 'Tony's Ring'. The place wasn't even half full. It sometimes went like that. It was early, yet. Still time to liven up.

Sharon and Kim were both on show, suitably dressed and made up as their alter egos, along with Hitler at the bar and a few others. 'Rock Hudson' and 'Marilyn Monroe' had been given the night off, but still plenty of staff were on parade for the number of clients in the house. Those with little to do spread themselves out, sitting at otherwise empty tables themselves instead of hovering awkwardly, ready to jump up keenly whenever the doorman led someone through the thick curtains that were there to keep the draft out.

Sharon and Kim were sitting on adjacent tables chatting about what they might do over the next couple of days. 'Tony's Ring' didn't open Mondays or Tuesdays, so they were free to get up to other mischief.

Right now, Kim was keeping her eye on two tables, each with a couple she was attending to. Sharon only had one table to look after, so when the tell-tale billowing of the curtain announced the arrival of new customers, she would be up quickly to receive them. It was her turn.

Although Tony had his favourites, he was a stickler for fairness. Each day before opening, lots would be drawn to establish the order of play. If a group of four came in, it would usually mean a bigger tip than from a lone punter. The staff were allowed to keep half of whatever tip they got for themselves. The other half would go into a pot to be shared equally between them all. The staff were paid the legal minimum wage, but the tips nearly always came to more. It was a good place to work if that was what you were cut out to do for a living. Even though it was only a four-day week, you could do alright for yourself if you didn't mind putting the hours in 'upstairs'.

A beaming smile on her face, Sharon groaned inside when she saw the guy she would have to serve pushing himself through the curtains. He called himself Paul, but that was not necessarily his real name. Some guys, usually the ones coming in alone with an eye on using the upstairs facilities, often wished to hide their true identity for their own reasons, matrimony being the most common.

Paul was well known for fancying Fifi, as she called herself when she wasn't 'wigged up' to look like her 'doppelganger' Marilyn Monroe. Fifi wasn't her real name, either. She adopted it for fun. It seemed to go with the extra service 'Tony's Ring' was known to offer upstairs to a lot of the takers.

Sharon showed Paul to his table with suitable panache, swaying her hips as expertly as Stephanie Star might once have done herself on a Paris catwalk.

'Very nice, Stephanie,' Paul said in appreciation, looking around the spacious pillared room before sitting down. Sharon, alias Stephanie Starere, knew that look and what it meant. 'No Marilyn tonight, I see,' he confirmed her suspicion.

Sharon pulled a chair back ready for him to sit, all smiles. It seemed, as she feared, he had come for an upstairs session. She was hoping his need was not great enough to look beyond Fifi for gratification. Professional or not, she didn't feel up to it tonight after the number of 'tricks' she had performed over the past few days. She needed a rest. Although the girls were allowed to be fussy about who took them upstairs, they couldn't be *too* fussy when things were slow at Tony's. Like tonight.

'She's not upstairs already, I hope?' Paul wondered.

'She's gone to Florida,' Sharon joked. 'Tony Curtis pulled her. They're off cruising on his yacht!' Keep it light, Tony had drilled into them if a client seemed to be getting too close to any of them. Fifi didn't seem to mind Paul's attentions, though. A big tipper, he didn't hold back with his money. Paul was a crane driver, one of those really high cranes. Apparently, he had told Fifi once, that if he wanted a pee, he just did it out of the window to save having to go all the way down and up again. And she had believed him! Fifi was quite a laugh on the quiet.

'No, sir. It's Marilyn's night off,' Sharon owned up. 'Now what can I get you? Don't say pizza. It's chef's night off, too.' She need not have asked what he wanted to drink. He always wanted the same thing. It pleased his sense of humour.

'Between the Sheets, please. Large.' There it was, said with a stupid grin on his face. 'And whatever you are drinking. One for Jane Russell, too. She's looking a bit deflated, probably because you got me instead of her.'

'That's her tough luck.' Always keep the punter happy with your banter was another of Tony's rules.

'Young Hitler's looking a bit left-out as well. Better get him his usual.' It was a running joke at the club, but one that kept Andrew, alias Hitler, happy. If Hitler himself had received as many 'Bouncing Bombs' as Paul had bought him, no dams at all would have survived in Germany during World War Two!

Andrew did very well for tips, too, along with the communal pot. Drinks bought by the customers for the staff never contained alcohol. They were just cleverly mixed to look like the real thing, charged at regular prices for the pot. 'Hitler' was a dab hand at that.

Tony himself never touched alcohol when at the club. Fake gin and tonics were easy to fabricate if someone wanted to treat him, the full amount of the price going into the communal pot. He was always on show around the club, periodically doing the rounds of the tables to make sure everyone was happy. Occasionally, if invited, he would sit down at a table for a few moments, acting the perfect host. He was a huge man, which had served him well in his earlier days as a professional wrestler. Now, in his late fifties, it could be said that he was beginning to go to pot. But he still had a presence. His size saw to that. Always sharply dressed, people knew who was boss. With Tony on parade, everything was under control.

Once Paul had settled with his golden cocktail in hand, Tony, seeing him sitting alone, drifted over to his table and joined him.

'How's it going, Paul?' Tony asked, sitting down. They shook equally large hands across the table. 'Have a good Christmas?'

'So, so. Spent it in Dover with the old folks. Don't see them that often.'

Dover docks were where Paul had learned his trade as a crane operator, a job that called for subtle reflexes and constant alertness. Hence, he totally abstained from alcohol during the working week, making up for it on days off. He was the sort of punter Tony liked, a big spender both downstairs and upstairs. Treating people to drinks one day a week barely dented Paul's payroll. 'Tony's Ring' was the perfect antidote to being stuck sky-high in a glass cabinet for hours on end during the week; the ideal place to let it all hang out. Being in demand on big construction projects around the country kept Paul away from home a lot. He wasn't married, so he was fancy free to go where the work took him. He had been in Manchester for several months and would be there for many more. Tony would be sorry to see him go when the time came, as he had more than once expressed.

'Marilyn's got the night off,' Tony told him. He prided himself on knowing the preferences of his customers. 'I expect that might have been who you were hoping to see.'

'No worries,' Paul responded. 'Thought she might already have been nabbed.'

'No. Quiet tonight. Work tomorrow for most people. What about you?'

'Just got back into town. Start again the day after tomorrow.'

'I'm sure we can sort you out later, if and when.'

'Thanks, Tony. I'll have a couple more of these and see how I feel.' He indicated his cocktail.

Tony nodded, giving Paul his hand again before moving on. He made a cursory lap of the occupied tables checking all was OK, stopping briefly at the solitary one-arm bandit where another regular loner was mindlessly inserting pound coins.

'Any luck, Jeff?' Tony asked, knowing Jeff had a 1 in 8 chance of getting something back because that was how the machine was set up. Even without being greedy, those odds reaped a sizable profit.

'Just about even,' Jeff lied, 'but I think she's about ready to drop the big one.'

The big one was a hundred pounds. And it dropped often and noisily enough for punters to believe they had a good chance of hitting it. Another example of Tony's idea of fairness.

Next, he approached Kim who was now sitting invitingly at the bar waiting for the front door curtains to billow. He alerted her about the possibility of Paul wanting to go upstairs to see how she felt about it. He discounted Sharon knowing she was fussy about Paul. 'You can't get near him after all those 'Between the Sheets' he drinks,' she had told Tony once. And once was enough. 'The smell of brandy and rum makes me want to puke!' Good enough reason to leave her out. Zoe, Tony's look-a-like Brigitte Bardot, who had just reappeared from upstairs was also discounted for the time being. But Kim was smiling. Paul would be more fun than hoping the bar would get busier. Sharon looked across at Kim, who gave her a reassuring wink to tell Sharon she was prepared to take Paul on should he be looking for action later. Sharon breathed a sigh of relief, blowing Kim a silent kiss for rescuing her from a possible sandblasting of stale brandy 'Upstairs'. With so few of the girls working tonight, Sharon would have felt obliged to answer the call had Tony insisted.

100

But as it happened, with Marilyn not being available, Paul wanted no more than a quiet drink with the stars that night. 'I'll be back next Saturday to see her,' he told Tony before leaving. 'Could you let her know, so she saves herself for me.'

'Will do.'

Marilyn would be happy about that. It meant a guaranteed big tip on top of the full works with Paul. The jackpot!

Chapter Twelve

The jumbo carrying Jenny Grant to Kenya passed a sister ship travelling the other way with Victor Rose aboard somewhere near the Tropic of Cancer over Southern Egypt. Neither was awake to acknowledge the happening. They were both flat out, sleeping off the results of British Airways' First-Class hospitality.

It had all happened so suddenly for Jenny. The chase from Cornwall to Marlsbury and the horror of Compton Stud, then this urgent summoning to Nairobi. 'It's safer having you out of the way over here,' Rose had barked to her. 'We don't want you cracking up if the law drags you in. You haven't bawled your head off to anyone already, have you?' 'Fuck you, too, arse-hole!' she had wanted to bark back but didn't. She was used to getting insults from the dumb shit of a man. Water off a duck's back now she would be as far away as possible from Marlsbury. If Edward's crazy wife could do that to Bahnlich, what might she have done to her given half a chance? Bahnlich was Stephanie's soul buddy by comparison to Jenny.

Safely tucked up in her flying cocoon with the crisis of Compton Stud behind her, she began to feel pleased something like this had finally happened. It had been on the cards for months. She couldn't understand why Edward should be so concerned about covering up what had happened. This was the perfect opportunity to remove the blight of Stephanie Star from his life. With no rebounds on himself. He had done all he could to save her from herself. Most showbiz watchers had known the golden couple's fairy-tale marriage had long been on the rocks. Time to own up. The tabloids were already all over it like a rash trying to drum up sales.

Had Edward put his mind to dealing with her sooner, Jenny thought, the better it would have been for everyone. There was surely enough money in the pot to keep both parties happy. Divorce was becoming far less of a stigma these days, even for those in the public eye.

Stephanie-bloody-Star was done and dusted by her own hand. No question! Once in police custody, she would be out of the picture for good. Then, perhaps, certain opportunities Jenny had been hoping for might open up for her. 'The icing on the cake!' she told herself.

102

Despite being the middle of the night, this blissful notion roused her to sit up and press a button for another gin and tonic. Things were good, no argument. How many women still clinging to the right side of forty could boast her position? As a member of Ludlow's inner circle, she had become accustomed to moving in style at the highest level. Look at her now, for instance. This latest move promised to take her ever closer to the bull's eye!

She finished her gin and tonic, taking the warm glow it had given her back to the horizontal as she lowered her seat again, snuggling up in a blanket to continue her happy thoughts.

She had no intention of remaining a mere cog in a wheel, no matter how fast it was spinning. She was, in depth, a businesswoman. She liked to build and control, and she was good at it. She knew that much about herself. How else could she have started her own temping business and become such a threat to established mainstream agencies within a couple of years? Ludlow had known what he was doing when he bought her out, even if she had to say it herself. It was her get up and go he wanted, her business acumen, not the business itself. Overnight, she had found herself in the big league. It was a good feeling. She liked it and didn't want it to stop. The hope was of better things to come. This chariot in the sky was taking her one step closer to achieving it, and it had nothing to do with 'temping'!

Ludlow had left Treetops for Nairobi in a state of nervous hope. If he was to be torn apart by the revelations of his vengeful wife, then at least a way was being prepared to limit the damage. He could rely on Gerald Silver to arrange an alternative to having HM Prisons provide for his comfort in old age. But the possibility was there should the diggers come by the floppy disc and manage to delve deep enough. He couldn't kid himself it wasn't. A certain metamorphosis would perhaps be called for, but he would still be a free man of sorts, if with a little less shine to his name plate. He would still be dancing to his own tune, hopefully one without the ring of a samba to it.

Stephanie had to be found first. Then have sense talked into her.

Two problems with no guarantees.

'I sent Rose back to do one or two things before all hell breaks loose,' a jumpy Ludlow told Jenny Grant, anticipating a minor backlash for seeming to doubt her ability to cope. They were sitting on the veranda of his suite at the historic Norfolk Hotel. Their view was of the lush courtyard with its colourful aviary and equatorial flora. She was more concerned with her boss's edginess right now to appreciate it more fully.

'I prefer you to be here with me,' he said, delivering it as sincerely as possible. Well away from Marlsbury, would have been a more honest way of putting it. He didn't want her saying the wrong thing to anyone. Safer to have her out of the country. 'No sense having you put through the ringer when this thing breaks,' he explained. 'The press'll be all over it. You'd be a prime target.'

He made it sound as though his only concern was for her, but she knew he was thinking more of his own skin, worried about what she might say if questioned. Too right. She wouldn't have held back. What was there to lose? Well, there was obviously something. Ever since getting off the plane he had been grilling her. The police couldn't have done a better job. She told him that if the press had pestered her for information, she would have told them to get lost. But he didn't sound so sure of her resolve. OK, she was glad she had been spared that possibility by being sent out here. But there had not been one word of thanks from him for what she'd been through at Compton Stud. She was paid to jump, yes. But covering up that horrific mess was beyond anyone's line of duty. One little word of appreciation would have gone a long way! And why all this? Trying to keep it quiet?

'There's absolutely no doubt about that tape?' he quizzed her for the hundredth time.

'There was no tape, Edward! I've told you a dozen times. The cow had smashed Bahnlich's brains out to get it, so she wasn't going leave it sitting around for people to find, was she?'

She was yelling with such irritation, he had to shush her. There were people in the gardens. She quietened herself to a hiss but didn't let go. 'She's murdered Bahnlich and wiped out your phones, and all you're worried about is a stupid fucking tape!'

He let her anger subside before responding. The physical damage didn't concern him, nor the communication problems so much now. 'All that stuff can be replaced in good time. What's on that tape is a different matter. And it could be bad news.' She didn't need to know about the disc.

Jenny couldn't hold herself back.

'Edward! You're not listening! She's just committed murder! Who's going be worrying about a fucking tape? When the police get hold of her, that'll be the fucking end of it!'

Jenny Grant had hardly ever spoken to her boss like this; fucking-this and fucking-that! It was only hours since she had got off the long flight. The g-and-t's and fine wine were egging her on.

'You don't fully understand, Jenny.' And he wasn't going to enlighten her, *fully*.

Through her tears, Jenny did not notice the patronizing look he was giving her.

No, she didn't fully understand. She didn't understand him one bit! Why hadn't he divorced the woman years ago and be done with it? He had enough grounds. That part of his life, or, *livelihood,* perhaps more relevantly, was history. Had the illusive knighthood he'd been hankering after stopped him? Vanity? Well, he'd got the fucking thing now, so time to get a life, Edward!

She emptied her glass in one gulp, trying to calm her thoughts. Okay, things could only get better. It was all over for Stephanie. She was done for. History.

Edward leaned closer, filling her glass without thinking. Bad move. She didn't need it and it nearly came back at him when he spoke again.

'I just hope Rose can get there in time to check on things before it's too late to do anything.'

'Thanks a lot!' she yelped, all restraint gone, the fine wine he'd just poured splashing everywhere, 'You make me go through all that then send that pig-brain back to check up on me!'

She slammed down what was left of the drink and turned away from him.

'Not check on *you*, Jenny. Check on the situation. What am I supposed to do for God's sake? What needs to be done now is best left to

Rose to sort out. It will probably need muscle more than brains when he finds her!'

She was hardly listening, nor was she seeing things clearly. The intoxicating view was wasted on her along with the fine wine. More tears were brimming up, to her annoyance. She tried furiously to blink them away. Why was she getting so upset? She was here, wasn't she? Away from the horror. First class to boot!

Edward saw the tears and tried to appease her.

'Listen, Jenny,' he started in conciliatory tones. 'I don't want you to get more involved in this thing than you are already. You've been great. I may not always make it known to you, but I'm really thankful for all you've done for me. Not just with this latest nightmare. Over the years, no-one could have handled things better for me, man or woman. Especially in recent months. I would have found it very difficult indeed to cope without you at my side.'

Jenny could hardly believe what she was hearing. This was a first, whether he really meant it or not.

'Compton Stud is no place for you at the moment,' he went on. 'I'm not sure if it will be for any of us again after this. God knows! Who could have guessed any of this? I thought it was just a fault with the telephone lines. If I'd known the real situation, of course I wouldn't have sent you there.'

She started to believe that now. Having her know what had happened to Bahnlich was perhaps not the best arrangement. If, as it was beginning to seem, an attempt was being made to cover up the situation, Jenny could see how it was better all round to have her out of the picture. And was she glad of this or what? Fuck, yes. These thoughts brought back the happier mood she had carried on the flight over. Without that sudden horror show of just two days ago, she wouldn't be sitting here in the sun right now, would she? Reasons to be cheerful, if not jubilant.

'What's done is done,' Ludlow said with resignation. 'It's down to Rose, now. Stephanie's got to be found and stopped, or…' he petered out.

'I hope she's fucking dead!' Jenny was thinking and meant it.

Ludlow leaned over and put his arm around her, making her body stiffen momentarily from the unexpected gesture. There was an awkward moment as she loosened up, making him realize his aim had been misconstrued. It was meant as a comforting thank you not as something more intimate. She leaned into him, softly yielding. For her, this felt different. He had never hugged her like this before.

Jenny carried her sexuality in a confidently subtle way. Ludlow had long thought she was suppressing the notion that an unashamed bout of all-out horizontal humping might be fun, might actually fulfill a human need other than that of procreation. She had her moments of coquetry, oh yes, but in no way was she, in the traditional sense of the expression, a prick teaser, as his wife had been big time when it suited her needs.

But not so Jenny.

You wouldn't call Jenny 'beautiful', not in the conventional sense, as Stephanie was. But she was attractive, and she kept herself in good shape, unlike Stephanie these days. Jenny was so tied up and anxious to keep on top of Ludlow's business affairs, she could hardly ever switch off. She had allowed little time for a social life, seldom letting her hair down, which had tended to make her highly strung, Ludlow sensed her tight web of sexuality might snap if plucked. He had always steered away from testing that theory. Mixing business with pleasure had been for his earlier years. His ego now outweighed his libido. This happy situation caused him far less emotional stress. With this unfolding situation, he sensed Jenny might be about to come out of her shell. She had achieved her career ambitions. Did she now want to be rid of the self-imposed chastity she had forced upon herself in her pains to get there? Was she beginning to crack?

In a sense, she was. She wanted sex. With him. This desire had grown the longer she had worked for him. But it wasn't sex alone she wanted. She wasn't angling to become just his 'bit on the side'. That could destroy everything. She was hoping she could provide something she knew had long been missing from his life. Love.

Edward thought he could see what might be on Jenny's mind. There had been warning signs. So far, her head had been keeping her heart in order, which suited his needs. Whatever might be rumbling beneath the surface, he was happy to keep their relationship afloat as it stood. There was to be no carnal side to it to upset the equilibrium despite the temptation of discovery.

By the way Jenny had just softened in the clutch of this latest unassuming friendly hug, he was sending out the wrong signals. He should be more careful. This was not the time, if ever there would be. His mind was in several other places.

'You've had a couple of very stressful days,' he said, removing his arm without the final gentle squeeze of her shoulder that might normally have accompanied the gesture. 'Why don't you go and rest up for a while? I've got some calls to make.'

In her drunkenness, she thought this might be it! An invitation at last. He would be following her to the bedroom when he was ready.

Wrong. The booze was fooling her.

Although she took time to prepare herself to receive him, as soon as her head hit the pillow, sleep, instead, took her.

Victor Rose arrived at Compton Stud around midnight on Monday. He planned to stay no longer than was necessary. It was a precarious operation. He didn't want to be seen anywhere near the place, so had left arriving there till the middle of the night for that reason. Neither did he want to leave evidence of his having been there. He wore surgical gloves and plastic bags over his shoes. He wasn't planning to move or touch anything except for the tape should he find it - and the contents of the safe.

He had a torch, but the house was miles from the road and other properties, so it was safe to switch lights on and off as he moved around. The studio area showed no signs of being used for months, so he didn't spend long looking in there. He didn't spend a lot of time delving anywhere, full stop. If Stephanie had found it worthwhile whacking Bahnlich to get the tape, she wasn't likely to leave it laying around for others to find.

For someone thrown into a state of high hysteria, Jenny Grant had summed up things pretty well.

He searched the whole property looking for tell-tale signs that Stephanie was still in the house somewhere but didn't really expect to find her and wasn't disappointed.

One thing Jenny *had* forgotten to check was the CCTV footage from the outside cameras. He would normally have bollocked her for such an oversight, but not in this case. He had almost forgot to do that himself.

The cameras recorded stop frame every few seconds onto VHS tapes. When they were checked later that morning at Gerald Silver's offices, there was nothing on them. A waste of money installing them!

The other thing Jenny had missed was the beached Range Rover at the back of the house, which probably meant she hadn't checked the stables either. How had the car ended up like that? Before Bahnlich got hit, or after? He shone the torch through the window. The keys were still in it. He guessed Stephanie had been at the wheel when it had happened. It wasn't likely to have been some crap burglar who couldn't drive trying to nick it. It had to be Stephanie. She hadn't driven for ages. Grabbed the keys and tried to do a runner. Had to be that.

So where was she now?

Long gone, he supposed. But he still trod carefully when he checked the stables. He didn't want her leaping out at him wielding a horseshoe hammer.

No worries. She wasn't there. Nor was one of her horses!

'Really?' he asked himself, trying to assess the meaning of it. 'Are ya kiddin' me she went riding off into the sunset like fucking Minnehaha, twenty-two grand stuffed in her pouch?'

Well, it had been something just like that!

He returned to the main house to tend to one more crucial thing before heading back to London to meet up with Gerald Silver. He needed to get into Ludlow's private safe to remove the contents. This he had left till last.

He checked his watch and got a shock before realizing he hadn't put it back 3 hours to British time. It was still pitch-black outside. Not yet 5 am. Good. He'd be well gone by first light.

The whereabouts of the safe was known solely to Ludlow himself apart from the company that had installed it. But they did not know the arcane process needed before it would open. Some other company had installed that. Even Rose had to be initiated into this before leaving Nairobi.

He stood for a few minutes studying the murder scene, committing it to memory. After due consideration, he stepped in and carefully removed the empty petty-cash box. It would be useful for the next task.

The custom-built safe was laid flat beneath the wooden tiles of Ludlow office precisely where he sat when at his desk. Its door opened upwards. Another unique feature was that the combination number would only activate the lock when the office door was opened at a precise angle to rest above a sensor hidden in the floor. Even a whizz-kid safe cracker would get nowhere without the knowledge of this finesse. It was probably also highly unlikely that a thief would go to work on the safe with the office door wide open!

Some eighty thousand dollars in various currencies nestled therein along with boxes of methadone tablets and buprenorphine patches prescribed to Stephanie in a forlorn attempt to ween her off heroin. Phials of the demon itself were there as well, as a fail-safe to control her rages and threats.

She could have as much of it as she wanted now, if she could be found. Anything to stop the threats!

Still wearing gloves, Rose emptied the safe as instructed, placing the contents into the petty-cash box. He put everything in the room back in order and took his leave. Within three hours, as dawn welcomed the London rush hour, he was ensconced in a Mayfair hotel, having transferred the haul into his room's own safe.

Within a further two hours, he had contacted the extra hands that might be needed in the course of the next few days. Their first task; to locate Stephanie. With little else he could do from his hotel room, he waited. And waiting not being his best attribute, he raided the mini bar.

Between 4.30 and 4.45 pm that day, Rose received a series of three calls on his portable brick telephone to which his only response was 'check'.

Soon after, he rang his boss in Kenya via the operator to report that Jenny had read the form well and that all the dogs were in their stalls ready to run. 'There's been no sight of the favourite,' he added, 'and no hint of the starting price in the papers.'

This coded news raised Ludlow's hope more than a little. Stephanie had not yet gone public with her threats. There had to be other things on her mind, he guessed. Like running from murder. Thankfully, that news hadn't broken yet either. Perhaps she had gone into hiding. But where could she go with that face of hers, drugged up or not? Most likely to her chat-up buddy on the tape recording? Her 'safe hands'.

Ludlow had been holding onto the hope that there was still a chance to make Bahnlich's death look like a burglary gone wrong as a trade-off with Stephanie. This could finally get her off his back once and for all. But realistically, what chance was there of that? Probably zero. He had to prepare for the worst; have arrangements in place to deal with all possible outcomes to lessen the blow.

That evening he received a call from Gerald Silver. 'The financial press believe they've got news of something,' he said enthusiastically. 'The phone hasn't stopped ringing about your supposedly 'secret' negotiations with the Kenyan minister. It's all going well. With a flourish, I've moved significant amounts of your sleeping assets into Isunti to help wise eyes think they've put two and two together about an impending big deal.'

Isunti was a company that the Wilson-Hughes group was about to take over. Stainless-steel tubing was practically all it produced. Hardly anything else left its factory floors. Isunti's capacity for increasing output was well-known among market watchers, as was the fact that virtually every foot of piping that rolled out of its mills in Osaka was destined for desalination plants or irrigation pumping stations around the globe.

'I also thought it was worth making a gesture to help throw another cat amongst the pigeons by sacrificing some of your holdings to buy Kenyan gilt-edged. That should also keep the pundits guessing for a bit longer. Another day like today and we'll have everyone believing we've pulled off the Kenyan irrigation deal already. Let's hope we've found your crazy wife before she does anything stupid, so you don't have to leave the party altogether!'

Chapter Thirteen

Peter Tyler got up much earlier than usual on Monday, anxious to get on with something that might give him a better idea of why Stephanie had been in such an anxious state.

He had his own set of keys to Hollom's Attic, which allowed him to come and go whenever it suited him to work on the Sopwith Pup or other projects.

But that was not the first thing on his mind this morning. He wanted to see if one of the second-hand tape recorders sitting around waiting for a buyer would play the tape he had found. That had to tell him *something*.

Most of the tape was salvageable once smoothed out, and indeed would play. Luckily, not too much of it had been damaged. There was silence for a minute or so, and then Stephanie's wavering voice could be heard quite clearly coming and going between ringing tones.

She was on the telephone!

'Brrr...brrr...major...brrr...brr...please answer! brr...brrr...wake up, please answer.!' Then came a brief sound like chips frying in a tunnel, before Stephanie again, breathing heavily.

She sounded frantic. Then came another woman's voice, annoyed, confused?

'Hello? Who is this?'

'It's me, major. Stephanie.'

'It's the middle of the night, for heaven's sake.'

'Sorry. Sorry. I had to be sure. I had to hear you say it. In case I got it wrong. So, it's true?'

A slight pause.

'Yes.'

Stephanie began to sob, barely controlling herself before asking: 'Boy or girl?'

'A healthy little girl. And that's all I can tell you. You know that.'

More sobs came before she could continue. 'Is she OK? I want to help her. Make it up to her now I can. I should have done it years ago, I know. But, it's been me, me, me all the time! I've been such I fucking wreck!'

'Stephanie! Calm down!'

'It's true! But now I know she's alive I want to do everything I can to help her, give her money, at least.'

'It's not that straight forward, Stephanie. She's now a grown woman. We can't just waltz in and disrupt her life by telling her she was adopted. It could cause huge problems for her, especially if she were to learn she was born out of... I have to say it, Stephanie, born out of statutory rape, which is exactly what it was. No getting away from it. You were only 13 years old!'

Tyler could hardly believe what he was hearing.

'I know all that! I'm not asking you to tell her the truth!' Stephanie yelled. She was losing it. 'That would destroy me, too! Stephanie Star, super rich fucking drug addict abandoned her baby and kept the world from knowing it. I couldn't face that. My life's in deep shit as it is already!'

More sobbing.

'Stephanie. Listen to me. Don't be so hard on yourself. You cannot be blamed for your childhood, for the way you were mistreated. I've delved into your records when you were known as Sheila Braithewaite. You're a tragic victim in all this, Stephanie. It's a wonder you survived at all with the abuse you suffered. No-one can blame you for going astray. You somehow slipped through the net of care at a very vulnerable, confusing age. It's those who failed you who are to blame. That you managed to put everything behind and achieve what you have in your life after such trauma is nothing more than a miracle.'

'It's a miracle I'm not dead, more like! Look at me! A hopeless junkie! Help me do something good for once in my life. And the only way, I suppose is with money. She doesn't have to know where it's coming from. A long-lost aunt or uncle, something like that. You must know what to do in situations like this.'

'It's not that simple, Stephanie, especially in the middle of the night. It needs thought. A clear head. I need to think about this.'

'It could have been left in a Will, couldn't it? I'll make a Will?'

'That's fine for the future, but think, Stephanie. You are still a young woman. If you want to do something now, anonymously, it will take some thought. Give me time. I'll try to sort something out. This is a very unusual situation.'

'All my life.....' Stephanie's sobbing stopped her going on momentarily, 'I wasn't sure if the baby had lived or not, didn't care one way or the other. I never saw it. They didn't show me...'

More lengthy sobbing accompanied by some shushing from the other woman. Eventually, Stephanie came through it. 'Where is she? What is she like? What is she doing? What's her name? I promise I won't go looking for her. How could I? I just need to know about her.'

'I can't tell you much, Stephanie. It's totally unethical. I can only tell you she's alive and well. And... I must be honest about this, with your history of drug addiction there's absolutely no possibility you would ever be allowed...'

'I know, I know. I don't have to meet her. All I want is to help her. Is she still in Sheffield, where... it happened?'

'No, she is not. I can tell you that much, but that's all. I've gone out on a limb for you with this, Stephanie, by acting completely alone as you had wished. None of my comrades know about this. You have a right to know your child survived. *Of course,* you do. But that's as far as it goes. I might have overstretched my authority even telling you she's a girl.' There was a garbled section for a few moments before the major's words came back clearly. '...in a quandary. Perhaps a monetary gesture from an anonymous source could possibly be arranged, but further than that, I just don't know.'

Stephanie jumped in clearly again.

'I would write a cheque now, if I could. But my account's been frozen thanks to my bastard husband! I'm deemed irresponsible. He's a control freak! God forbid he gets to know about this. I don't know what he'd do. I'll make a proper Will just in case...' The words faded again before coming back with a litany of accusations about her husband's dodgy dealings. It was very damaging stuff, if true. Was she making it up through malice? Everyone knew big businesses used every trick in the book. But his SODA charity? Drugs? Money laundering? It sounded like Ludlow was some big mafia kingpin, and proof of it was on a floppy disc she had innocently come by years back when her life had been in full swing.

The major's voice broke in.

'Stop it, Stephanie. I don't need to know all this. If you want to act on such matters, then take them to the proper authorities. They are beyond my remit.'

Stephanie started silently sobbing again.

'Please don't do anything silly, Stephanie. Give me time to think things through. Try to get some sleep. Next time, contact me in the way we discussed. I thought you were against using the telephone?'

'I know, yes, sorry. But I just had to be sure. As you probably know, my husband is in Africa, so there's no chance he can be listening in to us.'

But the late Tilda Bahnlich unfortunately could and had been.

Peter was stopped in his tracks. His mind was doing somersaults. Stephanie had been raped as a thirteen-year-old! Became pregnant. And all through her life she hadn't known if the baby had survived or not. Shit. No wonder the state she was in. 'No-one must know!' That made sense now, and he knew where she had been trying to go that morning? To the 'major', where else? Taking the tape and the 'fat' envelope. What a mess she had been in when they'd collided just minutes after crashing the Range Rover. What was she thinking, desperately trying to get to the major on a horse! Dressed like that!

He replaced the tape recorder where he had found it, his mind now doing the spinning.

By the time Martin Hollom came into the shop at 8.30 on the dot Monday morning, the tape was in a biscuit tin where Peter kept music cassettes and various bits and pieces for his Sopwith Pup project. He would decide what to do with it later.

'Up bright and early, Peter,' Martin remarked, not particularly surprised.

'Bad night's sleep. Thought I might as well get on with this.'

He told Hollom about seeing the stranded horse in the woods and the response he had got when he made the 999 call.

'So much for their concern! Don't know why I bothered.'

115

'S'pose they couldn't care less about chasing after her up there on her own patch,' Hollom reckoned. 'She's given them enough runaround as it is.'

True enough.

All through the day, Peter couldn't stop thinking about the revelations on the tape. At the same time, he was keeping a keen ear on every local news bulletin wondering if anyone else might have seen Stephanie's horse running wild.

That didn't happen until the following morning, and not exactly as anticipated. It came as an urgent traffic flash.

'All drivers using the Marlsbury-Septon road are advised to find an alternative route due to a serious accident involving a loose horse. The road is completely blocked in both directions. Diversions are being set up. More of that story as it comes in.'

'Did you hear that, Martin?' Peter shouted, an hour into a stint on the Sopwith Pup. 'That should set alarm bells ringing at the cop shop. Now the sods'll believe me!'

The next bulletin carried a fuller report. Apparently, a riderless horse had run into the road and two cars had collided head-on trying to avoid it. Both drivers were seriously injured, as was the horse. Sadly, it had to be put down. There was speculation that it belonged to the Ludlow family.

'Speculation my foot!' Peter sneered; glad he'd had the conscience and sense to make that call. 'I told the bastards!'

About noon, the shop doorbell rang, announcing Old Pikey. He'd been doing the rounds, spreading the news. He had seen the police dog unit heading out earlier. 'Probably them same sniffer dogs in The King's Head New Year's Eve,' he suggested. The horse had since been positively identified as belonging to Stephanie Star. Now the police were anxious to trace her.

'Is that why you're not at work today, then, Pikey?' Martin Hollom asked. 'What's going on up there?'

'That's it, innit?' Old Pikey replied. 'We've all been given an extra three days' holiday on account of this Knighthood business, ain't we? Mustn't grumble, but something funny's going on. I can smell it, can't I?'

And so could 'Coventry', the Southern Counties Champion Police Dog. She took off like a shot into the woods with her handler after one good sniff of the horse.

Meanwhile, Detective Inspector Jack Simpson had gone to Compton Stud to make inquiries, only to be confronted with very locked and silent main gates.

Before departing, he had faced a flurry of questions from a handful of journalists and a local TV crew that had gathered in anticipation outside Marlsbury Police Station.

The most persistent question was to learn if Stephanie Star been on the horse before it ran into the road?

Jack Simpson's reply was standard.

'At this early stage, we are looking at every possibility.'

'The horse was saddled up, so someone must have been out riding it, surely?' A hack asked.

'If it was Stephanie's horse, it must have been her, mustn't it?' From another one.

'We're keeping an open mind until we know more.'

At that precise moment, Coventry was leading her handler across the bridle path close to the point where Peter had first spotted the magnetic tape. Had he been more persistent in his search, it might have saved the need for sniffer dogs.

Not fifty yards further on from where he had unwound the tape from the horse two days earlier, Coventry suddenly sat down and started barking loudly enough to clear the woods of birds for miles, her tail whirling like a dervish.

There was Stephanie, as dead as dead could be, all shades of grey and blue, eyes open, face looking up, but chest flat to the ground. It was far too late for the kiss of life. The dog-handler simply activated his radio and alerted the emergency services.

At just after 2pm, with eyes wet from watering his cyder blossoms in the Turks Anchor, Martin Hollom charged into the back room to tell Peter the latest.

'They've found her! Dead! Up in Deadwoods! Yeah, Deadwoods. Appropriate, in't it?' He was spluttering over his words, more cyder than

117

sausage having passed his lips for lunch. 'Her neck's been broken. Some says it could be murder!'

Martin had scooped the airwaves with this news by ear-wigging the reporters on their hefty cell phones in the pub.

Peter's heart sank. He had started to suspect she might be dead. But not murdered. No way. Poor Stephanie. He chastened himself. Perhaps he should have made more of an effort to go after her New Year's morning. It had seemed pointless at the time.

'Who says it's murder?' he asked, disbelieving. No-one had been chasing her. He would have seen them.

A sudden thought came to him. Shit. He must be the last person to have seen her alive.

'It's that press mob. Going on about it being foul play.' Hollom went on. 'There's a load of them up at the Turks Anchor. I knew something like this was going to happen sooner or later. She's made a lot of enemies, that one. They reckon someone else was up there with her. 'Spect they've been pestering the coppers for more information. Ha!' He gibed. 'Or slipped Pikey a few bob, more like. Old Pikey knows all about getting graft from the press, don't he? Anyway, they're talking about other footprints being up there. Praps that Swiss woman topped her.'

Nothing had been on the radio yet about finding Stephanie, but Peter believed Martin Hollom had probably overheard correctly. *Someone else was up there with her!* It had to be Peter they were talking about. And the police must have known it was him because of his 999 call. Again, he was so glad he had rung them.

Victor Rose was also glad, but for a different reason. Stephanie was 'brown bread'! That had to be good news, didn't it? He called his boss to put him in the picture.

'She's been dead fucking days!' he roared, his tight grip threatening to crack the telephone's plastic handpiece. 'That's got to be good news, hasn't it, Ted?'

Ludlow got the point Rose was making. Five days had passed without any comebacks. No nasty phone calls from her 'safe hands'? He couldn't relax yet, though. But five days? There was still a glimmer of hope.

118

It took him a full minute to respond to Rose's optimism.

'Do something for me, Victor. Get onto Silver and tell him to prepare to cut and run. He must have heard the news himself by now, so he'll already be coming to his own conclusions. I can't face him myself right now. God knows what shit Stephanie's left behind her.'

Gerald Silver had indeed heard the news, along with most of the country, as would the rest of the world as it woke to a new day. Stephanie Star was still high on the newsworthy list, as much for her fall from grace as for her years at the top.   No escaping it.

Chapter Fourteen

In Manchester, England, Kim's ears pricked up when she heard the news. It was the first headline.

'Oi! Phoney!' she shouted from the kitchen of the rented flat she shared with Sharon. Phoney was Sharon's nickname from her school days. She was fed up with being called it, as Kim well knew, which is why she would use it when she wanted to get Sharon's attention.

Kim had risen unusually early for either of them, just in time to catch the midday bulletin as she put the kettle on. 'Did you hear that?'

There came no response, although she knew Sharon was awake. She made two mugs of tea using one tea bag. When it had brewed, she pushed open the door to the small bedroom using her shoulder. 'Stop faking it, Phoney. Tea time,' she sang, plonking one of the mugs on the upturned beer crate that served as a bedside table. She was wearing a long T-shirt with 'Hippie' printed on it under a drunken-looking unisex cartoon character wearing huge sunglasses giving a 'V' sign. Trying not to spill her own mug, Kim straddled across the bed, which was tight against the wall, shoving Sharon with her boney hip to make room for herself. Then, putting her bare legs under the covers, she sought a warm part of Sharon with her cold feet to rouse her.

'Oi! Fuck off, Burly!' Was the response.

Burly was Kim's nickname from schooldays, used equally to annoy. If Kim called Sharon 'Phoney', Kim got 'Burly' back. Nothing malicious in it.

'Your tea's getting cold.' Kim said.

Grunt.

'Guess what?'

'What?' Although awake, Sharon was not yet quite with it.

'Stephanie Star's dead!'

'What?' More enquiringly.

'Stephanie Star's dead.'

Sharon sat herself up. She was wide awake now.

'Shit! How?'

'Some accident on 'er 'orse.'

"Shit!" She was giving it some thought. 'Not drugs, then?'

'They haven't said. But, come on, what do you think? *Ride that Horse,* eh? Someone wrote a song called that, didn't they?'

'Dunno. What you on about?'

''orse! 'Eroin! You know!'

'Oh. Yeah.' It was sinking in.

'Surprised she could even get on a fucking horse these days, by all accounts.'

'Poor Steff. Is that all it said, accident?'

'Yeah. And that she was only 34. Can you believe that? I'll get a paper later. Might tell us more.'

'Didn't do herself in, did she, d'you think? Wouldn't be surprised with all that stuff going on about her in the papers. On the tele, too. With her getting nicked. A few nights ago.'

'New Year's Eve? No, they let her off. Drunk and disorderly, or somefin'. Don't s'pose that had anything to do with it.'

They drank their tea in silence for a minute or two with the duvet pulled up over their shoulders. Just their hands out holding their tea. There was no central heating.

They didn't sleep with each other, although they cuddled up in bed together like this sometimes when it was cold. They paid indirectly for gas and electricity through the landlord who hiked the price up, so they kept heating costs down as much as possible. They didn't spend a lot of time at home, anyway. There was an armchair divan in the so-called living room. Whoever came in first from their nightly outings would grab the bedroom. Whenever they came home together, the one who'd slept there last, kept it again for that night and so on. There was no arguing. They hardly ever bickered. They'd gone through school together and stayed friends after. They were both 20 now. Sharon, a few months older. They had been sharing this small flat for more than two years. It was one of seven similar apartments in a large, detached property in Manchester's southern suburbs that had been converted 'on the cheap'. Five of them had been built from rooms large enough to be divided up into bedsits. Sharon and Kim's had one of these. Plasterboard had been used for partitioning to save space. This allowed for visual privacy but offered very little in the way of sound insulation. The kitchen was built for single occupancy. Swinging a cat in it was not an option, the bathroom so compact that a person could be sitting on the pan and washing their feet in the plastic shower tray at the same time. There was a minuscule sink, but no shelf above it. That had sheared off from the plasterboard months ago due to overloading with beauty products and the like.

The girls made do fairly well all the same. It was a comfortable enough pad for their needs.

What helped make the lack of space go further, was they shared the same taste in clothes and make-up, swapping both with no hassle. They always went shopping together so that they could buy something they both liked and would wear. They were similar heights, around the 5'5" mark. Kim was a lot bustier but just as slim elsewhere. 'Top heavy' it had been said. Her legs were like sticks before she blossomed out. There had been a cruel joke going round that if you rubbed Kim's knees together, you'd get sparks across her nipples!

Sharing clothes usually worked out fine between them. Sharon didn't mind loose fitting tops. They made themselves up similarly, so only one jar of whatever was needed was bought at any given time. At present they were going through a pale-face punk phase.

The decoration of the flat reflected this. Rather the lack of decoration. Black drapes were pinned up everywhere. The one exception was a large poster of a supposed tennis player scratching her bare bum under her lifted skirt. They both related to this.

Their nicknames had caught on in the latter part of their school days. For Sharon, it was because from certain angles when the light was right, people would say she looked exactly like Stephanie Star. This became even more so as her face lost its puppy fat. Sharon was quite chuffed about this to begin with, to the point of deliberately trying to exaggerate the likeness by using the products Stephanie Star was advertising at any given time and copying the way she used them. That was when the nickname kicked in. Because Sharon was copying Stephanie, she became Ste*phon*ie. Soon after, just Phoney.

For Kim, it was slightly crueler. Her full name was Kimberley. Because of her big upper body, Kimberley was shortened to Burly. Both names had stuck.

'How did you get on last night,' Sharon asked. 'I didn't hear you come in.'

'I wasn't that late. 'Round three-ish, I s'pose. What happened to you? You crept off early. Bullet-head Jimbo was asking after you.'

'Yeah. I know. Wanted me to do a trick for some old geezer he was buttering up. I told him I was already lined up. Fuck him! He's getting out of order. Always hitting on me. I'm thinking about talking to Tony about him. You're alright. The prick seems to leave you alone.'

'Yeah, well. I'm happy about that. But Tony ain't going to get rid of him, is he?'

'I reckon he's on something. Have you ever looked him straight in the eye? Fucking freaky. He keeps on about working for him on the side Tuesdays and Wednesdays. Tony's got to be told about that.'

This suggestion was met with a shrug of the shoulders.

'You know Tony. He's alright, but what goes on outside club hours never concerns him. He's said as much. Jimbo's good news for Tony. One of the reasons there's never any real trouble at the club. Jimbo comes down so fucking hard on anyone who gets out of hand. Tony doesn't want to upset that state of affairs, does he?'

Jimbo, alias 'bullet-head' had been going 'straight' since working at Tony's. He had a history of violence and intimidation, qualities he seldom needed to put into practice at Tony's, thankfully for him. If he ever got started on a troublemaker, it would be difficult to stop him. His temper was always that close to the top. It wouldn't take much to see him back inside if he was ever to lose it big time. To have his crooked face standing over potential trouble was usually enough to quieten things down. It had to be said, one of the reasons things rarely got out of hand in the club was the threat of having Jimbo letting loose on you.

'Tony's Ring', had once been a snooker hall. For the sake of license as much as diversion, when the property was converted to its present purpose, a room was created to look like an *olde* English country pub bar sporting a full-size snooker table. The walls were of dark brown oak, its furnishings folksy armchairs and settees. It sported a roaring fake fireplace going full out winter *or* summer. The main area of Tony's Ring was all light blue and pinks and air conditioning. Laura Ashley wallpaper and drapes set the tone, with mildly erotic, but twee, framed posters scattered around to titillate the senses.

In another era the old snooker venue might have been transformed into a dance hall where the younger generation came to 'pull'. But Tony had pretensions of sophistication to lift his 'Ring' one or two steps higher. He wanted the place to attract a more mature clientele, so money was spent on creating a soft, sweet-smelling atmosphere, the piped music favouring foxtrots rather than jives. The doormen, as in bouncers, wore uniforms discreetly reminiscent of combat outfits, more camp than battle garments. Pints of beer were not available, only half-pints in stem glasses but charged at pint prices. Wine by the glass was not an option, only by the bottle. Tony's aim was to encourage well-lined pockets. How those pockets got that way was of no concern to him. No proper food was available, just those sad slices of pizza. This was an after-dinner hang-out. It didn't open till nine, and seldom got busy till the pubs were well closed. Monday, Tuesday and Wednesday it didn't open at all except on special occasions. For the rest of the week, particularly Fridays and Saturdays, it was pastel pink party-time downstairs, and unabashed knocking shop upstairs.

The waitresses and waiters were legally employed with up-to-date P.45 tax forms should they choose to move on. However, those forms would not reveal the true amount of earnings that came to them as tips. Moreover, neither would any of the remuneration coming from bonuses earned 'Upstairs'.

Those waiting in line to get a job at Tony's already knew, or soon found out, how rewarding the provision of these 'extramarital' services could be. Not knowing the ingredients of a 'Between the Sheets' or 'Bouncing Bomb' cocktail never stood in the way of getting a job as long as the looks and attitude of a wannabe were right.

Word got out early on that Tony looked after his workers, male and female. In consequence, there was always someone ready to fill a vacancy. This was usually accomplished by word of mouth. No advertising was really necessary, although he kept permanent ones running locally. They served to promote the venue as much as to attract suitable staff. For those with that inclination, it was known that 'Upstairs' at Tony's was a lot safer than working on the streets. Everything needed to cater for the different preferences and wallets was on site, including strong arms for protection against foul play if needed as provided by Jimbo and the doormen.

Tony's Ring was on the police radar, but there had never been any reports of trouble there. All the bills and necessary taxes were seen to be paid, plus a little on the side. It was a case of letting sleeping dogs lie. The police had their work cut out dealing with illicit sex going on elsewhere in the city, not just on the streets. Most of the resources were being employed in an effort to bring a gang of thugs to justice who were illegally importing young girls from Eastern Europe on a promise, only to entrap them as sex slaves.

Tony Ricartta, better known as Tiger Tony, had been a minor celebrity in the show-biz world of Wrestling. In the ring, he made himself up as a tiger from head to toe, giving himself a fake tail that he would swing around with exaggerated hip movements in celebration of any successful throw or submission. He was popular for his sense of playfulness, best illustrated when he had his opponent in a tight clinch from behind, when he would start his tail wagging feverishly.

Tony knew a thing or two about bouncing off the ropes and dodging blows, which had helped him steer clear of the law after quitting the wrestling game and entering the hospitality business. He still had all his marbles, and outside the ring and tiger make-up was very personable and approachable. His trade had made him adept at appearing fearless and aggressive, which stood him in good stead when it came to running such a business as Tony's Ring'. Few people messed with Tony. Jimmy, or Jimbo as the name had caught on, with his bent face had usually cleared any problems before Tony's 'charm' was needed.

Jimbo had all the qualities for ironing out disruption, whether at the bar, at the table or on the postage stamp of a dance floor. Trouble seldom went further than words. Only occasionally was force necessary to nip imminent violence in the bud, those moments usually triggered by alcohol overindulgence. Jimbo, alias bullet-head to the boys and girls who worked the floor at Tony's, was more than capable of limiting any inconvenience it might cause to other customers. Both doormen were also adept at stepping in on those occasions allowing normal service to be resumed as soon as possible. Generally, all clients respected the need for harmony at Tony's. Even habitual street miscreants tended to know their place, happy to keep a low profile. 'What goes on at Tony's, stays at Tony's' was one of the laws drilled into the staff, conveyed with a 'relax and enjoy' smile.

Tony's was one of the only such late-night establishments in the city, and not only Tony was anxious to keep his licence. His loyal customers would also hate to see him lose it. He advertised it as a singles club, although to call it a 'club' in the true sense of the word was a misnomer. No subscriptions were called for, no membership forms to fill in. Men weren't even required to wear ties: just to look presentable and not touch the 'goods' until paid for up front. The 'singles' part of the description was more or less correct.

Of course, those who came were not necessarily 'single'. They were perhaps looking for something they could not find in their matrimonial home, or perhaps escaping from something they could.

The clientele came from all walks of life, even from the higher echelons of local officialdom. Private booths were available where discretion was paramount. Tony went out of his way to keep a tight ship. No questions asked. The staff were well versed in turning a blind eye.

It was on the upper floor, 'Upstairs', appropriately called, where discretion became most necessary; and where Jimbo spent a lot of his time. Not everyone who came to Tony's knew of the services on offer above the dance floor. There was no hard sell. Tony was happy that the club passed as a convivial place to have a late-night drink if that's all a punter was looking for. As long as those who came could afford the inflated prices, all were welcomed.

After only a few visits, most previously innocent patrons would cotton on to what lay hidden 'Upstairs'.

Behind heavy curtains further along from the snooker room, those wishing to indulge in the forbidden fruits one floor up were taken through a door marked 'Private'. This opened to an awaiting lift. No stairs. People couldn't just drift up out of curiosity or in search of the toilets. The lift could only be operated from above for security reasons and would only come down by arrangement.

Once those had been made and a punter was in place to come up, Jimbo would send the lift down and be in attendance when it reappeared to take appropriate payment at a small counter reminiscent of a family hotel's reception desk. A row of different coloured keys were mounted on the wall behind it. From there, the customer would be invited to wait in a comfortable anti-room which not only provided its own small 'courtesy' bar, but also a television screen streaming non-stop hard-core pornography. All part of the service!

All six 'bed' rooms had ensuite facilities. No effort had been made to overly dress them. They were each decorated in their own colour. Customers had a choice of crimson, magenta, purple, pink, dark blue, or light blue. Green was seen as unsuitable for some reason. Everything in the rooms would be of its own colour; walls, floor, ceiling, doors, chairs (two in each), bed, mattress and linen; even the porcelain in the washroom was a matching colour. Soap, too. Everything! Tony thought it was a nice touch.

It was the amount of money passing hands upstairs that had given Jimbo the idea of trying something like this off his own back on the days when Tony's was closed. He would tread on Tony's toes. If it worked out and grew enough, he would move his act to a different part of the city to avoid conflict. Tony had taken him in and given him a job straight from a long stretch in the nick. Tony was alright. But that was a couple of years ago now, and Jimbo would love to get something going for himself.

He could poach some of the girls from Tony's to start with. He knew a lot of them were already working the streets on days off to earn a bit more. These were the ones he would be muscling in on first. He wasn't interested in handling boys and wouldn't be offering any of the poncy stuff Tony's went in for; soft music and cocktails. Street trade to start with until he could find a suitable place. Then, no frills. He might throw in some porn. That seemed to help the turnover at Tony's. He wouldn't have to buy any in. There was already a pile of it he could 'borrow' since he was the one in charge of it 'Upstairs'.

He already had his eye on a few of the girls to approach. He was looking for the most streetwise among them. Sharon and Kim fitted that category, along with a couple of Irish girls he thought he could talk into it. Those four worked the streets occasionally on their days off. He had already started to threaten them about it. In Sharon and Kim's case, they kept to a part of the city well away from Tony's nearer to where they lived, so they weren't really taking custom from Tony's. But he started putting the frighteners on them by suggesting they were. 'We can do whatever we want when Tony's is closed!' Sharon had argued when he'd confronted them in their favoured red-light spot east of the city.

'No, you fucking can't, big mouth!' he cursed back, grabbing her by her upper arms and pushing her against a convenient tree. 'You listen to me, you foul-mouthed cow! Anything you do outside Tony's, you do through me. Get it? Otherwise, you're out! I'll not let you slum it on the streets and comeback spreading the fucking pox around Tony's.'

That, of course, was a fair point.

Because of the nature of the 'Upstairs' services when dealing with random clients, Tony was strict about the health of his workers. Every week, usually on Thursday afternoon before things started rolling at the club, a surgery was held on site. A friendly doctor and nurse, both 'club members' themselves, checked out the whole staff for any signs of sickness, not just for venereal disease. Heavy colds and flu would not get the green flag either.

But Tony was fair. Anyone told to stay away for health reasons still received their official wage. Those with anything worse would get full health support. Any punter deemed to be responsible for bringing in an unwelcome ailment would not be allowed back until they were checked out to be clean. No hard feelings.

When bullet-head had calmed down, he let Sharon go and became more conciliatory. The time was right to hit them with his proposal.

'OK, so you want to earn more money on your days off. I get that. But not like this on the streets. Unprotected? How often have you been short-changed? Plenty, I bet. I can line up punters for you and make sure they don't do a runner. Tell me that's never happened? Without Tony's overheads, I can maybe pay you better rates, if you're in."

Oh, yeah? Sharon was thinking. And where would all this be going on? Some rat-infested dive. And of course, bullet head wouldn't short-change us himself, would he? Do me a fucking favour! He could never match Tony's for style and comfort, and if Tony got wind of what was going on, they might be kicked out.

Kim was having fewer negative thoughts. Street life wasn't as freewheeling as it sounded. Jimbo might be a prick, but as a minder he was worth the money. Much better to have him on your side instead of ducking and diving trying to avoid him. Tony had made it clear that what they got up to out of hours was none of his business. But things could change if Jimbo was trying to muscle in big time.

'He'll never leave us in peace until we say yes, Sharon, now he's started on us.' Kim reasoned. 'You know what he's like.'

'Fucking right, I do. He wants to own us!'

'Do you think Tony knows what he's up to?'

'Wouldn't surprise me one way or the other. Don't suppose he gives a shit as long it's not hurting the club. He's said as much, ain't he? But that depends on exactly what Jimbo's got on his mind.'

Had Tony fully realized what Jimbo had at the back of his mind, he might well have 'given a shit!'.

Tony's Club was set on a corner with a handful of shops on either side with flats above them. Access passageways led to garages and loading areas behind. None of the shops were doing all that well. A couple were boarded up. One had become a charity shop, which probably did more trade than any of the others apart from a betting office, which Tony owned along with a minicab business which the staff could use free of charge to get them home safely. Public transport had always stopped running by the time Tony's closed.

Originally there had been eight flats above Tony's place, each with its own brick stairway entrance at the back leading down to the garages. Over the years, as business 'Upstairs' grew, the dividing walls had been knocked through to inter-connect them. All but two of the back stairways had been blocked off now. One of these went up to a small self-contained flat where Jimbo lived. The other up to another one now used solely as a service area. Doors off Jimbo's place gave him the run of upstairs.

The service area housed washing machines, tumble dryers and all the cleaning tools and gadgets needed to keep a bordello spic and span.

Jimbo had keys to every door in Tony's Club, upstairs or down.

He was on site seven days a week keeping tabs on all the comings and goings. A skeleton staff were employed from Mondays to Thursdays to deal with cleaning and deliveries. All daytime activities.

What Jimbo was considering for his pimping business before encountering any unnecessary expenditure, was making use of one or two of the 'Upstairs' rainbow rooms. He had it all worked out. Entrance could be gained through his own flat without creating suspicion. Who was going to notice, let alone question the comings and goings?

What bullet-head had come to know, but would not accept, was that neither Sharon nor Kim liked to be told what to do. Being 'handled' was way off limits. That pair was not going to fall into his lap willingly.

At Tony's they could pick and choose whether or not they wanted to accept an invitation to go 'Upstairs'. Tony knew those two especially were happier working like that. Happiness meant less trouble and better business in the long run. Tony liked it that way. He understood why the girls were fussy about who they chose as clients, so he left it to them to say yes or no. No pressure. Tony would have hated having people calling him a pimp.

So, they didn't.

Sharon was one of the favourites along with Kim. They almost always had a suitable choice. When they didn't, very often they wouldn't choose at all, particularly Sharon. They would just work the tables and oblige on the dance floor if they preferred an easy night. Tony was happy to let all the girls do their thing. Sharon and Kim in particular were fun girls. Good at their job. They had more regulars than most of the others, which spoke volumes. Between them, they more than satisfied Tony's cash flow targets for 'Upstairs'.

Kim kept the subject of Jimbo going. More money would always be welcomed if Jimbo could come up with a better deal and the conditions were OK. But Sharon was not one bit interested in having bullet-head call the shots.

'He's an evil bastard,' she persisted. 'You wouldn't want to get the wrong side of that prick. So, I'm not going to chance putting myself in that position in the first place Anyway, I don't want to make a habit of street work, Kim, nor should you. It's alright for an occasional bit extra, but I don't want to put working for Tony's at risk. Once Jimbo got us at it, there'd be no stopping him!'

'OK. But what's he gonna do if we tell him to sod off.'
'We'd just have to face him down. Better that than slave labour.'
'He's your man for protection, though. Can't argue with that.'
'He's a control freak, Kim.'
'I dunno. I thought it might be worth considering.'

Sharon mulled it over, then said: 'Life would be fucking hell!'

They got by well enough, didn't they, as things were? At the forefront of her mind was the fear of upsetting Tony and losing their jobs. Because, at Tony's there was always the possibility, a sneaking hope, that one day the right bloke would turn up and whisk them off their feet. A rich one, preferably. Although thin on the ground, rich blokes did turn up sometimes at Tony's judging by the cars they drove.

So, it wasn't a total pipe dream.

Chapter Fifteen

While the creatures of the financial underworld surfaced to the new year and began to chew over the inference of certain sudden and unexpected movements in the market of civil engineering stocks and shares, some equally voracious subterranean insects were seen to have been investigating the bounty of Stephanie Stars rigid corpse. Studying the extent of these little busy-bodies' 'dig in' had helped determine the approximate time of Stephanie's death: sometime mid-morning, New Years' Day. It seemed her neck had been broken, possibly by her head's violent collision with the thick branch of an elm tree, directly under which her body lay.

Although the initial prognosis pointed to accidental death, the police would not be making a public statement until a full forensic examination could be processed. They were not yet totally disregarding the possibility of foul play.

Most of Marlsbury stayed glued to the radio during the afternoon so as not to miss any further developments in a fast-moving story. This promised to be the biggest news since the pumps factory closure. Bigger! It had begun to reverberate globally.

Peter kept his ears alerted to what was going on without overstating his keen interest. He left for home shortly after the 3 o'clock news bulletin. It was the only story on the air waves.

Sir Edward Ludlow had been contacted in Africa and informed of the tragedy. In spite of his shock and grave concern about his wife's terrible accident, he would not be cutting short his trip until a clearer idea of what had happened was known. The police were anxious to discover the whereabouts of a tall, well-built Swiss woman with short fair hair going by the name of Tilda Bahnlich, often seen in the company of the deceased.

Peter was just as anxious to make a discovery of his own. And that time had now come. As he headed home in the Tuesday afternoon gloom, he saw the bright lights of a television crew outside the SODA shop. And it wasn't the local news channel. It was ITN. He recognized the presenter. Proof that things were hotting up.

He covered the seven miles to Newton Stud in 23 minutes.

As soon as he got in, he went up to his room. He had to be quick because Gwen was due to turn up to look after his mother at any minute. And Gwen was nosy.

He was about to open the envelope when a twinge of conscience stopped him. Even though he knew Stephanie was dead, he wondered whether he should be doing this. If what was inside was construed as evidence, he was about to tamper with it! So be it. Given what Stephanie had said on the tape, he had an idea of what he might find in it..

He was in the loop, now. *No-one must know!* He was bound to keep Stephanie's heart-wrenching secret to himself.

It was still with a niggling sense of wrongdoing that he shook out the envelope's contents. There was a rush of relief to discover it hadn't been stuffed with drugs. He'd had a nagging fear that it might have been, knowing her history. Then what would he have done? Same went for the floppy disc. But that wasn't there, either.

What *was* in it, though, hit him like a shot in the arm. Wrapped in soggy newspaper was a wad of fifty-pound notes! Shit and fuck! Peter bristled, high as a kite. He had expected *some* money. But not *this* much. This was more than he'd ever seen, let alone touched. Bundles of twenties as well, still tightly hugging each other after being cocked in his shorts like a codpiece.

As deftly as the Artful Dodger, he carefully removed the damp newspaper and set about counting the money. By the time he had peeled each of the notes off and double-checked the count, he was salivating like Bill Sykes after a snatch!

Close on twenty-two thousand pounds!

No wonder Gwen had blushed after brushing her fanny against it!

The thought that now came to him made Peter, himself, redden. This was more than enough money to finish his Initiative!

Naughty! But it was hard to drive the thought away.

Did this major lady know about all this money? Stephanie had told her she wanted her to pass on some to the child. But *this* much? So soon after the phone call? And *would* the major find a way to pass it on? She didn't seem all that willing, listening to the tape.

For the moment, he would wait. Hold onto the money and see how things developed. Say nothing. Do nothing. Just listen. He would be

133

the safe keeper for the time being. Hope to find a way to come up with the right decision. Where there's a will there's always a way!

Pity no disc, though.

First, he had to decide what to do with the money right now before Gwen arrived. There was nowhere safe in the house. Gwen had a habit of going beyond her carer's role and giving the place a top to bottom makeover every week, often when he was out. There was not enough time to pull up any floorboards. It would have to be somewhere in his workshop. She rarely ventured down there. Even if she did, she wouldn't dare think of touching anything.

He spread the notes out on a bathroom towel then rolled it up, hoping this would help dry them out. This was only a temporary measure. He left it innocently rolled up on the bench next to his workout contraption. He would find a proper hiding place once it had dried out.

As he double padlocked the workshop, he heard Gwen's 2CV pulling up outside the house. She was already in by the time he came through the back door.

'What have you done?' she panted as soon as she saw him. She was red in the face, almost in tears.

He was so taken aback; he had no answer.

'They've found that Austrian woman. Murdered! Up at Compton Stud!' Gwen was completely pink in the face. Breathless. 'First Stephanie, now her!' she paused, waiting for his reaction. There was little. He was stunned.

'The police broke into the place and found her! They're now looking for a cyclist. They've given a description. It's you, Peter. What have you done? I knew there was something wrong when you came back with blood all over you. God!' The tears started.

It suddenly dawned on him why Stephanie was in such a state that morning. She had just killed Bahnlich! Possibly only minutes before he'd crashed into her. He was shaken. Gwen thought it was him who'd killed the woman and was already condemning him to the gallows!

'Gwen! Gwen. Listen to me,' he said, taking her by the shoulders. She looked up at him pathetically. 'I have done nothing.' Nothing that she was thinking of, at least.

'You were up there, weren't you? That's the way you always go. That blood! They're asking you to come forward.'

'I've already bloody come forward, if you want to use that word!' He was getting annoyed. 'I told them yesterday. Told them I'd seen her up there out of control with her horse.'

That took some of the wind out of her sails.

'You didn't tell me that,' she complained limply.

'Well, you're not a cop, are you?'

She calmed down, but the threat of tears remained.

'What would your mother do if anything happened to you?'

'Well, nothing has, has it? So put a lid on it!' His mind was ruffled all the same. Emotional stuff from Gwen was the last thing he needed.

'They can get in touch with me anytime they want, can't they? I'm not hiding from them. They know where I live. I've told them all I know, anyway.'

He tried to blank out Gwen's concern by mounting an attack on his personal work-out contraption. One thing he was not going to be bullied into was rushing to the police. He didn't see why he should change his routine to make their job easier. He couldn't remember if he had given them his number when he called 999, but he was pretty sure they could trace it if they wanted to. They had a pretty good idea who and where he lived, anyway.

The next morning before heading into Marlsbury, he unwrapped the banknotes and split them into two bundles. When blocking off the redundant fireplace in the workshop long ago with an old enamel-plated tray, he had noticed recesses in the fire bricks on either side up the chimney proper just above where the fancy tiles ended. That was a good enough place as any to hide the money. He managed to do this without smothering himself with soot. The tray wasn't fixed, just wedged in to stop the draft. He couldn't remember when a fire was last lit in it.

He was late leaving for Marlsbury. He went by the road route that avoided Compton Stud and Beacon Ridge. That area was bound to be teeming with police. The roads were dry which cheered him up. The sun had been in and out all morning.

He stopped on the outskirts of town to buy a newspaper. It was almost like old times. Stephanie Star's picture was on every front page.

135

The tabloids were screaming foul play, the broadsheets blaming her death on the poor horse. None of them were saying it outright yet, but, reading between the lines, the general consensus was that Stephanie was responsible for Bahnlich's death.

The Daily Telegraph coupled an early picture of Stephanie Star with a photograph of the freshly knighted Ludlow unveiling the 100th S.O.D.A. pump, with a sub-heading: 'Sir Edward Ludlow learns of double tragedy while resting at The Norfolk Hotel, Nairobi.' Lower down was a smaller picture of Tilda Bahnlich.

While its front pages had been making last minute space to carry a soberly worded report of this tragic affair, the financial pages were bubbling with speculation about the outcome of Ludlow's talks in Kenya and the unforeseen shifts in international stock markets, all seeming to suggest that the Wilson-Hughes Group was on the brink of clinching the multi-billion-dollar desalination and irrigation projects in East Africa.

The instant Peter entered Hollom's Attic, he read the owner's mind. His gnome-like joviality had gone.

'Hello, Peter,' he said with a tremor in his voice, busily tidying things that didn't need it to avoid direct eye contact. 'I suppose you know who's been round here looking for you?'

It didn't take much guessing, but Peter wasn't going to let on. 'No. Who? The Sopwith man?' he toyed.

'The bloody police, that's who!' Hollom barked edgily, moving the same box on its spot for the fourth time. 'It's been all over the radio. Haven't you heard? You'd better get yourself down there and see the buggers. I don't want them coming back here again. I'm trying to run a business!'

'Why should I? I've got no more to tell them.'

'That's not what *they* think, is it? Get yourself down there. Get them off my back.' Hollom had rarely been in such an uneasy mood. Something else was bothering him. 'You'll be getting me into trouble with the Social Security people next, if they find out you've been working here. Go and clear things up. The whole town's talking about you.'

'Let them. I've got nothing to hide,' he lied.

'Well, you listen to me, then. Either you go straight down there before they come back snooping around here again, or you can pack your things and get out of here for good. I've been doing you a big favour, Peter Tyler, and I don't want no trouble with the law because of it!'

Marlsbury Police Station was solid Edwardian red-brick, small windowed with the familiar blue lamp hanging over the steps up to the entrance.

Peter pad-locked his bike to the railings outside and bound up the steps with a carefree gait for the world to see. There was no-one behind the reception desk, so he rang the bell placed there to attract attention. A rather harassed looking young constable appeared from behind an inner door and apologized for keeping him waiting. 'How can I help you, sir?' he asked politely, his lower lip trying to locate the fuzz of a mousy moustache glistening on the upper.

'Peter Tyler's the name. I think someone here's been looking for me,' Peter told him, trying to sound as helpful as possible, although he was beginning to feel uncomfortable in the surroundings. 'I just heard something on the radio,' he white lied safely enough.

A hint of understanding cleared the furrow from the constable's brow. 'Oh, yes. You're the cyclist chap, aren't you?' That didn't take much detective work given the way Peter was dressed in his tight-fitting Lycra gear. 'Just a sec, I'll get the sergeant.'

He disappeared, returning almost immediately with a slightly older man about the same age as Peter himself. 'Mr. Tyler?' he asked rhetorically. 'Thanks for dropping by. I'm afraid the officer who wants to see you is out and about at the moment. Probably gone to see if you're at home. You could wait, but I suggest you come back in a bit. Everyone's a bit pushed today.'

Everyone might be a bit pushed, but no one was rushing to handcuff him, which was reassuring. 'I'll come back in, what, half an hour?'

'Better make it an hour. I could get another officer if you're in a hurry, but best wait for the Sargeant. Save you going over things twice.'

Tyler was thankful for that reminder. He would have to stick to his story when it came to it. So far, he was doing alright, he thought. Casual but concerned. There was just one thing. He wished he knew where 'the cyclist' had been seen. It was obviously him. But he couldn't think where.

He went over his movements on New Year's Day bit by bit. Nothing came to him apart from the car that had nearly hit him as he pulled out to turn up the track. That must have been it.

Detective Sergeant Simpson had been given the job of interviewing Peter Tyler. He was a big man, forty-ish, paunchy but healthy-looking, well-liked at the station because he was always happy to participate in whatever was going on. As a goalkeeper for the police football team, he took a lot of stick, since he wasn't too keen on diving. The best result of the season so far was what he called a draw. It was actually a 2-0 defeat, but he reckoned all teams had to give the police a two-goal start because his glasses were always steaming up or falling off. Besides that, they were the Law.

'Thanks for coming in, Mr. Tyler,' he said pleasantly, but with a grim smile. 'Nasty business all this. Two suspicious deaths discovered in the space of a few hours in a sleepy town like ours.'

'Terrible,' Peter managed to agree dispassionately.

Simpson lifted the flap on the counter and came out from behind.

'Do you mind stepping this way?' he asked, leading Peter through a corridor. 'We'll use one of the interview rooms. It'll be quieter there. Shouldn't take too long.'

Peter followed feeling peculiar, which was only natural, he supposed. There was something about the situation niggling him. Was it the smell of the place? He couldn't quite put his finger on it. Fresh paint?

The Detective Sergeant eyed Tyler up and down. 'I see you keep yourself good and fit,' he said, leading Tyler into a small, bright room, empty but for a table and three chairs. Bare walls. No distractions. 'I try myself,' he said, patting his paunch, 'but this gets in the way these days. I suppose it's all that mountain biking you do, if you know what I'm getting at? You were over Beacon Ridge way New Year's Day...' he looked down at his notes as if to check, then added: '...morning.'

'Yeah, I ride over that way 4 or 5 times a week,' Peter jumped in. 'Good work-out territory up there."

'And you rang to report seeing Mrs. Ludlow in trouble on her horse,' Simpson confirmed. 'She nearly knocked you down, apparently.'

'Yes, she did. But it wasn't till a couple of days later that I rang 999. It was after seeing her horse again without her on it. Whoever I spoke to here, didn't seem to take me too seriously. I think you should look into that.' Good to get that jibe in, Peter thought.

'Quite so. And we are. But on New Year's Day morning, did Mrs. Ludlow say anything to you?'

Peter pushed out his lips and shook his head slowly as if in thought. 'Just, that she was sorry.'

'Anything unusual strike you about her?'

'Well, she looked a wreck, if that's what you mean. I suppose that's not so unusual if you're to believe everything you read about her in the papers these days.' He was not going to let on about noticing she hadn't been dressed for horse riding. Why say more than necessary.

Simpson rose stiffly. 'I don't think I need to keep you any longer. If you think of anything else, just pop in. Bad case, this.' He opened the door and stood back to let Tyler pass. 'I'm guessing you'll be wanting to get back to your model making. Nice hobby, that. Still looking for a proper job, aren't you?'

Was that a crafty dig? It sounded like it.

'Yes,' Peter confessed, as though he was admitting to a criminal offense. 'Two years it's been. Nothing in these parts for someone with my qualifications. I do a few days part time in the bike shop during the summer. That helps a bit. Got my mum to look after.'

'That's bad luck, that is. Maybe something'll come up.' There was little concern in Simpson's voice.

Peter turned round to the sergeant when reaching the entrance hall, the devil in his eye, not able to resist an opportunity to stir things up for Ludlow. 'You know what I reckon. You'll find more drugs stashed out at Compton Stud than you will in a month of Sundays busting that crowd at The King's head.'

With that final kick for goal, he stepped nimbly out to find himself trapped by TV lights and clicking cameras. To his relief, they weren't there for his benefit. He had walked out into the glare of a police statement to the press. His way was barred by three flat-capped officers standing on the steps. He could either sweat it out or go back inside. He decided no movement was the best option, so he lowered his head and listened.

'All I can tell you at the present time,' Superintendent Warren, the officer in the middle, was saying, 'is that we are looking at two suspicious deaths. The situation is not yet entirely clear. Information is being processed as we speak. Investigations are continuing. There appears to have been a tragic series of events centering around the Ludlow property, Compton Stud.'

'Are you saying you're looking at a double murder?' someone hungry for sensation shouted.

'We rule nothing out at this stage, although that seems unlikely.'

'Did Stephanie Star kill herself, then, or was it an accident?'

'Stephanie Star's death is still unclear. Until all forensic evidence has been analysed, we shall be making no further comment.'

'There have been rumours of another person being involved,' an eager young woman thrusting out a microphone asked. 'Is that true?'

'That is pure speculation until we have all the facts before us.'

The Superintendent speaking had obviously not been told that the 'other' person in question had just been interviewed, and at that very moment was hovering behind him anxiously hoping the press out front had not twigged it either.

A few of the locals who were watching the spectacle did, however, spot Tyler. One being Old Pikey, who was particularly enjoying the cyclist's embarrassment at being caught like a rabbit in the headlights.

'If another person *is* involved, Superintendent, could it in fact be a case of double murder?' It was the same man who had already raised that question. Peter guessed what rag he might be working for: The Daily Scan. The guy looked like a scruffy wire-haired terrier, runny nose into the bargain.

'I can only repeat, that is speculation. But we are asking for anyone who might have been near Compton Stud over the New Year period to come forward if they saw anything that might help inquiries. This is a distressing series of events, and we hope to get to the bottom of it as soon as possible. I assure you we are doing all we can to do just that. Thank you.'

'Has Sir Edward Ludlow been told about the situation?' a familiar television reporter managed to get in as the three officers began to turn.

'Yes, we have made contact with Sir Edward and shall be keeping him informed of developments. He is understandably distraught.'

'Did he say when he will be returning to the UK, sir?'

'We did not discuss that. I am sure he is making his own arrangements. He is an extremely busy man at the moment, of course.'

In fact, Sir Edward Ludlow was relaxing on the veranda of his hotel room in Nairobi with the help of a large gin and tonic. However, his mind was racing. Was his charmed life about to implode? What could be done to lessen the blow should that transpire? Victor Rose along with Gerald Silver were doing all they could to avoid at least an embarrassing situation, but would it be enough to preempt a swift relocation from the world stage to a safe haven. The preparatory arrangements for that possible scenario would soon be in place.

Under the premise of grief, he had started this process by wisely withdrawing from the BBC documentary. Agreeing to such exposure had been an error, he had realized. Even more so now with the latest events. It was time to be more circumspect. A period of private mourning was called for, away from the public eye.

In Marlsbury, Peter Tyler had no chance of escaping the public eye. A salvo of flashlights dazzled him as the trio of police officers turned, all but sweeping him back into the station with them. He managed to sidestep their net and sneaked off on his bike without being apprehended by any of the loitering news folk.

He had only been back in the model shop in time to make his peace with Martin Hollom, when the doorbell rang to the entrance of Detective Sergeant Simpson.

'Sorry to trouble you again, Mr. Tyler,' he said apologetically, 'but would you mind coming back to the station? The Chief Inspector's got a few queries for you.'

Chapter Sixteen

While their suitcases were sent to Nairobi Airport, supposedly en route with their owners to Abuja, Nigeria, Sir Edward Ludlow and Jenny Grant were to be taken by helicopter to a spacious lodge on the banks of Lake Naivasha, a safe enough haven for the immediate time being, but perhaps not the ultimate one should things turn sour. Ernest McKintosh, S.O.D.A.'s big man in Africa, was engaged to assist in this diversion.

News travels fast in the jungle, and even though Nairobi was in the jungle no more, word had got through that market moves suggested Wilson-Hughes might be on the point of sealing the colossal East African irrigation contract.

Thus, when Ludlow walked out from the hotel into the mellowing African afternoon sun, grey-faced and suitable clothed for mourning in his darkest suit and black silk tie, he too was met by a similar barrage of cameras and pressmen that had captured Peter Tyler in Marlsbury. Despite having been told earlier in the day that the BBC documentary was off, Simon Dickson still pushed his camera crew to the front of the mob.

Ludlow was shattered by the aggressive questioning he had to face given his low ebb. 'No comment,' was all he could muster as Ernest McKintosh helped barge a way through to the awaiting SODA Land Rover, his escape route to the airport.

In contrast, it was perhaps noticed that his private secretary, who followed two paces behind him, did not appear to be suffering the same gloom. She was dressed casually in an olive-green safari outfit recently purchased in the hotel shop, paid for by room number. She carried herself with an air of self-control, fending off questions with a polite, winsome smile.

She could not deny that the news of Stephanie's death had put a spring in her step. If the press would like to make anything of the fact that it was just Jenny Stevens and Sir Edward Ludlow out here in Kenya together, then bring it on!

A police escort made sure the Land Rover had a clear run to the airport. Once there, they safely continued their diversionary journey, not by jet to Abuja, but by helicopter to the lakeside lodge that would be the couple's resting place until the next move was planned.

They arrived at the atmospheric retreat just as the sun was setting during that magical hour of approaching dusk that could induce meditation in those inclined.

Jenny perched herself on the colonial style veranda quite disorientated by the peace and tranquility after the clatter of the helicopter. The mad race to the helipad at Nairobi and the choppy flight up country had left her head throbbing like the thud of the helicopter blades that had propelled them. Now, her jet-lagged body was finding it hard to come to rest despite the beautiful landscape that stretched before her.

Before the sun had completely slid away, she thought her eyes were cheating her. The strangest combination of sights made her think she had begun to hallucinate for real.

The lodge was situated on a gently sloping hillside facing west, with the lake rising out of a feathering of wispy trees that stretched along the water's edge. As she watched the soft reflections of the sky in the lake, occasionally broken by flocks of birds homing in for the night, a silhouette of heads began to move from right to left above the foliage. One behind the other they glided as if bodyless, like targets at a fairground. Their gentle lolloping motion and their apparent height above the ground eventually clicked in her brain. She was not hallucinating. It was a column of giraffes, their bodies hidden by the foliage.

No sooner had she worked out that puzzle than another arrived. Beyond their heads, two bright lights appeared twinkling like stars bouncing on the surface of the lake. When the last giraffe head had passed, the lights disappeared only to suddenly return in the sky. Now, below them, the lake seemed to be opening up with a curious wave as if on cue from Moses. Thousands of birds were taking flight in opposite directions. Then came a noise. A rumbling echo from the distant mountains. An aircraft was approaching low over the lake, splitting the fleeing birds in its path.

It screeched overhead at an alarmingly low height, the noise deafening after the silence of before, and was heard to land almost immediately after it had passed.

As though aroused by the big flying insect, cicadas and frogs launched into their evening chorus with vigour.

About twenty minutes later, Jenny was introduced to Richard Whitton, the pilot who had managed to bring her personal flight of fancy down to earth. She was struck by how well he blended into the colonial architecture of the lodge. The only accoutrements missing from his tropical garb were putties to bottom off his loose-fitting khaki cotton uniform. He cut a romantic figure with his hair pasted down as he twitched his neatly trimmed moustache like an Errol Flynn about to swash his buckle. She felt he might squeak if she touched him. His skin was as smooth as waxwork, and he came with a fitting musty smell of pomade.

After a supper of locally sourced guinea fowl and root vegetables, the two men sat either side of Jenny in wicker armchairs admiring the night sky. The silence was not broken until a trolley of drinks was rolled out.

'Who wants what?' Jenny asked, offering her services as waitress. She was tired, but willing. 'I think I'll stick to G 'n T to ward off the mosquitoes.' It was that time of night.

The others joined her. After she had done the honours, Whitton asked: 'Will you be accompanying us to Mombasa, Jenny?' He eyed Ludlow tentatively, thinking someone should start up a conversation. He wondered if he had said the wrong thing, judging by the responses. Jenny's was visibly quizzical, giving Ludlow an expectant look. Mombasa was news to her. She thought the next move was to Nigeria. But, wherever? She was game.

Ludlow seemed momentarily uneasy.

'I think we can spare Jenny that inconvenience,' he said before Jenny could open her mouth. 'She needs a day or two's rest after all she's been through in the past few days. Don't you, Jenny?' He tried to give Jenny a sympathetic look, but the only thing it told her was that she was going nowhere for the time being. She was staying put and she had no say in the matter. But she had enough gin inside her to make an impertinent reply: 'And what inconvenience would that be, *sir*, pray?'

Simon Whitton was feeling awkward. He was not reading the situation at all.

'The inconvenience of standing to attention in the midday sun while drilling rigs for SODA are being unloaded and blessed in Mombasa Port,' Ludlow explained. 'My presence is called for publicity reasons. It will help boost the chances of sealing the irrigation project. It would hardly be fun for you, Jenny. Pure boredom.'

She didn't get it. One minute he was doing all he could to avoid the press, the next planning to meet them head on. Mombasa would be swarming with them when it was known he would be there.

He might have been reading her mind. 'As it happens, I haven't decided if I should make an appearance myself as yet,' he added. As it happened, he had. Mombasa was out.

Ludlow knew if he attended, he would be in the spotlight for all the wrong reasons. Jenny Grant need not be told that if he were to move from this present hideaway, it would not be to Mombasa, nor to Abuja, for that matter. He would be going to a completely different continent altogether. Alone. But the situation in Marlsbury had to be resolved one way or another before any decision like that could be made. Should all hell break loose, relocating anonymously to his ultimate safe haven would be difficult enough without having Jenny in tow.

Whitton himself was not yet party to the possible need for a completely different route map.

A telephone rang in the lodge. Ludlow was up like a shot.

There was good news and bad news.

'We've found her 'safe hands!' Victor Rose cried triumphantly, starting with the good news.

This was not strictly true, of course. Rose and his bloodhounds had not found Stephanie's so-called 'safe hands'. Rose was jumping to wishful conclusions with a wild leap of hope. The police themselves had not exactly 'found' Peter Tyler, either. He had walked into the police station of his own volition and walked out again shortly afterwards still a free man.

But Rose was convinced they'd got their man when he was told Tyler had been taken back in again. This time accompanied by a senior police officer.

'Guess who?' Rose could hardly contain himself, but managed to do so, briefly pausing for effect. 'You wouldn't believe it! That Tyler bloke. The one who gave you all that grief when you closed the Marlsbury plant! Remember him?'

'You're kidding me!' Ludlow's jaw dropped. Indeed, he remembered Peter Tyler. 'Of course! Of course! The one with the bike and the placards stirring up the shit.'

'Got it! He was up in the woods with the bitch just after she whacked Bahnlich, according to reports. Who knows, he might even have been in on it! Trouble is, the Law's still got him in for questioning.'

That was the bad news. It was any guess what Tyler might be telling them?

Several dollars' worth of silent telephone time passed before Ludlow spoke again.

'Where exactly are the bloodhounds?' he asked.

'One out front, one out back of the nick. Two more sniffing around the pubs to find out where he lives.'

'And you?'

'Ready for whatever. I'm moving down to the Stud to be on hand. I'll stay in the barn. Forensics might still be in the house. I can't do much up here in the city now, anyway.'

'OK. Make a point of introducing yourself to the cops. Pearson, I think is the man in charge. I've told them I can't get back for business reasons. Tell them I've sent you to represent me, and for them to give you all the help you might need. I'll tell Silver to confirm it with them. Keep your ear to the ground. You know the main aim now. But Victor, no unnecessary violence, please. Check Tyler out as soon as possible. Find out what he knows and what he's at. You've got a blank cheque to get him on our side if it's not too late and he's done his worst.' He took a breath. 'Tyler! Of course!'

Peter Tyler realized what it was about the interview room he disliked most; the bare brick walls, glazed deep brown up to about four feet high, then painted gloss cream up to the fading white ceiling. The corridors were the same, making the whole place reverberate with the brittle echo of an institution. Detective Chief Inspector Pearson was a slow-moving man, not through age, but through inclination. He was perhaps in his late forties and supported a full beard, so black it could have been dyed. It was neatly trimmed along the jawline with the cheeks above like hollow recesses that matched the rest of his angular features. He was overweight, not with a beer-gut, just fleshy all over. Like the famous

Marlsbury sausage, he was solidly plump, perhaps his best results coming from slow grilling.

One glimpse told Peter Tyler he was a thorough man.

He was not *hard,* although he sometimes chose to give that impression; more like, unmalleable in the line of duty. That side of him he was always happy to hang up at the end of the day with his trade-mark Barbour coat.

Bird watching was one of the Detective Chief Inspector's favourite pastimes. That and general wildlife appreciation. The local nature conservation club was delighted to have him as a member. Such an ally was of immense value in the fight against pollution and erosion of natural habitat. His voice carried weight whenever he spoke out against unnecessary building developments or overuse of pesticides and herbicides in farming. Tyler remembered Pearson speaking in sympathy with a group of enraged architects and artists who wanted Ludlow to re-site the giant satellite dishes he had stuck on the roof of Compton Stud without formal notification to the proper local authorities. Needless to say, the protest had not been successful. In fact, Pearson had earned a caution from those higher up for going into the public area with opinions that someone of his position should not expound. At the time of the Marlsbury closure, Tyler had sensed that the police were soft-pedalling on the demonstrators, putting it down to Pearson's influence.

However, Tyler was not going to be off his guard by thinking the man was a kindred spirit.

'Thank you for coming in so promptly, Mr. Tyler,' the Detective Chief Inspector said distantly as though he had something else on his mind. 'Please take a seat.'

Detective Sergeant Simpson was also present.

'I just want to clear up one or two points,' Pearson went on, taking a good look at his interviewee. 'Things have been developing so quickly today. Do you mind if we record this interview? Easier than writing it all down.'

'No problem,' Tyler replied, shaking his head submissively.

'Now, I've read the notes Detective Sergeant Simpson took down from you earlier,' Pearson began, then paused, still with that 'good look' at

Tyler, before continuing. 'Are you sure there's nothing you'd like to add? Anything you might have remembered in the meantime?'

Peter pretended to be reconsidering for a few moments and then shook his head confidently. 'Don't think so.'

Pearson fixed his look on Peter's eyes as if trying to identify a rare bird through his binoculars. 'It could be important to us. At the moment, certain things don't seem to tally.'

'No, I can't think of anything else,' Peter said quickly. Perhaps too quickly. 'Nothing that jumps out at me, at any rate.' He thought he'd put that in to allow himself room to manoeuvre in case, as it seemed, Pearson had something up his sleeve.

'You say you saw Mrs. Ludlow, that's Stephanie Star to most people, on the morning of New Year's Day, 1st January?'

'Yep.'

'You nearly collided with her and her horse, is that right.'

'Correct. I told the person on 999 about that after seeing the horse without her on it a couple of days later.'

'What time of day was that?'

Peter thought he would be a little devious. 'I'd guess early afternoon, but you can check the exact time with the 999 people. They ought to have made a note of it. But perhaps didn't, 'cos they don't seem to have acted on the information straight away, do they? If at all.'

Was Tyler being deliberately obstructive? Pearson wondered. It wouldn't do him any good if he kept *that* up.

'Not the time of the call, Peter. The time of day you bumped into Stephanie Star?'

'Ah. I can almost pinpoint that. I always try to leave my house around 10.20 and get to Beacon Ridge about 11, depending on the weather. So, I'd say it would have been between 11.10 and 11.20 that morning. I was slipping and sliding all over the place in the rain, hence the near collision.'

'Did you exchange words with her? It couldn't have been just 'Sorry', as you told the detective sergeant.'

'That was about it. She didn't hang around discussing the weather or wishing me a nice day, if that's what you're thinking. She was in a mad rush. I occasionally see her charging about in the woods, but not as desperately as that morning. I've often wondered if she wasn't trying to kill herself. Well, what can I say. That's why a rang 999 after seeing the horse riderless two days later. Why was nothing done about that call I made? Someone messed up there, in my opinion.'

Pearson had no argument to offer. But he wasn't going to bite. That matter was being dealt with elsewhere.

'Indeed, it seems they did,' he eventually admitted openly. 'I can assure you it is being looked into. But, back to the point. Are you absolutely sure Mrs. Ludlow didn't give you anything?'

So that's where this is leading, Peter thought. Why was Pearson asking this? A quick response was necessary.

'No. Why would she?'

'I don't know why, Peter. That's why I'm asking.'

'She didn't have time or inclination to give me anything even if she had wanted to. The horse reared up and she took off as if to say, 'don't ever get in my way again!''

'Which she had a right to say, didn't she? Since you were trespassing on her land, weren't you?'

'Come off it! Every biker and hiker goes up there. Public right of ways are all over the place.' But not exactly where he had been that morning, perhaps. He would have thought all the rain had washed away evidence of the precise spot. A vision of Stephanie hanging on for dear life as she disappeared through the trees came to him. Minutes later, she was dead! Shit. That was still a bit sobering.

Pearson brought him back from his reverie. 'Let's talk about Stephanie Star's husband, shall we? It appears you really don't like Sir Edward Ludlow, do you, Peter?' Pearson opened a folder in front of him as if about to prove it.

Tyler was not in the least bit surprised the police had a file on him, if that was what Pearson was looking at. The Marlsbury Pump closure demonstrations had been a group effort, although he, himself, had played a prominent part in it. Ludlow had seen no advantage in pressing charges against them for trespass and disorder. The publicity had been bad enough without any of the demonstrators ending up in prison.

If any had been, then Peter Tyler would probably have been the first of them.

'I've never made any bones about disliking Ludlow,' Peter was happy to admit without fear of failing a lie-detector test. 'I think he's an arsehole. I reckon he's done more harm to Marlsbury than the M33, let alone knocking down the pumps factory to make way for those eyesore boxes masquerading as houses.'

Pearson correctly translated this as an attack on the invasion of denizens that seemed to have coincided with the opening of the new motorway. He had been against that particular piece of road-building madness himself. It had taken out some prime bird-watching habitat.

He switched off the tape recorder.

'Not everyone approves of the way Sir Ludlow has chosen to do things in this area,' he suggested patronisingly. 'But there's little the likes of you or I can do about it. The man is very influential in case you hadn't noticed.'

Was Pearson playing 'good cop, good cop'? If so, when was the 'bad cop' bit going to start, Peter wondered.

Detective Inspector Pearson was thinking about the shooting parties he knew to take place in the Compton Stud woods when some of Ludlow's city cronies and media mates came to play. It sounded like a battle was going on up there sometimes, like a bunch of kids playing Cowboys and Indians but with real weapons. The local wildlife really suffered when all that went on. But nothing could be done to stop it. The land belonged to Ludlow, and it could be safely assumed all the guns were suitably licensed. 'I take your point about the motorway.' he confessed.

Peter was not allowing himself to be lulled into a sense of false security by this display of partisanship. He sensed Pearson was building up to something. He was right.

'What I want you to do, Peter, is go over your movements of New Year's morning one more time, just for me.' The bearded inquisitor reached over and took Detective Sergeant Simpson's notebook from him. Making a pointed display of ripping out the sheets that his colleague had painstakingly written on, he tore them into tiny pieces and dropped them into the wastepaper basket under the table. 'Let's start from scratch. Then there won't be any possible areas of conflict.'

He pushed the start button on the recorder and leaned back as if to say, 'no hurry'. The chairs in the room were not intended for relaxation, but Pearson made a brave attempt to settle down as if about to take a nap, going as far as to close his deep brown eyes.

It was only show, Peter guessed, and didn't last long. They opened again as soon as the story reached the point when he had nearly been knocked down by the car as he'd pulled out into the middle of the road to get a good run up the track to the ridge.

This seemed to be what Pearson had been waiting for. Peter had mentioned nothing of this to Simpson earlier. So, it had to be that. The driver of the car must have told the police about seeing him. Thankfully, it hadn't been someone lurking up in the woods who'd clocked the whole episode with Stephanie. 'You didn't mention this before, Peter,' Pearson emphasized. 'Why was that?'

'Didn't think it was all that relevant,' Peter parried. 'Why? Do you?'

'Everything you did that morning is relevant, Peter. We're dealing with an unfortunate set of circumstances here, and you seem to have got yourself caught right up in the middle of them, whether inadvertently or not. We're trying to put all the pieces together. Every little tidbit of truth helps us build the picture. Do you recall the time the driver tooted you so we can rule out the possibility of there being two cyclists and two cars doing the tooting at different times?'

Good cop, cynical cop, Peter was thinking.

'It wouldn't have been much later than 10.45, I'd say,' Tyler answered honestly. He felt that if he could remember all the exact timings that day, he was on safe ground. Just don't mention anything about Stephanie dropping something. He'd done nothing wrong. Had nothing to do with her death. Had been the good citizen and made that 999 call, thank goodness.

Who else could possibly have seen him that day and at what time? Whilst he had been hanging about in the woods in case Stephanie had come back looking for her package, he'd seen no-one. On his way home, he had been well covered with his cape against the weather, so good luck to anyone who could tell it was him.

But Gwen! She had been there when he got home. That must have been around halve two, three. God! I hope they don't start questioning her.

She'll crack up! All that stuff about me being covered in blood. Shit! I'll have to get to her before this lot does.

'Do us a favour, John,' Pearson said, having leaned over and turned off the recorder. 'Organize some teas for us, could you?'

When Simpson had left the room, Pearson continued on a different tack. 'Tell me about yourself, Peter,' he said like a benevolent personnel officer conducting a job interview.

Was this good cop again, or cynical cop, Peter wondered.

'Come on, tell me,' Pearson pressed. 'Off the record.'

'You probably know all there is to know about me with that thick file in front of you.'

'Ah, there must be more to you than all this stuff, Peter. Please give me more credit than that. A chap like you must have many aspirations.'

Peter didn't feel obliged to answer any of this shrink talk. But it opened up the chance to get in another dig at Ludlow. 'The only aspiration I have is to get the kind of job I spent seven years training for. Preferably, somewhere reasonably near to where I live. Not much to ask for, is it?' He wasn't going to say anything about developing his Initiative project. That was staying under wraps until it was ready to be safely patented.

'I suppose it can't help having a house-bound mother to look after. That must bring you down, sometimes?' Pearson poked.

'Not half as much as being thrown on the dole heap!' Peter snapped.

Detective Sergeant Simpson returned with three mugs of tea on a tray and a folded note. Pearson read the message before heaping three spoons of sugar into a mug with pictures of birds on it.

He switched the recorder back on and asked again: 'So what time was it when you arrived home on New Year's Day, Peter?'

Had Pearson forgotten Peter had already told him that? Or was it a silly attempt to trick him? Peter thought, *silly*, so he'd give a silly answer. 'Around two, I think, but it could have been a bit earlier. The latest it could have been was probably three-ish. because it was still fairly light given all the rain clouds around that day.'

Pearson made a doodle on his clock face. 'And what did you do when you got in? Be a bit more specific than just preparing your mum's tea.'

Peter was thinking there was no way anyone could know about Gwen being there. It was a bank holiday and her day off from caring for his mum. 'Not much else. Had a bath, tidied up, cleaned my bike up a bit more. That's about it, apart from going to bed.'

'And you went over to Compton Stud two days later, you say, when you saw the horse?' Pearson's glasses had slipped to the end of his nose, and Peter pushed back an imaginary pair on his own nose.

'Not exactly to Compton Stud itself,' Peter interjected. 'I took my normal run past the beacon on my way into Marlsbury by the long route. It was sunnier that day, if you remember.'

'How often did you meet Stephanie Star up there in the woods?' he asked.

Peter didn't expect that. But there was no delay in his answer.

'I've never *met* her as such unless you mean years ago when she opened Marlsbury Fayre and things. I saw her charging around on her horse occasionally, as I've told you.'

'I mean, there wasn't a sort of 'thing' going on between the pair of you, was there?'

'You must be joking!' Peter responded, suspecting Pearson might well be. 'What, do you think little old me was giving her one up there in the woods?' His frown turned into a smile. 'I wish! That would have made Ludlow sit up a bit, wouldn't it?'

'*You* tell me, Peter. You tell me. What am I meant to think? You're hiding something, aren't you? If it's not that, then what is it exactly?' He sniffed noisily, then flattened his palms together as if in prayer.

Peter wondered how he was giving himself away. Was it something on that note Pearson had just been given, or was he just playing a guessing game?

'We've got a nasty situation here, Peter. I would like to think you have absolutely nothing to do with this whole messy business, but you're not making it easy for me, are you? Or for yourself.' Pearson was shaking his head as he spoke, reprehensibly but with no anger, like a dutiful solicitor anxious to do the best for his client. 'As soon as you put your trust in me and tell me what this is all about, the sooner we can let you get back to your model making. Because we *will* get at the truth sooner or later, won't we?' Pearson rose to his feet without waiting for an answer. 'Will you excuse us for a few minutes, Peter?' he asked politely, stopping the recorder. At the door, he turned with another question. 'By the way, what size shoe do you take? Seven and a half, eight?'

Tyler shrank inside. Had he left footprints somewhere? Down by the stables when he'd looked over the wall? Surely the rain would have washed them away by now if he had?

'Usually size eight,' he admitted.

Once in his own office, Detective Inspector Pearson glanced again at the note Simpson had given him and said: 'Well, that seems to solve one of the mysteries, doesn't it? Who was it who managed to get through to Ludlow in Africa?'

'The Supe, herself,' Simpson told him. 'She reckons that about squares up the question of motive.'

Ludlow had explained why he thought his wife had killed Bahnlich and smashed up the tape recorder in the process. He told them about putting the phone tap on all the lines at Compton Stud. He guessed the forensics officers had already worked that out. The reason he gave for this was not exactly true, but it was believable. He'd said that it was in the hope his wife would reveal the identity of the person or persons supplying her with hard drugs. In which case, the information would have been passed on to the police to deal with. The belief was that sadly, in his absence, this must indeed be what had happened. Bahnlich had found out who the drug pusher was and paid for it.

'Sounds plausible,' Pearson surmised. 'She must really have wanted to stop what was on that tape from getting out to clout the Austrian woman like that.'

Ludlow had already reached that conclusion. Feeling he could be on a very slippery slope indeed; with trepidation he had asked the Superintendent if his wife had named names on the tape. When told the tape had not been found, he was relieved beyond belief.

'Whether or not the Supe thinks things are tied up,' Pearson said to Simpson, 'our Mr. Tyler is lying about something, isn't he? Or am I barking up the wrong tree?'

Simpson was undecided. 'Well, I don't see him as a drug pusher.'

'Nor do I,' Pearson had to agree.

'Not even pushing steroids, even though he's some sort of a health freak, isn't he? Nothing spare on him, flesh-wise?'

Something that the two men in discussion could not claim.

'Well, we can't pin her death on him unless he put the blinking tree in her way,' Simpson pointed out. 'And the forensics can't find any sign of him setting foot inside Compton Stud itself to have done the Austrian woman in, so where are we going with all this?'

'I just want to get the truth out of Tyler. Call it a hunch, but I think he's hiding something that might be relevant even if he's not a murderer or a drug baron!'

'If he was her drug pusher, he wasn't doing a very good job of it. According to her autopsy, she was in a shocking state of withdrawal when she died. Are you with me?'

'Yes, I'm with you, John,' Pearson said, mildly affronted his subordinate might be suggesting he was one step ahead of him. 'Was she looking for her pusher when she turned up at The King's Head on New Year's Eve seemingly out of her box? Everyone knows it's the place to go. Most of them in there are at it one way or another. We always find something there when we raid the place. Nothing too heavy, though. She was most likely looking for a one-off hit. That King's Head lot must have got the surprise of their lives when she walked in. Probably thought she was the cause of us barging in two minutes later. How stupid we were to let her go tootling off quietly back home! We screwed up there. Should have pulled her in. She might still be with us if we had.' Pearson considered those thoughts without too much regret. 'So, she gets home even more desperate for a hit and starts ringing round not knowing she's being recorded. Sometime later, she catches Bahnlich playing the conversations back, and wallop! Our Steff loses her head, charges off like the said chicken, tape in hand.'

'So, where's the tape now?' Simpson wondered.

155

Pearson took his point. 'In the boiler? Who knows? She wouldn't want to keep it, would she? So, it's no real surprise we haven't find it anywhere. The dogs would have sniffed it out if it had been up in the woods. Whichever way you look at it, she must have known she was done for. So, where are we with devious Mr. Tyler?'

'No point giving the tape to him. Even if he was her Mr. Fixit, he'd destroy it straight away, wouldn't he?'

Pearson had already come to that conclusion.

They were in his office on the second floor overlooking the police sports ground. He picked up his binoculars and followed a flock of birds against the reddening sky as they circled the distant bare trees.

'Lovely sight isn't it?' he said.

'It is, that. The old crows against the sunset.'

'Rooks, John. Rooks,' Pearson corrected Simpson knowledgeably. 'Rooks are gregarious, just like yourself. What we have downstairs in Peter Tyler is a crow, perhaps a carrion crow at that. A creature who prefers to travel singly but sometimes in pairs. Yet he does share one feature with rooks in being bare faced, if you get my drift. Take a look.' He handed Simpson his binoculars sensing his colleague didn't know what Pearson was talking about.

As Simpson struggled to adjust the binoculars to his liking, one of the telephones on Pearson's desk rang. He picked it up without announcing his name and listened. 'Make it six o'clock,' was all he said before putting the receiver down. 'Bloody press,' he said with resignation. 'Now there's rooks for you. Flocking round us for another statement.' He faced the window. Grounds men had appeared and were marking out new lines on the football pitch. 'Heard you drew at the weekend,' Pearson said, without a hint of sarcasm, taking back his binoculars and placing them on the windowsill.

'Yeah, two nil. Not bad, eh?' The Detective Sergeant grinned. The binoculars had told him nothing. He straightened his spectacles as if preparing for a save. 'If Derek hadn't missed that penalty, we would have won.' He could have joked about the police football team all day long.

Pearson smiled, thinking about trying to score one over on Peter Tyler. He picked up the telephone again and punched in a number. 'Can you change that press briefing to seven? Thanks.'

Simpson asked why the sudden change.

'I think six o'clock might be too soon for us to crack matey downstairs. We'll let him stew a bit longer and see if that makes him any more amenable to opening up with what he's been keeping from us.'

Simpson had already been looking forward to bed. It had been a mad day. This could only mean another late night.

'You can't tell me Tyler's been riding over that way so much just for exercise,' Pearson enlightened Simpson by way of thinking out loud. 'What better way to get at Ludlow than getting into his wife's panties?'

Whatever the true picture, Simpson was thinking, there was nothing Tyler could be charged with. Even if he had something going with the man's wife, so what? Nothing criminal in that.

'Latent cock holder or not,' Pearson joked, using two words where one would have done. 'I just want this strange bird to come clean. OK, so he might not be a real villain, but he's an anti-social little bugger, isn't he? Trying to use the opportunity with all the world's press around to drag up the Marlsbury Pumps closure stuff again. Well, I don't want him getting off Scott-free.'

Detective Sergeant Simpson regarded his superior with one raised eyebrow and pursed lips. He didn't think Tyler was that much out of order.

Pearson scratched the bridge of his nose, prompting Simpson to involuntarily reposition his spectacles, which had slipped again. By some miracle of gravity, they never seemed to fall off unless he was wearing shorts and kicking a ball about.

'One more thing,' Pearson went on. 'Get someone to go to Hollom's shop and find out how much he's been paying Tyler on the side. Then check Tyler's Social Security file to see if he's been declaring any of it. If he's got a bank account, get that checked. It's about time we made him feel uncomfortable for messing us around. Have we got any spare cells or are they still choc-o-block from New Year's Eve?'

'Most of that lot are out on bail.'

'Good. Pick one that still smells a bit and stick him in it for an hour or two. Give him the impression we might be keeping him in for the night. Then we'll have another go at him.'

With a final look at what was now a glorious sunset, he said: 'Right. Now the bloody press.'

Chapter Seventeen

Long before the press briefing at seven that evening, everyone in Marlsbury interested in knowing it had learned that the police were holding Peter Tyler for questioning. Old Pikey had seen to that. Sitting in his normal place in The Turk's Anchor, he had been offering snippets of information to reporters for discreet financial considerations. He had soon let it be known that he had worked at Compton Stud for years and knew a thing or two about the Ludlows. His actual knowledge was strictly limited, for the most part hearsay. But he had limitless imagination.

Detective Sergeant Simpson had paid another visit to Martin Hollom's shop, much to the owner's annoyance. He had learned precious little from Cyder Blossoms, who, although unhappy about what was going on, was not going to get himself into trouble by saying too much. That would have been stupid. Peter Tyler's behaviour had nothing to do with him, especially if the lad turned out to be a double murderer. If Tyler took money from his clients, then Hollom knew nothing about it. Model making was just the lad's hobby. No money passed between them.

'If you ask me, Sergeant,' Hollom confided, not wishing to appear totally unhelpful. 'I don't reckon he's got anything to do with what happened up there. He might hate Ludlow for putting him out of work, but he wouldn't be crazy enough to go getting mixed up with anything violent, let alone murder. He's all mouth, in my opinion. Give him a decent job and find a home for his mother to free him up, and he'd be a different man altogether.'

Thus spoke Martin Hollom.

'Can't buy you a pint, can I, sarge?' he offered as an incentive to get Simpson off the premises. It was approaching opening time and his Cyder Blossoms needed watering anew. 'But I suppose you're still on duty?' he added as a get-out clause. He would rather not be seen buying the police a drink. It might be misconstrued.

John Simpson had been on duty for more hours than he cared to think, and he wouldn't be finished for some time yet, the way Pearson wanted to stretch things out. With regrets, he declined the offer.

More people than usual were in The Turk's Anchor that evening, mainly due to the influx of journalists. But an extra smattering of locals had drifted in hoping to learn more of what had been developing. It was almost like wartime again, Old Pikey thought, the way people were talking openly to each other. A certain togetherness was running through the shocked community upon which some of the press were unashamedly scavenging. A few more days would see this initial co-operation with the media evaporate into mistrust. Its pervasive presence would begin to erode the goodwill of the inhabitants of Marlsbury and be seen as a heartless invasion of the town's privacy: a hindrance to its need to grieve in peace.

But until the novelty wore off, most people made the journalists feel welcomed, none more than the landlords of the public houses. The scribblers and snappers as they tended to call themselves were not shy with their money. It loosened tongues. No-one enjoyed the pleasure of their company more than Robby Pike who had to rely on his imagination as time went by to avoid repetition.

He kept his most creative inventions exclusively for the Daily Scan. They were the most generous. The more outrageous his claims, the better the pay.

But his tongue stopped wagging abruptly as soon as the six o'clock news glowed from the pub's TV screen with pictures of Compton Stud and Marlsbury. For the locals, seeing it on television was the final proof that what had happened was not just a bad dream. There were a few shocked responses when Peter Tyler was seen cowering behind the police spokesmen on the steps of the police station, looking *guilty*.

'There he is, that Peter Tyler!'

'Told you he was a queer one, didn't I?'

'Always summat a bit funny about 'im.'

At the end of the bulletin, came a late newsflash.

'In the last few minutes, we have received information that a man is being held for questioning at Marlsbury police station in connection with the deaths of Lady Ludlow and another woman. We understand he is a local unemployed man. A further statement is expected at seven o'clock.'

The twenty-five minutes Peter Tyler was left alone 'to stew' in the brittle interview room did but one thing: it convinced him to face down the deliberately slow-moving Detective Inspector's undisguised psychological front. His record of events would stay the same. He had done nothing 'wrong'. He was doing 'right' by Stephanie in keeping her distressing secret secure. Perhaps he should have already destroyed the tape. But it hinted at other secrets; Sir Edward-bloody-Ludlow's secrets! It would be handy to know a bit more about them. The tape was still at Hollom's Attic. Safe enough for the time being. As to the money, that was staying with him until he knew what he should do with it. He had no conscience about any of this. His mouth would be sealed. Stephanie's personal secret was safe with him, as it seemed it would be with the major, the only person who was really *meant* to know. What a life Stephanie had had! What suffering she must have carried through all the glossy magazine razzmatazz of her life. All the glitz. Was that traumatic part of her early life anything to do with her struggle with drug addiction? It couldn't have helped. Then the tragic end. Only hours after learning her child had lived. Poor, poor, Stephanie. He was already feeling duty-bound to find out who her daughter was. To get the money to her somehow. But that depended on unknown factors, one of them being the identity of the major. And then, would she tell him anything?

***

By six forty-five, Pearson was beginning to lose his patience with Tyler's persistent reticence. He was sure the lay about knew more than he was saying, but there was no charge he could lay on him. So, Pearson decided to shake him up a bit before going into the press briefing. There was to be no free ride.

'We'll be keeping you in tonight,' he told a startled Tyler. 'In case you should be worrying about your mother, we'll arrange for her carer to look after her overnight.'

Peter could not contain his annoyance, to Pearson's delight. 'On what charge?' he asked.

'No charge as yet,' Pearson shrugged. 'But we've got hours to decide that. Questions still need to be answered.'

'Fair enough,' Peter responded retaining his cool. 'Then you'd better go asking in the right places instead of kidding yourself you've got something on me.'

'Oh, I think we've got plenty of things we could come up with,' Pearson lied, seeing some of the steam going from his attack. 'Withholding evidence; obstructing the police in their line of duty; failing to report a crime; trespass; accessory to the fact after a murder. Take your choice. Oh.

And, of course, fraud. Taking money from the Social Services under false pretenses. You really ought to declare all your casual earnings, you know.' Pearson took a guess that Hollom must have been paying Tyler something under the table. 'Now you've got your boss Martin Hollom into trouble as well. He won't thank you for that.'

Tyler was not going to bite. Hollom paid him nothing. It was the other way round if anything. Clients gave Peter a 'donation' for putting their models together. The biggest percentage of this went into Hollom's pocket for the use of his space. It was all done on the quiet and Peter was sure Hollom wouldn't be stupid enough to dig a hole for himself.

Pearson could tell his tactics were not getting the result he hoped for. It suddenly came to him what it was about Tyler's face that he found curious apart from its apparent refusal to show emotion. And not just the eyes being unusually close together. It was the prominent high-arched forehead reminiscent of stone-age man, with a mouth being tucked so neatly under a fine nose, it seemed all the working parts of his face would safely fit under a single eye-patch.

What Pearson said next had the effect of pulling back this imaginary eye-patch and letting go.

'To give you something to think about, we'll be giving your house a thorough search shortly,' Pearson lied again, 'unless you want to tell us anything that would save us the trouble of messy your place up?'

Peter was quick to respond to it in as glib a manner as he could muster. 'Be my guest. You won't be finding anything under my mum's mattress if that's what you're thinking.' he said. 'So, I won't be demanding to see a search warrant. But please don't go giving her a heart attack. She's very fragile.'

It was not the response Pearson wanted nor expected.

'I've got nothing to hide,' Tyler went on, then added, hoping to make his lie more convincing. 'And I think you bloody well know it, otherwise you'd be asking me if I wanted a solicitor? Well, just so you know it, I don't need one.' He felt sure they wouldn't go looking up the chimney in his workshop.

'We'll continue later,' Pearson remarked as he left the room to go to the press briefing.

Almost apologetically, Detective Sergeant Simpson introduced Peter to his cell.

In the dank, heartless cell, he wondered if he should in fact ask for a solicitor. Surely arresting him like this was not on?

A thought suddenly came to him. Fuck! Fuck! Fuck!' he exploded inside. The newspaper the money had been wrapped in! He couldn't remember getting rid of it in his excitement. If they *did* search his workshop and looked closely at the damp War Cry, could traces of banknotes be spotted on it?

In the event, there was absolutely nothing to worry about. A search did not happen.

He was not made aware of this situation until his cell door opened soon after the press briefing had ended. Expecting to be confronted with another grilling, he was instead told he could go home. No charge.

Much to Pearson's annoyance, an instruction had come from above that Tyler should be held no longer. In fact, he should not have been held in the first place. There had been nothing to suggest he was involved with either death. The forensic evidence was conclusive. Stephanie Star's hand alone had killed Tilda Bahnlich. Traces of Bahnlich's blood were found on her hands and clothing as well as on everything she had touched in the beached Range Rover. Even on the horse's rein. Her own death was either an elaborate suicide or caused by misadventure. The latter was decided upon not only since it was the most likely, but also to save Sir Edward Ludlow further distress by introducing suicide as a possibility.

Peter Tyler retrieved his bike and managed to get away from the police station via the back parking lot without being hindered by the media flock. As another precaution, from there he took a local knowledge diversion to shake off any journalists who might have been hanging round to catch him leaving. In the dark it was easy. He had various routes he could take to get home.

When he arrived, Gwen was there as expected. She hit him with another surprise. This time non-physical. A woman police constable had been ringing.

'What was it about? Setting up a search?' Peter queried suspiciously.

'No, to ask if I would be here to look after your mum in case you were delayed at the cop shop.'

He could tell Gwen was anxious to hear what had been going on. His being at the 'cop shop' was sure to have done it. At least she wasn't close to tears this time, just bubbling over to hear about it.

'Well, as you can see, they didn't keep me in. I've done nothing and I haven't been charged if that's what you're so eager to learn. Disappointed?'

'Humf!' was all he got for that, so he asked how his mum was, to change the subject.

'Oh, she's alright. Hasn't got a clue what's been going on.' She frowned, and returned to her questioning: 'So why did you think the police might be wanting to come here to search the place? You hiding something in your pants again?'

'Leave off! No, I'm not. It's just that I was the last person to see Stephanie Star alive. You know all about that. That inspector what's-his-name threatened to have the place searched but I knew he was bluffing, that's all. Trying to squeeze more out of me, but I've told him all I know, and that's that. Can you believe he actually thought I might be having it off with Stephanie Star. What a plod! They're groping in the dark, trying to pin things on me because I've put their noses out of joint for saying they screwed up for not acting sooner when I told them about the horse. I just happened to be in the wrong place at the wrong time. Easy as that.' To convince Gwen further of his innocence, he added: 'Further to my question about a search, as I've told you a dozen times, I don't want anyone knowing about my Initiative project until I've managed to patent it. With the police nosing around the house having a good look at it and the press willing pay them for any bit of information they can get hold of, the idea could easily get out and be stolen. And on that subject, I'm trusting you to keep your big mouth shut if they start quizzing you!'

'I'm not going to blab to anyone, am I? I'm an interested party, myself. You promised to give me shares in it, and don't you bloody forget it!'

'I won't. Don't worry about that – as long as you behave!'

'How many?'

'How many what? Promises?'

'Shares, nitwit!'

'How many d'you think you're worth, then?' She had advanced him a couple of hundred pounds to buy materials. Not much in the grand scale of things, but it had helped push things closer to completion.

'Fifty-fifty,' she teased.

'Alright, I'll give you fifty, he teased back. 'Fifty out of a thousand shares when I release them on the stock market! Five percent.'

'Cheapskate.'

'Take it or leave it,' he continued straight-faced. 'It's a fair offer. You'll probably be able to retire on that. Maybe a bonus here and there to lessen my tax burden. You haven't got anything in writing, mind you. You'll have to trust my generosity. So, no lip, you hussy. And no leaping on me trying to ravage my body! Bloody baby-snatcher!' he added, to remind her of New Year's Day, expecting her to redden up. She did. Baby-snatcher indeed!

With that, he told her he was going down to his workshop to do some weights. 'They've had me sitting around all day at the nick. I need something to shake that off.'

'Did they feed you? You want me to knock up something?'

'No thanks. Don't bother. I'll grab a sandwich when I'm done. Are you still staying the night, since I'm not being kept in for murder?' he joked.

'If it'd been Sir what's-it Ludlow himself that they'd found dead up there, I bet you *would* still be locked up for murder!'

That might have been true once upon a time, but not anymore. He still had a petty urge to get back at Ludlow somehow. Having the 22 grand was not a bad start, let alone knowing the reason behind what Stephanie wanted done with it. Peter's lips would stay closed on both accounts. Some of the other things he had learned from the tape promised to be far more useful at getting back at Ludlow if proved to be true. Things the man would definitely prefer to remain 'offshore'.

The real reason Peter wanted to go to his workshop was not to exercise, but to destroy the newspaper that had been wrapped around the money. He had given no thought to its being the Salvation Army War Cry. But he soon saw why.

The paper was now virtually dry. Before tearing it up and burning it, he spotted handwriting on it. He would not have noticed, but for the fact that the ink had run. The writing was no bigger than the newsprint itself, perhaps to hide its being there, but it was still clear enough to read.

There was a telephone number and the words "Ring me *only* in an emergency. Major Wendy Clarke."

Salami! Had he heard Stephanie mutter the name somewhere on the tape? He thought she had, and it was beginning to make sense. Salvation Army! What's more, he now had a name and number to go with the voice!

Chapter Eighteen

'I'm not interested in any theories or personal battles you might be having with this Tyler chap,' Pearson was reminded the next morning. 'Leave that to the tabloids. I'd rather he sued them for the rubbish they've put out about him in the papers today than hitting us for holding him without a shred of evidence.'

At the centre of that rubbish, especially in the case of the Daily Scan, were headlines reading: 'Double Murder?' In slightly less bold print underneath came: 'Cyclist Held'. There was a photograph of the doorstep police announcement, with Tyler's head highlighted in the background. The caption: 'It's that man again! Remember the Marlsbury Demonstrations? See pages 5&6 for more.'

Those pages were covered with pictures of the demonstrations with Tyler made to look like the leading force against Ludlow, which was not too far from the truth.

The reader was promised the 'Full Story', which in fact mounted to little more than thinly disguised sensationalism stepping carefully around the laws of libel. There was also a picture in the later editions of Tyler's bike being removed from the railings in front of the police station 'for examination'. Another of a startled Martin Hollom shutting up shop with the caption: 'Where Peter Tyler worked *illegally*?' Hollom was blatantly misquoted as saying that he could not deny Tyler had possibly been having an affair with Ludlow's wife.

The whole article was nothing more than supposition. Tilda Bahnlich, a nurse employed by the ever absent Ludlow to help treat his wife's drug addiction, was reported as perhaps having discovered this secret affair by chance, which was possibly why it had cost the Austrian her life. According to Robert Pike, the head gardener at Compton Stud, Peter Tyler had often hinted at planning his revenge against Ludlow for closing the Marlsbury Pumps' plant. Could it be that striking up an allegiance with the man's wife was his first move? It had long been suspected that she was not in a happy relationship with her husband.

Before morning was out, most of Marlsbury had written Peter Tyler off. Being a market day, people had risen early and found plenty to talk about. Tut-tutting accompanied the parade of pigs being sold for slaughter. Many folk in the town thought Tyler would soon be going the same way.

But, to confound them all, shortly after midday, Peter Tyler walked into the Turk's Anchor as bare faced as one of Pearson's rooks.

He was feeling buoyant and confident and wanted it to be seen. Although he now had a name and telephone number for the other person sharing Stephanie Star's secret, he would let the dust settle over Marlsbury before any thought of making contact with the Salvation Army major. He needed time to consider long and hard about how to approach that call.

'Tyler's been released!' Victor Rose barked the news to Ludlow through his brick portable phone from the best suite in Compton Stud's converted barn. He had left London to base himself there to be onsite until things were sorted out. 'There's been no come-back from the Law regarding Tyler. Hopefully that means he's told them nothing. With her dead. his options have changed. He's probably weighing things up. Obviously knows you're out of the country. I told the Law you were on a flight and out of touch and to use me as contact. It seems the case is more or less done and dusted. Stephanie whacked Bahnlich and either topped herself or the horse did it for her.'

Ludlow took a moment to consider the news. What hit him most was that Tyler had kept his mouth shut. That could be an unbelievable bonus if Rose had got things right. There was still hope indeed.

'The police mentioned nothing of finding cash or a floppy disc, so it's my guess she laid everything on Tyler,' Rose continued with his take on the situation. 'One way or another, she plainly had him in tow. 22 grand to a bloke like him would buy a lot of loyalty. And get this, although it's a bit far-fetched even for the tabloids, they're putting it about that Tyler might have been having it off with your lovely wife!'

'Highly unlikely,' said the man of experience. 'But stranger things have happened out of desperation.' Ludlow paused for thought, then went on: 'With Stephanie dead and gone, he's more likely to run to the press than the Law, isn't he, whatever she wanted him to do. Different ballgame for him with her out of the picture. He could clean up twice. Twenty-odd grand for starters, then cash in on the scandalmongers. Nothing in it for him taking it to the police, even if that's what she'd wanted him to do. A bloke on the dole's going to cash in as much as he can. I would. Let's face it. Either way, it would fuck me up big time.' Ludlow's heart was beginning to race. This could prove to be very good news indeed, if he was reading things correctly. But they would have to act quickly. 'I trust you've already got someone watching Tyler round the clock?' Ludlow asked imperatively. 'Someone has to be on him night and day to make sure the press doesn't get to him before we do.'

'Working on it.' Rose confirmed. He accepted they had to grab Tyler as soon as possible, but not necessarily in a particularly humane manner. 'Karl, you remember, your wife's personal minder towards the end of her glory days, and Johann, one of our other security guys are already watching him. They're happy no-one's got to him yet.'

'OK. So far so good. But sooner or later one of the tabloids will come up with a sum to satisfy him, so get to him first and let him know I'll double whatever any tabloid offers. Tell him I hold nothing against him for whatever he had going with my wife. He can also keep the twenty grand you reckon she's given him for starters. I'm a generous man, tell him. He'll get much more if he can be persuaded to keep Stephanie's shit from the sensation-seeking press. He'd be surprised how happy I'll be to show my gratitude to him. In any way he wishes. Handsomely! Test him with a tax-free carrot and see what he comes up with. Play him gently. No need to go in hard until he shows his hand. A cool approach, Victor. Don't put the frighteners on him. The man already hates my guts, perhaps not totally without reason the way he sees it. Find a way to convince him I'm not all bad. Get him on our side with big promises. Offer him a blank cheque as soon as possible! Before the wrong people start hassling him.'

Ludlow did not know it, but one of those 'wrong people' was already in the process of hassling Tyler, perhaps not with promises of a blank check, but of a negotiable incentive to make him tell all.

It was the snotty-nosed Daily Scan journalist, no doubt one of those who had written some of the rubbish Peter had been reading about himself in the morning papers. 'Could I have a word, Mr. Tyler? Just a little chat?' the man asked with a smarmy grin. One glimpse of the blotchy skin of his cheeks suggested he led an unhealthy life. Peter Tyler felt an involuntary itch having him stand so close. 'Baker's the name,' he revealed, holding out a limp hand. Peter ignored it. 'Dick Baker. I think we can do business. I'm sure you could use some readies.'

Peter's first instinct was to tell the guy to get lost. But his second thought was more cutting. 'I'm all ears if you want to pay me five figure damages for libel out of court?' he said. 'For all the lies you've printed about me this morning!'

'Damages?' the man whined, as if affronted at being maligned. 'Ah. Editors. The bane of my life, Mr. Tyler. Always twisting words to find another angle. A little chat with me could rectify all that if you agree to sell us your story. Exclusive. In your own words, so to speak. We'd be very interested in your side of things, you know, you and Stephanie Star. I mean, why did they pull you in? Our readers have a right to know about that, and what really happened up at Compton Stud. You'd be doing yourself a great favour, telling us all. It's the perfect opportunity to clear your name.'

'Clear my name?' Peter huffed. 'Nothing *to* clear!'

'Ah. But that's not what people are thinking deep down, is it? Funny thing, people's attitudes. Once they've started believing something, it takes a lot of convincing to change it.' The Daily Scan journalist could see he was not getting far with Tyler. He tried another ploy. 'You've been wronged, Peter, if I can call you Peter.'

'Dead right, I have. And no you can't!' Peter virtually spat the words out, ignoring the cosying up Christian name approach. 'Wronged by you lot as much as the Law.'

'I was thinking further back than this latest business,' the man explained. 'You've been out of work for, what is it, two years now? That's a long time. Look at it this way. Not everyone in the world disagrees with you about Ludlow closing the local factory here in Marlsbury and moving the plant up north. Some people even blame him for the way Stephanie Star ended up. You are possibly the only friend she had in the end, if truth be known. Here's your chance to get back at Ludlow. Bring him down a peg while he's out in the sunshine lording it all over the place. He's not flavour of the month in the city all of a sudden, either is he? All sorts of rumours are flying about. You'd think his wife's death would bring him back, wouldn't you? But no. He's too busy? You've probably got your thoughts about all this, and the public would love to hear about it, I can assure you.' The hack wiped his nose with a grubby handkerchief. 'Tell all, Peter. It'll make you feel a hell of a lot better to set things straight. And you'll have some extra cash in your pocket. On the quiet, if you like. I can promise you. Think about it.'

Peter had already been thinking it could very well be a good way of getting at Ludlow. But not through The Daily Scan. That rag couldn't be trusted. He could end up being sued himself, if he wasn't careful, with the sort of way they twisted things.

'No deal,' he said.

'Hold up. You don't know what we're willing to pay yet,' Baker insisted, offering a business card.

'Your rag couldn't possibly come up with enough,' Peter sneered.

'Depends on what you're willing to tell us. Could be worth syndicating worldwide. You'd clean up!'

As Peter swung his leg over his bike ready to remove himself, he thought he would leave the man with something to chew over.

'Yeah, you're right. I've got plenty to sell,' he boasted, 'but bigger fish are already swimming in the tabloid pond!'

Even if Baker disbelieved him, it gave Tyler great satisfaction to introduce doubt.

As he rode off on his mountain bike, he passed a man not yards away in full leathers straddling a sporty trials motorbike. His helmet was reminiscent of the type worn by German troops during World War Two, often favoured by Hells' Angels. One of Baker's cronies, Tyler imagined. The biker was speaking into a handset. Not a brick cellphone, a distinctive walkie-talkie. Those things had also started appearing when the media circus had hit town.

Tyler had not gone more than ten yards, when he heard the motorbike start up and pull away behind him. That was the second time, now Peter came to think about it. It was the same engine crackle as he had heard coming out of the police yard the evening before. There was no mistaking the same irritating rasp coming from the exhaust.

It had to be coincidence; Tyler was thinking. No-one in his right mind would attempt to follow someone on a bike like that and expect it to go unnoticed.

All the same, Peter found himself testing the guy. He made a tour of the back streets, choosing a route no local would ever take if he wanted to go from A to B. Last night he had not been followed far. But today the bike stayed with him through all the turns, keeping a safe distance.

For some strange reason, it didn't make Peter angry, just curious. If it wasn't someone from the press, his next thought was that it was a plain clothes policeman. No. It had to be a newspaper hound. A runner for Baker, possibly, or for one of the other papers. But it was neither. It was Karl, one of Ludlow's security men. Stephanie's bodyguard in her heyday before things fell apart and Tilda Bahnlich moved in.

Just to confirm he was not imagining the whole thing, Peter thread his way back to the main street and parked up outside Hollom's Attic. He was not planning on going in, but the owner spotted him and came out, blocking the doorway. Hollom was not a happy man.

'I've been pestered non-stop all day because of you, lad! After the bleeding police it's been the damned press people. I've had enough of it, Peter Tyler. Don't you come back here no more. You're not welcome.' Peter had never seen Hollom in such a fury, and it wasn't an excess of cyder doing it. 'I can't see you being welcome anywhere in Marlsbury after what you've been up to. Leaving her body to rot up there. That's not human! Some people want you to swing just for what happened to the poor horse alone! Now, shove off! And don't come back!'

With that, Hollom went in, closing the door behind him.

Peter was taken aback. Hollom was not messing about. Things had hit him hard.

As Peter started off toward the road out of town, the motorbike revved up behind him again. Clear as daylight. He was being followed and whoever it was must want it known. Deliberate harassment? It smacked of Baker, trying to wear him down, perhaps. Should he confront the bloke or play him along? He decided on the latter. He was in that sort of mood. Up for giving this leather-clad pursuer a run for his money.

For a moment or two, it seemed he would have more than the biker to contend with.

There was a television crew loading their camera car outside the SODA shop surrounded by a bunch of nosy locals. As Tyler approached, someone must have spotted him, because all eyes turned to him and a woman shouted from the vehicle window: 'Mr. Tyler. One minute of your time?'

To avoid further hassle, Tyler turned into the first side street he came to, which, by good fortune, happened to be a narrow no-entry street. The camera car would not be able to follow. But it didn't stop the biker.

Better one playmate than a whole school of press monkeys, Peter thought.

Losing an overloaded Volvo Estate full of bag-eyed news folk was no problem. A trials bike was a different proposition. There was only one place that sprang to mind where this might be done. Deadwoods. And it could prove to be fun.

That fun did not really begin until the chase reached Ludlow's private airstrip which was on the route Peter chose to approach the woods. His tail seemed happy to cruise along behind without any thought of catching up with him or hiding the fact that he was there. Why? Peter asked himself again. To discover where he lived? He could understand the police not giving out his address. But with Old Pikey at the beck and call of every hack in town, it might as well have been lit up in neon lights on every street corner.

Getting to the airstrip from Marlsbury meant making a brief cross-country excursion. Peter knew the way like the back of his hand and thought he might be able to lose the biker on that stretch. Not so. He would have to wait till Deadwoods.

'OK, Helmut,' Tyler thought that an appropriate name to call him. 'You asked for it!'

There were one or two hideaways along the ridge skirting Deadwoods that he occasionally used for refuge against foul weather. If he could get far enough ahead of the biker to hole up in one of those unseen, he was on a winner. There was one place in particular where he would only need a few seconds lead to get off the track and in position out of sight. It was a well-chosen spot. If the biker was not paying complete attention, there would be quite a surprise in store for him which would entail the need for all his biking skills to stay aboard. The track turned drastically to its right. A sheer drop of nine or ten feet came directly after it. If he couldn't stop himself from going over it, Helmut would be in great need of that bullet-proof helmet of his.

Peter made his spot and pulled himself in with time to spare. To his delight, the motorbike chain-sawed past without hesitation and took off. That drop would have tested Evel Knievel himself. Somehow, though, this biker seemed to be up to the challenge. There was no crash, but the motorbike landed heavily. Its engine coughed and spluttered briefly, then choked and stopped altogether.

'Ah,' Peter thought. 'Gotcha!'

He wriggled out of his hideaway and went to the edge of the drop. Not twenty yards away, steam or smoke was rising from the distressed motorbike. The rider seemed unhurt. He was sitting on a rock poking at his walkie-talkie with a gloved finger. After putting it to his ear for a few seconds, he took it away and poked it again, more vigorously this time. He repeated this process twice more then slammed the handset onto his knee. No coverage? Too hilly? The wrong side of the ridge? Looking back at the drop he had just survived, he saw Tyler waving at him.

'Whoops,' Tyler shouted, grinning widely. 'Auf Wiedersein!'

He walked his mountain bike out of view before mounting it, then pedalled back the way he had come for a few hundred yards.

Once he was sure he was far enough ahead to be caught even if the motorbike could be started up again, Peter headed home.

He was feeling pretty pleased with himself for how he had dealt with his blatant pursuer when the intermittent wail of a distant fire engine came mingling in the wind. Within a mile or two of Newton Stoat, he could smell smoke. 'A bonfire out of control,' he was thinking idly, but soon learned differently. It was more like rubbish burning.

It was worse than that. A huge plume of black smoke was hanging over his side of the village and an acrid taste hit the back of his throat.

Panic seized him. Bright lights lit up fire engines and police cars blocking his street. Where his workshop had been, smoke rose from a tangled mess of gym equipment, bike frames and wheels.

Further up the road, his house was still in one piece. An ambulance was parked outside with the back doors open. Inside sat his mother with a mug in one hand and a tearful Gwen holding the other, both apparently unhurt. A nurse comforted them, trying to wave away the attentions of the objectionable Dick Baker of the Daily Scan.

'Piss off, you!' Peter shouted at the hack as he approached, pushing him away. 'Go!'

Baker was unabashed, but Tyler's actions did the trick. The scribbler withdrew to a safe distance, but still within earshot.

Not only was Peter's mother obviously unhurt, she also appeared to be enjoying the excitement and attention, wrapped snugly in blankets.

Gwen could not control her snivelling, occasionally giving Peter accusatory yet concerned glances as though suggesting he was to blame for what had happened. His mother added weight to this idea.

'What have you been up to, Peter? she asked almost gleefully. 'That old shed of yours didn't 'alf go up with a bang!'

He had no answer.

'And what's that contraption you've got taking up the living room? I wondered what those funny smells were. That's not likely to explode as well, is it?' she asked. Gwen steadied his mother's shaking hand because tea had started spilling onto the blankets.

Peter's mother rarely came downstairs these days, so she didn't know his Initiative was in the house. In the circumstances, he was so relieved he had moved it in. His workshop come gym did not require a lot of heating when he was working out down there. But fiddling with his Initiative during winter needed a decent room temperature. He would think twice now, however, about keeping the various tins of glue and dope sitting around in the house. The garden shed was a safer place for that stuff.

Detective Sergeant Simpson had been alerted along with the fire service.

'What do you think of all this?' he asked Tyler. 'Know anyone who might have a grudge against you?'

Peter took his time to find an answer. The shock was making it hard to think. All he could think about was the chimney. It didn't stop him coming out with a quip, however. 'Your Inspector Pearson, maybe?'

Simpson smiled at that.

'It'll be clearer when forensics have had a good look. Could have been an electrical fault, they reckon. Did you lay on the supply from the house yourself?'

'No, it's always been there. Ever since we came. Years ago. Never been a problem.' Not completely true.

'They've already looked in the junction box in the house, so they say. That cable was on its last legs, apparently. Hell of a long run down to the workshop. Exposed to the weather over the years. Does your insurance cover it?'

'Dunno. Possibly. But probably not. I'll have to check.'

As Tyler thought about it, his attention was taken by the tell-tale sound of a trials motorbike. As the engine cut, he looked up and down the road but couldn't pick it out with all the vehicles parked along it.

There was a tape bearing the words 'Crime Scene' around the remains of the workshop. From the front door of the house three people wearing masks appeared, clothed from head to foot in white garments which they began to peel off. The house had been checked over as a precaution. All appeared to be in order, apart from the number of tins and jars of inflammable glues and liquids scattered around the 'contraption' in the living room.

Relayed with no mincing of words, Tyler was told they should be removed before the house went up in smoke as well!

Peter took note, promising to take care of the problem straight away. Despite this all-clear, his mother was in no great hurry to go back inside. She was enjoying it too much in the fresh air with all the activity.

He got as close to the remains of his workshop as he dared to survey the damage. Arsonists could not have done a better job. It had been razed to the ground, right down to the last smoldering bricks of the fireplace! He was hit by a niggling thought. *Could* it have been arson?

'When the windows caved in, flames started shooting out of the chimney like a doodlebug!' said the village neighbour who had alerted the fire brigade. 'Whoosh! It went!'

Peter could picture it.

By ten that night, the firemen had wrapped their hoses and were gone. The crime scene tape was still in place to keep people away, but it seemed as if the cause was more likely to have been an electric fault. The flood lights had been turned off. Further investigation would continue in the morning and a final assessment made. Two unhappy junior officers were to be left in attendance overnight to keep an eye on things.

During the course of the evening more press people had arrived and left after gleaning enough information needed to piece their copy together.

Peter had avoided confrontation with them as much as possible, and once he and Gwen had moved his mother back inside, he shut the door on them.

Chapter Nineteen

When Peter drew back his curtains and looked out of his bedroom window the next morning, he could hardly believe what he was seeing. Apart from two police cars now alongside his workshop site, there was an incident vehicle and a television satellite truck with a camera crew already up and running. Directly outside his front gate was another TV crew and a gathering of anorak-clad reporters whose parked vehicles stretched beyond Gwen's Citroen 2CV on the other side of the street.

Inevitably, it seemed, there among the bunch was Dick Baker, looking more dishevelled than ever. Surely, he couldn't have been out there all night? Would he ever give up?

Sitting astride a trials bike, his feet on the pedals, an elbow on the roof of Gwen's 2CV keeping him upright, was a man dressed in full leathers, not the one who had tailed Peter the day before. The helmet was different, and this biker was stockier. There was a similarity, however. A walkie-talkie was hanging around his neck.

There was a movement within the pack of journalists. A flash went off. Tyler had been seen at the window. He quickly closed the curtains and went downstairs to see if Gwen was up. She was.

'For Christ's sake don't go out the front door,' he beckoned her. 'The bloody wolf-pack are all over the place.'

'I know. I've seen 'em,' she said. 'So, what's this all about, Peter? Are you going to tell me, or what? First the police taking you in, and now your place burnt to the ground.'

'Obviously some nutter did it. I can't see it being an electrical fault. Mind you.' He couldn't really rule that out. All the wiring was yonks old. In the house, too. Perhaps that ought to be looked into? 'Perhaps some crazy horse lover got it all wrong and took umbrage. I reported Stephanie Star's horse running wild as soon as I saw it without her on it. What more could I do?'

That was the best he could come up with. He couldn't tell her exactly what was going on, because he didn't know himself.

'Well, I hope the house is safe, if only for your mum's sake.'

'They gave it the all-clear, didn't they? I suppose I'd better get rid of all the paint pots and stuff, though. Should have done that last night. I'll do it in a minute.'

'I'm not talking about that. What if someone did do it and try again on the house? Something's going on. I'm not stupid. You've not been yourself since New Year.' Gwen's face was reddening.

'No-one would be so mad as to try anything like that with people inside. They've already got all the bloody attention if it was an animal rights protest. That's usually why they do it. It must be all over the papers today with that lot outside.'

'There was a bit about it on local TV this morning. Even a picture of me and your mum sitting in the ambulance.'

'There you go. Fame at last! Best you stay here today, then. You'll be in their sights. You'll get bombarded. If you do have to go out, don't say much. Just that we're all alright and that we hope the police get whoever's responsible if they talk about arson. Something like that. I'll face them later when I've had a chance to think about what to say. Hope that gets rid of them.'

'Well, I'm not bloody-well going anywhere today,' Gwen hastened to tell him. 'I'll stay and look after your mum. Her heart rate's really picked up after the excitement. She can't stop telling me what a naughty boy you are!' She joked.

'Yeah, alright. Don't push it, red cheeks,' he countered.

The telephone rang.

Peter looked questioningly at Gwen as if to ask if she expected a call. She pushed her lips out as if to whistle and shook her head a couple of times.

Peter grimaced. He supposed he ought to take it in case it was something important. Mistake. It was Dick Baker.

'I hope you managed to get a good night's sleep, Peter,' the reporter said, as if they were old mates. 'Have you given thought to the proposition I put to you? Exclusive. Nice earner.'

How do these people get his phone number, Peter asked himself, cursing inside.

'Not interested!' he responded forcefully. 'And while you're on the phone, get this into your thick skull. Print any more of that rubbish about me, and I'll be suing you for an even nicer little earner!'

He put the receiver down before Baker could come back at him, waited a few seconds, then picked it up again. Satisfied that the line was clear, he left the receiver off the hook to stop any more calls getting through.

He was truly pissed off with the situation. His workshop gone with everything in it, not just the money. Although it wasn't his, really, it was still a disaster. Then his bikes, his models, his work-out equipment. All gone. Perhaps most of all, his *place*. His man-cave.

Again and again, it hit him how lucky it was to have moved his Initiative into the house for the winter. Otherwise, that too would have gone up in smoke. Even twenty-two grand paled at the thought of that! 'Don't dwell on it,' he kept telling himself, standing over his Initiative. Yeah. It wasn't his money. But it might have been, if locating Stephanie's daughter turned out to be impossible. Now what? Be thankful for small mercies! His Initiative was still in one piece.

The bigger mercy was no-one had been injured. He wasn't thinking of himself, but of his mother and Gwen. He probably never showed it enough, but he was really pleased to have Gwen around. Looking after his mother alone would have been impossible. The washing and cleaning, the bedpan scenario. Meals and health checks. Gwen was a brick.

Coming out of his reverie, he looked down at the list of things still to be done on his invention. It was no good. He couldn't put his brain into focus. He still had to find a way to synchronize the rotation of the three propellers in an energy efficient way. He needed his own unique control system that wouldn't encroach on gaming consoles that were springing up all over the place. There was still a way to go before the Initiative would be ready for commercial production. First, he had to prove it would fly! Well, he knew it would fly, but the weight of the onboard battery was still a concern. For its ultimate purpose, it had to be compact and light, yet still have the power to lift the extra weight of a remotely controlled camera. That was what would make his Initiative unique. The final stream-lining necessary to bring it all together in a good-looking aerodynamic piece of kit would follow once all the technical components were in place. He would probably have to strike a deal with a high-end injection-molding company when it got that far. That's when costs would hit the roof. He had been thinking he might have 'borrowed' the 22 grand to help him through that stage. No hope of that anymore.

Losing the money was more than depressing. He knew his Initiative would eventually come together, and what a leg-up that cash would have been! He wasn't yet ready to run to the Daily Scan inventing stories to raise funds. 22 grand. Gone. 'Jeez!' That really hurt.

He stared at his creation, frustrated. He couldn't free up his mind enough to work on it. But one thing he could and should do was get rid of everything inflammable hanging around the living room; the dope, the white spirit, the various glues and paints. He knew they shouldn't have been there in the first place. Into the garden shed they would go with all the other odds and ends.

Minor problem: the shed could be seen from the road. This would mean exposing himself to the mob outside.

'Sod 'em,' he thought, as he started to gather the stuff up. 'Needs must.'

Gwen gave a silent nod of approval when she saw what he was doing.

As expected, even before getting to the shed, all and sundry started calling out to him.

It took him three runs to complete the task and by then he had come to the conclusion that perhaps it was as well to face the relentless mob. If he made a statement, it might get rid of them.

A group of them had stationed themselves by the incident vehicle still parked by his burnt-out workshop. They quickly joined the others, seeing him present himself at the garden gate. Cameras and microphones were thrust in his direction as the barging crowd jostled for position. Standing back from them, Peter noticed, was the leather clad biker last seen up in Deadwoods. He had neither microphone nor camera, but the familiar walkie-talkie to his ear.

To a barrage of questions thrown at him, Peter held his palms up as if to push them back.

'No questions,' he said forthrightly. 'All you're getting is a brief statement so you can pack your bags and go home.' He waited for his words to sink in before continuing. 'As you can imagine, I am truly pissed off with what's happened down there.' He waved in the direction of his wrecked workshop. 'Your time would be better spent pestering the police to do their job and round up the long-haired crazies who I suspect are responsible. I am of course truly sorry about the horse having to be put down, but in case you didn't know it, I was the one who alerted the police about it running wild two days ago. So, if anyone's to blame, it's the cops for not acting sooner. Two bloody days it took them to get their act together. Two days! That's gross neglect if you ask me. Stephanie Star might not have been flavour of the month with the drugs and everything, but her horse could have been saved.' He took a breath, which allowed time for an onslaught of questions. The one that caught his ear most was: 'Were you having a thing with Stephanie Star?'

'I told you, I'm answering no questions,' he said forcibly. 'I've done enough of that at the nick. And they've got a bloody cheek sticking me in a cell trying to pin murder on me. Same as you lot with the stuff you've been putting about in the papers. My solicitor will be looking into all that in due course.' He had no real intention of wasting his time and energy with lawyers. What chance did a bloke like him have down that route? 'One last thing you might want to better your time asking is where has Ludlow been while all this has been going on? Anyone thought about that? What's keeping him away? His wife has died. What's he frightened of?'

He turned and walked toward his front door quite pleased with himself for throwing in those last few lines. There followed another burst of questions. He looked back, shook his head irritably and said: 'Enough's enough! Clear off!'

Back inside, he wondered if any of what he had been saying would make the evening news. 'Shit!' he suddenly thought. He should have mentioned Inspector Pearson by name as the culprit for his wrongful arrest. That would have been another good wind-up. Too late, unfortunately.

Gwen was regarding him questioningly as he walked in.

'Well, I made my statement,' he told her.

'I know. I was watching through the window. What did you tell them? Nothing about the blood you had on you that day, I bet.'

'Leave it out, Gwen. What's your point?'

'You know.'

'Well, if it *was* blood, it must have come from the horse's rein when I grabbed it. It's a wonder she wasn't smothered in blood according to what she did to that Austrian woman. So don't *you* keep trying to fit me up with murder like the law tried. I've just been bollocking the police, if you must know, about not acting quicker to save the horse. Other than that, I told them all to piss off.'

'Well,' Gwen said, peeking out from behind a curtain, 'they haven't taken a blind bit of notice. Some of them seem to be drifting off, though. Looks like the forensics people are wrapping up. There's a bit of action down where it's cordoned off.'

Gwen was thinking correctly. The reporters were now gathering around the forensics team who had taken their masks off and were in the street climbing out of their protective garments.

Twenty minutes later, there was a knock on the back door. A female member of that team was standing there now clad in a full-length anorak with barely more than her feet showing. She had come to confirm that there was no clear evidence of the fire having been started deliberately. It seemed to have been caused by an electrical fault. The area where it began was around the only socket in the place, which seemed to have been powering several appliances: a power drill, a heater, a kettle and a battery charger. It was too difficult to establish if the building had been broken into. A report would be made, but it was thought no further investigation would be found necessary.

Before taking her leave, the forensics officer held out an envelope with a business card attached.

'I was asked if I would hand you this,' the forensics woman said. 'It's from some leather-clad courier guy on a motorbike. Said he didn't want to bother you anymore than you had already been by the press. I

182

wouldn't normally have helped but he said it was important and when I saw who it was from, I thought I'd better.'

Tyler looked at the card, frowned and swallowed hard. Was he seeing things?

In raised bold golden print, the card announced: Ludlow Media Group. Beneath, in smaller script came, Victor Rose, Vice-President, Entertainment. There was a city of London address and telephone number.

'If there was ever any doubt about it, Ted, there's none now,' Victor Rose said into his brick cellphone, finally getting through to his boss's safe haven in Kenya, 'Tyler is definitely in it up to his neck! We found the money. All twenty-two grand of it! And you'll never guess where. Up the fucking chimney in his man-cave! The first place we looked. What a dickhead!'

Rose thought it best to start with that part of the story given his boss's anxiety about violence. 'But no tape, no disc.' he was unhappy to report. 'We pulled his place apart, but no show. He must have stashed them somewhere else. We're quite certain he's not gone running to the press. We've tapped his phone, got two guys watching him closely. And guess what?' Rose paused, as if waiting for an answer.

'Enlighten me' was all he got.

'It's the stuff of make believe. You couldn't invent it.' Which was exactly what Rose was about to do, as his boss suspected. The news would soon be out, but it was perhaps better coming from Rose.

'Only hours after we got out of his place, it seems some horse-loving brigade got in and burnt his place to the ground. So, if the other stuff had been there and we missed it, it ain't there anymore!'

If the money had been found during the sort of search he knew Rose to be capable of, so would the tape and disc. So why had he taken the risk of burning the place down? He knew it had to have been Rose. He was too much of a Maverick, sometimes. It sounded like he'd gotten away with it. But Rose, oh Rose. Would he ever learn to control himself?

It made sense that Tyler had been wary not to keep all his eggs in one basket. With the money gone, which Ludlow presumed to be payment for his 'safe hands' services, what would Tyler's next move be now he was out of pocket? Run to the highest bidder? He had to be reined in as soon as possible.

Victor Rose might have been reading Ludlow's mind through the silence coming down the line from Africa.

'I delivered a note to Tyler expressing your deepest sympathies and all that,' he told his boss. 'Thanking him for being a good citizen and regretting that he's got himself innocently caught up in this sordid business. I stressed you were a generous, unforgiving man with all you told me to tell him about compensating him.'

'Have you told Silver about this?'

'Will do, now I've spoken to you.'

'Well, do it straight away, so he's up to speed. Let's hope Tyler's in the mood to get rich.'

Rose went on to explain that the crime scene at Compton Stud had been done with. A clean up was now in progress. Tilda Bahnlich's family, what there was of it, had been informed. Arrangements were being made to have the body flown home to Austria.

Peter read the note the forensic officer had given him again and again, trying to understand the significance of it.

Dear Mr. Tyler,

I am sending this communication to you on behalf of Sir Edward Ludlow, who is unfortunately indisposed at present in Africa representing his charity S.O.D.A., as you might know.

He has asked me to convey his utter disgust for what has happened to your property, possibly at the hands of deluded animal lovers. He also sincerely thanks you for alerting the police about his sick wife's traumatic behaviour, and for telling them about seeing her riderless horse running wild. That anyone could misconstrue your actions as neglect is beyond reason. You behaved as any good citizen should.

In conclusion, he would like to offer you compensation in some way for your loss, and for being a concerned acquaintance of his now tragically deceased wife. Perhaps, most of all, he appreciates that you have not given way to pressures from the press to make easy money out of the recent tragic state of affairs and events that you have found yourself so innocently caught up in.
Yours respectfully,
Victor Rose

The note was type-written and signed with a squiggle that only just resembled the name.

On another sheet in compact handwriting was a postscript which read:

For your information, I add that Sir Edward is even more thankful than it might sound from the above, especially for not running to the press. It's bad enough already with all the shit going on in the papers trying to dirty his name – and yours, as it happens. So, keep your nose clean and don't go telling stories about any shit his wife paid you to spread about. Expressly, keep that mouth of yours shut and he will more than make up for any money she gave you, as well as upping anything the tabloids might be offering you many times over. Think about this. Seriously. I would, if I were you. You've got my card, so get in touch if you want a quiet life. The sooner the better.

Then that squiggle again.

Chapter Twenty

About mid-January each year, Tony would set about making arrangements for his upcoming birthday to be celebrated at his club in the outskirts of Manchester. These would usually be spread over the weekend closest to the actual date. A live band would be booked, usually the same one, 'Heir O' The Dog', a quintet he had become friends with over the course of his career. They were perfect for a night of fun, playing for laughs and dressing to match. Well-known stand-up comedians would also appear, making for non-stop fun. Most of the guests were, or had once been, involved with show business one way or another. Out front minor celebrities, or behind the scenes pullers of strings.

'Tony's Birthday Bash' was by invitation only. Professional caterers would be brought in to provide gourmet finger-food and a first-class drinks service. Money was not spared; no soggy pizzas nor fake 'Between the Sheets' cocktails in sight.

This year, 1988, being a leap year, the 'bash' would occur on Tony's actual birthday date. Even though this fell on a Monday, Tony's Ring would be open to host this extra special celebration.

Tony had been born on 29th February 1928, which had also been a leap year. Although he would have experienced only 15 of those actual dates, on the next occasion it would herald his sixtieth year on the planet. A double landmark worthy of extra effort.

What Tony had thought of arranging for this notable year to add to his usual 'unmissable' celebratory day, was a contest to crown the best look-alike famous person living in or around the Manchester area. Any look-alike was welcome, be it film star, politician, sports star, criminal; anyone past or present who most people would know. A job at 'Tony's Ring' would automatically be offered to the winner should that person be interested, but what was usually more of an enticement to encourage contestants to chance their luck was the promise of something like an all-expenses paid Mediterranean cruise or a holiday in Tenerife for two if they won.

Before the actual birthday bash, Tony had decided the contenders should be whittled down to six. This year, the rainbow rooms were given a Spring clean and kitted out with new bed linen and given over to the finalists to make themselves ready to present themselves, with the option of staying over should they wish.

To get the ball rolling, during the weeks before the big day, adverts would be run in the local papers to attract contestants. Tony was especially hoping for anyone who could come close to looking like himself, or any of his 'famous' friends who had been invited to sit on the judges' bench. He thought having at least one of the judges judging his or her own lookalike would be fun. A nice touch.

Guests would be encouraged to come in fancy dress themselves, not to the extent of wearing masks and wigs, as perhaps the ornate invitation cards might suggest with its image of a Venetian masked ball emblazoned on them. Tony thought 'going posh' like that would add class to the event.

Tony's idea for Jimbo, much to Jimbo's discomfort, it must be said, was to have him dressed as Quasimodo, right down to a false humpback. Without too much imagination, Jimbo's facial features fitted the bill in an amusing sort of way. This was not his own opinion, of course. He saw himself more as a Steve McQueen character. The money was always on Tony winning that argument when the day came.

The girls and boys working out front really looked forward to Tony's birthday bashes. Although they were strictly on duty, it was more in a theatrical manner. The catering staff did most of the hard graft. The staff lookalikes' role was to ham up their adopted persona a little more than usual. On bash days, they were essentially there as entertainers, and the more they entertained with their role playing, the bigger the tips. All of them always did very well by the end of play. Some even topping as much as a month's normal wages. And all theirs, no divvying up on Bash days!

Sharon usually came out top of that league, but always shared it with Kim. That was their way. Share and share alike. But Sharon would get tea in bed more frequently as reimbursement. That was until in Kim's opinion the balance had been paid off.

'What shall we do with our 'birthday bash' money this year?' Kim wanted to know. They would always do something special with their sudden riches. It was never anything like repainting the kitchen or starting a savings account. They never spent much time in the kitchen, and they

187

were optimistic enough to believe the future was a long way off. The furthest they ever got to thinking about that prospect was daydreaming about when their knights in shining armour would eventually come along. And those dreams tended to come along in more of a flurry around the time of Tony's birthday bashes because there were usually a few candidates who might fit that role in attendance on those occasions, a smattering of fairly well-known personalities among them, some rich and single. The problem was, if any of the 'possibles' showed particular interest in the girls, it was most often because of the star they were pretending to be, rather than themselves! All playacting, on both sides. No real future in that.

They never gave up hope, though. It added extra interest to Tony's special celebrations. They would prance around strutting their stuff, quietly assessing the possibilities, at every opportunity exchanging notes. Once, Kim thought she was on to a winner. The guy had come back several times after and taken her Upstairs. But he hadn't yet invited her out on a date away from Tony's. He was in his early thirties, good looking, fit, and had his own company, so he had told her. She had 'waxed lyrical' to Sharon about him so much that it seemed the guy might be about to come between them. That was until an article in the local papers changed everything. It revealed that he was on remand for crimes related to persistent car theft. Bad enough. But it was the fact that he was married with two children that had really upset Kim.

Since then, they had decided that a little more discreet vetting should be applied before getting their hopes up too high about anyone they fancied who might fit the bill. Tony, without knowing their precise reasons for asking, was usually happy to help out in this matter to some extent. Sometimes, even going as far as to warn them with a subtle: 'Be careful with that bloke. All is not as it might seem.'

Tony was protective of his own by nature. Perhaps not a father figure to them, but close-on.

Sharon's father had disappeared under a cloud when she was about seven. She had long known why, and it still didn't sit comfortably with her. As seven-year-old's possibly generally do, she remembered loving her dad more than her mum. She spent more time being cuddled by him than her.

By the time she was approaching nine, she had begun to sense there might be something wrong with all his 'cuddling'. She couldn't remember how it happened, but one day everything went wild in the house. There were shouts and screams, pots and pans crashing. She had been sent to her room and she could see two police cars outside. She never saw or heard from her father again. All her mother told her was that she loved her very much and that her father was a bad man and had been taken away.

Sharon learned later that he had not so much been taken away as disappeared. He had absconded to avoid prosecution for child molestation. Whether he had left the country was not known. It was assumed he had, because to this day his whereabouts had never been discovered.

Sharon's mum, Susan, had done her best to bury the episode and bring Sharon up as best she could. But single parenthood is never easy.

To help out in this situation, Kim's mum, a close neighbour and friend of Susan had looked after Sharon as a child whenever necessary. Before long, Sharon and Kim had become inseparable. They really clicked; had the same sense of fun, dreamed about the same things, shared the same thoughts and feelings as they went through puberty. They were like twin sisters by then, apart from their looks.

Once of age, these two tearaways couldn't wait to move out and make their own way in life. Although Sharon's mum had eventually moved away from the district, she still kept in touch with Kim's mum from time to time. Their conversations usually got around to wondering what *that* pair of theirs were getting up to?

And it could be fair to say that the pair in question were making sure that what they were getting up to went no further than *Tony's Ring*.

Peter Tyler had a decision to make.

There was more to the Ludlow letter delivered by the forensics officer other than bullshit sympathy for his workshop being burnt down. There was a definite edge to it. A threat. Ludlow was a worried man, and it wasn't too difficult to work out what it might be. Tax havens and shell companies sprang to mind. Possibly drugs? Why else would he be coming on like this? 'For your loss.' Come on! Do me a favour! Ludlow must know about the 22 grand Stephanie had dropped. That amount of cash doesn't go missing without being noticed. From what she had been saying on the tape her finances were frozen. It sounded like she didn't have two farthings to rub together, so where had that money come from? Another reason for killing Bahnlich? Did Ludlow think Peter was in cahoots somehow? He was shit-scared about *something* for Rose to come on to him in the letter the way he had.

Major Wendy Clarke was meant to be the recipient of the money, but only in passing. The Salvation Army had done a good job tracing Stephanie's daughter. But that seemed to be as far as it was going with the major. She showed no interest in Stephanie's rant about Ludlow's dodgy dealings. Not in her remit. Abalone? Good name for a shell company! Hide your money somewhere nice and sunny. Tax-dodging. Peter's meagre Sopwith Pup cash earnings weren't in the same league, but he would bet he'd be the one to get caught out long before Ludlow ever did!

In the light of the note, he needed to be very cagey indeed. 'Compensation'? A certain amount of sparring might be necessary to keep Stephanie's daughter out of the picture, otherwise Major Clarke might suddenly jump into the ring with a head-butt.

As he read the note again, Gwen came through wondering what had been keeping him. He tried not to give away the turmoil going on in his head.

Had he got this right? All Stephanie wanted was to secretly help the child she thought she had lost as a thirteen-year-old. Ludlow thought she was about to stab in him the back by exposing his corrupt Charity. The major was to act as courier for the 22 grand. 'No-one must know'. Ludlow knew nothing of the child, nor did Stephanie want him to know, or anyone else for that matter. No-one apart from the Salvation Army. Safe hands and honesty. The first place anyone would go for such help.

That had to be it. That was the situation. He was convinced he was reading it properly.

Again, Peter Tyler was thinking, say nothing, do nothing. Listen. Add to that; keep your nerve! Could he go along with this? 'More than the tabloids might be offering'? Ludlow's words. Could Peter do it? Take the money and run? It would be under extremely false pretenses. But what a result to dupe Ludlow if he could he get away with it? Could he really justify selling any of this tell-tale stuff to the press, anyway? It was virtually all hearsay. OK. The tape stuff was real, but he would feel like a real prick giving that to the press. A moral shit-bag. Stephanie was clearly under stress. Plainly didn't want her secret made public. In equal measures, neither did it seem like Ludlow want *his*. Moreso, perhaps, because he was still of this world!

Did Peter have the moral edge to justify misleading Ludlow if it meant the child could be helped anonymously, as Stephanie had wished? There must be some very juicy data dotted about on that missing disc for Ludlow to be so desperate to outbid the tabloids.

If a thought bubble could have been floating above Peter's head right now, it would be saying; 'Could Tyler's Initiative soon be up and running!'

But there was a spanner in the works. The 22 grand was gone. Should something be said about that? That Stephanie had given it to him only for it to have gone up in smoke? Would that endorse his position as her confidant in Ludlow's mind? Give him more weight? Possibly.

What was in his best interests? How should he go about any of this?

These considerations were suddenly put into focus by Gwen.

'Come on, out with it!' she said nosily, having left him in his deep thoughts long enough. 'Now what? Love letter from forensics?'

'Mind your own business,' he told her, playing her along by holding up the printed note in front of her rosy cheeks and folding it playfully. 'Wouldn't you like to know, miss nosy pants?'

'Hmph!' came a disdainful grunt. 'Suit yourself.'

'OK, you win,' he smiled, ending the game by offering the typed note to her. He had shoved the handwritten post-script into his pocket while she was at the window. 'What do you make of that, red nose?'

Gwen read the note, her eyes widening the further she got into it. She looked up at him,
gob-smacked. 'Is this for real?'

'That's what I was about to ask you.'

'Who gave it to that forensics lady?'

'Some bloke on a motorbike,' he told her. 'But it was sent by this man.' He handed her the business card as the realization came to him. 'Those bikers have been following me ever since I left the nick the other day. I thought they were to do with the Daily Scan.'

'Ludlow Media Group!' she chirped, screwing up her nose. 'Looks genuine?'

'Appears to be,' he mused. 'Why wouldn't it be, I suppose. News travels fast these days.'

'So, what's all this about not running to the press to make easy money?' she was keen to know. 'I knew you had *something* up your sleeve as well as down your pants that day! What did our Steff tell you while you were holding onto her bloody reins?'

It was perhaps best to be frugal with the truth. 'Nothing that made particular sense.' he said. Stephanie's panic-stricken secret, *no-one must know*, he would kept to himself. Honour among thieves?

'Well, she must have told you something 'sir what's it' didn't want you to know about.' A statement as the glow on Gwen's cheeks weakened.

'That's what I'm trying to figure out,' Peter admitted. 'Her garbled words came at me like machine gun fire. None of it made sense, except her saying sorry a dozen times. I was more interested in keeping out of the way of the horse than listening to her. It bloody nearly clobbered me. Imagine it. It could only have been minutes before that she had killed her nurse. No wonder she was in such a state.'

'Well, you should put your head together if Ludlow seriously wants to compensate you.' Gwen's mind was racing. 'I told you more than once you ought to go to him with that Initiative of yours. What a chance now! He's filthy rich! Get him to sponsor it if he wants to help you out. That's not asking much. And get him to put some bloody double-glazing on this place before your mum dies of pneumonia. What a godsend this could be! If he means it. Get rid of the damp and liven the place up. Forget doing anything to that wreck of yours down there. It's a wonder it didn't go up in flames years ago. Do this place up instead and get somewhere else to finish your Initiative. Get it out of here like the forensics people told you.

192

I didn't like to mention it myself. What about Hollom's Attic? He wouldn't mind, would he?'

That was questionable, but Peter let her spout on. However, he had in fact already been thinking something along the same lines as Gwen about looking for a sponsor before any of this had happened. Ludlow hadn't exactly jumped out at him as an obvious target. But now, with this landing in his lap. Temptation indeed. Once launched, everything else would fall into place. New workshop, new house, new life. He would be his own man by then. Home and dry. The world would be his oyster. Or maybe his Abalone!

'Yes, yes, Gwen.' He finally brought her bossing to an end. 'All in good time. You can spend your cut on a new damp course if you so wish!'

'H'mm' and a middle finger was all he got for that.

He had a restless night mulling over his situation. What could he do about it? What *should* he do? The shock of everything that day was messing with his ability to think clearly.

It wasn't much better when he got up in the morning. But the conclusion he *had* arrived at during the night was back to; do nothing. Let things unfold in their own time. To some extent, the Salvation Army Major was still in the picture. But perhaps not so much now with Stephanie gone - along with the twenty-odd grand! What would she be inclined to do? More to the point, what *could* she do? Not a lot. The case was closed for her, really?

It was a matter of wait and see. But he couldn't wait too long before letting Victor Rose know what he was going to do one way or another. He would have to pick his words very carefully, because he would be committing himself to a very big bluff.

That night, Gwen went back to her own place on the edge of Marlsbury; a one-bedroom flat with all mod cons in the first new block to be completed where the pumps factory had once been. When she arrived at Peter's house in the morning, she asked him to check his telephone line.

'I've been trying to ring you,' she told him. 'Wanted to know if you needed anything brought in from the supermarket.'

He lifted the handset and put his ear to it. Nothing.

'What's going on now?' he groaned. 'Something else to bloody fix!'

At least he wouldn't be bothered with nuisance calls from the likes of Dick Baker while the line was down. Maybe he should leave it like that for a while. It might discourage them further.

'I bought a few things you're running short of, plus some Marlsbury sausages for tonight,' she told him. 'The bill's on the table.'

'Thanks for that. I was wondering what to do about grub tonight,' he said. 'That note from Ludlow has been on my mind non-stop.'

'Well, don't sit on your arse thinking about it for too long in case he changes his mind. You keep on about him owing you. So, cash in! What are you waiting for? If he genuinely thinks you've been a good citizen, go for it. What are you being so shy about? That's not like you.'

He nodded slowly, distracted. It wasn't that straight forward. She didn't have the full picture. Nor was she going to get it!

'Well, the phone's put the kibosh on ringing from here, hasn't it,' he pointed out. 'I'll do it from town later. Try to find out what's happened to the line here at the same time.'

A stifled 'Hymmph' from Gwen. 'I'll be staying the night,' she announced as she disappeared upstairs to deal with Peter's mother's needs.

When Peter wheeled his bike out to ride into Marlsbury, he was confronted by the leather-clad biker who'd gone flying over the ridge the other day.

'Good morning, Mr. Tyler. My name is Karl,' the man introduced himself before Peter had swung his leg over the saddle. 'You remember me? I am the one following you. Oops! In the woods. Mr. Rose send me. He tries to ring you but phone not working.' The man spoke with a slight accent. German? Slavic? 'He would like meet you today. You say time. He send car.'

It took a few moments for Peter to gather his response. His first instinct was to be churlish. He was annoyed at being confronted like this. Suspicious, too. But he didn't want to overreact. He found himself looking around as if seeking the right words. In so doing, he caught sight of Gwen at an upstairs window. He was sure her cheeks were glowing.

'Why?' he heard himself asking. Was this his opportunity? Or was it a trap? Things were moving fast. Not what he had anticipated. Ludlow was plainly eager. 'What's it about?'

The biker shrugged his answer. He was a mere messenger. 'Sooner the better, he say.'

Was sooner the better for Peter, though? At least he wouldn't have to chase into town to make the call. Another glance up at Gwen. He guessed what she'd be egging him on to do. The idea of reporting the telephone line fault could wait. Ludlow's offer might not.

'Where? And when?' Peter asked.

The biker shrugged again. 'Big house?' It seemed a guess. 'He send car now?' he questioned, waving his walkie-talkie to illustrate how this could be arranged.

With another look up at Gwen, he said, 'OK'

He took his bike back in and told her what was happening.

'If I'm not back within a couple of hours, send for the cavalry,' he joked, refusing her offer to come with him brandishing a rolling pin.

Chapter Twenty One

Peter felt quite strange to be sitting chauffeur driven on the back seat of a Range Rover as it drove through the gates of Compton Stud. It had occurred to him that he had never ever been in the back seat of any car, let alone one that had once carried supermodel Stephanie Star around. It could even be the same one he had seen stuck on the parapet edge that fatal day. These things were built like tanks compared to Gwen's runaround 2CV. A few scrapes underneath wouldn't have done much damage to it.

Like an angry wasp, Karl's trials motorbike had followed them all the way from Peter's place to where the Range Rover now pulled up at the huge barn that had been converted into over-spill living quarters for photo shoots. The driver, who happened to be the other biker keeping tabs on Peter now shed of his leathers, led the way upstairs. At the end of a long corridor, he knocked on a door, opened it and beckoned Tyler to go in. With a brief nod to the man inside, he closed the door, remaining outside.

Victor Rose greeted Peter from behind a narrow table which was not much wider than an ironing board. It was more a work surface than a table. Set against the wall beside it was a refrigerator, then came a compact stainless-steel sink and drainer overlooking the least appealing side of the main house itself through double glazed windows. A quick look around told Peter he was in a very comfortable pad, complete with signed photographs scattered around the walls. Up-market publicity stills of famous models. Samples of past photo-shoots.

Through an open doorway on the furthest wall, he could see an unmade double bed. He imagined there to be a bathroom off that room making the whole place a very livable self-contained apartment.

'So, Mr. Tyler?' Rose pronounced, as if Peter had set up the meeting and should be the one to start proceedings. The manner of the delivery suggested Rose had watched too many James Bond movies.

'Indeed,' Peter responded after a pause, and 'indeed' was all he was willing to come up with in the present circumstances. The sparring had begun. This was Victor Rose's show. It was up to him to make the first move.

'Drink?' he proposed, shaking a tumbler side to side invitingly. 'I can offer you whisky, gin, wine or beer. No cyder I'm afraid.'

Why would he think Peter would want cyder?

'Coke,' Peter replied, and thought of adding 'the liquid kind' as a subtle hint that he knew Rose must have dabbled with cocaine given his card put him in the entertainment business. 'Diet if you've got it.'

'No can do, I'm afraid,' Rose explained, trying to ignore his guest's wardrobe. Tyler had made no concessions to the nature of their meeting. He was wearing a parka over mud-splattered cycling gear. The cleaners would have to be called in after his visit. But at least Tyler had come at the first bidding, which encouraged Rose to believe he was here to do business. 'Tonic water is the only soft drink in the house.'

'That will have to do, then,'

'Ice and lemon?' Spoken like a true barman.

Tyler nodded. 'Thanks.'

'I'll join you,' Rose said, doing the honours. 'Sure?' he asked again, unscrewing a bottle of Gordon's gin and topping up his own glass. Tyler declined. He needed to keep a clear head.

Rose was doing his best to be congenial, but the effort seemed to be wasted on Tyler.

'Have a seat,' he prompted, indicating one of the bar stools at the table. He would normally have offered an armchair, but not the way Tyler was dressed.

'Thanks for coming,' the host said, settling on a stool opposite Tyler, who immediately drew his own stool back. The table being so narrow, the men were in danger of smelling each other's breath. 'Karl mentioned I tried to ring you several times, I believe? The receiver was either off the hook or your line is down.' He knew full well it was the latter of those options, since he had instructed Karl to shin up the telegraph pole for that purpose. That way, tapping the phone was unnecessary and no business with the press could be done using it.

'It was only to invite you here. Best we sort this out face to face.'

'Sort what out, exactly?' Peter was thinking but said nothing. He was waiting for clues. Something to pin his bluff on so he had a better chance of getting away with it. Reassurance of this had to come from how Rose chose to proceed. This sartorially dressed man was only the go-between, but his postscript to Ludlow's note suggested he had more than just the pulse of his boss's wishes.

'Well, here I am.' Peter agreed, implying he was all ears. 'Nice place you've got.' Over to you, Mr. Rose, his raised eyebrows invited.

'Let's get down to basics,' Rose suggested in response. 'Whatever your relationship with Sir Ludlow's wife, and whatever she might have told you and, *given* you, you are not being blamed.' He gave Tyler a meaningful stare before adding; 'Are you with me?'

Peter gave a brief nod.

'Good. You got my note,' said knowingly, not as a question. 'Well let me reiterate, in spite of what the press might be saying about you, Sir Ludlow considers you to be an innocent party in this particularly seedy business. His crazy wife's condition these past months has been deteriorating to the point of self-abuse and make believe. You probably got the gist of this yourself when talking to her. She was becoming more and more confused, convinced that her husband was trying to kill her. Did she tell you that? And so the threats started. She was going to tell the world this and that. Bring him down. Wreak havoc. All based on fanciful paranoia. Not a shred of truth in any of it that could be proved in a court of law. Just vicious threats from a sad junkie. Well, you must know yourself how mud sticks.' Rose saved himself from adding, since your clothes are covered with it, before getting at what he really meant. 'Have you seen what they're saying about *you* again in the papers today? Is it all true? I very much doubt it. The same with Sir Edward. Like you, he could do without any more disruption to his own life than there is already with what his stupid bitch of a wife has done.' Rose downed his gin and tonic in one go and poured himself another. 'Of course, the gutter press love all that stuff, and it's plain from the attention they're giving you that they're willing to chuck money in your direction to get their hands on any tittle-tattle you might be able to tell them. So, thank you again, for keeping your mouth shut. Wise move. As a warning, no apologies for having to point this out, you won't know what hit you should you try to get rich on her lies. Sir Edward has the best lawyers in the country. Mud-slinging impostors would be brought to justice. So, steer clear of that temptation for your own good. Sir Edward is more than ready to compensate you for your cooperation. He can do far better than the twenty grand his wife gave you to stir the shit. Oh, yes, we know about the money and the other 'stuff' she gave you in her paranoia before topping herself. And that's what we think she did. Topped herself. Couldn't face the music after whacking her nurse. The long and the short of it is, fighting you and the tabloids in the courts is the last thing Sir Edward wants, if that's where you were thinking of going with all her lies and hearsay. He would rather divert that expense in your direction in payment for your complete discretion. So, enough of this time-wasting bullshit.'

The 'other stuff'? Rose must mean the tape? Did they think he had the disc, too? Playing the tape in court, clever lawyers might claim it was hearsay from a troubled mind. Words spouted under duress, with absolutely no proof or substance. But it could open up a can of worms if investigated properly; be very uncomfortable for Ludlow at least. Abalone alone might be enough if the authorities could get into it. The floppy disc was different. If it had 'stuff' on it, that wouldn't be hearsay. That's what was causing Ludlow's grief. That's why Peter was here.

They obviously thought he had been the one talking to Stephanie on the tape, and it must stay that way. Keep the Salvation Army out of all this, which is what the major herself appeared to want. Having told Stephanie about the child being alive and well, it seemed that was enough. She wasn't happy about taking things further.

But Peter was guessing that was not what Stephanie would settle for. She wanted something done to help her child. What mother wouldn't? Her despair on the tape said it all.

Peter was trying to add things up. Ludlow knew nothing of Stephanie's child, thinking she had 'paid' Tyler 22 grand to safeguard the incriminating tape and illusive disc in case anything should happen to her. Now it *had*, big time indeed, Ludlow thought Peter was about to spill the beans by running to the police or worse, the press. For his silence, Ludlow was promising to offer him 'compensation' for his 'losses' far in excess of anything the press would pay out. This could be thousands!

'I'll own up,' Peter said, hoping to sound cocky, thinking that was the way to go. 'I don't particularly like Ludlow, in case you hadn't realised it. Ask anyone in Marlsbury if you've got any doubts – or the police, for that matter.' He thought he would slip that in for what it was worth. 'A couple of years ago, nothing would have given me more pleasure than to see Ludlow ruined. You probably remember that period? You were always at his side. Funnily enough, at that time I thought you were no more than a bodyguard.' Without knowing it, Tyler had stolen Rose's habit of punctuating his words by flexing his shoulder muscles. Rose seemed to stiffen in recognition. 'Now I can see you are much more than that.' This was a deliberate sop. An effort to suggest he had no axe to grind with Rose himself. 'I am also a different person to how you might have seen me back then. I have softened a touch since those days. That is not to say I'm now your boss's number one fan. To be more specific, I still think he's a bit of a prick. He has things to answer for. A knighthood for fuck's sake. How much did his charity have to pay to get him that, I wonder?' The mention of charity seemed to hit a note with Rose.

'Anyway,' Tyler continued. 'Disliking the man is one thing, but do I have any particular allegiance to his wife? Not particularly. Tell him that. Why she singled me out to help her I'll never know. Look where it's got me. All my stuff up in smoke,' he was about to mention losing the 22 grand but stopped himself for some reason. Did Rose need to know just yet?

'So be it. My workshop's gone,' Peter continued, 'but not certain stuff as you call it. But now, since Stephanie is also gone, I have no real interest in any pointless crusades. That wouldn't get me anywhere, would it? Especially since, as unlikely as it might seem, out of the fire, as it were, I find myself sitting here on the threshold of far greater riches than the 22 grand Stephanie gave me to comply with her wishes of exposing to the world what a devious bastard her husband is.'

Rose shook his head irritably but said nothing. He had been wondering when Tyler would mention the money. Had he guessed Rose had rescued it and gone on to set fire to the place himself? It seemed not.

Tyler's confidence was irking Rose. He expanded his chest like a frog's throat, fighting an instinct to grab Tyler by *his*. But grin and bear it he must. No violence was his instruction, however much he felt the threat of it would be a more fruitful path to silencing this scruffy piece of shit before him.

'What it boils down to, if I've got this right,' Peter went on, hopefully in a reasonable manner, 'is that you have invited me here to discuss to what lengths the Ludlow Group might be willing to go to 'invest' in my future, and as well, I suppose, in my trust? Are we on the same page?' Reference to the 'Group' was a canny move, the way Peter was thinking. Investment was at the forefront of his mind as much as compensation for his workshop. He could sense Gwen egging him on.

'How much?' Rose asked bluntly, trying to cut through the waffle, anxious to get an idea of what this smug parasite thought his trust was worth.

'I am not stupid,' Peter declared. 'It's completely by chance that I'm sitting here in possession of something Steph gave me the 22 grand to keep in a safe place until needed.' He thought using the familiar 'Steph' might lend weight to the lie. 'Stuff that would clearly mean big trouble for her husband.' No reaction from Rose. 'Well, the bad news for me is that the 22 grand she gave me went up in smoke with the rest of my belongings. The bad news for Ludlow, and what turns out to be very good news for me, is that the tape and disc did not. They were put in much safer places. A case of not keeping all my eggs in one basket.'

Rose had been waiting for Tyler to open up about the money being burned. As suspected, the tape and disc must have been hidden elsewhere.

'How much?' Rose snapped again, all but choking on his drink in his impatience. 'You must have a figure in your mind to cover compensation for your shack of a workshop and for handing back everything the bitch gave you?'

Peter was feeling slightly more at ease with how things were going. He took a sip of tonic water then leaned on the narrow table with one elbow facing out into the room to avoid direct eye contact with Rose.

'The way I see it,' he said, 'that dosh, all 22 grand of it, was legally mine until it went up in smoke. Paid in advance for services to be rendered. Now, I could continue to render those services out of duty to my client, even though she is now sadly deceased. But I would get nothing but trouble if I did that, you seem to be telling me. Now, I could easily fail to render those services since I am in no danger of any come-back for my negligence. This decision depends upon the extent of the investment, compensation, whatever you want to call it, Ludlow is prepared to come up with. I feel 22 grand is a mere starting point before the cost of replacing my workshop is taken into account. Then, if Sir Edward Ludlow were to be feeling particularly concerned about my well-being for all the stress this business continues to cause me, further consideration would be thankfully received. But I must be honest and tell you this straight out, he gets nothing back accept my word and my trust.'

'OK,' Rose snapped, after downing the rest of his drink without mishap. 'Let's stop all the crap. Whether the position you find yourself in is by chance or design, it's in nobody's interest, least of all yours, to have Stephanie Star's bullshit hit the headlines. Now, this is me speaking, not Ludlow. That bitch of his had completely lost it. She was out of her mind. All sense of reality gone. Giving you 20 odd grand with no guarantees must have told you she was off her fucking head, right? Fucking crazy. You know it. Threatening to ruin the man who had pulled her out of the gutter and made her what she was, or *had* been. Why? She probably didn't have a clue herself. She was off her fucking rocker. Sick. And nasty with it.'

Tyler felt his deceit was gaining firmer ground. Rose's stance was telling him there were probably even more skeletons in Ludlow's cupboard than Stephnie had garbled to the major. But there was already plenty to go on.

Rose must have been referring to just that when he continued.

'Look, does Ludlow want any of this dragged through the papers and courts?' Rose argued. 'Of course, he fucking doesn't. Does he want to have his business affairs and charity accounts put through the ringer to the delight of his competitors and the horror of his investors? Something that could take years to fight in court and could write millions off his holdings? What do you think? All thanks to a junkie wife who didn't know her arse from her elbow. Again, of course he fucking doesn't. No business wants that sort of scrutiny. Legit or not!'

Rose had coloured up. But not quite as much as Gwen did when agitated.

'No? Well let me say this again to be sure you're hearing *me* straight,' Rose continued steely eyed. 'If you ever think of going anywhere with her threats of blackmail, forget it. Because you will be a dead man if you do. I'll see to that. That's a promise, not an instruction from above. This comes from me. And I'm not pissing around. So, bear that in fucking mind.'

The three large gin and tonics were doing the talking. The aggression was genuine, but it quickly subsided as Rose went on like a bank manager setting up a loan.

'Whatever you want for this trust of yours, you'll get. Trust *me*. That's *his* insurance, and likewise, *yours*. Break that trust and you're gone. Be wise, which is what I think you already know is the way to go. But don't fuck around and don't be too greedy, understand? So where are we in this little discussion?'

Out of the blue, Peter surprised himself wishing Gwen was by his side. She wouldn't hold back. She'd have a better idea of how to negotiate this situation. He was more circumspect himself, suddenly nervous. Was this really happening? It was beginning to sink in that it was.

This would be a serious turning point in his life if he could carry it off, and he seemed to be getting away with it. So, perhaps it wasn't so strange he was feeling nervous. But there would soon be no turning back. It would be too late to say: 'Sorry, Victor, old son. It was all a big bluff to wind you up.' That would not go down well at all.

'You ask me how much?' Tyler eventually spoke. 'I don't bloody know how much, do I? I don't know how much it would take to rebuild my workshop. I don't know the worth of the mental stress I've been put through. And most of all, I don't know exactly how much he wants Stephanie's 'lies' kept from the police.' He thought he'd mention police instead of the press, although it amounted to the same point he was making.

Tyler had a pretty good idea what he wanted, but he might get more if he hedged his bets.

203

'Let me tell you how I see it,' he continued in this vein. 'Once a 'settlement' is agreed beyond doubt, the tape and disc will never see the light of day as long as I live to a ripe old age and die of natural causes.'

'OK. You get the 22 grand up front. No questions asked. It's yours.' If Tyler was to play ball, it was an easy starting point. Rose had carte blanche from his boss to tie Tyler up for as much as was necessary. But from his own perspective, Rose would prefer to settle as little as possible on the creep. 'Any way you want it: cash, cheque, overseas account, you name it. Next, your workshop. Whatever it costs to rebuild it. Again, in any way that suits you. Both gimme's. Now, your turn. You've got to help me. This stress and hardship bollocks you talk about. Where are we at with that?'

Peter was trying to sense the limits Ludlow had set Rose. It was already beyond anything he had anticipated. But more was in the offing. He could tell.

'Well,' he said, frowning in the hope of showing no sense of being happy with the way things were going. 'I've been out of work for two years or more, as I'm sure you know. Ever since Ludlow moved the factory to Manchester and started building boxes on the old site to make himself richer. There are no jobs for the likes of me around here, so the stress and hardship 'bollocks' I've been caused might be eased if I could start my own business. Work for myself. That's why I mention investment. Proper investment. If I suddenly had large sums of cash appearing, people would be asking where it had come from, and why. If I start a company with investment from Ludlow, I'm sure it can be all done above board as a sort of venture-capital deal, if that's what you call it? That way it wouldn't put a dent in his personal wallet, either. It would be a mere pinprick of a tax loss for whichever one of the Ludlow Group he wanted to use. With the right amount behind me, I promise you my business wouldn't fail. It might even end up making Ludlow that much richer!' Gwen would be proud of him for that suggestion.

Rose was not expecting a proposition like this. His own company indeed. This scruffy git wasn't short of grand designs.

'What sort of business are we talking about?'

Tyler wasn't going to tell Rose the ins and outs of his Initiative. Ludlow was the only person for that.

'Model aircraft,' was all he was prepared to admit right now.

Victor Rose thought he was hearing things.

'Come again?' he said.

'Model aircraft. Proper fliers.'

Is this guy for real? Rose asked himself. Here he was, threatening to pull the trap door from under Ludlow and his millions, and all he wanted in life was the chance to make toy airplanes! He couldn't credit it. The man was a fucking yo-yo!

Did Victor have good news for his boss, or what?

Chapter Twenty Two

Sharon was curled up beneath her duvet on the settee in the living room just stirring from her dreams. The last one she had been enjoying, she thought, but it was slipping away. She was struggling to hang onto it. She turned over and stretched her legs trying to bring it back. No use. It had evaporated. She was now half awake. Why was it always easier to remember bad dreams, she was wondering? Or was it just her?

With the dream gone, she started to think about the day ahead. It was Tuesday. No Tony's. A day off, which pleased her. No doubt it would please Kim, too. She hadn't been feeling all that well of late. On Sunday, Tony had spotted her nose running and told her to go home early to bed with a Beecham's powder. She had the beginnings of a cold. Now it was in full flow.

As was their arrangement, the first to get home after the day got the proper bed. Kim had grabbed it and she was still in it. On Monday, Sharon had taken bowls of Kim's favourite soup into her, cream of tomato with crusts of toast floating in it. Three times! That was all she wanted; all she could keep down. Tonight, Sharon thought she might try her with something more solid, like rock salmon and chips with a gherkin. They both liked that.

Sharon was going to have another day to herself, so how to make the most of it? She had been thinking about getting a small tattoo on the back of her neck, but it was perhaps better to have Kim with her for that in case she fainted or something. The other thing she had been toying with was getting more ear piercings done on her left ear. She only had the conventional one hole in that ear compared to seven on the right. Although she quite liked the imbalance, it would make a nice change to be able to swap it around a bit.

These thoughts of the day were milling around idly beneath her eyelids when a salvo of sneezes erupted from the bedroom followed by a sharp curse. 'Shit!' Then came a more studied groan of concern: 'Oh, shit!'

'Gawd!' Sharon muttered to herself. 'What's she done now?'

She swung her feet off the settee still clinging to the duvet. She had no idea what time it was. The goth drapes over the window did their job fit for the blitz blackout!

'What's up, Burly? You've prob'ly woke the whole house with ya yelling.' Sharon had no need to yell herself. Kim was barely three feet away on the other side of the plasterboard wall. There had been no danger of waking other people. It was past noon. The only people still likely to be in were the Fenshaws, two floors down on the other side of the entrance hall. And they were probably deaf judging by the sound level they always had their tele turned up.

They were a nice old couple, though. Always asking how Sharon and Kim were when they bumped into each other. And never complaining about them when they came crashing in sometimes in the middle of the night. That's when being deaf would come in handy.

Sharon got to her feet and pulled back the drape a touch from the window to let some light in, wrapping the duvet around her naked body. Just her head and feet were showing. There was a dustbin lid sized clock on the wall. It was getting on for half twelve.

She could hear Kim shuffling about in the compact bedroom muttering 'shit' to herself every five seconds. Sharon thought she might have pissed in the bed or something by the way she was pulling it about.

'Is it safe to come in?' she asked sarcastically, as if suggesting Kim might have a bloke in there. 'You haven't been breaking the rules, have you?'

'Ha, fucking, ha!' came the response. The next moment, the bedroom door opened, and a bundled-up bedding sheet came flying out. 'I've just come on with a vengeance! It's all over the mattress as well. I've been trying to turn it over.' That would explain the huffing and cussing.

The room was like a crime scene with blood in evidence and clothes strewn everywhere.

'Jeez, Kim,' Sharon said, sarcasm gone. 'Get yourself in the shower. Soak the sheet while you're in it to get the worst of it out. I'll go to the launderette later with it. I'll make up a full load and have a quick go at the mattress before turning it over.' Kim was making puffing sounds of compliance. Sharon would sort it. You could rely on that. 'That was a bit sudden, wasn't it?' Sharon asked. 'You weren't due, were you? You usually send me smoke signals.'

'No warning. No guts ache. That's something at least. Sore throat, though. Bit of a headache.'

'You're run down. 'Spect I'll be getting it next. Anyway, get yourself cleaned up. I'll do a bit of shopping while I'm at the launderette. Whatcha fancy eating later? Don't say tomato soup again. I could get some fish and chips. How's that sound?'

'Don't know. A gherkin, maybe.'

'Well, that's a start. I'll give Tony a ring and tell him you won't be in Thursday.'

'He's probably already guessed that, sending me home Sunday.'

'I'll tell him, anyway. Might take the opportunity to give him a heads-up about what Jimbo seems to be playing at.'

'You'll get yerself into trouble, Phoney. Jimbo'll give you hell if he finds out you grassed on him!'

'I don't give a toss. Jimbo's at my throat enough as it is.'

Kim waddled to the shower room while Sharon put the kitchen light on and set about making some tea. A few more 'shits!' were heard above the sound of the electric kettle boiling. 'Daft fucker,' Sharon muttered, smiling to herself.

Ten minutes later, the pair sat at either end of the settee with their feet up, hands wrapped around mugs of tea. Sharon had turned the mattress over, ensuring the wet patch was covered with a towel underneath, then tucked a clean sheet in around it ready for action. Filling the laundry bag with the dirty clothes scattered about the room had to wait until Kim had got herself back into bed.

'I'll bring some Lemsip back. I know you like that. You even guzzle it down when you haven't got a bloody cold, ya daft fucker. You wanna be careful you don't o'd on it!'

'Put a bit of gin in it and I might!'

Conveniently, the launderette had a payphone. Sharon rang Tony to tell him about Kim's condition. Her complaint about Jimbo hassling the girls to work for him on the days Tony's Ring was closed fell on fairly deaf ears. As long as it didn't interfere with the running of the club, Tony had no reason to step in.

'Never known you to hold back, Sharon. Just tell Jimbo you're not interested.'

It wasn't that easy with Jimbo.

Ludlow had felt a wave of relief flow through him when Victor Rose relayed the essence of his meeting with Peter Tyler. It sounded like immediate disaster had been diverted. Perhaps life as he knew it was not about to collapse.

The errors he had made along that road, some serious and now regrettable, were still reprehensible as the law would see it, even though some of them belonged to his earlier years. The well-used side-stepping tax evasion practices favoured by the rich and famous that sent the Chancellor of the Exchequer chasing shadowy figures through a catacomb of blind alleys was not his main concern. He was well ahead of the game in the Teflon world of offshore banking and shell companies. It was a different case with Ludlow's venture into pharmaceuticals. Despite the enterprise being short-lived during the hey-days of his Stephanie Star creation, should the arteries of corruption burst and be exposed to light, the discovery of illicit border transportation and money laundering would stick like proverbial shit to a SODA disaster-relief blanket. That would be the end of Ludlow's charmed life.

With this possible eventuality pounding in his chest, Ludlow found respite with the prospect of Rose managing to rein Tyler in. Their meeting had been recorded in its entirety, so nothing would be missed.

'One way or another, Stephanie seems to have enlisted Tyler to do her dirty work for her.' Rose expounded. 'Now she's dead, he's got greedy. But not too greedy by the sounds of it, with his toy airplanes. Should be easy to tie him up legally on some deal or other.' Rose would love to tie Tyler up and throw him into the North Sea with a weight attached if it was down to him. 'He's chomping at the bit to get his teeth into your wallet. But not so keen to hand over the tape and disc.'

'First things first, Victor. If he wants my wallet to keep his mouth shut, I'll stuff it in as far as it'll go! We can worry about the disc and the tape in due course.' Ludlow was beginning to see an end to the uncertainties. Money was no object. 'Keep humouring him. Keep telling

209

him I'll make him a rich man any way he wants. But first I need to see him to establish how this is to happen. If I'm the only person he'll talk to about this, tell him he'll have to come out here to Africa. I'm staying put until we can clear this up. So, make him feel important. Lay some cash on him up front. Spoil him. Tell him, if he plays ball, he can move his stuff into one of the studios at Compton Stud since his workshop's gone

and work from there. Move in. Stay there, if he wants. Tell him he can have one of the executive suites. Show him around. And when you've finished tying up all the loose ends, get him on a plane. First Class. Keep buttering him up. Convince him I'm serious about this, but I need to discuss things face to face if he's to become one of the family.'

That prospect gave Victor Rose palpitations.

It would be an unpleasant few weeks for Rose sitting in for his boss's absence. 'Sir Edward will not allow his private grief to interrupt S.O.D.A.'s charity program' was the official line on Ludlow's absence. Unofficially, he was safely holed up with Jenny Grant on the shores of Lake Naivasha, suffering not grief at the loss of his wife, but a festering anxiety of what she had left in her wake.

The tabloids had slowly eased up on sensational stories about the junkie life of Stephanie Star, one-time beauty queen, supermodel, Lady Ludlow for just one day. Unverifiable stories suggesting deviant sexual activities in her later years abounded for a while that even had Victor Rose wondering. Ludlow was more interested in learning what the inside pages of the broadsheets were saying. The motives behind sudden violent up and down market moves of companies linked to the Ludlow Group were being questioned. Why should the criminal behaviour of the CEO's wife cause such turmoil? The rumours and leaks surrounding the massive East African Irrigation Project were also muddying the market waters. The week had seen an unforeseeable climb in the value of Wilson-Hughes share prices, and then, overnight, it was almost Black Monday again for its investors when it transpired that a Dutch company had won the huge irrigation contract.

Just before that news broke, for those who could put two and two together but couldn't quite show it made four, it seemed an unusual amount of market movement had been in evidence to the benefit of certain offshore shell companies that couldn't be investigated because they suddenly ceased to exist.

Smoke was coming from computer terminals in the city with so many fluctuations.

An inquiry was inevitable but short-lived. Nothing untoward could be hung at Wilson-Hughes' door, although, losing investors thought they could smell something very shitty on its doormat.

'We're clean,' Gerald Silver reported to Ludlow. 'With a little help from our friends in the press. The speculation worked a treat for us. Just as well we held back and didn't cut and run completely too soon. When all's said and done, we haven't come through this too badly.'

'I'm thankful you stifled my panic,' Ludlow admitted. 'What would I do without you, Gerald?'

'That's what makes my garden grow, Edward,' Silver pointed out. And he was not only talking about the substantial fees that were part of his parcel. With his finger on the pulse of all Ludlow holdings, his personal portfolio expanded whichever way the market moved.

An attempt had been made to keep the time and location of Stephanie Star's cremation a secret. But in the world of 'payola', news got out. Journalists outnumbered all other attendees, although they were kept away from the short service itself. Stephanie had no direct family, and few friends left who wished to 'see her off' in the glare of publicity. Just Rose, and Karl on his final duty as the supermodel's long-serving bodyguard of earlier years. That duty having now been passed further up the minder chain to the holy Lord himself. There were no major 'celebrities' of great interest to the photographers and cameramen, most of whom had been sent explicitly in the hope that Ludlow himself might have slipped back into the country to be present. Even Simon Dickson and his BBC film crew had turned up with a view to talking him into continuing the postponed documentary. But it was not to be.

The funeral service was simple and brief. Within three hours of the curtains closing on Stephanie's coffin, Rose was at Heathrow Airport about to face his next task, which he saw as no less irksome than the one he had just overseen: sitting alongside Tyler for the long flight to Nairobi.

Ironically, as baggage was going into the hold of their jumbo, a coffin rather less ornate than Stephanie Star's was being carefully loaded into a freight plane at another part of the airport en route to Zurich.

It departed with no great ceremony to be collected by whomsoever had loved Tilda Bahnlich.

With the slayer and slain dispatched in a seemly manner to meet their makers, there had been nothing to delay Sir Edward Ludlow's most faithful, if sometimes uncivil, servant from leaving the dust to settle over the satellite dishes of Compton Stud now closure had been reached.

Out of respect for his late wife's victim, so the story went, and the tragic stain left hanging over the property, the offices were closed for good. All business interests there were terminated. The staff released. The way Ludlow had been thinking, he might never see *England* again, let alone Compton Stud. The bulk of his empire might have been salvaged, but his credibility in Paternoster Square was far from stable as yet, Third World Saint or not.

The city of London perhaps did not breed paragons of virtue, but certain codes of conduct were encouraged by those who jobbed there. Sympathetic observers were willing to believe Sir Edward's judgement had been understandably clouded by the heinous crime committed by his wife before her sudden demise. With all that coming on the very day he had been knighted, his mind must have been in utter turmoil. It was easy to see how his optimism for sealing the irrigation deal had got out of hand amid all the speculation surrounding him and it.

It was argued that the press, particularly the British, must at least share some of the responsibility for getting the wrong end of the stick and fanning the flames of optimism suggesting Wilson-Hughes' Holdings were about to clinch the deal.

The cynics, of which there were many, especially those speculators who had been caught out by such an unforeseen turnaround after days of exceptional gains, considered Ludlow's reasons for not returning to the UK to be more transparent than the lifts at Lloyds. But not even the most misanthropic of them came close to the real truth behind his panic sell-off. It had nothing to do with the irrigation project.

Nevertheless, his credibility had been severely wounded. Thus far the bleeding seemed to be under control. The next step being to ensure gangrene did not set in, hence the need for direct consultation with Peter Tyler.

Initially, Peter had wondered whether he should agree to travel halfway round the world to meet Ludlow. It would take him out of his comfort zone and be certain to mean another cross examination. But having come this far, he had to show confidence. Gwen had sealed it.

'Bloody hell, Peter!' she had yelled, 'You've made it! He wouldn't offer you a place to work at the Stud if he wasn't serious! Don't forget I've got shares!' Her encouragement wouldn't stop. 'You are going, aren't you?'

He toyed with her.

'Going where?'

'To see Ludlow, pillock!' she blurted. 'In Africa. That posh bloke Rose has been round since you were last here. I thought he had come to see you, but no, it was *me* he wanted to talk to. Very polite, he was. Knew my name, and all. He asked me if I wouldn't mind moving in to look after your mum while you were away with Sir bloody Ludlow! 'Cept he didn't say *bloody*. You tell me nothing, do you, Peter *bloody* Tyler? So, I won't tell you how much he offered me for my troubles. You can stay away as long as you like!'

Peter had mentioned the situation with his mother to Rose, partly to bide his time before making up his mind about agreeing to go. He didn't want to appear over keen. But his mother's care had to be addressed before he could ever think of going. He hadn't expected Rose to jump in and sort it out directly with Gwen. So, he couldn't use that excuse for not agreeing to go. His mother would be in safe hands. Gwen herself had got the whip out to see him gone, because she would be quids in!

'You've got lift off, Peter. Don't miss the boat!' she chirped, mixing up the metaphors. She was chuckling spontaneously. 'It's going to get everyone in Marlsbury guessing when this news gets out. They'll be stumped! You and Ludlow! You'll be on the front pages again. I can't wait! People won't know what to make of it!'

Peter had never known her to be so excited. Amazingly, her cheeks hadn't turned red.

'I don't care what they make of it,' Peter responded, perhaps without complete candour. 'No doubt Old Pikey'll be having a field-day dreaming something up to entertain the tabloids again.'

Gwen went on happily. 'The posh bloke also said double-glazing and damp-proofing was going to be done before too long and wanted a look around to get an idea of what it might cost. Took his time about it, too. Seemed quite interested in your Initiative. Or, should I say, *our* Initiative? And don't you forget it!'

Tyler wouldn't mind betting Rose was taking his time sniffing around for something else he would have found a lot more interesting. Once again it was just as well he had hidden the tape at Hollom's Attic.

Gwen was in a very chirpy mood. Rose must have offered her way over the odds.

'Mind you,' she said, hoping to wind him up a bit more seriously. 'I'd still like to know what you had stuffed down your pants New Year's Day. I never found any dirty magazines in the house.'

'Nosy cow!' he snapped, hiding his good humour. 'It was a Dutch porno mag. That's why I hid it. I didn't want it giving you any wrong ideas about coming on to me again!'

Gwen pulled a face and reddened up at the thought.

The furthest afield Peter Tyler had ever flown was Southern Spain for his holidays, packaged at school holiday peak-times on a bucket-shop charter flight. This sudden long flight to Kenya seated in first class was a new and unexpected experience for him, not to say a guilty indulgence. Who could have believed it? Such luxury! Beautiful air hostesses running around after you as if you were royalty. He could take plenty of this treatment! This was his breakthrough.

As long as he could keep on his toes.

Throughout the journey, Victor Rose was touchy. The reason was quite conspicuous. Whereas he, himself, was dressed immaculately with his perennial sense of occasion, like a master of ceremonies at a prize fight, Peter Tyler was slumped in his baggy tracksuit looking like a soiled towel thrown into the ring.

Rose sat bolt upright like a sartorial punch-bag, elbows pulled in as if to dodge an incoming blow, even though there was first class space between them. What pissed him off even more was Tyler's constant aggravating smile. How he would love to wipe that off the prick's face. The day would come, he promised himself. He had this geek of a smart-arse well sussed.

When the nose-wheel touched down with a judder as the jumbo landed at Nairobi Airport, a certain foreboding shook Tyler. Ludlow was a worried man because Stephanie Star had been giving him the runaround with threats of who knew what? Now that Peter had picked up the baton, he had to be sure he could keep on track. One thing *was* clear. He didn't trust Rose one bit. Something irked Tyler about him. He didn't want Rose anywhere near them when it came to his confrontation with Ludlow.

Chapter Twenty Three

'Peter!' Sir Edward Ludlow pronounced from the verandah of his colonial hideaway arms outstretched as if Tyler was a long-lost son. The dust created by the adventurous way Ernest McKintosh had locked wheels to bring the Land Cruiser to a halt still hung in the still air as Tyler and Rose approached the atmospheric hunting lodge.

Peter nodded guardedly in response to Ludlow's greeting, but said nothing, not ready to reciprocate the camaraderie just yet with the history between them. The man must have mistrusted Peter as much as Peter mistrusted him. It was too early for any buddy-buddy stuff. He needed a chance to feel his way and was too tired to make the effort right now.

A table had been laid for an *al fresco* breakfast or lunch. Tyler didn't know which. His body clock was all over the place. But there was an extravagance of fruit and flowers in the most perfect of settings overlooking a lake that expanded for miles to the foot of distant mountains shimmering in the haze. 'Bizarre,' Peter was thinking. 'One minute, Marlsbury, the next *this!*' It was hard to get his head round it.

'You don't mind my calling you Peter, I hope?' Ludlow asked, a certain intrigue in his manner. He was trying to gauge his guest's mood. Peter saw it as soft soap.

'Be my guest,' he replied flatly, no friendship conveyed, which, in consideration, was perhaps not the best strategy when all was said and done.

Now the man was in front of him, Peter felt he should be less circumspect. Ludlow already had the look of a defeated man. His face was gaunt, grey and blood-drained, defying the tan of weeks in the African sun. Peter felt boosted by this. But he wouldn't get carried away just yet. Let the other man do the talking to start the negotiations, show his hand first. Once again, Peter would wait.

'Good,' Ludlow said, drawing the word out as if uncertain about its sentiment. 'Well, let's get you settled in straight away.'

Sensing Tyler's negative attitude, Ludlow withdrew the hand he was in the act of offering to his guest and instead extended it to introduce a man who stood in attendance beaming, dressed in a loose one-piece cotton garment. 'This is Ashura. He will show you to your quarters and *assure*,' he stressed the word with a smile, 'your every need is catered for during your stay. When you are ship-shape, come back and join me. I'll show you around.'

Ashura gave Peter the briefest of bows before leading him through open double doors into a voluminous room, the walls of which were covered with a miscellany of horns, tusks and animal heads interspersed with well-stocked bookshelves, paintings and photographs of the 'hunt'. Armchairs and settees were scattered at one end around a free-standing open fireplace that had a manually operated spit, presumably for roasting the catch of the day. The fire wasn't lit, and Peter couldn't imagine it ever needing to be for any other purpose. It was exactly what you might expect to find in such a captivating lodge. A large dining table made from one chunky slice of what must have been a huge hardwood tree took up much of the other end of the room. Several candelabras were spread along it, new candles in place. Backup for power-loss? In the centre of the room stood a full-size snooker table, the baize of which looked well-used. From the cross beams of the arched timber ceiling, whirring fans hung, creating a warm breeze hardly matching the coolness of the shaded verandah outside. The room perfectly demonstrated the romance of life in the tropics.

Entering one of the many doors that led off from this master living room, Peter found himself in a small anti-room, where he supposed coats, boots, bags and the like were meant to be left. But it possibly also acted as a buffer to noise from the main room. Through another door was a comfortably laid out bedroom, a mosquito net currently gathered above the bed itself like an awning. On the far wall was a long window with a mesh grill as a barrier to these and other insects. One corner of the room was partitioned off with a wicker screen. Hidden behind this, for modesty's sake, was the ablution area; flushing toilet, sink and an ancient enamel bath. The room had its own hanging ceiling fan and a portable candle stick on a bedside table, safety matches alongside. Thin rugs covered parts of the wooden floor which helped muffle the creaking floorboards as he moved around. The place had a damp, musty smell suggesting it had not been occupied for a while.

The window looked to the back of the lodge where another building, less impressive than the lodge itself, sat among trees and bush, distant mountains again beyond. Servants' quarters, no doubt.

Peter helped himself to a bottle of water from an ice bucket which sat on a rickety bamboo table. He had been drinking bottled water the whole trip, but none tasted as good as this one. As he drank, he considered almost with disbelief how he had come to be standing here. It had happened so quickly. He was exhausted mentally and physically with all the travel, but to his amazement, any nerves he might have had about facing Ludlow seemed to have gone. Having been brought out here, first class, let it not be forgotten, self-confidence was growing in him. He looked up at the gently whirring ceiling fan, thinking: 'I could get used to this'.

His thin lips widened into a smile as he ran the taps behind the wicker screen. Deep rusty water spurted out before running clear after a few seconds. A sign declaring *Not for Drinking* was hardly necessary. He gave his face and hands a quick sluice then made his way back out to the verandah with a nod to Ashura, who quickly rose from a seat near the door and accompanied him.

Conversation stopped as Tyler appeared.

'Ah, good,' Ludlow said, rising from his seat. 'Thought you might have nodded off. It's been non-stop for you for the past couple of days. I appreciate it.'

Peter didn't think he'd been gone that long. In any case, he wasn't ready to nod off. Tired as he was, too much adrenaline still ran through him.

The pilot who had flown them from Nairobi had now joined the party on the verandah, as well as a woman who seemed familiar to Peter. Ludlow noticed the long look Tyler was giving her.

'Jenny Grant, my private secretary,' he explained, trying to sound jolly. 'My Girl Friday. Better keep yourself in her good books. I have to!' he joked, laughing nervously. Apart from Richard Whitton, the pilot, no one else joined in.

Brief nods were exchanged between Jenny and Peter, who was still trying to place her.

'Do you mind if we take a stroll?' Ludlow asked pleasantly, hand outstretched toward the verandah steps. 'Lunch isn't quite ready. It'll be closer to dinner, in fact. Sorry for the delay. You must be famished after all that rushing about. I know I always am. Grab a beer if you fancy one.'

Without prompting, Ashura took a Tusker from the nearby cooler, de-capped it and held it out to Peter, smiling broadly to display a full set of brilliant white teeth. Ashura looked in his fifties, but was nearer seventy, and nimble with it. Not an inch of spare flesh. 'Thank you, Ashura,' Peter said appreciatively. He didn't normally drink beer to quench his thirst, but his throat was already dry again and the beer was ice cold. Yes, this way of life could grow on him.

Ludlow politely urged his guest to lead the way down the steps.

'This will give you a chance to acclimatize,' he said after a few strides. 'It will also give us a chance to get acquainted. As we must.' They were sauntering. The slow pace suited the thought processes going on in their minds. Ludlow assumed they were reading from the same book. It was now a matter of deciding how to turn to the next page.

'Lovely place, this.' Ludlow expressed. 'I come here whenever I need to get away from it all,' he revealed. He had a few other equally exotic locations around the globe that provided even more seclusion. But no need to mention those. 'Let's face it. I've been lucky. Right from the start.' They had passed through a small copse of mango trees and were now standing by a swimming pool. A bare-chested attendant was scooping leaves from the surface. He shouted: 'Jambo, boss!' giving a wave.

'This is Peter, Jabali,' Ludlow shouted back. 'He's staying with us for a few days. Make sure he's safe.'

'Yes, boss,'

Ludlow turned to Peter. 'Take a dip whenever you like. And if you want a massage, Jabali's your man.'

They walked down the gentle slope toward the lake which was misleadingly further away than it looked from the lodge. They stopped in the shade of a tree whose foliage spread out conveniently like an open parasol.

'Let's face it,' Ludlow went on. 'I was spoilt rotten as a child. I think that's the right expression. Everything I wanted, handed to me on a plate.' Peter wasn't expecting any of this. Did the man think Peter was a shrink? He guessed there was a 'but' coming. And it did. 'But overindulgence can be a drawback in later life, when you have to face the real world.' Try deprivation, Peter was thinking. 'My acceptance to Oxford University promised a delay in preparing for the future,' Ludlow confessed happily. 'The laxity of imposed discipline beneath the dreaming spires did nothing but encourage my ingrained indulgence in everything hedonistic. Don't forget the 'sixties' were running rampant at that time.'

The track suit Peter was wearing was becoming more and more uncomfortable in the heat, so he relieved himself of the top. His intention had been to buy a light cotton outfit as soon as they had arrived in Nairobi, but he hadn't been told a private plane would be waiting to whisk them away immediately. Passport formalities had been arranged for them in a V.I.P. lounge so they had hardly left the tarmac before being on their way again. He was still uncomfortably warm with a vest and a long-sleeved shirt on. England had been sub-zero yesterday when they had left. The combination of sleeplessness, sun, and his subterfuge was making him feel quite loose between the ears. Sunstroke? He wasn't wearing a hat, but he had only been in direct sunlight for ten minutes. He dismissed thoughts that he might have been drugged. He looked at the beer label. Five per cent. Quite pokey. That must be it. On top of everything else, he was half-pissed.

They started walking again. Further down the slope to where mudflats of the lake began, a picnic table made from logs stood in the shade of another tree. Peter headed for this, ignoring Ludlow's inclination to lead him in a different direction. While his host looked on, he unceremoniously removed his shirt and vest as though preparing for a medical examination. Within seconds he began to feel better. There was a slight breeze coming off the lake.

'You'll soon get used to the heat,' Ludlow remarked, having to raise his voice a little. The tree was alive with twittering birds although there wasn't a feather in sight, just dozens of strange looking straw baskets hanging from it, bouncing about like balloons in a ballroom.

'Weaver bird nests,' Ludlow explained just as Peter saw flashes of orange and yellow darting about between them. 'You haven't chosen the best place for a quiet chat.' He smiled.

Peter didn't care about that. It was cooler in the shade. The sun was almost directly above them. Not surprising, since they were virtually sitting on the equator.

'I loved every moment I was up at Oxford.' Ludlow picked up where he had left off. 'I felt no privilege at being there. It was my right, was it not? That was my attitude. A lot of my contemporaries felt the same, I'm sure. Fairly soon after finding my feet, it was nothing but fun and freedom. My 'métier' fell into my lap. I soon knew what I wanted to do with my life, so I didn't waste time swatting for diplomas.'

They started strolling back to the lodge.

'I got into magazine publishing through university stuff. Then music. It was more fun than work. Vocations usually are, are they not? I went at it hammer and tongs, became a slave to making life at Oxford the real world, not merely a dress rehearsal. I wouldn't be where I am today without those years of wheeling and dealing at Oxford. I didn't so much *study* business there. I put in into practice, honing my talents in areas where failure did not necessarily mean loss of face but rather experience gained. There were few failures at Oxford. They came later and are at the root of what brings bring you here now. I took my eye off the ball and allowed myself to be led astray. But let's not go there.'

They had reached the steps to the verandah. Before going up, Ludlow said: 'I understand you have ambitions, Peter? You could be more like me than you think, just haven't had the leg-up that I had. Till now, perhaps?' Ludlow smiled. 'Let's talk more about that after lunch. OK with you?'

Was there any choice?

Peter felt Ludlow was trying to justify his position in life, at the same time as suggesting, in the words of ABBA, that it was a rich man's world. A world which Peter could become part of should he answer

Ludlow's SOS call. Peter must fight his inbuilt urge to dislike the man. Be civil, without giving the impression he was going to be a push over. That was the name of the game.

But suddenly, all Peter wanted to answer was the call to sleep. Excusing himself, he skipped lunch or dinner or whatever it was meant to be, settling for a bowl of fruit in his room, where the first thing he did was strip off and take a shower. A banana and a half later, he was flat out beneath the mosquito net in deep sleep, so exhausted, the stress and uncertainties of the past days blanked out.

He woke in a sweat. It took him a moment to remember where he was. It was a mosquito net covering him, not a shroud! Africa!

He had been asleep for hours. Dawn had long gone.

Peter had another quick shower, rusty water or not. He needed to freshen up and get his mind back on track.

Breakfast passed pleasantly enough. He was up late, so he ate alone on the verandah with Ashura, as promised, taking care of his every need.

With morning ablutions done, Ludlow took him on another stroll under a clear blue sky. Care-of Ashura, Peter was now wearing what looked like a full-length cotton night-shirt. Nothing under it.

'It will keep you cool, Mr. Peter,' Ashura had told him. 'Called *kanzu*. Look fine!'

'Thank you, Ashura. Much appreciated.'

Some soft leather flip-flops were also provided.

Once the manicured gardens of the lodge had been appreciated and left behind, Ludlow said: 'I fear there's been too much bad blood between us, Peter. I accept the Marlsbury pumps closure was at the root of it, but I feel you were a little unreasonable. You didn't see the bigger picture. If you'll excuse me saying, you were perhaps too busy waving banners at the time to have noticed my father's pump business was becoming worn out. A great, profitable family business in the years after the war, but running out of steam by the time I took over. My father had paid little attention to the advance of technology. Perhaps you don't know it, but there was a saying that went: 'A job at Marlsbury Pumps is a job for life'. Well, it had been for a lot of the workforce who'd been with the company since the very beginning. Most were ready for retirement and, I might say, very happy with the generous compensation paid. Most had also taken out the company pension plan, which set them up very well for their later years. Moving the business to an area of unusually high unemployment at the time, I was able to take on the Japanese at their own game by building from scratch, incorporating all the new technology. No complaints from those who relocated, I can assure you. I wish you had considered moving up there with us. You would have been a bright young addition to the fold with ideas of your own, no doubt, about how the company could further embrace the digital age. As I remember, you were top of the class after serving your apprenticeship. I hope you realise that your daily release studies came at no little expense to the company. It's probably too much to say that you *owed* the company to relocate with us. But what is done is done.

'I do appreciate your dilemma at the time. You had lost your father at an early age, I believe, and had a handicapped mother to care for. Yes, I am quite familiar with your CV. Not a happy situation. But you must have realised you were fighting a losing battle organizing all those demonstrations against closure. What can I say? I'm sorry it hit you so hard. I'm just happy your bitterness has not clouded your reason enough to stop you coming out here to give me the opportunity to hopefully put things right between us.'

Hearing all this as the pair strolled towards the beautiful vista of Lake Naivasha made Peter feel weird; strangely detached. He had moved on. All that bickering with demonstrations was more than two years ago. And yes, it had been a losing battle. But the weight of recent circumstances bringing him out here *had* changed things. Perhaps even more than Ludlow himself thought. It was a totally different landscape now, and his ploy of letting his host lead the way seemed to be working.

'Now, about your business with my dear wife,' Ludlow continued, not totally free of sarcasm. 'I suppose you realise I'm going to expect a little more from you than just your silence before *real* trust between us can be achieved?'

Ludlow wondered if Tyler had heard him. It seemed he might be talking to a brick wall. His darling wife had made a very strange choice of accomplice, he was thinking. But it made sense, he supposed, to pick someone as disgruntled as the cyclist who had led the protests?

Peter had been thinking of Ludlow's words: 'put things right between *us*'. He finally spoke.

'I came here at your behest because we're in a situation that needs sorting out, a situation that I did not personally create, nor, quite honestly, wished to be in. There's no need to go over all that Marlsbury pump closure stuff again. It shouldn't be too hard to work out why your wife chose me to twist the knife into you. She was plainly worried something might happen to her. She was terrified of you, you must have known that. But as I've told your man Rose, and as I suspect he has relayed to you, I am not stupid. I've got no real allegiance to your wife. Your *late* wife, I should say. And just to put your mind at rest, I hadn't been fucking her, if that's what you've been thinking. Ours was a purely platonic relationship. But what she thought about you was not so *pure*. Acidic, I would have said.'

Ludlow nodded heavily. At last Tyler was talking.

They were now almost at the edge of the lake, which caused a flock of wading flamingos to up and away. 'Let me remind you,' Peter went on, 'So far, I have made absolutely no demands on you. OK, I might have come round to doing so in due course, but you've preempted that by bringing me out here. Rose told me you were ready to *generously* out-bid any offers I've had coming in from the press as well as reimburse the money your wife gave me that went up in smoke. She really had it in for you, didn't she?' Ludlow nodded in acceptance. 'So here we are now to talk about the *generous* offer you had in mind to ensure the situation is well and *truly* sorted.' Ludlow was still nodding. 'Well, I can promise you I'm not expecting anything close to what your wife must be worth, although she didn't know exactly what that figure was because you had craftily frozen her accounts. And that truly *had* pissed her off. Abalone came high on that list of her complaints I suppose you know?'

Ludlow was not too amazed Stephanie had pulled Abalone out of her memory. It was where most of her wealth had been stowed before several smart moves had sent it in different directions.

'Let's face it,' Peter thought it was worth repeating, 'you don't trust me, and surprise, surprise, I don't trust you. On that front, I guess you could say we're in total agreement. So, if we work on that assumption, we can move ahead.' Peter inhaled a deep warm breath. 'As I guess you suspect, your wife shared more than the existence of Abalone with me. All that stuff is in a safe place, I can reassure you. More than safe. Belt and braces. Rose tells me if I don't play ball, I'll be a dead man. But then so would you be, to all intents and purposes. I guess you suspect that. So, let's be frank about this. We will have to rely on trust if we are both to lead as long and happy lives as our consciences permit. Don't you agree?'

Ludlow nodded again. This was progress. Next, how to manipulate a failsafe means of guaranteeing Tyler's trust? Conscience would have nothing to do with it.

Chapter Twenty Four

The hours of deep sleep Peter managed to enjoy under the mosquito net over the next few days did more than revitalise him. They introduced a new spark of optimism in him. Gwen was right. This really could be his lift off if he could keep an equal head and not be too greedy.

Ludlow had been concentrating his thoughts on Tyler's 'belt and braces' remark. A first reference to the floppy disc?

They had breakfasted and now sat alone on the verandah.

'Peter, I am truly grateful you decided this was the way to go. Of agreeing to come out here, not as a holiday freebee, but as an opportunity to fulfil your life's dreams rather than staying put and overseeing the demise of mine. The promise of riches is a strong motivation. You are only human, Peter, I'm very glad to say.' As if to celebrate that sentiment, Ludlow rang an ornately etched glass bell and within seconds Ashura was in attendance with a tray of drinks.

Both men declined alcohol for the sake of clear heads more than time of day. The host had Planter's Punch, his guest fresh lime juice and soda, no sugar. They clinked glasses. The atmosphere was relaxed.

What the multi-millionaire said next changed it for Peter. He nearly choked on his drink but managed to disguise the shock by pretending he'd swallowed a lump of ice. 'You probably didn't know that my late and dearly departed wife used to refer to you as her 'major' whenever she wanted to taunt me. I sometimes call my people 'lieutenants', you see. It was her little way of ridiculing my style. But perhaps 'major' is perhaps not a bad rank for you to have now you're to be part of the team?'

Peter's fake coughing gave him time to gather his thoughts. 'You can call me whatever you want, but I'm not sure about being part of a *team*,' he replied, gathering his composure. 'I see myself more as a one-man-band. Independent.'

'You can be part of a team without losing your independence.

'Don't see how.'

It was no sense arguing, thought Ludlow. Tyler was going to be attached to a team whether he realised it or not, with a virtual collar around his neck.

They fell silent for a few minutes. What if the real major *did* suddenly come out of the woodwork? Peter was thinking. He would have to be ready for that. Deny knowledge or have a believable answer.

Ludlow's own thoughts were still with the proposed virtual collar. He was playing with certain ideas of how tight it should be.

Peter moved to a swinging couch suspended from large iron hooks on the ceiling of the verandah. He pushed himself gently back and forth without taking his feet from the floor. This not only created movement in the air around him, but also gave his neglected leg muscles the impression they were being exercised. The movement was quite silent apart from a click from the hooks above.

Inside the house, the overhead fans were droning away. The whole place felt empty but for the two of them and Ashura, who sat patiently at the end of the verandah out of earshot.

Somewhere within, Peter heard a floorboard creak. Ah, they were not completely alone.

Victor Rose had shifted his muscular weight while there was a break in the conversation. He had been instructed to listen-in discreetly. The wooden walls of the lodge were suitably thin to allow this unseen.

Jenny Grant and Ernest MacKintosh had been taken on a sightseeing flight by Richard Whitton to keep them out of the way while Ludlow got down to business with Tyler. The less they knew, the better.

'So, Peter, tell me about this project you have in mind. Something to do with model aircraft, isn't it?'

'Not just any old model aircraft.'

'Elaborate. I mean, small models, large models? Copies of classic aircraft, like the Sopwith Pup you'd almost finished before you got kicked out? A small-minded man, that Mr. Hollom.'

That was a bit of a shock. So, they knew all about Hollom's Attic. Fortunately, it would seem they hadn't searched the place. He probably wouldn't be languishing here if they had, that was for sure. A better place than a biscuit tin would have to be found to hide the tape! To be on the safe side.

'Not a bad man, really, Hollom. Just too much local cyder.' Peter said. Not a bad man at all, in fact, as long as he kept interlopers out of the back room. 'My project is an original conception. But first, tell me one thing. Is Victor Rose trustworthy?' Ludlow raised his eyebrows. Where was this going? 'If not, could you tell him to clear off from behind the wall? I'm not prepared to discuss details of my invention with anyone other than yourself. I'm sure you understand the hazards of disclosure?'

Ludlow realised Tyler had sensed Rose was listening in.

'Trustworthy? Don't doubt it. You have to trust *me* on that. I asked him to lend a discreet ear to our little chat. It could prove invaluable should our own memories falter.'

'So, do I take it you are not recording this conversation? I thought perhaps you might have a hidden microphone somewhere. You know, like you did at Compton Stud?' Just a mischievous reminder, but every little nudge added weight to his position.

'Alas, no such facilities here. We shall have to put trust in our word and a handshake. Whatever you want and agree upon, Rose will be party to making sure it happens. He is a team player. The very best. So, what are we talking about? A new concept, I gather, a new sort of model flying machine? Tell me more.'

Peter had been mulling over how to make his pitch. How to make it sound businesslike and plausible.

'The project is virtually ready to be launched, barring one or two technical loose ends. I need the wherewithal to streamline the design and seal its copyright. That's for starters. Then, to take it into production and marketing. Once it's out there, I'm convinced it will gather its own momentum. There'll be no stopping it!'

Ludlow adjusted his position in his armchair. Passion and self-confidence. He liked it, *but*... 'Forgive me for asking, but isn't the model aircraft market well covered already. There's all sorts out there. Have you been to Hamley's recently? How will this new concept of yours compete? There's only so much you can do with model aircraft.'

'There's nothing on the market to compete! My Initiative, I'm thinking of calling it: Tyler's Initiative. As I say, it's a different concept, in a new field of its own. Hamley's, Macy's, every model shop around the world will be fighting for the retail franchise. But that's not the real market for it. I've been working on it for months. Already spent a fortune on it – a fortune for me, that is.'

The passion wouldn't go away, Ludlow was pleased to hear. Hatred was not the only driving force behind Peter Tyler, happily. This opportunity to build a better life for himself had completely blown away any conscience he might have had for not answering Stephanie's call to stir up the shit.

'Money is not your problem anymore, Peter,' Ludlow endorsed this perception. 'Selling your Initiative might be.' Ludlow smiled charmingly. 'Just *how* different is it?'

There was no point holding back anymore. Ludlow could hardly steal the idea. And Peter had to face it, his Initiative stood a far better chance of success with the weight of Ludlow's industrial clout behind it. Better than settling for a lump sum and going it alone. He found himself getting excited, Victor Rose listening in or not!

'At the root, it's a complex arrangement of transistors and microcircuits. You obviously know all about transistors, solid state and light as a feather. The biggest headache is the weight of the batteries needed to drive the system. Best if you think helicopter, Chinook, in particular, which has two props, right? OK. Now add another.' He had the self-satisfied look on his face of someone who had just planted the word *zigzag* in the bottom corner of a Scrabble board. He waited for a response.

'Go on,' was all he got.

'OK, so where would you put it, this third prop?' It was a perfunctory question. 'Well, I'll tell you. Equidistant from the other two at an angle of 120 degrees, the three props forming an equilateral triangle, similarly geared and powered but controlled remotely, either individually or in concert. I imagine you might have an idea what this means?' Another pause to see if he was getting through. Another 'go on' was what he got, but this time with more interest and a slow nod. 'Apart from going up, down and forward, the Initiative will be able to go left, right, backwards, directly from a standing point, stand still or spin on the spot if you want it to. Completely maneuverable in any direction, at speed! All controlled by a handset. Every geek and enthusiast in the world will want one!'

Tyler's passion was not ill-founded, Ludlow was beginning to realize.

'It seems to me you could have a good thing going here, Peter.'

'I *know* I have!'

'But have you thought of taking the idea further?'

'*Of course* I bloody have!'

'I can see great potential if it'll do what you say it will. Battery weight might not be such a problem. You've no doubt heard of lithium cells. One of my electronics holdings is in the forefront of that research. In fact, there's nothing your Initiative needs that can't be found somewhere in one of Wilson-Hughes' enterprises alone. Have you grasped what we could be into here?'

'Excuse me?' Peter snapped. 'We? What do you mean by *we*? This is my invention. You can have no claims on it whatsoever. That's for starters!'

'Ok. Ok. Keep your shirt on. I'm not going to steal anything from you,' Ludlow patted the air with his palms as if surrendering. 'Listen. You're going to need all the help you can get with this, not just money. If you want to buy that help from elsewhere, it's your prerogative. But it's a tough world out there. I don't want to throw money at you and have you taken to the cleaners by some shark and have you keep running back to me for more. That would be a waste of time and money. Not what I'm about. Nor should you be. You're going to need help and know-how to get this up and running, so be careful who you choose if all you want is money and decide to take the idea elsewhere. Be aware contract lawyers don't come cheap, either. That's another minefield you'll have to negotiate. I'm just saying, I've got all the set-ups you could possibly need under one roof. You must know that. And let's face it, you've got enough on me to keep me honest. Think about it. You won't get better support anywhere else. Whichever company you took this to would want its own interests and profit margins met. Some of the parts you'll need will almost definitely have their own patents to deal with. Batteries included, so to speak. Can you handle all that on your own? Do you want that bother, even? How good a businessman, are you?'

Tyler was silenced. He got what Ludlow was inferring.

'I won't beat about the bush, Peter. I'll tell you what I think straight out. You're not being ambitious enough. I can see the bigger picture. And I promise you'll get a more secure deal with me than trolling through the Yellow Pages. That's not just because of what happened back in Marlsbury. I believe this Initiative of yours – good name – could have more potential than you possibly think, and if some third party is to make money from it, why not Wilson-Hughes? We can give you a first-rate management team of your choosing to look after the nitty-gritty that *your* invention needs to take it to a level well beyond that of the sophisticated toy market you're possibly thinking of.'

Tyler liked what he had been hearing, but he had a point to make.

'I can assure you that I've given plenty of thought to my Initiative beyond than of sophisticated toys! However, I wouldn't mind betting that ten times as many model Spitfires have been made than the real ones. So that market is not to be sneezed at. My Initiative might not be the Spitfire of its time, but it will reach for the skies none the less in its own inimitable way. I see it as becoming another workhorse for national security, just as the Spitfire was in its day.'

So, Tyler was already thinking about the bigger picture. National security indeed? 'Tell me more.' Ludlow wanted to hear it from the inventor himself.

'The prototype I'm working on is just to prove the principle works. To be honest, for its full potential, a fourth prop might be needed. Batteries are one of my main concerns right now. Lithium, you say. Interesting. Suitable lift capability will be needed to carry extra weight.' He paused, for effect. 'I'm talking of a camera on gimbals.'

The men's eyes met.

Peter went on: 'Every police force in the world will want one – two! The armed forces. Crowd control. Sieges! Terrorists! Surveillance!

231

You name it! Anywhere you couldn't put human eyes, send up a Tyler's Initiative with its multi directional camera!'

'Brilliant!'

'The Grand National, water sports! *Any* sport you couldn't otherwise cover from the air. Endless uses.'

Ludlow nodded with growing respect. His mind was up and running like his days at Oxford.

'Whatever you want, you've got it,' he said genuinely. 'You could be onto a big winner here. If you want Wilson-Hughes to fund it and look after your legal interests, all costs will be met. You keep control. Move the bulk of your prototype into Compton Stud. That's as secure a place as any to get things finished without the danger of prying eyes. I'll always be at the end of a telephone for anything you want or need. *Anything!* I'll put Karl and Johan at your beck and call. Victor, too, for anything those two can't sort out. Once you've got your prototype up and running, three props, four, either or both would be good eventually, we'll go full ahead to streamline designs for all its diverse uses. I promise you now, I am ready to put a couple of million into this if you want Wilson-Hughes aboard. So, tell me, how would you like to proceed? Do we have a deal?'

Peter had given thought to this many times when scrabbling about in his living room with only the occasional financial input from Gwen. He had always thought no partners, complete independence.

However, had things had just changed! A couple of million! Fuck me, Gwen! Wait till you hear this!

'Wilson-Hughes, it is,' he answered with genuine enthusiasm 'As soon as you like!' He then did something he would never have thought possible; he offered his hand to Ludlow!

After the last night at the lodge, Peter journeyed by road back to Nairobi accompanied by his new business sponsor. It was thought a good idea to be seen together in a casual manner. After an overnight at the Muthaiga Club, Peter would be taking a flight back to London with Victor, who had already departed the Naivasha lodge with Jenny Grant in the Wilson-Hughes Jetstream to arrange those details in advance. Ms. Grant couldn't wait to get away from the place. The days she had spent at the hideaway had not been so romantic as she had been hoping. As soon as Tyler had arrived, she had been told to make herself scarce. Very irritating! She was being side-stepped; had no idea at all why this strange troublemaker had been welcomed with open arms. Tyler's Initiative, the product, would be taken into her confidence once Tyler had departed.

Ludlow had prepared a draft statement for Jenny to run her eyes over before he delivered it publicly. Then she would know all. In it, he would officiously 'come out of mourning' for the loss of his wife and declare that the time was now right to reveal he had been in delayed negotiations with Peter Tyler to finance an innovative product of his, which, Ludlow could not stress strongly enough, would take the world by storm.

'We have to prepare the way for your sudden change of fortune, Peter.' he had explained. 'Our association might appear unusual to some watchers. We must show that it is well founded rather than some shady collusion, don't you agree? A joint venture based on a sound product that will be economically beneficial to both parties. The exact nature of our venture need not be made public until you are absolutely ready. Don't worry. You'll have your own company and control; sensibly, with limited liability. Perfectly legit and in the open. I'll arrange the accounting so that you have a steady income of your choice and ensure that the bottom line never leaves you with a tax burden. How does that sound?'

Peter had to admit it sounded good. Unbelievably good. If Ludlow was true to his word, of course. And why wouldn't he be? Especially if his own companies would be in on the profit? That outcome might lessen the blow should Tyler's dubious shenanigans ever get out. But once Ludlow had gone public with his proposed 'investment' and their 'partnership' was signed and sealed, Peter reckoned he would be home and dried. No turning back. For either of them!

Ludlow's own motives were firmly fixed on saving his own skin. So far, so good. This situation with Tyler had fallen into his lap. The man was proving to be his way out.

Once brought up to date with what had transpired from the meetings in Kenya, Gerald Silver had started juggling a lot of figures to clear the way for the forthcoming joint-venture. He also recommended that Sir Edward should continue his discretionary absence from the UK.

'The situation has been defused for the time being, it seems, but we can't be sure that Tyler is completely fail-safe as yet,' warned Silver, who was not only a shrewd reader of financial matters, but also had a keen nose for character assessment. They had talked at great length about how to approach the manner of 'investment' in their inherited 'Initiative'. Silver thought he had hit on the perfect combination of tact, generosity and insurance. To set the plan in motion, it entailed Sir Edward talking to his affiliates in Bolivia. Ludlow was one step ahead of him. He thought making a discreet trip there might prove more expedient.

'Not such a bad idea,' Silver agreed. 'I'll leave that to your discretion.'

Apart from Bilochem Pharmaceuticals Industries being based in La Paz, Ludlow did a certain amount of personal banking there; very personal banking, for such a day as this. The bank Gerald Silver suggested for the devious account needed was an obvious choice, because Bilochem itself owned it. Without fear of comeback, Peter Tyler would be established as a loyal customer of the past two years. More precisely, his account would reveal to have been receiving regular monthly payments of one thousand pounds in pesos from Bilochem Pharmaceuticals ever since losing his job at Marlsbury Pumps. For no better reason than disguise, the account was then moved to Lichtenstein.

It would be an opportune way of establishing Peter Tyler as a long-standing beneficiary of one of Ludlow's darker enterprises. One of those, incidentally, that he thought his late wife had paid Tyler to expose in her place! Nice touch?

'Very affordable insurance,' Silver concurred.

Some of the accumulation of Peter Tyler's newly found wealth would soon find its way into a brand-new company account registered in Switzerland as 'Tyler's Initiative. Ltd.'. Boosting this account would be an additional twenty-two thousand pounds, to all appearances made to look like clean money acquired from Ludlow's Venture Capital coffers. Peter Tyler would not be told the ins and outs of various other safeguards unless his attitude of cooperation changed for the worse. To learn that his own skeleton now rested in the Bilochem cupboard might make him think twice about threatening to open it!

Chapter Twenty Five

The weather in the UK was depressing after sunny Kenya. However, it did not dampen Peter's spirits, especially when he saw Gwen glowing from behind the front window as they pulled up. The burnt-out wreck of his workshop caused nothing more than a brief shrug now. C'est la vie, he told himself. Happily, the members of the press had all gone.

He had been surprised how reassuring it was to see Gwen again looking her jolly, nosy self.

As a joke to impress Gwen, Karl, who had picked Tyler up from Heathrow in the Range Rover, jumped out and ran round to ceremoniously open the passenger door for him, doffing a peaked cap.

Gwen guessed it was a wind up. Karl couldn't hold back a smile as he got back into the driver's seat.

The mistletoe had gone, but she still made a grab for Peter as he walked in.

'Get *you* in a flashy Range Rover! Can't you open a bloody door for yourself nowadays?'

'My new status doesn't call for it.'

'Shut up! Your chauffeur looks a bit off, too.'

Karl was in his usual black leathers. The peaked cap was worn just for a laugh.

'How'd it go, you lucky devil?' she yelped. 'I want the works! Every last detail. And is that my present?' Gwen had noticed a duty-free carrier bag.

'What present? You think I had time for shopping? It was a business trip. Nothing but hard bargaining none stop.' He enjoyed teasing her. 'Apart from sun-bathing and gin and tonics, of course.'

'Oh, yeah? You don't look very sun-tanned. And when did you ever drink gin and tonics? Playboy!'

'I could get used to it, though, now I'm going to be a company director.' He pulled a bottle of Gordon's Gin from the bag and handed it to her. 'There you go. Courtesy of my new-found wealth.'

Her eyes lit up. Not for the gin.

'So, it's on? You've done it? He's going to back you?'

'Big time! I couldn't believe it. He really likes the idea. Thinks it's got great potential. Which of course, it has.' He took another item from the bag. 'I bought this as another thank you for giving me a push.'

She pulled a puzzled face. It was a stick painted in the colours of the Kenyan flag with what appeared to be hair hanging from it. She played with it for a second.

'What is it?'

'A flyswat. It's for pestering me non-stop to take the thing to Ludlow. No flies on you, Gwen!'

She grinned, making a pretend swipe at him with her new toy.

I was only thinking of my own future. 10 percent, don't forget!'

'Five!'

'Eight?'

'Six!'

'Seven?'

'Six!'

'Six and a half?'

'Six!!'

'With bonuses?'

He grimaced, then smiled with resignation. 'As long as you type the odd letter for me.'

'Done! Shake on it.'

He did.

She grinned widely.

'You're not much of a businessman, are you? I'll have to watch your back for you, ya wally! I would have settled for five percent. Too late now. Six and a half it is.'

'Six! And no lip, if you want to keep your job.'

'You forget. Your nice Mr. Victor Rose is employing me now. You won't have the time to look after your mum yourself if you're going

237

to be a fancy executive. You've got me here for keeps, chum! So, get used to it.'

'If I must,' he groaned. But she knew he was happy about it. She didn't know yet, though, that he would be relocating to Compton Stud for a lot of his time. Too soon for him to own up. 'How *is* mum, by the way?'

'Sleeping.'

'Recovered from all the excitement?'

'I think she misses it. Keeps talking about it, anyway. She's not convinced about having work done on the place, though. We've had workmen in measuring up the windows for double glazing. She'll have to be moved about when they come to fit the things. Either from room to room or to a hotel for a few days. Up to you.'

'She can have my room while they're doing hers. I'll be kipping at the Stud quite a bit from now on. I've got all hands-on deck to help me finish my prototype as quickly as I can.'

'Bloody heck, Peter. You really have made it!'

'I'll be virtually moving into the place for a while. We'll see.'

'I've always wondered what Compton Stud's like inside.' She ventured hopefully.

'I'll be happy to tell you all about it when the time comes!' Best to nip that idea of Gwen's in the bud!

'Huh!' Not a grunt of pleasure.

'I don't suppose the old girl has missed me at all, has she? Probably pleased as Punch to have you around full time.'

'I've had no complaints,'

'I've thought about selling this place in due course. Buying something newer, closer to amenities for you, since I seem to have got you for *good*!' he breathed a mock sigh. 'Start thinking about where you might want to be. Doesn't have to be near Marlsbury particularly. But nowhere too foreign. Bath? Wells? They could be nice. Not too far away.'

'Jumping the gun a bit, aincha?'

'Just saying. Things are on the up. It's only a matter of time. I've already outgrown this house now my workshop's gone. If you're going to be a permanent fixture, let's make sure you'll be happy. Life might not be all roses being my dog's-body.'

'I'll give you bloody dog's-body! I'll be cracking the whip, don't you worry. I don't want my six and a half percent going down the drain!'

'Six! Seriously, though. This place is miles from the shops, let alone the doctors. Once the finances are in place, it'll make absolute sense to move. It'll make life better for all of us. The work Ludlow is paying to have done here will obviously up its value no end. With everything else that's on the cards, we'll be able to afford something decent.'

Gwen liked the sound of 'us' and 'we'.

Peter could forgive himself for feeling optimistic. He felt fairly sure he wasn't jumping the gun. He had nothing in his pocket just yet, but he trusted that final handshake with Ludlow in Nairobi. Two million!

Peter had pulled this off.

Ludlow was thinking something similar.

He had reigned Tyler in.

During the following days and weeks, Peter moved everything to do with his Initiative into one of the smaller studios at Compton Stud. With Karl and Johan stationed on site, Tyler had been happy to agree it would be a far safer place for him to finish the project. He was also provided with one of the self-contained apartments in the converted barn for the convenience of staying over whenever he wished.

Peter Tyler was over the moon and why wouldn't he be?

As his association with Compton Stud leaked out, half of Marlsbury now began to wonder how Tyler had conned his way into Ludlow's good books.

He had been given the virtual run of Compton Stud's facilities, always under the watchful eyes of Karl, with Johann never far away. The offices and living quarters of the main house were closed down and out of bounds for the time being. But the rest of the property was like a 5-star hotel. The gymnasium was kitted out to suit Olympians. Peter made full use of its facilities, usually in awe of Karl's superior performances. That man was like a rock! Close on six feet tall and all muscle.

There was an indoor swimming pool, a viewing theatre with adjoining lounges, one with a self-service bar still well-stocked even though the last photo shoot had been months back. Outside was another pool, covered at present, two tennis courts and a slightly 'sunken' area for croquet or badminton. That area had more often been used as a spillover for camera crews and models to relax or party in. It had also once been overlooked by a beached Rang-Rover!

A first-rate kitchen was installed in the converted barn, manned by professionals whenever the place had been hired out. That was still fully functional. With Karl and Johann on hand to do the shopping and cooking Peter was on cloud nine.

How damp and depressing his own place now seemed by comparison. But improvements were on their way. Going back after a session at Compton Stud brought home to him how much the changes were needed. His workshop had become his real home. With that gone, his life had changed dramatically.

Ludlow would bear the cost of rebuilding it, but Peter had asked for the main house to be damp-proofed and double-glazed first. All was in hand.

After paying homage to those charred remains, Peter wondered if he actually wanted it to be rebuilt. Would he ever need it again? Being allowed to hang out at Compton Stud had changed his perspective. That place stank of extravagance and know-how. And now Peter was tapping into some of it. All he needed was to hold his nerve for a few more months; weeks, maybe.

Things quickly started moving apace. In no time design experts for the Initiative's various components were employed alongside others engaged in making the whole thing aerodynamic.

As Ludlow had pointed out, the Wilson-Hughes Group had everything needed to put Tyler's Initiative into production in one or other of its associated companies scattered around the United Kingdom.

Whereas what Peter Tyler called his 'bedstead' prototype had been held together in part with super-glue and cello-tape, the patented model would be transformed into a masterpiece of spot welding and weightless fusion. Looking more like an upside-down version of H.G.Wells' Triffid, the 'bedstead' would perhaps one day find its way into a museum.

When Tyler took it to the air on its maiden test flight, the witnesses were in open-mouthed amazement. The inventor himself had tears in his as he steadied the prototype in a hover at about twelve feet above their heads, spinning it rapidly and seamlessly! Then up as straight as an arrow rotating in the opposite direction!

'Patent that!' Peter had cried in jubilation, rocking his Initiative back and forward with ease, flying as high as a kite himself. 'It works!' He sounded more surprised than any of the others. 'It bloody well works!'

'*Verdammte holle,* Peter!' Karl whistled. 'You soon rich man! Champagne tonight!'

'*Henkell Trocken*!' Johann chipped in.

The only person not enjoying the show was Rose. The success of the 'launch' now meant the conning bastard would be getting his foot further through the door!

Within days, Peter was handed a series of contracts to sign. The ones that most interested him were patent and copyright agreements. Things were moving fast.

With these signings, a welcome easing of Karl's vigilance seemed to have arrived. It must be said, being now well and truly tied to Ludlow, why would Peter Tyler ever think of rocking the boat? He would be even less so inclined if he knew he now owned certain bank accounts in Lichtenstein and Switzerland full of dirty money attached to drug trafficking.

As the weeks went by and all his demands were met, the trust grew in both directions. However, every room in Tyler's house had been bugged discreetly during the measuring of proposed double glazing and damp proofing work. A receiver was installed neatly out of sight behind the dashboard of the Range Rover, connected to its rather special radio aerial. One of Karl's duties was to monitor conversation when Tyler was in the house in case he was ever to let slip anything concerning the tape or disc.

The apartment in the converted barn, once the domain of executive clients during the studio's heyday, gave Peter a buzz he had never experienced before. Kenya now seemed like a dream. The promises made there unreal. But here he was. Ludlow had been true to his word. The apartment was pure luxury, just a few steps across to the former studio-cum-cinema in the main house which had now been transformed into the ultimate workshop.

Peter Tyler was beginning to enjoy life.

'Tony's Ring' was gearing up for the 29th February celebrations.

Despite running advertisements in all the local Manchester newspapers, the response had not been as Tony would have wanted for his sixtieth birthday bash.

None of the hopeful contestants for the 'lookalikes' competition came close to passing as Tony himself or as any of his famous friends sitting on the judges' bench. As much as he had tried to vary his choice of the final six contestants, he felt it would be unfair to exclude three of the hopefuls on the grounds of repetition. By far the four best lookalikes putting themselves forward were all would-be Elvis Presley's. The other two selections were only slightly more passable than the rest of the rather disappointing turnout. However, one of those was a rather busty Brigitte Bardot, which opened the opportunity of comparing her to the 'in-house' Bardot, who would of course be on duty on the big night. It seemed as well to have at least one female contestant. The last of the six, was a fairly standard Charlie Chaplin. It was the baggy trousers and bowler hat that did it for him, not so much his looks.

Jimbo, as Quasimodo, did his best to act as caretaker of the six finalists. Each was allowed to bring one person along with them to help out with costume and make-up. The rainbow rooms became a hub of fun and laughter. Of course, there was a nice prize to be won, but there appeared to be no bitter rivalry amongst the contestants. It was already fun having made the final six. There was only one of them taking himself a little too seriously. One of the four Elvis's. He seemed to see his chances better than the others because he thought he sounded more like Elvis when he sang. The voice would be the deciding factor if it came to a tiebreaker.

'Upstairs' would be running its free bar service to liven up the occasion, but not the pornography normally at show on the monitor. That was given over to a wide shot of downstairs, where much revelry was going on.

Sharon and Kim, along with the rest of the staff were working their socks off putting themselves about, posing and dancing with as many of the guests as possible; perhaps giving more attention to those seen as being most worthy of the extra effort. Particularly the e*ligible* ones?

The band played, the comedian joked, the best fancy-dress couple won a prize, the said singing Elvis won a trip to Tenerife. Tony appeared in his famous tiger outfit and was about to do his party piece of carrying off the house 'Brigitte Bardot' with his teeth, when he collapsed.

Three hours later, in Manchester General Hospital, he died.

Chapter Twenty Six

Before Spring had officially arrived with the clocks going forward an hour, Wilson Hughes value on the Stock Market was showing signs of recovering from the jitters. A certain amount of back-pedalling also became evident with respect to Ludlow's questionable misinformation about the Kenyan irrigation project. On different pages, there were column inches devoted to the revelation that, despite Peter Tyler's former undoubted hostility, he was now eating out of Ludlow's pocket.

For Peter, to have Ludlow's millions behind him was like sticking two fingers up at the tabloids for all their libelous insinuations.

Ludlow had gone one better in consolidating their connection in what had become dubbed his 'Nairobi Declaration'. In it, he had taken great pains to announce that he would be instructing his solicitors to issue writs of libel against the Daily Scan on behalf of his new business partner.

Opinions changed overnight about Tyler. Even Detective Chief Inspector Pearson thought perhaps he had got it wrong about the man. Was it this Initiative thing of his that Tyler had been keeping quiet about? Pearson had known all along that he was hiding something. So, that was it. Tyler had been in cahoots with Ludlow all the time. Little wonder then that he hadn't been pushing himself to find a proper job, the sly fucker.

The staff at Compton Stud had been given notice not to return after the dramatic events there. Something like this had been anticipated, of course, after the two deaths, but it had still come as an aggravation to Robby Pike. He had been the head gardener there for a long time. Not so much of a surprise for the cleaners and stable girls. Everyone was being handsomely compensated. The most surprised, and very happily so, was Mary Sutton, the erstwhile telephonist. She had been about to tender her resignation by post without turning up for work after the New Year's holiday. This meant that instead of receiving a bollocking from the stuck-up Jenny Grant for giving short notice and getting just a paltry week's back pay, she had received a full three months' compensation along with the other staff.

In all its former purposes, Compton Stud had been closed down. Just one phone line was reinstated after Stephanie's brainstorming attack on the exchange. There was no need for four lines anymore. Also, one could be more easily monitored; a precaution Ludlow insisted was kept in place for peace of mind.

Karl and Johan had proved to be more than adequate assistants in the final stages of putting Tyler's Initiative together. The three of them formed a good working relationship.

After weeks of industrious harmony behind closed doors, anticipation was growing that Tyler's Initiative Mark I would soon be ready for the Birmingham NEC launch.

Peter Tyler was in heaven.

But then, a bombshell fell onto the doormat at Newton Stoat!

'A bumper crop of post arrived for you,' Gwen had told him as soon as he came through the door on his latest visit to see his mother. 'Most of them look like begging letters from charities. What do you expect now you and Ludlow are all over the newspapers? People must think you're a bloody millionaire already. There's also one from the BBC! I was going to steam it open, then thought, why bother steaming it. Just open it. If I'm to be your dog's body, I need to know what's what while you're away on business.'

'So, what's it say?' he asked, playing her along. He knew she wouldn't dare open his letters.

'Couldn't find a letter opener, so you'll have to look at it yourself and let me know. I need to be kept up to date, being a shareholder.'

He picked up the Kenyan fly swat and flicked her shoulder with it.

'No lip! Know your place. Nothing in writing, don't forget!'

'The post is on the living room table,' she told him with a scoff.

Gwen was right, most of the envelopes had charity logos on them. There was even one from S.O.D.A.! Someone had got their wires crossed there, he thought.

Discarding the charity mail casually as he went through the pile, he suddenly went stiff, the blood draining from his face. In his hand was one from The Salvation Army, his name and address handwritten carefully in pen and ink. He stared at it, frightened to open it. Thank goodness Gwen hadn't come through with him and seen the shock it had given him. He shoved the envelope down his trousers, the back this time. His mind was racing. There was no doubt who the letter had come from. *Confidential* was underlined on the front, *From Major Wendy Clarke* on the back under the Salvation Army's Blood and Fire emblem.

He took a deep breath. Think, he told himself. What was in the BBC letter? Could he pass the shock off on that? He opened it quickly. Possibly. It was short and to the point. A certain Simon Dixon would like to interview him as part of a television documentary he was making about Sir Edward Ludlow..

Just in time. Gwen had now come through.

'Have a look at this,' he said, trying to disguise his unease.

She took the BBC letter and read it. 'Blimey. That's not so bad, is it? What are you looking so panic stricken about?'

'They'll be digging up all that buddy-buddy stuff with Ludlow again,' he suggested, trying to make that seem the cause of his unrest. 'How come I'm now hanging out with him all-of-a-sudden? I can do without any of that nonsense. They can go and take a running jump!'

'Wouldn't it be good publicity for our Initiative? Millions would get to know about it overnight.' The *our* went unnoticed, or at least unchallenged.

'Exactly! That's not what we want until we're completely ready. Ludlow knows all about publicity. That side of things is down to him. He'll know when to start pushing it. So don't you go blurting about it to anyone yourself. Otherwise, I might have to reconsider your five percent.'

'Six!'

With the Salvation Army letter digging into the small of his back, he didn't want to continue the usual banter.

Blood and fire! Was that an omen?

As soon as he got into the Range Rover, Peter handed Karl the BBC letter.

'Look at that,' he said. 'And be sure to let your boss know I'll be telling Mr. Dickson to piss off and mind his own business.'

Karl knew already about the letter since he'd been listening in and had been wondering if Peter would mention it or not. The notion of 'not' had gone through Peter's mind, but he decided it was just as well to let Karl know he wasn't going to go telling tales to the BBC.

During the drive back to Compton Stud, Peter's mind was racing. He was silent, but that was OK. The pair weren't great conversationalists. Why had the major written to him?

He suddenly needed the toilet and urged Karl to put his foot down.

When they got back, he made straight for the privacy of his flat to relieve himself before opening the letter.

*

Dear Mr. Tyler,

Please excuse my writing to you. I thought I might have heard from *you* before this.

I suspect you know who I am and why I am contacting you. We urgently need to discuss a certain issue, don't you think!

Given your recent travels and reports I have read about you in the newspapers, I sincerely hope you have not taken it upon yourself to reveal anything of a certain person, sadly no longer with us, may have told you. If you have broken that confidence, you have also broken mine, and the hand of common law will come down hard on you. Confidence is sacrosanct!

I need to be reassured that the matter I refer to has gone no further than the two of us. A decision has to be made as to how this delicate situation can be resolved, as indeed it must. *Without* disclosure, I stress.

You will perhaps understand that? Why this should be done in complete secrecy.

The most discreet way of contacting me is not by telephone or letter, but by putting a note in my collection box. This need not be on a bank note (although by all accounts, you could afford it to be). On it, give me a time, date and place, obviously somewhere suitably convenient and inconspicuous, and I shall be there.

I go collecting in all the public houses in Marlsbury on Friday nights. Sunday lunchtimes I am in the square with the Salvation Army Brass Band. Your choice.

If I don't hear back, I shall think the worst of you.

Yours *sincerely*, Wendy Clarke.

*

She sounded very pissed off. But Peter felt he had a few days' grace before he would have to respond to the letter. His approach needed thought. Face to face would prove awkward with Karl and Johann likely to be at his shoulder. First, he had to let her know he'd received the letter. Tell her he was not only a friend, but the obvious go-between if Stephanie's daughter was to be contacted. He knew Stephanie's secret and it was safe with him. She had given him money. Wendy Clarke didn't need to know all the details about it going up in smoke only to be later reimbursed by Ludlow himself. She might not appreciate the irony.

To be honest, Peter was more than curious to know about Stephanie's offspring. He would love to meet her under some pretence. Winning the Pools or a lottery wouldn't work. The money couldn't just fall into her lap. Long lost uncle? The major had seemed none too keen to deal with the situation herself. Until now? Otherwise, why had she written to him? He was more than relieved to know she wanted to keep the matter between the two of them.

In a way, he felt duty bound to help the girl, and he could afford to be magnanimous now with all that had been going on. For that, he needed the major's say-so. He could do nothing without knowing who the girl was.

He decided Sunday lunchtime would be the best time to make contact, when she was with the band in the square. There would be a better chance around then of getting his friendly 'minders' off his back for two minutes. He had an idea about that.

'I'm thinking of going to Marlsbury on Sunday,' he told Karl. 'Show my face. Surprise a few people. I suppose you'll be wanting to come goose-stepping along with me?'

'Ha Ha. You take too personal, Peter,' Karl protested with a broad version of his irritating smirk. 'I look after you. Make you safe. Many people like same service. You lucky rich man. But too much angst. Not made for games you play.' He indicated with a nudge of his head that Peter should follow him. 'Come, you more lucky today. I show you something.'

The *something* was a brand-new Jaguar motor car, sleek and black.

'Your new auto.' Karl announced proudly.

'Mine?' Peter queried, astonished. 'Why?' He was thinking it was a complete waste of money for him to have his own car. He couldn't drive. But why should he worry? All executives had one.

'Company car. Tyler's Initiative,' Karl explained, conceding, 'Good car. Like Mercedes.'

'Better!' Peter argued, still thinking about the extravagance. But at least it was British extravagance.

'I drive you to town. Show off. You big chief, now.' Karl joked, offering another service. 'You want to learn drive? Sit in front. Watch me. Easy. Automatic.'

In summer, the centre of Marlsbury sprouted teashops with tables outside and various knick-knack stalls in the square on Sundays to encourage passing tourists. In winter, the only things to bring people into town were the pubs and the annual food fair towards Christmas time.

Summer or winter, the one attraction that could always be relied upon on Sundays come rain or shine, was the Salvation Army Band playing in the square.

'We're going to The Turk's Anchor for lunch now things have calmed down and the cops and tabloids have eaten humble pie.'

Karl cocked his ear and frowned. Humble pie? He got no explanation, just a smile.

As they drove into town, Peter told his leather-clad friend to park somewhere in the streets behind the pub. 'It'll be a lot easier today. The square's closed off on Sundays.'

Karl obeyed without a second's thought.

A less likely couple had never been seen climbing from such an elegant car. They looked more like showroom thieves.

The pub suited them better.

Karl turned a few heads, and not just female. He had a striking appearance, shoe-horned top to toe into soft leather; handsome, in his own dark way. Piercing eyes. With his chauffeur's peak cap removed, he looked closer to the stud he sometimes hinted at being.

Peter was hoping to cash in on Karl's appearance and ego, banking on one of the local girls latching onto him to free up the few minutes' breathing space he needed. And things could not have turned out any better.

Janet Tomlinson was in the pub. As soon as she saw Peter come in accompanied by this new hulk of a man, she made a dive for them.

'Well, Peter!' she expostulated, hardly glancing in his direction. 'Who's your friend?' She was into leather. 'You haven't gone all YMCA on me, have you?'

Karl frowned, seeking help from Peter. He didn't understand what she was talking about, but he sensed where she was coming from.

'Don't mind her, Karl. She likes to play games,' Peter explained, getting a smile from Janet which said; 'Dead right, I do'.

'Karl, meet Janet, Janet, meet Karl.' The two shook hands and all three smiled.

'Pleased to meet you, Karl. Peter's been keeping you a secret,' Janet drooled ostentatiously. 'And what do *you* do?' she added suggestively.

Karl didn't get the innuendo. Peter stepped in.

'Karl's my guardian angel. He looks after my welfare, don't you Karl? Karl's a trouble-shooter. He understands English perfectly, so don't be trying to take him for a ride with your sweet talk!' Peter added a smile to his double entendre as he went to the bar to order drinks; coke for Karl, 'Between The Sheets' for Janet, of course. What else?

Within minutes, the Salvation Army band could be heard striking up in the square. Peter gave it a moment, then excused himself to go to the toilet. The newly acquainted couple were getting on fine and hardly noticed. 'Good start,' Peter thought.

Instead of going to the gents, he walked straight through the saloon bar to the back exit and made his way to the square.

There were only a few people standing around listening to the brass band. Peter strolled up and joined them. He studied each of the women in uniform, trying to pick out which of them was Wendy Clarke. She spotted him first as he had expected she might, with all the pictures of him that had been in the papers.

She approached him rattling her collection box, nodding recognition in time to the music.

A slight woman, not much over five feet tall, she had a pleasant face with lines of caring rather than worry. What was showing of her hair from under her hat was white. He put her in her early sixties.

He checked the name on her badge and gave her a reciprocating nod before slipping his donation into the collection box.

The five-pound note was wrapped around a message written on note paper. It was to the point:

*

'I am being watched. Our secret secure. I now have the wherewithal to help the child in total anonymity. Both short and long term. With your blessing, I will need her identity, of course, so yes we should meet. I will contact you again by this familiar method once I can arrange a safe time and place. Thank you. Peter Tyler.'

*

He thought he would indicate he was up to speed with how she and Stephanie had communicated. It would give him more substance.

He felt that was all he needed to write to reassure her he had kept his mouth shut. Whether she wanted the child helped financially or not was her decision. He hoped she would. He wanted to meet the girl. He was thinking it might be in his own interests as well as the girl's.

Major Wendy Clarke nodded in thanks before moving on with a shake of her box.

If she was reluctant to let him know where to find Stephanie's daughter, he might put his foot down. After all, it was Stephanie's last wish, was it not?

Peter quickly retraced his steps to the bar, where Karl and Janet had been joined by another couple from the cycling club. They all seemed to be getting on fine.

Karl gave Peter a look suggesting he'd been a long time in the toilet.

Peter fobbed him off. 'You're looking upset, Karl. Sorry if I've come back so soon. Think I'd leave you all alone with Janet for any length of time, you randy foreign person?' He leaned toward Janet conspiratorially and whispered loudly enough to be sure Karl could hear: 'Unless Janet would like to be left alone with you, of course.' Then back to Karl, 'Can't you relax for two minutes? You're not on parade now. How many times must I tell you I'm not going anywhere? Don't forget, I can't drive, and I haven't got my bike with me!' Back to Janet. 'Karl's under orders to make sure I don't run off with my Initiative and make someone else a millionaire.'

Janet tossed the remark aside.

'I thought S.E.L. was already filthy rich enough?' she often spoke of Ludlow by his initials.

'Whenever was a rich man ever satisfied he had enough?' Peter quipped. 'I'll be feeling the same myself before too long, I expect.'

The trio continued to banter their way through another round, being joined occasionally by well-wishers, most of whom did not hold back from telling Peter of their surprise at the turnaround in his fortunes. 'Good on ya!' was most people's message for him. 'You ought to sue that Daily Scan for all the stuff they printed about you.' Ludlow was already threatening to do that, he was happy to tell them.

Just after two o'clock, closing time, while Janet was powdering her nose, Peter told Karl he would wait at the front of the pub while he brought the car round. 'Unless you want an hour or two with Janet?' He added, not just as a joke, but to test how receptive Karl might be to such an idea. 'Get on someone else's back for a change!' Another innuendo. Spotted this time.

'Ha Ha,' Karl replied. 'You want play games with me too much.'

'Don't know what you're missing.' Peter teased.

When Janet came out of the ladies' toilet, the pair had gone from the bar. She rushed out to find Peter standing on his own. 'What happened to you two?' she asked, looking up and down the street. 'I thought you'd done a runner on me. Where's that Karl?'

Peter said nothing. His ploy was showing promise. To answer her question, he pointed.

The Jaguar was coming round the corner with Karl at the wheel. It slid to a silent stop beside them.

'Wow!' Janet exclaimed as Karl got out and made a theatrical show of opening the door for Peter to get in. 'Are you guys serious!?'

She laughed. She had every right to at the sight of these two characters and the purring elegance of a car that was probably designed for government ministers and the like. 'Is it bullet-proof?' she joked.

Peter appreciated Janet's reaction. She wasn't the only one gawping. Half the people spilling out of the pub were, too. If this wasn't the final proof of Tyler's change of fortune, nothing was.

Two weeks passed before Peter was ready to meet the major. It would be another test. Not quite with the same stress and deceit associated with the meeting in Kenya, but not all that far off. Once again, he would have to make his story believable. One big difference this time? This meeting would be for the benefit of someone else. Mostly.

It was on the third Sunday after passing on his first message to the major that the eye-catching Jaguar again pulled into Marlsbury. Karl was quite happy with these occasional jaunts into town.

He had not yet seen his way to giving into Janet's sexual pleasures, although it could be seen they both enjoyed each other's company all the same. Karl was even 'cottoning on' to some of Janet's innuendos. He found her 'right up his street'.

It was not too much of a surprise that Janet was already in the crowded pub when they walked in, turning heads as usual. Their miss-matched styles of dress never ceased to guarantee amusement.

'Are you two blokes having it off?' Janet asked mischievously as she joined them. 'Karl won't invite me to the Stud. Is that what this joint venture of yours is all about, Peter? Y...M...C...A...' she began singing. 'I hear you spend a lot of time in the gym together.'

'Sadly, Janet, sometimes, as James Brown would have it, 'It's a man's, man's world.'

'But not always, eh?' Janet came straight back, smiling impishly.

Picking a suitably moment when the Salvation Army were in full blast, Peter once again excused himself and slipped out to give the major his new message. Scribbled on a five-pound note, it read: '2 pm. Next Friday. NatWest. Marlsbury.'

During the week, Peter primed Karl about going into town. 'Got to see the bank manager to let him know I'll soon be writing some big cheques. Best to warn him,' he had bluffed. 'I don't want any of them bouncing!'

As they drove in to Marlsbury, he told Karl it was best to meet him in The Turk's Anchor after he'd found somewhere to park. The Jaguar pulled up outside the NatWest Bank that Friday just after 1.55 pm. Double yellow lines and Friday traffic would keep Karl suitably busy and out of the way for a while. Add to that, finding a parking space. Depending on that and what the major had to say, he might even beat Karl to the pub. 'Don't know how long I'll be. That's down to the bank manager. See you in the pub later.'

'Take you time but not spend too much money!' Karl said as the Jaguar purred on its way. 'Maybe Janet is there to teach new swear words.'

As Peter was hoping, the bank was fairly empty. Four chairs in an appointment alcove were all free. He sat in one, drawing another close to him. Pulling a small knee-high table alongside, he spread out some copies of the contracts he had recently signed to give him a reason for being there, keeping an eye on the entrance.

At exactly 2.00, Wendy Clarke walked in. He was pleased to see she had come in street clothes, not her uniform. With a slight nod, he bade her sit in the chair he had placed so that she would have her back to the entrance.

'Should I suddenly ignore you and gather my papers, don't be offended,' he explained without looking at her, sliding some bank brochures across to her as added decoys. He wanted to cover his tracks should Karl decide to come checking on him. 'Just act as though you don't know me, and don't look round. I'll be up and away before you know it. As I mentioned, I'm being watched closely. Ludlow would love to know why I'm talking to you. So, we have to be extremely discreet. Agreed?'

Wendy Clarke nodded nervously. He could see she was unsure who should start the proceedings?

'Thanks for meeting me.' She barely whispered.

'Likewise.' he responded. 'What would you like me to do?' Straight to the point.

She stared at him as close to distressed as anyone could be without breaking down, it seemed.

'I should have tried harder to help her,' Wendy Clarke uttered as if from within her own private confessional.

'You shouldn't take it to heart,' Peter said comfortingly. 'Stephanie was perhaps beyond help. But at least she was lucid enough to want to help her child. We're both in accordance with that, aren't we?'

'Yes, of course. But should she find out that her blood mother had to abandon her can often mean long lasting emotional disruption for a child. Knowing Mrs. Ludlow didn't want the child's true identity to be revealed encouraged me to go ahead with tracing her. But then the murder. And Stephanie's own death. Well, that changed everything as far as I was concerned. Imagine what that might do to her daughter, if she ever found out her mother was a drug addict and murderer! That's why I wrote to you needing to know the truth of your involvement.'

Peter was nodding sympathetically. 'Of course, I understand. But I nevertheless have a duty to Stephanie. She made me promise to help her child. Gave me money. Discreetly of course. I pledged to do it anonymously, and I stand by that. So, where are we with this? What can you tell me?'

The major seemed to be morally compromised. Could she believe him.

'Stephanie Star's real name before marriage was Sheila Braithewaite. I suppose you already knew that.' He didn't, but he took note. It was the first clue he needed. 'The child was taken away from her at birth, a healthy girl, but premature. A breach baby. It was a very difficult birth by all accounts, with serious complications, poor girl. Life-changing surgery was needed during and after the baby was delivered. Sheila was barely thirteen years old. Until a few months ago she had apparently shown little interest in knowing if the child had survived or not. She had wiped the experience from her memory. But how could she forget such trauma? Is that what caused her drug addiction? The guilt? Her husband knew nothing of the child, and she wanted it kept that way to the point of paranoia. As you must know, her marriage was no more than a sham.'

The major looked Peter in the eye. Unknown to her, he had gleaned a lot of this on the tape. He urged her to continue. He could see she wanted to.

'What confuses me is that for the world to see is that you are now in partnership with her husband! You *must* assure me again that you have told him nothing of this?'

'I have disclosed absolutely nothing to do with Sheila Braithewaite to anyone. Nor will I. Especially to her daughter should I ever be allowed to help her as her mother wished. Stephanie gave me a large sum of money for that purpose. All I need to know is where I might find her and that you have trust in me. Also, I will search high and low at Compton Stud to see if I can find a draft of the Will Stephanie talked to me about making. Did she mention making a Will to you?'

Peter thought a white lie about a Will might move things forward. He already knew her answer would be 'yes'.

He got confirmation in a gentle nod.

'I'll look into it now that I can roam the house without suspicion.' This was another lie, of course. He could not roam the house without suspicion. That was not the way he would be 'looking into it'. He was toying with a different possibility. 'How much have you discovered about the child?' Peter went on. 'Do you have a name and address? Does she have a job. Ambitions? Anything extra you might know like that would help. I have to tell you I've no intention of sending a large sum of money unannounced to her through the post. A more subtle approach is called for, don't you think? Less suspicious. Does she have aspirations, do you know? How deeply have you managed to dig?'

He sensed the major was beginning to believe he genuinely wanted to help, in spite of what she might have read in the papers about him. She answered him willingly enough.

'I've no more than scratched the surface. But it appears the young woman had a job as a night-club hostess-cum-waitress until it ceased trading. Her comings and goings since have been difficult to pin down. It is feared she might have taken to the streets in Manchester. That's as far as my searches have got me and frankly as far as I feel I can take them. The child is not a child anymore. She'll soon be 21, an adult.'

Wendy Clarke raised her eyebrows interrogatively, brushing imaginary creases from her Marks and Spencer's slacks. She seemed yet to be convinced she should say more. 'Can I trust you to help her under your own steam? But *Anonymously*, I must stress. Because I feel I cannot properly assume the authority to take this matter further now Mrs. Ludlow is deceased.'

Peter put his thoughts together like a counsel for the defence about to pull a cat out of the bag to seal acquittal. He had been hoping the ploy would not be necessary, but he was fairly sure it could settle the deal he was hoping for, so he went for it.

'Yes, you can trust me,' he said as earnestly as possible. 'And this should convince you.' He leaned across the low table and handed her an unsealed envelope. Inside was a floppy disc he had recently bought from WH Smiths upon which he had typed some high-tech jargon. He had cut it in two. 'Stephanie's possible blackmailing disc,' he lied. 'You probably know what I'm talking about. She might have told you she thought she had thrown it away. She had, but I found it and as you see destroyed it. I hope this helps you make your decision. Do as you will with it. I don't want to hold it any longer. It has been burning my fingers.'

He saw surprise, dread then relief run across the major's brow. To consolidate his apparent confidentiality and concern, he stressed: 'And yes, I promise I will act in total and utter anonymity!'

The major slipped the envelope into her bag and fished out a prepared note. It read:

'Gloria Shaw. Last known address, Ardwick Court, Kings Avenue, Manchester.'

Chapter Twenty Seven

Sharon and Kim sat at their usual table in Ches's Cafe.

'Bacon sarnie!' Ches shouted from the compact kitchen tucked away through a door-less doorway behind the serving counter. Kim got up to fetch it. There was no table service at Ches's. She knew the sandwich was for her. No other customers were in the place. Three o'clock had passed. The cafe would soon be closing.

Sharon was already well into her beans on toast.

Although they had a passable kitchen of their own back at the flat, they hardly ever bothered to cook there. Microwaved ready meals were about as far as fine dining took them at home, not many takeaways, either. Too much trouble lugging them home and usually cold when they got them there. The nearest Indian and Chinese places were a good mile away.

At Tony's Ring, there was the non-stop supply of pizza to feast on, mostly the passed-sell-by-date kind. The staff could help themselves to them at that point. Hungry punters never outpaced the stock at Tony's.

'Do you want another tea?' Kim asked as she plonked herself down. 'Ches is about to empty the pot. Last chance, he says.'

'Go on then,' Sharon replied after a moment or two, as if the decision had been difficult to make.

'Yes, please, Ches!' Kim shouted, not seeing Ches. He was already cleaning up out back in the Kitchen.

'Coming up!' he shouted in response.

Five minutes later, seeing they were still eating, he brought two steaming mugs over to them.

'You girls must be at a loose end,' he said, squeezing himself down at an adjacent table. Portly would be a kind way of describing Ches. He was rotund and rosy cheeked beneath a virtually hairless scalp that always bore the heat of the kitchen on its perspiring brow. Breakfasts were his busiest times. His wife, Sue, helped out from six till noon, keeping the influx of building trade workers happy. Lunch was a much quieter time. Ches could handle that himself.

'Any news of what's going to happen to Tony's Ring?' he asked. 'That was a bit of a shock, weren't it? Him dropping dead like that?' Ches knew the girls worked there, and were hookers on the quiet. None of his

258

business. He had been to Tony's on occasion and seen them all dressed up as their doubles. He liked them. They were always laughing and joking about their antics. Although they never spent much money with him, they were regular customers and never came at busy times taking up space.

'Yeah, well. We're out of a job, in't we?' Kim speaking.

'Not opening again, then?'

'Don't look like it.'

'What's going to happen to the place, then?'

Sharon shrugged her shoulders. Kim said: 'Ain't got a clue.'

'Don't you need a couple of waitresses, Ches?' Sharon joked.

'Yeah, right.' Ches smiled. 'Where would I put you?'

The tables were so tightly spaced, at peak times when the place was packed, the customers had to pass the trays and plates back and forth across the tables themselves.

'You're a good-looking couple. It shouldn't be too hard to find yourselves something.' He nodded toward Sharon. 'You might have to keep that wig you wear at Tony's, though, Sharon! Unless you can find yourself a punk pub, somewhere.'

'Thanks, Ches,' Sharon responded in good humour. 'I'll bear that in mind.'

'So, what you reckon's gonna happen? None of Tony's sons thinking of taking it on? It's got to have been making money with what they charge for a drink there.'

'All we've heard is it's closing down.'

Sharon and Kim had decided not to say anything about what Jimbo had in mind, should anyone ask. Until Tony's wife, Luludja, decided what she wanted to do with the place, which wouldn't be until after the funeral, Jimbo would still be living there.

What Luludja had already made clear to those involved, however, was that a night club and knocking shop it would be no more. All that had been Tony's idea after he had quit his money-making career play-acting in the wrestling ring. The club had presented a different stage for him to strut his stuff, surrounded by his make-believe stars without the usual mock hissing and booing typical of a wrestling crowd.

Once or twice a year, if someone hired the entire club for a private party and dug deep enough into their pockets, he would oblige requests to appear in his trademark 'tiger' regalia allowing guests the chance of a photo-opportunity. As usual on those occasions, he would exit with a roar (his famous *miaow*) dragging off one of his 'star' waitresses apparently by the teeth, as he had been attempting to do when he drew his last breath.

Forever the showman.

Tony would have been happy with the way he had passed away. Happier still, perhaps, if he had actually managed to get his quarry off the ground for his last hurrah. But even the slight weight of lookalike Brigitte Bardot had been too much. Nevertheless, it was sudden, and had happened while he was in the throes of doing what he had always loved doing, play-acting in the ring.

Not many people knew it, but he had been riddled with arthritis for years. Those years of bouncing around the wrestling ring had left him with two frozen shoulders, sciatica, tennis elbow: the works. To cope with these ailments, he had become addicted to anabolic steroids. He could not shake them off. Eventually, with that final 'miaow' his heart had given up on him.

What a way to go!

He had been married to his wife, Luludja, Lulu he called her, for thirty four years. Like him, she came from Romany stock. They had three boys and one girl all in the same number of years. Soon after Aishe, the last born, arrived, it was discovered that Tony had become impotent. For a week or two there was an uncomfortable hiatus of doubt about the paternity of Aishe. To everyone's relief, especially Lulu's, with suitable blood tests, it was proven that Tony was indeed the father.

Luludja had wanted done with Manchester for some time. The sale of the club, adjoining shops and flats, all of which she was now the sole owner, would provide ample funds for her to up sticks and relocate to her chosen beach in Slovenia or Croatia, two countries with prevailing sunshine and family connections. Aishe, with husband and five kids, would sell or rent out her own crowded semi-detached house and move into what had been Tony and Luludja's spacious family home. This showy detached house which some said could be seen from space when lit-up at Christmas time was situated in a favoured residential area in Manchester's suburbs. The three sons, neither of whom had the inclination to follow in their father's footsteps, were behind their mother's decision to close and sell up. There would be funds enough when split equally to expand their joint used-car businesses, which traded successfully in different parts of the city.

Supermarket chains were the front runners in bidding for the site. The area was thin on the ground for grocery stores and would benefit hugely from a modern convenience store, like a Tesco's or Sainsbury's. Not a superstore. The site was not big enough for one of those, but big enough to suit the needs of the district, including space enough for modest off-street parking. It shouldn't be too much of a problem acquiring the few shops still trading independently either side of what had been Tony's Ring.

It would take time to sort all this out, which would give Jimbo an opportunity to see if he could get his own version of a knocking-shop going. He had to get things moving as soon as he could. To his advantage, he now had seven days a week to work with, not just the days Tony's had been closed. Another bonus was that he would be in total control until a sale of the premises had been sorted out. His idea was to re-establish a less fancy Upstairs business with the aim of moving operations to a different location when the time came. He reckoned he had at least a couple of months before any change in the situation would arrive. Possibly more.

He had a head start. The years of managing upstairs had left him with a long list of names and contact details, carefully recorded in his 'green' book. Not all customers were careless enough to leave evidence of their true identities 'Upstairs' but an amazing number of them had been. The girls were asked to sneak this information if at all possible. It was accepted that punters often used false names when trading upstairs. Jimbo preferred to know exactly who they really were. Insurance, he called it. Just in case of come backs or mishap. He also took note of a punter's preferences, which service was required, which girls, how often. An expanse of information was recorded in Jimbo's 'green book'. Very colourful reading it was, too. Upstairs, the girls went by the colour of the room they habitually used, not by name. Sharon, for example was Magenta; Kim, Blue. Then, Red, Pink, Yellow, Orange. No Green. That colour was kept for Jimbo's book.

Luludja had the agreement of her children that in the period before the site could be sold Jimbo should continue to live upstairs on a wage to ensure that squatters didn't move in or vandals wreck the place. This, of course, suited his own objectives perfectly.

Within days of Tony's wake, the only way into the premises was through the door to Jimbo's own flat, then onward to the rainbow rooms. All other routes had been locked and barred.

Going through the green book page by page, Jimbo first selected the most regular clients. Some of these were not surprisingly alarmed to get the call, since they believed their previous visits had been incognito. Jimbo was unabashed to reveal that their patronage had not been forgotten, and that despite the demise of Tony's downstairs, the Upstairs show would go on. The big differences being that entrance would be gained via stairs at the back of the property, bookings being taken by telephone call without the mandatory purchase of expensive drinks.

Keeping the same girls was not strictly necessary, but highly preferable. They already knew the ropes and had their regulars. Some of them, however, had not been completely won over by the new arrangements now Tony himself was gone and downstairs closed.

Particularly Magenta!

She had already had her doubts about being in the grip of Jimbo before Tony died. This new regime would mean being even more answerable to him. Kim was less doubtful. It would be better than working the streets full-time. They had to earn a crust. They could probably find jobs as barmaids, but that wouldn't pay much. With Jimbo, they'd be call-girls, still with their own rainbow room. Being a call-girl sounded a bit posher to Kim. She had visions of them becoming the next Christine Keeler and Mandy Rice-Davies, swanning about with the rich and famous.

'Oh, yeah!' Sharon brought her down to earth. 'With fuck-face Jimbo pulling our strings! Sometimes, Burly, I think you really are a daft fucker!'

'Nothing wrong with dreaming, Phoney!'

In the end, basically to keep him from pestering them, they thought they might as well give Jimbo's new venture a whirl until they could sort something out more attractive for themselves. The territory being familiar helped that decision. Sharon insisted this would only be a stopgap, thinking they could always pull out if they found themselves sitting around with sore arses waiting for the phone to ring.

Two new street girls were enlisted, because 'Marilyn' and 'Brigitte', alias Yellow and Red, were not interested in the new set up.

They had decided to take their chances in London. Sharon was thinking that wasn't such a bad idea but at Kim's insistence agreed to give Jimbo the benefit of doubt for the time being and see how it worked out. They wouldn't exactly be signing a contract. That word had different connotations with Jimbo. 'Ownership' was closer to what he had on his mind.

Sharon would never let that happen if she had anything to say about it. Never. Full stop!

Chapter Twenty Eight

There were many companies in the United Kingdom capable of providing top-quality injection molding. Peter had been pleased to discover that three of them were attached to the Wilson Hughes Group to a lesser or greater extent, one of which was based in that part of the country he was seeking a reason to visit: Manchester. So, he made sure it was that company that got the Initiative's 'fuselage' contract.

'We're going to Manchester, Karl,' he told his inseparable guardian with a brightness in his voice.

Karl took the unexpected news philosophically without bothering to ask why. The reason was soon explained.

'I want a closer look at this injection molding procedure being used. I need to get familiar with that side of the business. It's different to the nuts-and-bolts stuff and printed circuits I've been busy with myself. You might find it interesting, too.'

'In Germany they make best. We should go Munich, not Manchester. Many industry,' Karl pressed, smiling like an alter-ego. 'Then make quick trip to Vienna for proper cream tea, not like Betty's in Marlsbury.'

'I thought people drank coffee more than tea in Austria. The tea I've seen you make for yourself here looks like weak piss!'

Karl shook his head. 'You English,' he said, adding enigmatically. 'Tea bags.'

Hoping to locate Gloria Shaw was his real reason for wanting to go to Manchester, of course. But he needed a smoke screen, so why not injection molding, something of genuine interest to him? Good cover.

If he needed to stay longer to achieve his main objective, he also had an excuse to look at how the progress of the relocated Marlsbury Pump plant was coming along. He had seen plans for it, and it looked interesting enough. Being all steel, glass and straight lines, it was nothing like the original Victorian brick plant. Quite impressive in fact.

Sheila Braithewaite's baby had been given the temporary name of Gloria by the team who had delivered her. On that day, 6th May 1967, the dark clouds and thunderous lightning overhead Sheffield hospital had matched the wild cries and writhing of the young mother during a lengthy, difficult birth. With no response to the pinpricks and bum-smacks from the motionless little blood-covered grey creature that had refused to come forth without a delicate incision precisely administered mid push, the doctors and nurses were ready to accept defeat. But then, drowned by young Sheila's screams as the doctor fought to repair the extensive tearing caused by the cut, the baby girl slowly shed her dreadful cast of blue-grey as she coughed and gurgled and at last began to hiccup her way into the world.

Stephanie never saw her child. As far as she was concerned in her traumatic state, she didn't want to. She thought it dead, and, to her guilt and shame towards the end of her own life, had always been happy to believe it.

Gloria was the choice of name on her tagged toe. Mr. and Mrs. Shaw, the overjoyed couple who were soon to become her adopted mum and dad, had been more than happy to keep the name.

Stephanie never healed completely, neither mentally nor physically. The experience had all but brought both mother and child to death's door.

'Please use the utmost delicacy, Mr. Tyler,' the major had stressed. wondering if she had done the right thing in releasing the confidential information. But who was she to stand in the way of Stephanie's wishes, if the outcome would be for the child's good?

Peter had assured her with the sincerity of a monk that he would tread very carefully. And he had meant it. But the coming of Gloria Shaw promised to offer up a compensatory thorn to stick into Ludlow should Peter's new world collapse around him.

Karl chauffeured Peter to Manchester in the company Jaguar.

Their hotel overlooked Piccadilly Gardens in the centre. Immediately after checking in, Peter phoned the desk, inventing a complaint so he could be moved to a different room on a different floor. He preferred not to be in the one he had been given adjacent to his minder. Space between them would suit him better.

Once safely settled, he unfolded a map of the city and laid it on the bed feeling he should perhaps be rattling a Dry Martini, shaken not stirred.

One part of the city in particular interested him. As he prepared for the evening, he put his knowledge to the test, glancing down to check he had got certain routes correct in his head so he wouldn't have to pull the map out in the street.

He knew precisely where the target address lay. Whether Gloria still lived there, he would have to wait and see. It wouldn't work to dive straight in. A soft approach was the best plan.

Staking out would have been easier with a car, but that was out of the question. In his wildest dreams, he couldn't think of having Karl along for *that* ride.

Victor Rose had set up a meeting for Tyler at the injection molding company. Although Ludlow had suggested companies in other cities might have been better options, Tyler had stuck to his choice. 'Suit yourself if it gives you a hard on!' Rose had responded irritably. 'If you think you know better than your boss!' Rose had been growing to dislike Tyler even more now the Initiative was looking to be a success as the weeks had gone by.

'Sorry to disappoint you, fag end, but I think you'll find I'm my own boss,' Tyler had come back at Rose, knowing it would truly wind him up that it was known he had once 'fagged' for Ludlow at boarding school.

The meeting was set up for early afternoon the next day. Peter's real business would be undertaken late at night, when good-time girls came out to play. Hopefully, Karl would be tucked up in bed by then.

It had taken a couple of weeks for Jimbo to get his own idea of a brothel going. At first, punters were suspicious of the new arrangements. The closure of Tony's Ring had attracted a lot of local press. The idea of having to get into the Upstairs Rainbow Rooms via the outside back stairway instead of the discreet interior lift put customers off. Jimbo did all he could to explain that everything was the same once inside, but this took time to get through. And it wasn't quite true. It was *not* exactly the same once inside. There would be no foreplay, so to speak, with soft music, free booze and the girls fancy dressed as stars. It would literally be an in-and-out job. Punters were not encouraged to hang about before or after services had been provided.

The girls sat around wrapped in shawls waiting for action. Heating had been reduced to a minimum since the club had stopped operating. There was no dressing up, no pretense of being anyone but themselves.

Sharon, however, did continue to wear her Stephanie Star wig. She considered it to be her trademark disguise. Worn only for business. Without it, she felt she could walk the streets incognito as her own person.

What Jimbo did keep the same was screened pornography on tap. Not so much a welcome for the clients, more to put them in the mood to get on with it. Payment in cash up front upon entry.

Business continued at a slow pace, being now conducted solely through telephone bookings. Even Jimbo began to see the girls' point of view that it was a waste of time sitting around waiting for no reason.

There were no 'walk-ins' anymore. Most of the clients gave at least a day's notice for an appointment. Some even booked a regular spot, to coincide with their domestic arrangements. As long as the girls were on site in good time to meet prearranged bookings, all would be fine. But watch out, if they weren't!

In case rush bookings came in, they were told they had to be near their telephone early evenings. This idea immediately put Sharon's nose out of joint. Not only did Jimbo still want control over their movements, but with rush bookings you never knew who the geezer was you might be lumbered with. Jimbo would always be around should muscle be needed. But why take the risk? It was not the way Sharon wanted to work.

The two new street girls Jimbo had signed up had no access to a phone other than a public call box, so they took off to another city without notice. They didn't hang around to be faced with Jimbo's known violent temper.

While he was still trying to come to terms with this setback, Sharon and Kim decided it was a good time to rub salt into his wound. They told him they would only be on call the same days they had worked for Tony. That was Thursdays to Sundays. Jimbo eventually went along with this arrangement since bookings hardly ever came in before the weekend. He, himself, was getting pissed off sitting around waiting for the phone to ring at the beginning of the week. So, he could see it made sense. And he couldn't afford to lose Sharon and Kim. They took most bookings, usually from good paying regulars. Somehow, he would have to get hold of one of those new mobile phones that were all the rage. That would help.

At weekends, he thought he would be able to keep four girls as busy as they wanted to be. But this wouldn't start happening until after Tony's wake had come and gone.

The funeral itself was an event that made the local TV news, so well-known was Tony as a showman. The occasion did not disappoint. As had been Tony's wish, his coffin sat in the middle of a replica wrestling ring adorned with the cups and trophy belts he had accumulated over his active years. Laid across the coffin itself was one of his famous 'tiger' leotards. This fitting display was mounted on an open carriage drawn by four horses of Romany stock.

As a gesture to the closing of Tony's Ring, Luludja thought it would be a 'nice touch' to have as many of the famous 'stars' who had worked there follow behind the family's open carriage in one of their own, 'Just to add a bit of colour', because Tony would have loved that. No-one could have guessed how many other horse-drawn carriages and caravans would follow on behind. It was like a scene from 'How The West Was Won!'. Then came the limos bearing various minor show-biz personalities who had befriended Tony over the years. Other mourners walked behind this procession along streets that had become lined with onlookers attracted by the spectacle.

Not a royal funeral, but one fitting a former king of the wrestling ring.

Tony's Ring was the obvious venue for his wake. This would be his last fling and it would be packed out. No gatecrashers would find their way in. Security was tight.

The streets around it were also crowded with rubber-neckers trying to get a glimpse of the   celebrities. They were soon gone once the carriages had been trotted off, leaving all evidence of having been there to be scraped up by a group of lads bearing shovels and brooms. Generously rewarded for this task, they had been engaged to follow the parade pushing wheelbarrows to clear up horse droppings and litter. With so much interest in the event, Lulu did not want to give the press any opportunity to besmirch Tony's big day.

Lulu spared no money in laying on a good spread at the wake. There was still enough booze left in stock behind the bar, but she had ordered plenty extra to be sure no-one went short.

The same location catering company familiar with show-biz events that had been engaged for the fateful birthday bash was brought in again. It seemed fitting.

Not a sad pizza in sight.

The rainbow girls, as Lulu liked to call them, were kept busy circulating non-stop with trays of drinks and snacks, always available to pose as usual for photographs with guests. Jimbo was in charge of keeping the girls on their toes, but he was more interested in identifying any of those guests present whom he knew to be familiar with the services offered Upstairs. There was strictly no such 'catering' available today, of course. Jimbo wasn't that crass, although the thought had occurred to him. Luludja had no idea he was attempting to keep that part of Tony's Ring active for as long as he could once downstairs was closed.

What he had gone ahead with, however, was having business cards printed to discreetly hand to known punters so they would know it was going to be business as usual Upstairs until further notice. 'Rainbow Loft Conversions still open for business' the cards announced. 'Ring Jimbo for more information.' He had already handed out a few at the church, before and after the service, and now had his eye on a dozen or so more at the wake. It was a friendlier way of passing on the news than cold-calling punters who had no idea their phone numbers and sexual preferences had been stored in Jimbo's little green book.

The day went well. Tony would have been proud. Next morning, after one final clean-up, Jimbo made sure industrial padlocks and bars went on all doors at ground level. Access to the entire premises would now only be possible through Jimbo's personal flat, where he would reside until such time as the property changed ownership.

Tesco's seemed keen to outbid all-comers to acquire the site to make way for one of their first Express stores. All the adjacent shops in the parades either side of Tony's would need to be bought out for this enterprise to happen, which might hold up negotiations because one or two of them were holding out for a better deal. Jimbo knew they would eventually succumb and at that point he would have to move on. His problem would be having the wherewithal to set up somewhere else by that time. Otherwise, it would be back on the streets.

Sharon had soon become pissed off with Jimbo's call-girl set-up, let alone his bullying and threats. Providing for her regulars was fine but doing tricks with some of the unknown telephone punters Jimbo came up with was not to her liking at all. Jimbo didn't give a fuck who he stitched the girls up with. It was money in his pocket, whoever he brought in.

At Tony's you could see who the potential clients were, and you could take 'em or leave 'em. Tony was good like that. Even on the streets you had a choice.

So, even before Tesco's had moved in and Jimbo out, Sharon was back on the street working her old patch again. Not exactly behind Jimbo's back, because he didn't own her, despite thinking he did. But there was no point winding him up unnecessarily by advertising the fact. It would be like waving a red flag at a bull. Kim was less fussy but would always cover for Sharon whenever she could, to calm Jimbo down. The loss of the security Tony's Place had given him was making him unstable, just as he had been in his younger years before being locked up.

There was nowhere in Manchester that Sharon and Kim knew of where they could find work as 'hostesses' with anything like the set-up of Tony's Ring. The few pubs that offered similar services were all well-staffed, with long waiting lists. Wanting to work together made finding the right sort of place doubly difficult for them.

They kept their eyes on the small ads for jobs in case something turned up. In the meantime, they knew they could get by without being at the beck and call of Jimbo. The problem was, Jimbo was finding it difficult to get by without *them*.

He hadn't planned well enough ahead. Without Tony's, he was just a pimp demanding protection money from girls. He was an intimidating bastard, putting the frighteners not only on the girls, but on potential customers as well. It was almost impossible for the girls to pick up work without cutting him in. And dangerous for them if they did.

The area they concentrated on was in a run-down part of town well known as being a red-light district. Trade was almost exclusively drive-by's. One pub still existed in the area, used mainly as a hangout for the street girls between tricks. Not much went on upstairs.

It was one of the pubs Peter Tyler had circled on his map.

'I'm going out to get myself laid tonight,' Peter fore-warned the Austrian to pave way for his disappearing act should he be caught red-handed.

'Not bad idea,' Karl concurred. 'Same thought I had. But it rains. Plenty girls in bar. Why get wet outside?'

'Not my type. They're looking for businessmen. Pricy.'

Karl seemed confused. 'What mean 'pricy'.'

'Expensive. 'Mucho gelt'!'

'Huh!' Karl scoffed. 'You got plenty 'gelt'.'

And, as Karl pointed out, Peter was also a businessman, although no-one in this hotel would have guessed it unless they had recognized his face from seeing it in the papers. He still insisted on his track-suit attire. Smart hotel girls would not go for that look in a hurry. It was off-putting. Out of place. Something he was actually beginning to accept more than a little these days. 'You enjoy yourself here, Karl, my man. I feel more like an adventure. Know what I mean?'

Karl thought he did. 'I put on peak cap and you sit in back. We let Jaguar do the pulling. What you say?'

'No way. Tell you what. You take the Jaguar, if you like. See how you do cruising. I'll rely on my own devices. We can compare notes over a late breakfast.'

Karl chuckled, thinking Tyler had made a deliberate pun. '*De-vices*'. He struggled with making one himself with the word. 'You risk knob on the streets, then maybe have to squeeze it in de-vice, nicht!' He made twisting movements with a clenched fist, grimacing as though the outcome would be painful. 'In Austria, we have tight control on night girls. Is better.'

Peter didn't argue.

Peter asked Karl to drop him in one of the parts of the city known for its street life which was nowhere near his ultimate destination. It was only just after nine and still quite busy.

'Don't catch anything,' Karl joked. 'You crazy man.'

'Yeah-yeah. Perhaps.'

As soon as the Jaguar had disappeared, Peter waited for the first taxi to come looking for a fare.

'Do you know any night clubs around here?' he asked the driver.

'Nothing round this way, guv,' the cabby replied. 'I'd have to take you into the centre. Used to be one called 'Tony's' not too far from here, but that closed a few weeks back. I think it's going to be a Tesco's now, which'll be a bit handy for me. I live nearby.'

'Well, I don't really want to go into the centre. Do you know a pub called 'The Black Swan'? I think that's somewhere around this way.'

'The Black Swan it is, then. It's not that lively a place, if you're looking for action. There's another one not all that much further, might be better for you.'

Peter thought he knew the one the cabby was talking about, but he didn't want to go there just yet.

'The Black Swan's fine. Only looking for a quick pint.'

'Got yer!'

After being dropped, he ignored the pub and walked a few hundred yards until he found himself in a residential area of the suburbs. Wide tree-lined streets with large, detached houses sitting back from the road.

'Ardwick Mansions' was a Victorian edifice with a steeply pitched roof and dormer windows all round. It stood on a corner, which gave it added distance from its neighbours. Its porch was lit unevenly by an 'olde worlde' lamp that had lost several pieces of its stained glass.

Making his first walk pass, Peter could see a line of bellpushes which corresponded to the major's findings that the house was divided into bed-sits.

Lights were on in several windows which would seem to fit into the picture. Reggae music drifted down from one of them, but not loud enough to disturb the laced-curtained feeling pervading the street.

At the end of the road, he turned and went back. No-one was out walking. This was automobile territory. Most of these seemed to be parked in garages or driveways, which, together with the mature trees all along it gave the street a sense of 'mind your own business'.

Having got a feel of the place, he decided it was time to move on. It would be almost ten by the time he reached the other pub the taxi driver had mentioned. The one he was more interested in checking out.

It was on the edge of the red-light district in a pretty grim part of town pointed out by the major. Most of his knowledge had come from her searches, with his own map-reading thrown in. The district was not much more than a wasteland of railway arches and bridges straddling a downtrodden patchwork of streets that had been cut off by an elevated dual carriageway with an access roundabout in one direction, a disused canal and railway tracks in others.

It was fairly apparent why the street girls had chosen this enclosed zone to market their wares. Most of the cars driving into it looking for action entered via a road leading from the roundabout which then had to curl round beneath the elevated section before it showed itself on their patch. This meant they had a quick preview of vehicles heading their way, and if any happened to be police cars paying a visit, it gave the girls extra time to clear the pavements before they arrived. There was a stairway leading up to the main road and paths through to the canal, all of which were well trodden on such occasions. There was also the pub to disappear into should that be the nearest option. The odd unmarked squad car got through, but generally the cops weren't too hard on the girls. It was the pimps they were more interested in nabbing.

Peter arrived over a railway footbridge into the dank streets, the houses of which opened directly onto the pavements. As he followed his mental map to where he would find the pub he was targeting, he sent one young girl diving for cover. Appearing from nowhere without a car not looking like a normal punter, she took him as being bad news. The Law in plain clothes? On closer examination, his tracksuit told her he wasn't. He was just about to say something, but she beat him to it. 'Piss off, weirdo!' she bawled. She never went with blokes without cars. She could have been no older than sixteen.

Two more girls were standing in the doorway of a defunct hairdressers next to the pub.

'Looking for a girl?' one of them asked, cold bloodedly. She wasn't fussy about his bike gear and tracksuit top. She wasn't exactly dressed elegantly herself in a short black PVC coat and knee-length boots with little else beneath, it seemed. She must have been freezing. It wasn't a particularly warm evening.

'Not for the minute, sweetheart,' Peter found himself saying in friendly tones, as if thankful for not being told to piss off a second time. He smiled at them briefly. One looked twice as old as the other. Neither of them could be Gloria Shaw. Of that he was certain.

A car cruised by with its passenger window down. Two men inside. The older woman in PVC skipped to the gutter and walked alongside it, peering in. After a few seconds, she waved the kid over and as the back door opened, they jumped in. Two happy hookers!

Another car arrived, stopping about fifty yards away. The figure of a woman stepped out of the darkness of one of the railway arches and presented her face at the driver's window. Whatever he saw, he didn't like, for he drove off without taking her on board.

Peter strolled up to her, immediately seeing her trouble. She was well into her fifties. In the low light, she could even have been a bloke.

'Looking for me, honey?' she asked, ever hopeful. She had a sympathetic smile, but that was about it. Hard times. Peter felt sorry for her.

'No, someone else. You looked a bit like her from a distance.' The second sentence was complete fabrication. So was the next. 'My regular girl. Gloria. You know her?'

The hooker pulled a face. No working girl used her real name. And there were no Gloria's on this patch. 'Never heard of her,' she said curtly. 'Try me for a change. Anything you like. I ain't fussy.'

'Thanks, but no.' He wasn't *that* sorry for her.

He decided to make a quick tour of the neighbourhood.

An assortment of girls lurked along the wet streets, scattered like an unruly platoon on manoeuvres, armed only with the will to survive. Most were holed up in dark corners, well-chosen strategic positions for advance or retreat.

Peter was propositioned several times, and when it seemed appropriate, he took the opportunity to ask about Gloria. But he soon realised it was a waste of time. Using a name just created suspicion. No-one knew her, or they weren't saying so if they did. He didn't look like a father, but he might have been a disgruntled boyfriend. He could even have been a plain clothed cop, tracksuit or not. So why take chances? The biggest puzzle; he was on foot.

Ten minutes later he had worked his way back to the pub. A sign hanging outside said, 'The   Mitre'. The pair he had seen getting into the car earlier were just being dropped back on their spot. 'That was quick!' he thought. The woman waved the car goodbye. Short and sweet. She seemed well satisfied.

He followed them into the Pub. They made straight for the 'Ladies' while he shuffled to the bar and bought himself half a pint. The place was fairly busy, but he found a corner seat where he could keep a casual eye on the comings and goings.

There were more women than men, some of them looking barely of age.

Of the men, one stood out. This guy was chunky but gaunt looking, with arms and neck covered in tattoos. He was talking loudly and sounded Scottish. His face had been through the wars. At a guess Peter put him in his late thirties. His tightly cropped red hair was splattered with gaps like a wheat field after a storm. He seemed to be giving a dark-haired punkish-looking girl a hard time, although she didn't appear to be too concerned about it. She obviously knew the man; had heard it all before?

The bar was unadorned. A proper local that had seen plenty of wear and tear. Peter's impression was of familiarity. It was not unlike 'The King's Head' in Marlsbury – full of misfits and ne'er-do-wells?

He had no sense of being alienated as a strange new face. Without compromising his usual garb to make it more suited to a night out on the town, no-one had paid his entrance too much attention. Those who did were probably thinking he must have left his bike outside, perhaps with the thought that it might be worth nipping out to nick. All in all, he felt happily anonymous. Quite obvious was that no-one recognized him.

He pretended not to seem interested in what was going on but could not help noticing the Scottish guy turn to a girl who had just come in. She went directly to him. Few words were spoken, but, discreet as it was meant to be, money was passed to him. No diplomas for guessing his job description! With a nod, the guy turned back to the girl he was sitting with. He now started pointing a finger at her like gunshots.

Peter couldn't hear exactly what was being said, despite his Scottish brogue being as raw as jute.

Looks had clearly not been this man's priority in life. His forehead was a battlefield of scars, his nose pushed almost flat.

Peter got up for another half-pint, taking his time as he sidled past the Scot on his way to the bar. He didn't catch much of what was being said, but what he did tell him enough of what the finger pointing might be about.

'Where's that cow Sharon? I'll dip her dugs in acid if she's trying to do another runner!' Not nice at all. 'Two days it's bin!'

'We don't get into police matters,' the major had told Peter. 'We just do the best we can for the girls' welfare if they'll let us. There are a lot of foreign girls, too. They are even more difficult to help, of course. As soon as they see our uniform, they disappear.' She had been talking generally about prostitution. How younger and younger girls were being groomed against their will. 'They're too afraid to come forward, so how can we help them?'

Some of the girls coming and going from the pub were prime candidates for salvation if ever he saw them. Underage, under protected, and under siege by leeches like this guy with his threats.

'Unfortunately, Stephanie's daughter would seem to have hit rock bottom. I don't know what to say. Even the job she had in the nightclub was probably not all it might have seemed, but at least it kept her off the streets. The police know it's going on, of course,' the major had said, 'but how can they stop it completely? They can't be everywhere, for goodness sake. If the girls are caught, they pay a fine and the pimps have them back on the streets the same day. It's these sex traffickers that must be stopped. Once the girls get caught up in the business, it really is a one-way street for them. They need to be helped, not punished. Often, they come from disturbed or violent backgrounds and believe the pimps are a better option than going back to whatever they ran away from. I don't know how you intend to find her, but one thing you might want to try is checking out our Friday night soup kitchen. It's quite popular with the homeless and the sex workers.'

Peter was suddenly thrown from his reverie.

The Scottish thug had leapt to his feet, upturning his chair in the process. 'Come here you little cow!' he yelled, bringing conversation in the bar to a momentary halt. When people saw who had caused the eruption, they went back to minding their own businesses. The girl who had supposedly
gone missing for two days had just walked into the pub as defiantly as a fox.

Peter froze. It was like an ice pick had been driven into his spine. The Scot was not the only person who had been looking for this girl. This had to be Gloria, alias 'that cow Sharon'. Take away the rainbow-coloured punk hair and black lipstick and there she was, Stephanie Star, Mark II. Gloria Shaw as he knew her. Even the bunch of rings punched through her ears couldn't take the likeness away. It was staggering.

The look of 'fuck you!' on her face as she walked in suddenly changed to one of 'for fuck's sake, not again' when she saw the Scot.

As the pimp lumbered over to her, she stood her ground defiantly, letting rip a string of expletives to ward him off. Not a chance! He grabbed her by the rings of her ear, twisting until blood came. 'Where the fook ha *you* bin? Go missin agin an' you's in the fookin canal!'

He was hurting her, but she didn't give him the satisfaction of screaming. No-one stepped in to stop him. No-one but Peter Tyler, that was. It must have been some sort of animal instinct he didn't know he possessed. He got up and moved quickly forward. By the time he got to them, the pimp had let go of the ear and Peter found himself confronting the man face on. So alien did this budding challenge appear to be to the Scot, that he just stood and gaped. Was this wimp of a guy serious? Was this a do-gooder who'd lost his bearings?

With every eye in the pub on him, Peter was now wondering what on earth had induced him to interfere? Dutch courage? He'd only had half a pint!

'Steady on, squire,' he said, adding somewhat inanely, 'don't damage the goods.'

Whatever the Scot thought of Peter's banal words, they seemed to do the trick. There was nothing but violence in the man's eyes. No point trying to reason. Peter suddenly felt totally ridiculous and inadequate playing the hero.

'Piss off, wanker!' Sharon hissed with feeling, aiming it directly at Peter in case there should be any misunderstanding. Was she sensing an even uglier situation was developing and wanted to diffuse it? 'I ain't your fucking goods!'

Jimbo seemed to like her words. He looked Peter's garb up and down, smiling without opening his mouth. 'On yer fookin bike!' he threatened, clearly undecided about turning his back on a confrontation. 'Before I change ma mind.'

'Fair enough.' Peter nodded, happy to accept the non-violent route. 'I was just making my way to the bar.' He lied.

With another half-pint in his hand, he returned to his seat. So much for chivalry. Where did that streak come from all of a sudden? He would have to curb it. This was not the time nor place to test it.

As much as he tried to disguise it, he was unable to take his eyes off Sharon. There could be little doubting it, she was Stephanie Star's unsuspecting daughter, Gloria. Beneath the punk make-up, there was no mistaking it. It was magnetic.

Sharon kept throwing quick glances at Peter as she faced down the threats being aimed at her. What was with this guy? Was he some sort of crank? Only a nutter would try to take Jimbo on. Yet somehow, he seemed familiar. Was it something to do with the way he was dressed? Weird.

Peter could see her interest in him. Whether she had recognized him or was just irritated by his constant eyeballing, she didn't let on to her pimp, which was encouraging, at least.

After about ten minutes of what looked like a pretty one-sided intense discussion, Jimbo latched onto another girl who had just come in and Sharon quickly left the pub. With Jimbo's attention drawn to the new girl, Peter gave it a minute, then slipped out unnoticed.

It took him a while to find Sharon. She was holed up in one of the arches with the other girl who had been sitting with Jimbo when Peter had entered the pub. They were sharing something out. Peter didn't expect it was Smarties.

'How's your ear, Sharon? Still bleeding?' he asked like a bright new pin.

She didn't know for sure, but it sounded like he was taking the piss. He made her feel uncomfortable, that much she did know. Anyone who'd go face on to Jimbo had to be mental. This bloke could be trouble.

But she had dealt with worse.

'Are you trying to piss me off, or what? You don't know how close you came to it back there.'

'I think I do. I don't know what happened to me. But you seemed to be in trouble until you called me a wanker. That wasn't very nice of you, was it?'

'If you're that sensitive, you shouldn't be out after dark, chuck!'

This drew giggles from the other girl.

'Shit or get off the pot,' Sharon suddenly said, putting a hand to her damaged ear. 'If you don't want a seeing to, fuck off. You're in the way.'

'I don't want the two of you. I'm not that weird.'

'Haven't you looked at yourself lately?'

'I dress for comfort,' Peter didn't mind the banter. 'Your ear's still bleeding, by the way. It needs disinfecting after that prick's fingers have been all over it.'

'Are you me fucking mother, now?'

'Just telling you. So, can we leave your chum and go somewhere?'

'Where's your car?'

'It's not with me. Haven't you got a place we can go?'

'I 'ave, but we ain't! If you want comfort, you provide it. Otherwise, it's just a hand job. Where do you think you are, Romeo? Bleedin' Mayfair? There in't nowhere comfy round 'ere.'

'A hand job it is then.'

Sharon exchanged glances with her friend and shrugged. 'We do get 'em, don't we, Kim?'

'He seems harmless enough,' Kim shrugged.

'Needs must, I s'pose.' But Sharon had her eye on the prize. This bloke was from down south. She could probably get away with charging him double. He was definitely the gullible type to get up thinking he could take on Jimbo.

Sharon put Peter as coming from London. She couldn't hear his West Country twang. She started walking deeper into the arch. 'Come on, lover boy. Over here.' she said, jerking her head.

Two minutes later, she was jerking something else.

He wondered about the ethics of what he was doing, but felt it was the best way to convince her he was harmless.

'That'll cost you twenty quid,' she said when it was done. 'You had more than your money's worth eyeballing me all night in the pub. I ought to charge you double.' She already was, at twenty quid.

It was safe sex, if completely mercenary. Sordid. Under the arch with the noise of traffic and dripping water from above, the squelch of rubber gloves from below. She was taking no chances. He didn't blame her.

She had no idea, but better times would soon be up for grabs for her. It was only a matter of how to convince her to reach out and take them.

The deed done he took out his wallet while she peeled off her gloves. He was expecting her to discard them there and then. But no. As if placed for that explicit reason, like dog-litter bins in a park, there was a convenient waste bin hanging on the wall outside the arch. She dumped them in it, then seeing his open wallet, put her hand out.

He counted the money into it: 'Five, ten, fifteen, twenty....'. At twenty, she was about to fold the notes up, but he stopped her. 'Hang on. You're a bit keen, aren't you? You said double.'

She gave a look of disbelief. 'What?'

'You said you ought to charge me double for eyeballing you all night. It was hardly all night, but I don't want you going around telling people I'm a mean git. I've got my good name to protect. So, double it is' He waved his head about airily, hamming it up as if he belonged to the upper classes. 'Do you think I can't afford it, daaarling?' he gibed.

'Get you, yer daft fucker. But thanks. Anytime.' She didn't know what to make of him. Weird? Yes. Threatening? No. Loaded? Maybe not, but he had plenty enough for now. She'd seen what was in his wallet. She liked this part of his 'style'. Forget about his dress sense, something was still niggling her. What was it about him? Had she met him before? Not round here, that was for sure. But she was certain she had seen him somewhere. She was about to ask him what part of London he was from, when he spoke.

'So how much do you make on a good night?' Kim drifted over to them. Nothing had happened for her in the interim.

'What's it to you?' Sharon responded, dodging the question. She didn't normally want to get into a conversation with a punter once they'd paid up. On this occasion, it was the opposite. This guy wasn't a normal punter, that much she knew. Forty quid for a hand job!

'I'm interested, that's all.'

'You seem interested in a lot of things that don't concern you.'

'What you charge obviously does concern me.'

'Don't tell me you want to be a fucking pimp? Daft fucker!'

'Do I look the type?'

'Not much. Not enough scars. But that nearly changed in the pub just now.'

'Thanks for helping out with that. You ought to get away from that creep.' He turned to Kim. 'You, too, from the way he was having a go at you earlier.'

'Fuck me!' Sharon swore resolutely as if she had just seen the light. 'You must be the Sally Army in disguise? Out to get your oats while trying to mend our ways at the same time. Shouldn't you be working the Friday soup kitchen? Is that where I've seen you before?'

Peter was taken aback by that sudden reference. It could have been expected, he supposed.

'Now you've got me down as both the Good *and* the Bad. What about the ugly?'

She thought about it for a second. 'Naa. You ain't so bad. Just a daft fucker.'

'Daft enough to give you forty quid for a hand-job, I accept. So, how much do you usually make on a good night?'

Sharon gave Kim a shifty look, so he guessed a bare-faced lie was coming. 'Hundred, hundred'n ten. Summat like that.'

Complete fantasy. Way over the odds, he reckoned. But he liked her ambition. He needed that for her to take the bait.

'And that's a good night, right?' He asked as if for confirmation. 'Like a Friday or Saturday?' She nodded with a look that suggested she thought he actually *believed* her. He took his time before making his proposition. 'OK. A hundred and twenty quid if you spend all tomorrow night with me in comfort. Proper job. Rubber, but no gloves. That's my offer.' He said it as if it was his final bid at an auction.

Was this guy for real?

'You provide the comfort?' She wanted to know before bringing down the hammer.

'I provide the comfort.'

Her face was illuminated for a second by the lights of a passing car hitting the dank roof of the arch. He thought he saw doubt. But the businesswoman in her prevailed.

'Done,' she agreed. But there was a proviso. She was wary of going in completely headfirst. He seemed all right, but you never could tell. 'On one condition.'

'Go on.'

'I bring my friend.'

'As long as it's not your mate Jimbo!'

'Daft fucker!' she laughed. 'Do me a favour! Kim, here.'

'I can't handle two of you!'

'She won't get in the way. Will you Kim? Just for security.'

'What about my security?'

'Daft fucker,' she said again, laughing.

'Same price?'

'Same price.'

'Sounds like a bargain,' he said, thinking of saying he *could* perhaps handle the pair of them after all, because Kim had bigger tits. But he thought better of it. Best not test her sense of humour any further for the time being.

It would have been the wrong time for it anyway, as it happened.

'Shit!' Sharon barked, her eyes in a squint looking over his shoulders. 'You'd better scarper quick. Jimbo's on the fucking war-path by the look of 'im.'

Peter glanced over his shoulder. Sure enough, Jimbo was thundering down the street towards them.

''Op it!' Sharon urged. 'He won't piss about with you now you're outside. There's steps up the other side of the arch to the left about fifty yards. Go!'

'Room 526, Swan Hotel, eight tomorrow?' he said, looking her in the eye, unmoved. He wasn't going until she agreed. 'Hundred and twenty,' he reminded her. She gave a sharp nod. He gave one back as if to seal the deal, turned, and was through the arch before Jimbo got to Sharon.

'Why'r ya bin gassing with that prick?' He growled, suspicious, and not shy about it. 'Wha-the-fook're you's up to!'

'What the fuck're you up to yerself, knob-head?' The only way was to stand up to Jimbo. 'Always putting the frighteners on punters? I've just done a trick with him. You've just pissed off a fucking gold-mine, wanker! Probably never see him again, thanks to you.'

'Where's the fookin' money, ya cheeky cow?

This was something Sharon wasn't going to argue about. She took a ten pound note out and handed it to him. She knew that would quieten him. That was her regular rate for a hand job. She wasn't going to tell him she'd copped forty quid!

'Now fuck off and leave me to it, you're like a fucking voo-doo man, scaring punters off.'

'And you's. Don't you be fooking disappearin' agin!'

'Don't be surprised if I do!' Sharon was about to answer but stopped herself. One thing was sure. She *would* be seeing that punter again, as long as he wasn't stitching her up. And she wouldn't be sharing any of the hundred and twenty quid with Jimbo, not a penny, no matter what!

Chapter Twenty Nine

Sharon and Kim thought they'd make a night-out of the occasion since there was a hundred and twenty quid in it, much more than they would normally make together of a weekend working the streets. They got to Peter's hotel an hour before he was expecting them and went straight to the bar. The idea, apart from living it up a little with a cocktail or two to get in the mood was to suss out if they could spot any girls working the place. And they didn't mean as waitresses. They had made no concessions to their street wardrobe to blend in better with 'the discreet charm of the bourgeoisie', the more conventional guests who usually frequented 5-Star city hotels. These two black-clad punks, dressed purposely that way so as not to be mistaken for hookers, looked especially out of place in the soft plushness, drawing more than the occasional glance. Were they groupies to some heavy metal band playing somewhere in the city? Or perhaps members of a punk group themselves?

Both Sharon and Kim felt perfectly at home being stared at. Tony's had cured them of any embarrassment they might have had about that. Wearing tutus and skimpy tops, Sharon looking like Stephanie Star, and Kim fighting to keep her tits in as Jane Russell, they were a non-stop floor show. Eyes were never off them as they moved around. It was all good fun, and they couldn't get enough of it.

The Swan Hotel's décor was perhaps 4 stars up from Tony's place, but not so you would notice after a couple of drinks if your mind was on other things. The present customers didn't look that much different to some of those found at Tony's.

But Tony's was a night club, with the rainbow rooms upstairs for the use of, 'rented' by the hour, not the day. The girls who worked the hotels might themselves have been 'rented' by the hour, but the hotel rooms were respectably booked by the day.

Sharon and Kim looked around for any likely suspects. It would be interesting to know how good the trade was. They had thought about trying to break into the hotel circuit themselves after Tony's place had folded. But generally, they found that side of the business was sewn up by gangs. These two wanted nothing to do with gangs. It was bad enough having

Jimbo at their throats thinking he owned them. Sharon was entertaining the idea of moving away from the city to get him off her back completely. Kim was still wavering. Jimbo was no more than a chancer trying to go it alone after losing the safety net of Tony's to cling to. But he had become a dangerously *unstable* chancer. Tony had been his life safer. With him gone, Jimbo had returned to being a loose cannon.

At 5 to 8, Sharon went to the front desk and asked to be put through to Mr. Peter's room, 526. Peter was the only name she had for him.

'Who shall I say is calling?' Carol, the receptionist asked, trying to hide her suspicions behind a professional smile.

'His expensive lay,' Sharon was tempted to say, but stuck with 'Sharon'.

'Are you expected?' Another polite smile from Carol.

I fucking hope so! Sharon suddenly thought but answered yes.

She was handed the receiver once Peter had confirmed Sharon was *bona fide*.

'Hello, Romeo, it's me, Sharon. You haven't been having it off with the receptionist, have you? She sounded a bit put out when I asked for you.'

'Which one?' he replied, equal to her tease.

'Ha bloody ha. Nice one. Anyway, thank Christ you're there. It suddenly hit me that you might have been taking the piss.'

'Now, would I do a thing like that? Just get in the lift and come up to the fifth floor. 526 is on the left as you come out. I'll leave the door wedged open.'

She handed the receiver back to the receptionist, who now had raised eyebrows. Perhaps she had overheard some of the conversation.

'Thanks, Sharon. Have a nice day,' Sharon mimicked aloud, sensing she wasn't going to get the sentiment from Carol herself.

Sharon went back to the bar to tell Kim it wasn't a wind-up. 'Give it an hour or two before you come knocking. And try not to get too pissed. I'll leave the door open somehow, if I can, but it probably self-locks, 'cos he's leaving it wedged open for me to get in. Just hammer on it if I can't. Anyway, that's where I am. I see you've got your eye on that bloke in leathers who's just come in. You might even get lucky yourself. But don't you dare leave the hotel without me, OK? And don't spend all the money I've given you. This is a working gig! See you in a bit.'

Three minutes later, Sharon walked into room 526 acting like a little girl lost. It was more than a room. It was a suite. Her eyes lit up, but she held her tongue. She didn't expect this.

Peter was surprised to see her alone.

'Where's your minder?'

'She's got her eye on some guy in the bar. We couldn't spot any other girls on the game, so I think she could get lucky. She usually does with bazookas like her's when she puts her mind to it. It's all right. I don't need a minder. I think I can trust you. I've got to in a place like this, in't I?'

'Never be fooled by appearances.'

'Don't worry. I think I've got you sussed.'

He pointed to a bowl of fruit on a table set with two chairs.

'There's something for you over there.'

Under the bowl was a pile of banknotes.

Sharon's eyes lit up anew. She went to the table, picked up the money and counted it. It was all there. One hundred and twenty pounds!

With a sly look on her face, she turned and made for the door. 'Nice doing business with you. Tara!'

At the door, she turned, giggling. 'Had you there, didn't I?'

'It would have been your loss, punk! Easy come, easy go.'

'Money up front. I like it.'

'I thought you might. I didn't want you worrying about our agreed fee, since it's probably double what you earn in a week on the streets!'

So, he'd sussed her?

'I take it you're not worried about getting value for your money?'

'Nope. If I don't like food in a restaurant, I go elsewhere. Same difference.'

'Well, you'll have to tell me what you like, and I hope you're hungry.'

'All in good time. A start would be taking your coat off.'

Her coat was black and looked far too loose on her. It might have been her mate Kim's, but he guessed it was the punk style she was into. She took it off and threw it over one of the twin beds, revealing baggy black slacks underneath as well, the crutch of them nearly down to her knees. Peter thought all that loose punk stuff had been last year, if not even earlier. It was far from becoming, but somehow went with the rest of the camouflage.

'Kim'll come up later, so don't be alarmed if you hear someone bashing on the door while we're at it. She won't get in the way. If I know her, she'll dive straight into the bathroom for a soak. We've only got a poxy shower in our gaff. Having said that, we might not see her till the morning. She's after pulling some bloke she's seen in the bar, if I know her, as long as no hotel hookers turn up.'

Peter shrugged. 'Good. I wouldn't want to think she's been banished back to the streets around that pub of yours. This is much more salubrious, don't you think?'

'Course it is, whatever that means. But it's not our patch. We'd be treading on some big fat toes if we tried it on in this place. There's worse than that Jimbo fucker out there, ya know.'

'I have my doubts about that. You've got to get rid of that arsehole.'

'Tell me about it!'

'No, you tell *me* about it. And anything else. We've got all night. Make yourself at home. Make the most of it.'

She took his words to mean get on with it and started to pull off her top. He stopped her before the under-layer of black came off. He could see she was wearing no bra.

'Hang on. No hurry. Have a drink first. Comfort I said. Remember?'

287

Her eyes sparkled when he opened the minibar. It was loaded. She wanted rum and coke.

'Have you eaten?' he asked as if it was the next most important thing in the world. She had, but she could always eat more. A sandwich would have done, but he ordered steak and chips for two, well done. She asked for a bottle of Mateus Rose. That was the only wine she liked apart from champagne, and she didn't have the nerve to ask for that. Besides, it tended to give her the farts, and that wouldn't have been nice in the circumstances.

The meal and the wine arrived courteously on a trolley. Peter added to the waiter's custom smile by tipping handsomely with a request to leave the clearing up until the morning.

The food befitted 5-star room service and left Sharon with a warm glow.

She didn't know how to handle this treatment. It was so uncommon to her, it made her suspicious. What did this bloke really want? This wasn't the normal procedure. There had occasionally been similar foreplay on occasion at Tony's; punters buttering her up downstairs at the tables. But as soon as they got her upstairs it was down to business. She felt unusually safe with this guy, for some reason. He had to have money, but there was a kink in him somehow. And gnawing at her was still the feeling she had seen him somewhere before. But he was no movie star.

'What is it with you?' she had to ask. Call it curiosity. 'I suppose you know you're a bit weird.'

'It has been said.' He was thinking of Janet Tomlinson.

'Are you always like this before you get it up? Steak and chips first?'

'All the time. Better than oysters.'

'Daft fucker,' she said, giggling.

With the rum and coke and half a bottle of wine on top of the cocktails in the bar, Sharon was feeling relaxed and quite happy with her lot. In fact, she had to admit she was actually enjoying herself. Out of interest, she got up and went to the wardrobe, wondering what other clothes he might have in there. She couldn't believe it. There was just one tracksuit similar to the top he was wearing. Same make, same colour. No trousers. Perhaps they were in one of the drawers?

'Christ!' she said, turning to face him. 'What is it with you? Why don't you buy yourself some decent clothes? Why'd you go around like that?'

That was fine coming from her, with her black lipstick to boot!

'I'm eccentric. I don't want people to know I've got money.'

'Huh!' she snorted, smiling broadly. Her teeth were just like her mother's. 'It's a bit of a give-away, chuck, in't it? Staying in a hotel like this. What must this room cost? Is it all on company expenses? Is that what the fucking safe's for in the wardrobe?'

She had never seen a hotel safety deposit box.

'Got it in one. But it's my own company, so I'm the one who pays in the end.'

She grunted harmless disbelief.

'It's true. I promise. You're looking at an eccentric man of the world. Anyway, you can't shout about my wardrobe. Your clothes aren't exactly Marks and Spencer's. What are you trying to hide?'

She giggled. 'Perhaps you'll see in a minute if you ever get round to it.'

But she decided not to wait. Instinct told her to take the matter into her own hands. She made a display of coolly stripping off the rest of her clothes, dropping them in a clutter onto one of the single beds then spreading herself out provocatively on the other. He couldn't think why he had asked for a twin room. Ignorance? Decorum?

She was quite at ease being splayed out starkers. She knew she had a stunning body and wasn't ashamed of showing it, although she would never present herself like this for any of her usual class of punter. But with the amount of money she had in her pocket tonight, she'd walk up and down the corridor like it if he asked her to. At one point she had been thinking this strange bloke might be some sort of porno freak who wanted to take pictures. Her fee would have been further upped if that had been his game. But there would be no showing her face! Nothing to worry about, however, there was no suggestion he was after anything like that. She was satisfied he was pretty straight. Weird, but straight. The other thing that was again weird; she was actually enjoying herself. Having a bit of a laugh. If she played her cards right, she might be able to talk him into becoming a regular. With him happy to pay over the odds, she wouldn't have to look for much else to survive. That would suit her down to the ground. Even if it didn't last - nothing ever did, did it? - it could be her first step to moving on. Then Jimbo could really go fuck himself!

With this thought playing on her mind, she was ready to please him, however necessary. It wasn't just the booze talking. This Peter might be a bit weird, but he could be a step towards her way out.

She wasn't going to egg him on any more than she had already. She knew he would come round to it in his own time. She just lay there ready and willing for whenever and whatever he wanted.

For a hundred and twenty quid she could wait.

First, there were three things he was particular about, two of which she never worked without anyway – cleanliness and proper precautions against the dreaded AIDS. She approved of that sort of fussiness. The third she had never encountered. The general nature of her work had never called for it, and a normal punter would have been told to 'fuck off!' if he had requested it. But for Peter, in the warm comfort of this hotel suite, she was happy to oblige.

'One thing, Sharon,' he said, as nonchalantly as if asking her to type a letter, 'could you go and wash that clown's make-up from your face? It doesn't do your drop-dead gorgeous body any favours. It would be nice to see a bit of colour in your cheeks, for once. You can leave your black nails on if you like. We don't want the place stinking of varnish remover.'

The black lipstick Sharon wore when working the streets was not just for style, it served to put punters off from trying to kiss her. That was a definite no-go area.

She slid off the bed pulling a mock sulky face, growling at him as she went into the bathroom. She was in there for longer than he would have expected. He could hear the shower running, then the hair dryer. When she came out, she was smelling of roses, not nail varnish. Hanging her head to one side in a seductive pose, she adopted a smile. 'Clean girl', she bragged. Peter was stunned. It was the self-same famous pose and smile that had launched the young Stephanie Star onto the world stage, and Sharon-stroke-Goria had fallen into it so naturally. The likeness was unbelievable. Without knowing, it was her own mother she was impersonating! And it was oh so easy for her. Despite her standing enticingly naked before him, he could not take his eyes from her face.

All he could do was nod. 'Beautiful,' he said.

While he was gawking, she hit him with a surprise.

'Whey-hey! I've sussed out who you are.' She was now smiling broadly, and as if to seal her discovery she slapped the cheeks of her bum in celebration. 'You're that Peter Tyler bloke who's been in all the papers. I knew I'd seen that face of yours somewhere! So, you ain't been kidding me. You *are* fucking rich. *And,* you knew the *real* Stephanie Star! You wouldn't believe it but I used to dress up as her doppelganger at the club where I used to work! Fuck me!' She suddenly went silent for a moment, then asked excitedly: 'Is it true you were giving Stephanie one?'

He guessed she would eventually work out who he was. But hopefully she wouldn't get anywhere near close to guessing the explicit reason he had come to Manchester.

'That's for me to know and you to find out,' he hedged. 'And yes, I can see that you do look a bit like her now you've washed your make-up off. So, they called you her doppelganger, did they?'

'All the fucking time!' she swore. 'But can't complain. It got me the job and paid well while it lasted. I'll tell you about it sometime. For two years or more I had to dress up as her most nights. She's done well for me as it happens, has our Steph!'

'So, you've been taking money under false pretenses?'

She pulled a face, shrugging, 'Yeah. S'pose so. My nickname's Phoney. Call me that if you want a kick in the balls!' She tip-toed over to the uncluttered bed.

'Shall we?' she invited, pulling back the covers. 'I've never been to bed with such a rich geezer before. Perhaps I shouldn't tell you this, but I think it's turning me on.'

He wasn't all that rich just yet, but happy that the notion turned her on. It was the opening he needed. The haunting music of Mark Knopfler echoing magically from the house radio gave Peter his own warm glow of recognition. The words were almost too coincidental. Sharon, Gloria, was not so far away from him with her tunnel of love, and she seemed more than ready to escape the dire straits she found herself in.

The music was helping, but he himself had been turned on long before joining her in the bed. He couldn't have been aroused more as he lay there looking at her face, noses almost touching. He tried to kiss her on the lips, but she was having none of it, even though she could tell he had cleaned his teeth. Old habits die hard. It was an involuntary action on her part. In order not to have offended him unduly, she gave him a peck on the cheek and joked: 'Don't know where you've been, do I?' She giggled. 'Or where you might be thinking of going!'

It didn't upset him. She was being cautious. 'Fair enough.' She *was* a professional, after all.

After less time than he would have liked, she pushed him away with hands set as claws gently scratching at him, and said, 'Leave it to me, then.' She set about some sure-fire tricks she knew would get him going and within a minute he exploded in a blaze of ecstatic groans. But it didn't stop him. He wriggled and thrust until, to her infinite surprise and joy, she had joined him in perfect coitus. By now, the claws had left red marks on his back and their mouths were pressed together with sounds like cars backfiring each time they tried to take a breath,

'Wow!' Sharon barked, pressing her head back into the voluminous hotel pillow. 'Did you rise to the occasion, or what?' She blew out air as if in amazement. 'Where did *that* come from?'

It wasn't a question asked of Peter. She was asking it of herself. Something definitely *had* turned her on! 'I've never had anything like that, chuck! Even doing it on me own!'

Peter was left in no doubt that she had enjoyed the encounter. It must be a nightmare going through the motions just for a crust of bread, on uppers or not. What a way to have to make a living!

He was hoping he could change that for her.

The bedclothes had been discarded in their sexual enthralls. They lay naked side by side on the bare mattress. He wasn't that much longer than she was. The room was warm. It would take them a while to cool down.

'How long have you been on the game?' he asked, staring at the ceiling, wishing there was a mirror there.

'Why? Are you gonna tell me I ain't got the hang of it yet?' she joked. 'It seemed good enough for *you*. I thought your eyes were going to pop out of their sockets!'

She pretended her feelings had been wounded and started playing with the remote control tuned into the radio.

'Now you're the one being a daft fucker. Of course, it was great, although a bit like being screwed on a trampoline, especially with all the rubber. You'd just as well take your gloves off now. Your black nails have completely cut their way through!'

The remark made her chuckle. It was good to know she could still laugh at herself.

'Daft fucker, yourself,' she said, smiling. 'Catch me not giving value for money! I'm a hooker, not a fucking housewife!'

'Are you planning to stay a hooker all your life, then? Or have you got other plans?'

'All my life? I'm not 21 yet. Give us a sodding chance!'

She turned, rose onto an elbow, and looked him straight in the eye, frowning. 'You sound like a bloody probation officer. Of course, I've got plans. But it takes money, don't it? Tell me another way I can make this sort of dough?' Especially the amount she was getting out of him for the night.

'That's all well and good. It won't be long before you find you've reached your sell-by-date in your chosen profession.'

'Thanks a lot, chuck!'

'It's not exactly the safest business to be in, is it? Not if you're looking for a long and healthy life. And that's without having blokes like Jimbo around. I'll say it again, you ought to get away from him.'

'Yeah, and thanks again for the advice. Any other ideas?'

Peter shrugged. It was too soon to risk making pertinent suggestions.

'I thought not. Anyway, I get rid of him and another one takes his place. I don't want to sound fucking obvious, but that 'other one' ain't gonna be you, if that's what you're thinking. You ain't the type. And you're rich. Anyway, why are you so worried? It's life, in't it? I can take care of myself. I've managed so far.'

Peter thought she probably could, up to a point.

'A few more punters like you on the go and I'd soon have a bank balance.' The smile returned to her face and then left to become more serious. As serious as Peter had seen it in their short acquaintance. 'That's an invitation, in case you missed it. Call me anytime. I mean it.'

'Talking of invitations, what's happened to my double date? Or was that a wind up?'

'No wind up. She must have pulled. But she could come knocking at any time. She knows where I am and she won't leave the hotel without me. So, brace up if she appears. Don't worry, she won't try to join in.'

The next thing she said came out of nowhere. He didn't know how to read it at first.

'You married?' she asked, matter of fact like. It took him a moment to accept it as an innocent question. 'You doing the dirty on a nice faithful wife stuck at home with the dishes?'

Peter shook his head. 'Not *that* type, either. Still feeling my way. I'm not that much older than you, you know?'

'You're not secretly one of these rich nutters who goes round trying to reform hookers on the quiet, are you?'

'I wouldn't be screwing you if I was, would I? As a married man or a reformer.'

'You'd be surprised. I've even had married vicars with their skirts up paying their way.'

'Real ones, or people dressed up to look like one?'

She chuckled. 'Daft fucker. You can talk about dressing up!'

'As you keep saying.'

She got up and went to the toilet. When she came out, she stood in front of the long wardrobe mirror, half-twisted her body and looked over her shoulder at her buttocks. There was a faint imprint of the toilet seat on them. She rubbed them to get rid of it and then asked in all sincerity: 'Do you think my arse is too big?' It was as though she was asking a girlfriend.

'A bit,' he lied, getting the sort of response he had hoped for.

'What do you mean?' she said vainly, looking at him through the mirror. 'It's not, is it?'

He went to her and stood behind her, testing each cheek with a squeeze. 'As arses go, it's not bad, I suppose. It could maybe use a bit off the sides. Other than that. Perfect.' He put his arms round her and gently held her breasts. 'These are little gems, though!'

'Wait till you see Kim's,' she thought gleefully.

They remained like that for a while, looking at each other in the mirror without embarrassment. He had a strange face, she was thinking, like a pinched angel. His body was amazing. Taunt. He wasn't much taller than her, but he was all muscle. He was nothing like what she classed as a businessman; not like any she had entertained, anyway. Could he just be impersonating the bloke he said he was? Just like *she* had, pretending to be Stephanie Star. Bluffed his way into the hotel? She would almost have liked it better if he had. That would be a fucking hoot. A good sketch. Something Kim would like, too. It would make no difference to her if he couldn't pay for the room. She had her hundred and twenty quid.

But no. Of course not. It was definitely *him*. Peter Tyler. She began to wonder again if he had actually slept with Steph. Slipping a hand behind her, she made him flinch by squeezing his balls.

'Help me think better of you, Peter,' she said like a school mistress. 'Tell me you really did fuck Stephanie Star. I promise it will get you brownie points, especially if you tell me I was better.'

Peter felt another lie would do no harm. There wasn't an ounce of jealousy in Sharon.

'Promise you won't tell anyone else? Total secrecy between you and me? Not even Kim?'

'I promise,' Sharon herself lied. 'Cross my heart and hope to die.' She kept nothing from Kim, as Peter might have guessed.

'I did, and you were far, far better. No comparison.'

'A very good reply. How many times and where.'

'Oh, I didn't bother counting. All over the place. In her bedroom when her old man wasn't around, which was quite often. In the gym sometimes between press-ups. In the stables, on horseback, in the woods. She was a proper goer on the quiet, but nowhere as good as you, with your professional dexterity. We even managed it on my bike once, although that was a bit awkward.'

'Fuck off, ya daft fucker!' A tighter squeeze coming as payback for teasing her.

'I don't know what to believe now,' she said, letting him go. The whole length of their bodies was touching. 'As long as I was better at it than her, that's all I need to know.'

'Much better,' he told her, taking his leave for the bathroom.

When he came out, she was waving the hotel registration card. 'I'm not snooping, Mr. Tyler,' she said with her mock posh voice. 'This was staring at me on the desk. Can I keep it as a memento to remind me you shagged me? Just in case you disappear into the sunset.'

'As long as you don't tell anyone about me and Stephanie.'

'Of course not," Sharon lied. "But what's the problem? It was in all the papers.'

'All hearsay. How would you like it if people said you were sleeping with a junkie?'

'Huh!" she guffawed. "I might not have *slept* with 'em, but I wouldn't be surprised if some of the punters I've seen to weren't junkies. You could be on something yourself for all I know. Uppers of some sort, I would have said, if you'll excuse the inference.'

He rubbed his hair as dry as possible before throwing down the towel.

'I promise you I'm not on anything. I also promise you I'm not going to suddenly disappear.' He smoothed his hair down with his hands.

He was pink in the face from his hot shower. 'Same time, same place, same price tomorrow night? You're worth every penny' He wasn't just saying that to win her over. He gave the bedside clock a quick glance. It was close to one o'clock. 'That in fact would be later on tonight, not tomorrow. I've got a meeting in the afternoon otherwise we could have made a day of it. What do you say?'

She liked the 'worth every penny' remark. He could also tell she was keen about a repeat performance. Another big pay day at the forefront of her keenness, probably. But there was also something else in her naked demeanour. She was shaking with delight like an excited little girl who had just been told she could have a pony for Christmas. There was no mistaking she was getting off on his 5-star attention.

'If you still need to bring an invisible accomplice, that's OK by me.'

'Daft fucker!' she said, adopting another drop-dead gorgeous Stephanie Star pose, pouting her lips. 'I did think of trying modelling once, you know. But it's not all Vogue cover stuff, is it? Unless you hit the top. Fat chance of that! Most of it's about getting up at five in the morning and standing around all day in stuff you'd never want to be seen dead in yourself. And you can't eat fuck all in case you put on two ounces!'

An opportunity had opened up for Peter to innocently investigate.

'It wouldn't be so bad if you got on the right circuit. Your body's not too bad for your age.'

'Cheeky fucker! What do you mean 'for *my* age'?'

'Models are getting younger and younger these days. It might not be too late for you.' Another tease.

'Well, do I or don't I have potential?' She asked as she spun round in full fantasy whilst aping an announcer: 'And now, ladies and gentlemen, introducing Sharon Shaw, the face of the future.'

'I think you could have if you were prepared to knuckle down. It's not all glamour, as you've said. You could be advertising cars, wallpaper, cough mixture; anything.'

He sounded so serious, she stopped play-acting, falling into a natural pose that would have floored Michelangelo. Whatever else God had done to this child he had given her outstanding beauty. Peter suddenly felt immense affection for her. He wanted to make her happy. 'Now why do you think I couldn't take my eyes off you in the pub, even with that clown's make-up of yours?' She shrugged her shoulders and pulled a face. 'I tell you what,' he thought she was in the right mood to test going the whole hog, 'with the right make-up in the right light you could be made to look just as good as your doppelganger did when she was first discovered. Some people might even think you were her daughter, but for the fact that Stephanie Star didn't have any kids. Could be something to build on. That likeness. Who knows? Especially in the *au naturelle.*'

'You're just looking at me arse again. Winding me up. I'll get Kim to sort you out if you don't watch it!' she gave herself another look in the mirror. 'Come on. Be serious. I've already been passing meself off as Steff for two years or more. I've had enough of that. Honest. Tell me, do you think I could make it as a model as meself? Sharon Shaw? Not a super model like Steff was, but at least one that didn't have to get up at dawn and put crap clothes on. I could handle wallpaper, if it came to it!''

'Listen,'' he said, sensing the idea wasn't necessarily a pipe dream. 'As a freelance, you could pick and choose jobs once you'd done the rounds and made a name for yourself. Just like you've been doing with your current profession,' he joked. 'And you'd have to put a stop to that. Or think about being a bit more discreet. Like you've been tonight, I hope.'

She shrugged her answer.

'A short, sharp course at a modelling school would do you no harm. You'd soon catch on. You're a natural, from what I've seen of your capers tonight, and I'm not referring to the horizontal ones!'

'Can a model earn what you're paying me for tonight, given it's night-work, mind you?' She laughed at herself. 'You know what I mean.'

'More, if you knuckle down. And you wouldn't have that prick Jimbo breathing down your neck. Please tell me he hasn't made you entertain *him*?'

'No fucking way! Is that what you think of me?'

298

'Glad to hear it. No brownie points lost there, then.' That was one thing less to worry about in getting her away from the thug. 'There is something you should perhaps consider if you want to have a go at modelling.'

'Oh, yeah?' She was ready for another wind up. 'What's that then?'

'Tidy up that ear with all the holes drilled into it. All that chain mail you've had hanging on it makes it look like a colander! It would limit any chances of a Cosmetics contract, which would be a shame with that gorgeous face of yours.'

She fiddled with her ear lobes. It shouldn't be too much of a problem. She always managed to fill the holes in when doing her Stephanie Star act at Tony's. Easy-peasy. The wig helped as well.

Peter knew Photoshop would do a proper job on her ears if it ever came to it.

With those thoughts lingering, they had one more session then crashed out with an in-house horror movie flickering over their shameless bodies.

Chapter Thirty

Peter was woken by a chambermaid barging into the room at the same time as she was knocking. 'Solly,' was all he heard before the door closed again. She would have been even 'sollier' if she had switched on the light and seen the naked state of the room more clearly. He looked at the glowing bedside clock. 10.35. Perhaps businessmen were supposed to be up and away by that time.

He put his head back on the pillow. It had been quite a night. Fortunately, the appointment he had arranged wasn't till the afternoon, so no rush. He had plenty of time to get himself together.

He must have disturbed Sharon. He felt her shift. She was still naked, as was he, tight up against him with an arm across his midriff, snoring. She seemed to have taken up most of the bed. One of his legs was hanging off the side. He had a strange sensation. Feeling down his body, the situation was explained. He had two arms across his midriff! Neither of them his.

What the hell...! It gave him a start. Swinging his legs off the bed, he jumped up. Of course! In the dim light, hardly any bed clothes in sight, he could see another naked body. Kim. Sharon must have let her in while he slept. Why not use the other bed, for heaven's sake? God knows how Sharon coped being squeezed in the middle.

He let them sleep, going to slip a 'Do Not Disturb' sign outside the door as he should have done the night before, then made for the bathroom.

He took his time cleaning himself, running over the events of the night. He was pretty pleased with the way things were working out. A plan was formulating. An intriguing way was opening up of how to answer Stephanie's wishes to help her daughter. And what a way it would be to do it! He felt sure Sharon would go for it. She certainly had the credentials. It was almost a natural progression from 'posing' at Tony's, blatantly playing the lookalike. She had pulled it off there in the flesh, so why not in the wider world of fashion magazines?

The plan would sit happily alongside Peter's own pretenses. A useful card to have up his sleeve?

When he walked back into the bedroom now wearing the hotel bathrobe, he felt overdressed. The room was extremely warm. Both the girls were sitting up in the bed, legs covered with a sheet, but breasts bare, drinking tea. Peter now understood the remark Sharon had made about Kim's big 'bazookas'!

'Hello, Peter. I'm Kim,' she said, noticing him looking at them. 'Big, ain't they. You tried grabbing them in your sleep last night. That'll cost you next time.'

'My pleasure, Kim. I'm glad you thought I was asleep,' he responded.

'You cheeky, sod!'

'Don't listen, Kim. He's winding you up. He's like that.' Sharon explained.

'If you want to charge me, I'll have to deduct it from Sharon's fee. What do you think about that, Sharon?'

'Too late. You've paid me already, remember. Anyway, keep your hands off her. You're *my* client.' Then to Kim, gently pinching one of her bare 'bazookas'. 'And you, Burly. Keep your tits to yourself. You're just my minder.'

'Now, ladies,' Peter interjected once Kim had stopped wobbling gleefully. 'No fighting over me.'

'Daft fucker,' said Sharon, holding out her cup to him. 'Any chance of another cuppa, chuck?'

There wasn't. The pot was empty. So, Peter set about making some more. He could use a cup himself.

Kim was much fleshier than Sharon all over, from what Peter could see. With the ghostly white punk make-up that was fading now, the pinkness of her skin below the neckline and the blue of her lacquer-weary hair gave her the look of a melting Neapolitan ice-cream in desperate need of a lick!'

'So, Kim. Where did *you* spring from?' he asked, sitting at the end of the bed after replenishing their cups, using a glass for his own tea since the room only catered for two guests. He was slightly ashamed to be thinking it was perhaps a pity Kim hadn't turned up earlier last night.

'I got up and wedged the door open for her,' Sharon explained, maternally. 'Couldn't have her running about the streets looking like that. She might have got lumbered.'

'She might well have got lumbered with a surprise in here if I'd tried to jump on you in the dark and missed.'

'By all accounts you *did* try. But nothing surprises Kim, does it, Kim?'

'So, they say,' Kim admitted, laughing, which set off her pink parts wobbling again.

'Well, I hope I don't get charged triple for the room. The maid poked her nose in uninvited just now while you were both asleep.'

'Sod her! She won't say nothing' Sharon scoffed. 'She's probably on the game herself. 'Spect a lot of them are in this place. Two or three stars up from Tony's, though, eh, Kim?'

'And the rest.'

Peter had already booked the hotel for another night, so there was no hurry to quit the room. Approaching noon, having breakfasted on room service, Sharon and Kim, now all punked up again, said they were going to make a move.

Their hopes were raised when Peter made a withdrawal from the safe deposit box in the wardrobe. He noticed their expectant looks.

'What?' he asked. Then answered for them. 'Put your greedy little eyes back in their sockets. I've got stuff to do today. Expenses. Nothing more for you, Sharon, until tonight. Same arrangement? I'm happy to pay up front. But not *this* much up front.' The girls pulled sulky faces. 'Have we got the pleasure of Kim's bazookas tonight.' He wanted to know.

'She's fixed herself up here again, ain't ya, Kim?'

Kim nodded matter-of-factly. 'Some leathered-up foreign fucker. He was all right, though.' She didn't own up about only charging him her normal rate. Nothing like as much as Sharon had conned out of Peter.

It took no guessing who that 'foreign fucker' had been!

'I wondered about him,' Sharon said. 'Right up your street, Kim. He looked as much out of place as us. What was his excuse for being here?'

'Said he was a roadie for some German group trying to make it over here. The Studs, he called 'em,' Kim giggled, wriggling into her coat. 'He wasn't bad himself!'

The girls chuckled as they went out the door.

'Tara, Peter. See you at eight,' Sharon said, with a wave goodbye. 'Don't be late! Or I'll be charging you overtime!'

During the course of the day, Karl learned just how boring printed circuits and injection-molding could be. Peter showed more interest. But during the guided tour of the factory, his only questions related to which countries produced the raw materials being used. The UK was preferable, after that came countries where civil rights were well established. His little contribution to a better world. The company he had chosen was as close to being as solid a British firm as Peter could wish. 'You would have been good German fifty years ago, Peter.' Karl gibed. 'You like proper businessman today. Good fuck put your head together.'

Or two or three, Peter was about to boast, but didn't want to go into the niceties of last night. Nor did he mention that he knew Karl had not gone short himself.

Peter excused himself early that evening. 'I'm entertaining again at home. I anticipate you might be doing the same.'

Karl gave him a carefree shrug. No words.

But it didn't work out as anticipated. Sharon didn't show, with or without her Neapolitan friend.

Perhaps she was into business she couldn't refuse. But he couldn't see why she would turn down another night in comfort for top cash guaranteed. Something must have gone wrong. Jimbo? He sincerely hoped not. But it that's what is was.

By eleven, he had long given her up, thinking he would have to stay an extra day in Manchester if he was to get through to her. But then the hotel phone rang. It was Sharon, and she sounded distressed. 'Something's come up... sorry...'

He heard a scuffle. 'Give me that, you cow!' Jimbo's voice, in the background, suddenly coming closer. 'Right, you ponce!' Loud and clear. 'You want to fuck around with my 'goods', you pay *me*. Understood? You think I don't know what y'r fooking game is? Think again, weirdo!'

Peter *was* thinking. Fast. Jimbo had Sharon, and she wasn't happy.

'You want to see her looking nice again, you come *here*, to your favourite arch! She does tricks when and where I tell her to. Get that into your thick skull. And bring cash. Plenty. You *owe* me. Understand? Be here in an hour, or she gets it and I'll be after you's next!'

'Alright! Calm down,' Peter's head was reeling. This wasn't meant to happen. How had the prick found out? He knew Peter was interested in Sharon, perhaps thinking he was a pimp? 'Don't lay so much of a finger on her if you want any money from me,' Peter threatened, convincingly enough. 'Not a penny! One hair out of place, and you get zilch! And worse!' Not so convincingly.

'One hour!' Was the response.

'Let me speak to her.'

'Go fuck yourself, weirdo! One hour, or she gets it!'

The phone went dead.

Sharon had been whimpering in the background. Had Jimbo got at her already? Could Peter buy him off? Daft thought. Thugs like Jimbo didn't go away.

He alerted Karl, who had been sleeping. 'Got to go out, Karl. Need you and the car. Can you get yourself together? Ten minutes? Fifteen?'

Without questioning, Karl said he could.

'Girl trouble,' Peter explained once they were in the car, without going into detail. This was something he had to sort out himself. They got to the red-light district early and cruised the streets close to 'The Mitre' pub. It was long past closing time, but a few people were still milling around it. Peter kept a keen eye out for Sharon just in case she'd shaken off Jimbo. But no sign of her, as feared.

At the given time, he asked Karl to draw up quietly close to the said arch and douse the lights.

No-one was hovering outside it. He left the car and walked a few paces so he could look inside. Deserted. What was going on? He was dead on time.

As he edged further into the arch, a car's headlights passing by from somewhere lit it up for a second. And there Sharon was, at the other end, motionless. No Jimbo?

'Are you OK?' he asked suspiciously as he rushed towards her. He couldn't see her face. Then another car passed, its headlights bouncing off the dripping wet bricks and he caught a glimpse of it. It had been pummelled. Her eyes were so swollen, he couldn't be sure she could even see him. All the rings had been ripped from her ears. She was in a mess. But no tears.

'What happened?' he asked, as he got to her.

'I didn't tell him anything…. look out!' she cried, too late for him to heed the warning. He was winded by a vicious blow to the ribs from behind. The next thing he knew, he was thrown against the wall of the arch. He jerked a knee up in reaction, but Jimbo was too smart to be caught that easily. The knee caught his thigh instead. His immediate reply was to throw a fierce head butt.

Peter felt something crack between his eyes, and knew he'd be looking like Sharon within seconds.

'You interfering fucking prick!' Jimbo snarled, spit spraying all over Peter's face, lifting his own knee now, scoring a direct hit. Peter tried to bend forward to ease the pain, but he was being pinned by his shoulders in no gentle way against the wall. 'No-one takes fanny away from me, you interfering prick!' He head-butted again. Peter's head was lowered this time, which was good news for his nose, but not so good for the top of his skull. He was nearly knocked cold. Suddenly, he felt as sick as a dog.'

Sharon tried to pull Jimbo off, getting another clout herself for her troubles.

'Where's the money?' the pimp roared, clawing at Peter's tracksuit. It didn't take him long to realise there was no wallet. 'Where is

305

it? His voice echoed from the walls of the arch as another knee went into Peter's groin. No answer came. Peter could barely manage a groan. His idea of negotiating a settlement away with the fairies.

Then his worst fears were realised. An evil-looking knife blade flashed before his eyes, sending him instantly to jelly.

Before he knew it, he was on the ground. Was this it? He hadn't felt a thing. No pain, and as quick as lightning he was rolling free.

For a second, he saw Jimbo's scarred head being thrust back. Karl had arrived on the scene. He had his knee in the small of Jimbo's back with a grip on the wrist of the hand with the knife so fierce that Jimbo couldn't move it. Which was perhaps just as well since the point of it was now barely an inch from his own face, the blade sharp enough for back-street lobotomy.

'Just one excuse, scheis-kopf!' Karl said coolly in perfect Anglo-German, over-powering the pimp with such force, there was no further struggle. Jimbo was out of shape and in full submission.

Karl's rapid intervention sparked Sharon off. She could see out of her puffy eyes well enough to seize the situation. Her chance to give Jimbo payback. Whatever happened now, she wasn't going to let him fuck up her life any longer. She would be away from Manchester, whatever happened. Fully determined to take this last chance to get back at him.

She hadn't seen the knife in Jimbo's overpowered hand. But she could tell Karl had him arm-locked in total submission on the damp ground. Perhaps she wouldn't have cared if she had seen it. From behind Karl, she sent her Doc Marten boot up between Jimbo's legs with a great lunge into his balls. It was a direct hit and carried such force that it jerked Jimbo's head forward. This sent the sharp point of the knife clear through his left nostril and out the other side of his nose like a Polanski scene. Only worse. Now it was Dali's turn. The blade didn't stop until it had sliced across Jimbo's left eye and reached bone. The scream was as terrifying as Munck's!

Karl released his hold. It was needed no more.

Jimbo's pains weren't over yet. He sat up, shaking and groaning, hands like claws clutching his skull. Sensing he was no danger Sharon came at him again with a boot to the other eye to more screams echoing under the arch.

In the full throws of yet another kick, Karl grabbed at her making her boot miss, the momentum of the weighty Doc Marten as it swung in mid-air sending her flying.

Jimbo was yelling blue murder, hands to face, burbling through blood, his knife now laying harmlessly on the cobble stones beside him, touched only by his own hand.

'Let's go,' Karl commanded coolly. 'Before police come.' Peter and Sharon were still on the ground. It had happened so quickly. Sharon got up then tried to help Peter struggle to his feet.

Some girls had appeared to see what all the noise was about. None of them was ever going to lift a finger to help Jimbo. They were soon gone. Nothing to do with them.

Sharon wouldn't let go of Peter. 'Don't go without me!' she pleaded, Then, seeing how beaten-up he looked, breathed: 'Shit!'

'I hope I don't look as bad as you.' He managed to joke, blood all down his front.

'The bastard!' she hissed. Karl started dragging Peter away. She hopped along beside them for a few paces then turned and ran back. 'Sharon!' Peter shouted, but it didn't stop her.

She was shaping up like a footballer taking a penalty, and by the sound of the roar next heard, she had scored.

'You coming with us or not?' Peter shouted, taking the words out of Karl's mouth.

'Fucking right, I am!' she swore, catching up with them again. 'I'm history here if he ever gets hold of me again!'

She wanted to pick up a few things from her place. Not a lot. There wasn't much she couldn't do without. She had to leave a message for Kim, who fortunately had missed all this. Just as well, perhaps? 'I don't know how the fuck Jimbo found out. I didn't tell him, neither did Kim,' Sharon wanted it made clear. 'She went straight to her mum's soon after we left you this morning.'

Sharon would let Kim know what had happened as soon as she got a chance. The main thing right now was to leave a brief note and get the hell out of Manchester. She wiped the dried blood from her face, then took a damp cloth and did the same for Peter.

Having been able to clean themselves up enough, they got back into the hotel without creating any interest. It was way gone midnight. Very few people were in evidence.

Sharon found it hard to get to sleep. She was paranoid Jimbo would come after them.

Peter had to calm her down all through the night. He promised they would be leaving first thing in the morning. 'Don't worry. Jimbo has got bigger problems than looking for you. It'll be weeks before he sees anything again with that boot of yours.'

'That bastard heals!' Sharon said. Neither Peter nor she had seen the shocking damage the knife had done. That eye would never heal!

She was desperate to get out of Manchester for good and kept telling Peter so all through the night. 'It's the only way,' she was convinced, which made Peter's task a mere formality. His invitation sounded like pure generosity.

'You really mean it!' she cried, jumping at his offer. He promised to find her a place down South. She was about to say he owed her because it was all his fault for keeping her out all night but thought better of it. No point pushing her luck. Fuck Jimbo! He had it coming. This was her chance!

'Anywhere'll be good enough till I can sort myself out. I'll pay you back.' She gave that some thought. 'Somehow,' she added. It shouldn't be too hard for him to guess what that 'somehow' would have to be. And he'd be happy with that.

'Relax. We're in this together. Once away from here, first thing in the morning, we'll sort something out. Don't worry, I'll look after you until you find your feet. I feel responsible. It's my fault in a way this has happened. But don't expect too much of this five-star hotel treatment.' She could hardly take this in. He was serious. She didn't need the 5-stars, just some place where Jimbo couldn't get to her. Making do didn't worry her.

Never had. She always had her body to fall back on, literally! Her looks had been dented, sure, but that didn't matter too much. It wasn't her face punters wanted. Her face would heal soon enough, anyway. Forget all that stuff they were fantasizing about last night, Pure make-believe.

It was as if he was reading her mind.

'When your face gets better, we'll get you a new wig to cover your ears. Who knows, we might still be able to make a model out of you. Body stuff. Underwear. Stockings and shoes.'

Teasing her again? Another wind up?

'Why me?' She wanted to know. It was all too good to be true. He'd barely known her twenty-four hours. 'I'm not that good a fuck, am I?'

'You are as it happens. But sex is not the be-all and end all in life.'

'Huh!' It came out as a puff. 'It is when it pays the rent.'

'You must start concentrating on what other talents you might have. Getting off the streets must be the first move. I'll help. After last night, we're blood brothers.'

Where was all this interest in her coming from, Sharon was wondering? What was in it for him? Not pimping. His mate Karl had more credentials in that department. Whatever Peter Tyler was up to, she felt she could handle it, could always do a runner, if need be. That was her perennial get-out. Something was telling her maybe not this time, though. At least not for a while. This weird fairy godfather who had drifted into her life couldn't have chosen a better time.

'I've been thinking about all that stuff we were talking about last night,' he said in the early hours, sensing she couldn't sleep from the way she kept shifting about in the bed. 'You know, that modelling stuff. I know we were having a laugh, but it's not such a daft idea now your time in Manchester would seem to have been cut short.'.

'Daft fucker! Modelling? With a face like this? Looks like I'm wearing horror mask!'

'Not immediately, daft fucker, yourself. When you get your looks back. Something to look forward to. Something to cheer you up.'

'I'm gonna need some of that. The sooner the better.'

'It'll take a little working out, but I've had an idea that could pay dividends as well as being fun.'

Just the thought of a bit of fun made her feel better. 'Oh, yeah?' she asked suspiciously. 'Depends what I have to do?'

'Just be yourself, basically. Keep play-acting at being a young Stephanie Star as you've been doing, use your uncanny likeness to make people sit up and take notice. And I think I know someone who will sit up and take notice even more than I have. Someone who could give you a big leg up, like he did for Stephanie herself!'

Her damaged ears pricked up at the outrageous idea.

'Are you fucking serious?'

He nodded, the swollen features of his face creasing in an impish grin.

'You *are* serious, aincha, ya daft fucker?' She looked doubtful. 'With a mug like this?' She was about to pull a face, but the pain stopped her.

'Once it heals. A month, two months?'

'Why?' Again, it was an obvious question.

Peter thought about it. How should he put it? Theatrically, he decided, to disguise the truth in it.

'It could put you in the fast lane to that glamorous world that's full of more *real* phoney's than you might think, and be the sort of challenge I would enjoy taking on to test my creative management initiative. I'm sure we'd make a good team. Most of all, it could be fun.'

'If you say so.' A twinkle peaked through the bruised eyes. 'Sounds like a laugh. That's if I can ever pass as a teenager again, not someone near her sell-by-date, as you so nicely suggested.'

Had Jimbo plied much more violence to her face that possibility might well have been in question. Even as it was, it might take more than a couple of months for her looks to return. But there was no hurry. The idea that was germinating in him needed some head scratching.

Karl kept eyeing Sharon's puffy face in the driving mirror as they drove down the M6. How had Tyler got mixed up with this punk kid? She promised to be nothing but trouble. But perhaps it was understandable he should want to get her away from Manchester quickly. Safer that way for all concerned, himself included. But Karl knew the pimp would not be able to take things any further with this business for a very long time, even if he chose to.

Sharon was not so sure. But that worry was for the future as she snuggled down in the back of the Range Rover trying to ignore her throbbing injuries. Not least of these was her aching right hip. It felt like she might have dislocated after swinging her Doc Martin and missing! It was probably only a pulled muscle but painful, none the less. That sketch now amused her. 'Did you see me go flying?' she asked Peter, being careful not to laugh.

'I did,' Peter answered, holding back a smile as he nursed the bridge of his nose. 'It wasn't very elegant.'

'You would have taken pimp's head off had boot connected!' Karl joined in.

'S'what I was trying to do!' Sharon pointed out, the brief conversation cheering her up. 'Got him when I went back, though! There was blood everywhere.' Jimbo's blood. That thought made her even happier.

She started thinking about all the wild promises Peter had come out with when they'd been screwing each other. The idea of fooling people had grabbed Sharon as a harmless pastime if it was going to give her a free ride, whatever her benefactor's reasons. She'd been doing it long enough already. Keeping her looks under wraps for a while would do her no harm while the mess back in Manchester sorted itself out, and she was happy Peter was thinking along the same lines. But why? She kept asking herself. Was he honestly feeling responsible for what had happened? Or could it really be that he fancied her? Either way, she'd take it.

Chapter Thirty One

'Belfast, tomorrow morning' the ops man in the control room of Little Eaton Aerodrome said down the telephone, and another twenty pound note would arrive in the post. Easy money. If the 'Daily Scan' was that interested in the movements of Ludlow's private aircraft, then why not cash in on it?

Zurich and Bordeaux had been the two previous messages, false alarms. Ludlow had not shown. He had been away now for months and there had not been more than a whisper about his whereabouts. Dick Baker wasn't letting go. He was sure there was still a story in it,

This time the twenty pounds paid off, Ludlow was heading for home. So much for trying to slip into the country through the back door, he should have run the gauntlet of Heathrow's newsmen and been done with it. Better than being snapped at the end of a telescopic lens on his own airstrip looking shifty, virtually arm in arm with his secretary, Jenny Grant. In all the years of watching, Dick Baker had never seen Ludlow on such intimate terms with the woman in question. Victor Rose was there with the Rolls Royce to collect them looking peeved, which made another happy snap for Baker. He was building quite a colourful portfolio on the itinerant businessman and his entourage. Daily Scan readers loved a sniff of scandal, particularly if the rich and famous were involved. There was still plenty running in this story that could be made to sound very titillating.

In Manchester, Jimbo's one eye opened wide as he turned to the centre fold of The Daily Scan to see Tyler, the weirdo he thought was a would-be pimp propositioning that cow, Sharon. Even his empty eye socket was trying to open up under its NHS eye-patch! He knew who Ludlow was, of course. He was always in the papers. This Rose character was somehow familiar, too. Something to do with the huge pumps factory Ludlow was having built in Manchester? Jimbo looked hard at the guy. Something was nagging him. His sharp clothes? Then it hit him. Tony's! This ponce had been Upstairs on occasion at that time, calling himself Randall. How could he forget him. Randall went for boys.

So, Sharon's weirdo was part of this lot. The fucking 'in-crowd'! But what about her? Where was that cow?

This one-eye-catching report steered clear of libel in favour of speculation. The Scan had started treading softly.

Ludlow had gone in big with injunctions and lawsuits on several counts of defamation of character against The Scan. The wise money was on him to win. He wanted more than a categorical retraction of the lies printed around the saga of Compton Stud. He was after blood, 'I'll sink the bastards!' he had vowed. 'Then rub their noses in it!'

Jimbo had been thinking along similar lines in his quest to settle his own grievances.

Jenny was happy to live with what the tabloids were putting out. Let them get on with it. The rumours developing around her involvement with Sir Edward Ludlow were causing her no discomfort.

She was sitting with him behind the tinted windows of his Rolls Royce heading for Septon railway station, being dropped off to go to London. He had things to do at Compton Stud having been away for so long and it suited him that she never wanted to set foot in the place again. She couldn't after what she'd been through. Instead, she was heading for her flat in New Kings Road, Fulham, or Flahum, as she could sometimes be heard pronouncing it. 'How long do you need to in be in that hellhole?' She asked, not understanding why he would want to go there at all himself.

'For as long as necessary,' he replied, loosely trying to hide his irritability at being questioned. 'This will probably be for the very last time, as I've told you. We've been through all that. Don't concern yourself. Compton Stud will never be the same for any of us, especially with its new resident, Peter Tyler, making a nest for himself there. Apparently, the place has become a hive of activity. He hasn't been wasting his time. I have things to discuss with him.'

'Well, he's welcome to the place.' That was Jenny's opinion. Even so, she still could not understand why Edward owed such a big favour to Tyler as to be giving him free run of the property. This 'initiative' project sounded all well and good on paper, but she'd had doubts from the outset about it ever paying for itself despite all the positive reports coming in about it. Tyler was no more than a nerd to her! There had to be something more to investing so much in this Initiative toy of his, as she saw it. Was it just to keep Compton Stud running as a tax loss now the dishes were to come down?

'Will we hang onto to the Stud indefinitely?' Jenny had asked, having taken to using a 'we' as often as possible where a 'you' might have been expected. A subliminal reminder to Edward of how she placed herself these days. He sensed this and it irked him. It was not exactly how he saw things.

'Oh, I don't know, while it suits me, at least. If Tyler's Initiative pays off, as looks very likely indeed, I might do some sort of deal with him if he wants to stay at the place. Let him take care of all its ghosts and skeletons.'

She could go along with that idea, as she could with another prospect that Edward had run by her during their cozier Kenyan moments. With his life in London seemingly turning sour, moving head office to Zurich had become a likely option, discreet accommodation attached.

The Rolls Royce turned off the Septon bypass and headed into the centre of the town.

'Should I be thinking of putting my flat on the market?' It was a question asked of Edward to keep the subject of their relationship at the front of his mind.

'Let's not get ahead of ourselves, Jenny. You might find yourself stranded without digs in London,' he was quick to point out.

That would never happen. She was not thinking of *selling* her own place. Letting it would be the option she'd go for should things progress the way she was hoping.

'I could always move into Knightsbridge?' She suggested, knowing he would never get rid of that fancy fortress, no matter what! Which was true. But Ludlow's Knightsbridge apartment would always stay as what it had been designed to be, a bachelor pad. His *pied a terre* in London.

'I don't think that would be wise with all this court nonsense going on. The press hasn't given up yet, as you know. They are still hounding me. Some hack might get onto it and read it the wrong way. That wouldn't help matters.'

It might not help certain matters, but it wouldn't do her own ambitions any harm. The sooner the papers went big on their 'new' relationship, the sooner she would like it. Stephanie had been dead long enough for the mourning period to be over. It was about time Jenny started to press her own claims.

Ludlow had seen this eagerness in Jenny growing, and it had concerned him since that very first soft fall at the Norfolk Hotel in Nairobi. Moreover, during the heady days that followed at the lakeside lodge. It had been on his mind at the time that he might live to regret it, but with the passage of Peter Tyler through Africa and a 'lifesaving' solution apparently reached, a surge of euphoria had hit Ludlow, sparking off that now regretful spell off impulsiveness that had lowered his defenses and let Jenny through.

He had been in the wilderness of uncertainty ever since learning of his wife's death. Now, with the sense that he had escaped being nailed to the cross, who could blame his sudden flip to sexual insouciance. Tyler's initiative, lower case 'i' as much as upper, had come to his rescue. The man had something to sell apart from his *silence*, and it was cheap at half the price. How fortuitous! Tyler was human. He preferred to grab the opportunity to enhance his own chances in life rather than answering Stephanie's vengeful call to destroy Ludlow's.

Jenny was in the right place at the right time to catch her boss in this uncommonly carefree mood. And he did not hold back! His sense of survival had sent him headlong into the comforts of Jenny's welcoming arms. He had been in raptures while it lasted, lost in the ravages of shared carnal bliss from one full moon to the next.

His relief had been palpable to Jenny only hours after Tyler's arrival, and she was still not party to the whole truth behind it. But why should she care? Whatever it had been, she was only too thankful to be on hand to reap the results of Edward's eagerness to come on to her.

It began one evening after dinner on the veranda of their hideaway, one particularly hot and humid evening after an especially well-wined dinner. Edward had only just returned, Jenny thought from South Africa via Nigeria although it had been from Bolivia, and he was uncommonly pleased to see her again. The lodge was empty but for two of the staff. The cook had fallen asleep in the kitchen after preparing their meal. Ashura, the houseboy, was at his post on the veranda steps all but asleep himself.

The pilot who had recently dispatched Ludlow had not even cut the engines before heading off again, Nairobi bound.

The playfulness was triggered innocently enough by Edward.

'I suppose you realise, Jenny,' he confessed after his fourth Brandy. 'The meat we ate tonight is meant to be a rank aphrodisiac according to local legend. Crocodile claw! I didn't like to mention it to you before.'

Ashura had never witnessed such drunken scenes that followed. The Bwana and the red-faced lady charged about the veranda on all fours clawing at each other's clothes. They must have forgotten about his silent presence, or thought he was sound asleep, and he was happy to keep it that way. This pair needed the voodoo man if any did!

The chase ended in the lady's boudoir, taking a swift turn to the ultimate sexual pairing. Ashura could have been forgiven for thinking it was all a bit desperate, plainly something they had both been crying out for. They were together all the way with mutual contentment. How different to that first night in his matrimonial bed!

For Jenny, it was not so much the intense passion of the moment that she had been craving, as the moment itself. She was not virginally untouched, although it had been a long, long time since she had engaged in any sexual 'fumbling'. And that's all it had been. This had been different. A fully consummated coupling that had left her a-tingle. She had been longing for this day, this chance to ruffle the sheets of Edward's neglected love life. No wonder she was in ecstasy, screaming louder than the baboons of Treetops' water hole.

Her moment had come. Her body was shaking with the indescribable glow of release. She lay beside him in the heat like a puppet with its strings cut.

From then on, for her, things would never be the same between them. When bodies did that, it was for keeps.

'Did we mix our drinks or something, last night?' Ludlow muttered casually over breakfast.

'Or something, I think,' she answered with a grin.

'I seem to have a terribly sore head this morning.'

'No wonder!' Jenny thought. She had a sore fanny to go with it! 'We were a bit rumbustious. I think that's the word,' she said, trying to wrestle some charm from those penetrating eyes of his. 'We should try it again, soon.'

And they did, each time with a little less desperation on Jenny's part, and decreasing passion on his, until the pleasures of the original lunacy were not only gone for him but being replaced by thoughts of what his irresponsible lust might ultimately cost.

Long before their subsequent departure for England, Edward had begun to convey to Jenny through various means, some reasonable, some not, that he considered their 'mad' affair had run its natural course. She was bright enough to see what he was getting at, but not about to acquiesce in the suggested conclusion. Okay, for propriety's sake, she could understand it might make sense to perhaps cool things down in public. But unseen in private, nothing was going to change as far as she was concerned. She was not going to be picked up, pawed over, and dumped like a centrefold playmate.

No siree! She had other ideas.

The Rolls Royce pulled into Septon Station approach and double parked. No porters came rushing, so Johann, the driver, went looking for one.

Septon was hardly a city, but it was a busy place, like Soho compared to Marlsbury as far as entertainment went. The station was always bustling. London being not much more than an hour away by fast train.

'Are you sure you wouldn't prefer to go to your parents for a while?' Edward had suggested lamely. 'You did cut short your visit last time you saw them.' He knew her mind was made up, but it would have been preferable to put some distance between them for a while. 'It must be lovely in Cornwall at this time of year.'

'No, I couldn't face being down there right now. I feel I should be close to you. For your sake as much as mine.'

'For heaven's sake Jenny. Think! The press will be all over me once they know I'm back.'

That thought worried her less by the minute. 'Who cares what the press thinks about us?'

His silent glare told her enough was enough.

'I will see you in a few days, though, won't I?' she pressed, the crocodile in her rather than the secretary doing the talking.

'Once I'm freed up, I'll get in touch. Keep your phone charged. Look, you'd better run. We're causing a bottleneck.'

She knew he was giving her short shrift. He never worried about holding up traffic!

She leaned over to give him a kiss, putting an arm around his neck to get it. His cool response to this innocent movement smacked of rejection.

'Not now, Jenny,' was all he said, shrugging her off.

She didn't like it.

An hour later, Sharon and Kim appeared from the same station Jenny had earlier entered after having been so rudely sent on her way.

The two newcomers were in a far happier mood.

It was Friday, the weather was fine. Sharon had skipped the afternoon modelling class Peter had fixed for her since Kim had come down for a few days. They were as chuffed as two kids playing hooky from school.

For a few weeks now, Peter had rented a two-bedroomed flat for Sharon in Septon, which had its own front door and back garden. The hotel room near Paddington Station was OK during the week while she was on the modelling course, but he thought it best to get her away from London at weekends. Safer. He had given her more than enough money to get by on. But street life in the Paddington area was quite busy and he didn't want her getting any ideas. It was better for him, too, having her closer to Compton Stud.

It was the first place Sharon had ever had that she could call her own, even though Peter came and went at leisure. There was plenty of room for the two of them not to be on each other's toes. She felt like a queen. All that space and privacy! 'It's only temporary,' he told her. 'Like a box compared to the place you'll be able to afford one day if you knuckle down.'

He steered away from hinting he might be planning a longer relationship with her by using 'you' instead of 'us'. But that was exactly what he was beginning to feel. She had become 'special' to him. He felt, or rather hoped, in one way or another they were in for the long haul together.

She couldn't believe Peter was for real. All this! For what? She could tell he was growing to like her, going soft on her. Why? And what a weird way it had all started. She had to pinch herself sometimes. He wasn't exactly the handsome knight in shining armour she had often dreamed about, but he had certainly come to her rescue like one. Maybe that's the way things happen sometimes, like in fairy tales. She had no complaints. His attentions made her feel secure, even his stupid orders about keeping off the streets. She didn't tell him half the things she got up to in the evenings. She couldn't go out for fish and chips without him jumping down her throat. But it was nothing like the Jimbo situation, thank God. The further behind her all that got, the happier she felt. Peter was a bit like an old woman, sometimes, but his heart was in the right place.

She wasn't planning to go back on the game if she could help it, should that be what was concerning him. She would be a fool with all this going for her.

Peter was looking pleased when he wheeled his bike into Sharon's hallway that Friday evening.

As he closed the front door, she came through to him from the kitchen. He had his own key, but he always rang twice as he entered so as not to scare her. She was still a bit nervy about the 'Jimbo' thing. So should Peter be, she thought, wondering if Jimbo had sussed out who he was.

'You're looking happy,' Sharon greeted Peter, pleased to see him. 'Sent that guided missile of yours to the moon or something?'

He had tried to explain his Initiative to her, but guided missile was how it came across to her. 'Ludlow is back!' he said with relish. 'Your punk days are numbered!'

He leant over to kiss her, but she had turned and was leading him towards the small kitchen. It wasn't a snub. She hadn't seen the peck coming. If she had, she would have accepted it without fuss. She never denied him being lovey-dovey, whenever he wanted to be. She didn't go out of her way to encourage it, but she wasn't going to stop it.

'Wash your hands' she told him, running the hot water tap. She hated the smell of his bike. 'Then close your eyes.'

That combination generally meant only one thing.

'Give us a chance,' he bickered. 'I've just ridden twenty miles!'

'Stop moaning! You're meant to be fit.' she snapped, leading him through to the living room with her hands over his eyes. He could smell candles burning.

'Oh no! Not the wax treatment!' he whined.

He heard someone smother a guffaw. Not Sharon.

'Ok. You Can open your eyes now,' she told him, singing a fanfare as she whisked her hands away 'Da-darrr!'

On the table in the middle of the room stood a bottle of 'Methode Champenoise', three glasses and an iced cake covered with candles. Sitting at the ready was the buxom figure of Kim, still wobbling from the thought of wax treatments.

'Ey-up Peter! Pull up a chair. I've been dying to get started!'

Peter greeted Kim and then looked at Sharon. 'What's all this in aid of?' he asked. 'Your birthday's not until Sunday.'

'In aid of!' both girls chorused, breaking up. 'That's a good one,' Kim screamed. 'Gawd! 21, Sunday! She'll be too old for it soon, won't she Pete? Bloody geriatric!'

'Oi!' Sharon barked like a sea-lion. 'Watch it, Burly! Or I'll kick you back out onto the streets.'

Kim creased up again, shaking the top half of her body vigorously from side to side for Peter's benefit to make her gold-top breasts bounce about even more generously under her loose sweater.

She handed him the knife. 'You do the honours, Pete. I might injure myself. I'm no good with knives.'

Sharon was eager to pour the drinks. 'I love opening champagne,' she bubbled. 'It makes you feel all sort of special, don't it? The good things in life, and all that.'

'Classy!' Kim romanticised. 'Proper stylish.'

The cork came out with no finesse, most of the first gush missing all three glasses.

'Careful!' Kim shrieked.

'Whoa there, boy!' Sharon coaxed. 'In a bit of a hurry, isn't it? Just like you Peter! Underneath the arches,' she sang. 'I dream my dreams away!' Another fit of laughter grabbed the girls.

'You two've been at the drink already, haven't you?'

'Only one or two. Couldn't wait, could we?' Kim said. 'We haven't seen each other for a while.'

'Got things to celebrate, haven't we, Kim?' Sharon said, holding up her glass. 'Here's to the BIG NEWS!' Peter raised his eyebrows. Had she gone out and got herself a modelling contract on her own? But it wasn't that. It was much better news, much, much better.

'I haven't got AIDS!' she cried 'The results came through this morning! I had a test done. First since Tony's. Great, in't it? It'd been worrying me. Been losing weight, see. Probably the Jimbo thing.'

Peter raised his glass.

'I ain't got it neither.' Kim boasted. My ma made me have a check-up. I ask you! How could I have it with my size? Honestly. Look at me.' She weighed her breasts in her hands. 'Have a feel, Peter. You don't get many of these to the pound!'

To the hundredweight, more like! Peter was thinking.

Both girls looked at him expectantly. 'Well?' they asked in unison. Peter eventually realised what they were getting at.

'What are you looking at me like that for?' he replied, pretending to be affronted. 'I haven't got AIDS! They always screen me when I give blood.'

They finished the make-believe champagne like three clean bears round a pot of honey and then opened the next. Peter sipped at his. He wasn't exactly a big drinker. But the girls went hammer and tongs at it, determined to have a good time.

He used to dream of situations such as the one he found himself in later that night, sandwiched between two wanton naked bodies. But in the event, he found it more than inhibiting. He finally fell asleep locked into Sharon with Kim bringing up the rear, only to wake in the middle of the night facing the other way, the three of them clinging to each other's anchor points like a bobsleigh team. At least it was a double bed this time.

'This game you want to play with that Ludlow toff ain't really a game, is it?' Sharon asked with insight the next morning. 'What's it all about?'

All three of them were now lying on their backs, Kim was snoring. 'A bright future' Peter explained minimally. There was no need to burden

Sharon with the whole truth, nor give Kim an inkling of it. 'I tell you, it's not what you know in this world, it's *who* you know. It goes even further. It's what you can get from who you know.'

Sharon blew out air as Peter went on.

'Because of who you look like, I think with a little bit of encouragement my partner Sir Edward Ludlow might be talked into helping me turn you into another Stephanie Star.' He thought he'd exaggerate his partnership connection to Ludlow to add weight to his plan. 'If not a supermodel for the catwalks, then at least a grass-roots model for one of those catalogues that come through in the post. He's got the know-how and the right contacts. I've got a feeling I can make him go for it if it's not too traumatic for him to see a replica of his wife when I show him your photos.'

'Daft fucker. You're bonkers. You're talking like a loony.'

'It's not bonkers at all. You *could* make it as a model if you wanted. That wasn't bullshit I was on about up in Manchester.'

By her standards, she had already made it. Within the space of weeks, here she was going to modelling school being showered with attention and money. Not that she couldn't handle more if it was coming her way. But she couldn't see what he was suggesting coming off. The odd shag had gone to his head.

'Do I get famous and all?' she bartered jokingly, playing him along.

'Down to you if you think you're up to it. It's not all glitz, as you know, having your name it lights.'

She wouldn't mind taking her chances.

Chapter Thirty Two

For the next week or so Peter went back and forward between Compton Stud, Septon and his mum's place in Newton Stoat, usually on his bike. But he needed the use of Karl and the Jaguar for a run into Marlsbury at one point. Martin Hollom had news for him.

Peter hadn't seen the old sot since being shown the door months ago.

'You're looking well, lad,' Hollom greeted him, cap-in-hand.

'Not so bad yourself,' Peter lied. 'But that cyder'll get the better of you one day.'

'Oh, I know lad, I know. But at least I'll go with a smile on me face. Just like you will yourself now, s'pose. You're doing all right for yourself at last, in'cha?'

Peter nearly said: 'No thanks to you.' But that would not have been fair.

'I've had the Social Security people nosing about the shop, but I ain't told them nothing.' Hollom went on.

'Well, you wouldn't, would you? You're not that stupid. You'd get done for hiring slave labour!'

Hollom let the remark pass.

'Anyway, seems you've had a bit of luck,' he said. Peter took notice. 'You know that old man you've been making the Sopwith Pup for? Well, he's gone and died and left you the damn thing so's you can finish it. You'd just as well take it away with you. It's cloggin' my place up.'

It was good that Hollom was talking to him again. He seemed to have mellowed in the interim, not asking for all his other bits and pieces to be removed, nor to give him the shop door key back. Peter was in his good books again, which was good to know.

'Stop off at the airstrip, Karl,' Peter said, after they had dismantled its wings to get the Sopwith into the car. 'I'll finish it there when I get a chance. There's that workshop under the dis-used conning tower that I can use. The strip's the place it needs to be when it's finished. No point mixing it up with the Initiative stuff at the Stud. Shouldn't take too long before I can give it a go.'

323

Ludlow's private Cessna was parked up in the only serviceable hangar in use at the airstrip.

'When's Ludlow flying off again?' Peter asked Karl innocently as he went back to his car, hoping to learn something prior to a meeting that had been set up between them for later that day. 'Any idea?'

'Who knows?' came the non-committal reply. 'Ask yourself when you see him. Maybe next time he flies off with Sopwith Pup by mistake!'

Peter got his point, but the Pup wasn't quite that big.

'Ah! Peter. How nice to see you again,' Ludlow said charmingly as Tyler entered the studio workshop at Compton Stud. It was their first meeting since Nairobi. 'I was just taking a look round. It all seems very productive. Good to know you haven't been wasting your time. Nor have the salespeople. Orders are coming in, you'll be pleased to know. There's been a great response since the Birmingham Trade Fair.'

Peter was pleased to hear that. 'Mark II is shaping up now as well.'

'I thought I could see signs of something new developing,' Ludlow said. 'Looks interesting. Not for the domestic market. Far more heavy duty.'

'Yes, indeed. I'll be relying on your experience in due course about how to proceed with marketing. There's something else I also want to run by you when you have a quiet moment. Something a little more delicate, but something that I'm convinced will tempt your indulgence.'

Ludlow looked at Victor questioningly, as if in reprimand for not having been forewarned of this new demand.

Peter could not help noticing.

'This is something that has recently come up,' Peter responded. 'Rose knows nothing of it, neither should he.' When Peter was ready to introduce Sharon, complete with her mother's famous hairdo, he wanted to be alone with Ludlow, as they had been on the shores of Lake Naivasha, but with the paper-thin walls. 'I want this new project to be kept between the two of us. Completely. Once I've explained what it is, you'll see why. It'll be up to you to decide the way to go with it, depending on how impressed you are. And I'm sure you'll be very impressed indeed.' Peter concluded inscrutably.

By the sound of it, whatever Tyler was dreaming up, Ludlow had a feeling he would be obliged to go along with it. Delicate? It didn't sound too much of a threat. He would pass his judgement in due course and probably indulge Tyler for the sake of a quiet life.

'Do you plan to be staying here now you're back in the country?' It was a reasonable enough question for Tyler to ask of his business partner. 'Otherwise, how do I get in touch with you about this? I'd be quite happy to sit with you on that creaky verandah in Kenya again, if necessary. Or anywhere else you prefer as long as big ears here isn't hiding in the cupboard.' A nod toward a disgruntled Rose
caused Ludlow to smile, knowing from past experience how fussy the man was about protecting what he considered to be his intellectual property.

'You still have my private UK cellphone number I presume?' Ludlow asked. 'Use that as soon as you are ready,' Ludlow responded with a smile. 'Don't leave it too long. I shall possibly be off on my travels again soon. I can assure you it won't be to Naivasha, though, unfortunately.'

As soon as he had a chance that afternoon, Peter slipped out of Compton Stud via the stables and cycled head down through the ferns up to Beacon Ridge. Once under cover of Goodwoods, he stopped for a brief look back to see if there was any sign of Karl following him.

There was not. Life had become less restrictive since Tyler's Initiative had hit the financial pages.

Happy about that, he cut across to the bridle path and made his way deep in thought until he found himself alongside the tree where Stephanie had met her death. Had he been aiming for it purposely? It was not on his normal route. Stephanie had been on his mind. He had arrived there subliminally. The tree was surrounded by layers of flowers and photos of young Stephanie, with messages left by sad and devoted fans.

He got off his bike, laid it flat and studied the homages for a minute or two. So much had happened since that fateful day. Peter was a changed man. His grievances with Ludlow were not gone but had no real impetus any longer in that direction. He was far from squeaky-clean himself. Taking advantage of another man's fear and shortcomings through the chance death of his wife was not exactly the noblest of acts. Although he had not exactly instigated that deceit himself. Just slyly egged it along.

He now faced a minor dilemma. To answer Stephanie's wishes to help Sharon in a meaningful manner, he felt he would have to disregard her plea of 'no-one must know'. It was tricky, but he felt Ludlow would have to be enlightened. How else could any of Stephanie's wealth be released without Ludlow's complicity?

Peter had an idea about how that might be achieved.

Stephanie could be hurt no longer by Ludlow knowing her secret. During her life she had kept it for her own sake, not for Sharon's, or more correctly, Gloria's. It was that person who mattered now; the one who 'should not know' her true identity. He had given Major Wendy Clarke his word, and he would stick to it. Knowing Sharon as he did now, even if he told her outright who she really was, she would call him 'a daft fucker' and leave it at that.

He doubted he would get the same response from Ludlow once shown photographic evidence. In the flesh, there would be no question at all.

It was time to come clean. He felt his Initiative had now established himself enough as a partner to own up to certain misconceptions that Ludlow had created for himself. There were still those elements of Stephanie's conversation with Major Wendy Clarke that Ludlow would not want exposed and investigated. Therein was the bargaining chip that would justify the risk of putting his proposition forward. False in application, but honest in purpose. He felt confident Ludlow would go along with quietly setting up his newly acquired stepdaughter in some way in exchange for all threats removed.

Let bygones be bygones. In which case, what good reason for Ludlow *not* to help Sharon? In spite of how it had come about, Tyler and Ludlow were now partners in business. Perhaps they could now join in an endeavour that would help cleanse both their consciences, to a greater or lesser extent?

What Peter Tyler had in mind was a lucrative modelling contract for Sharon. Something Ludlow could orchestrate with ease. He could still pull all the strings. Even without the extraordinary bonus of having

Stephanie's famed looks, with the weight of Ludlow's connections, Sharon's success could be manufactured at the drop of a hat. With the body she possessed and a little application she'd be a winner. All she had to do was stay on her feet and smile!

Peter would naturally offer himself up as her personal manager to guide her through the pitfalls, keep her on the straight and narrow. She was a free spirit, which he loved, but it could mean danger if and when money began to flow. Although she was streetwise, she would be like a kid in a sweet shop once the world opened up for her. Peter wanted to be around with a steady hand when that happened.

The success of this scenario rested on his next enterprise. More hands-on this time: devious, but with a pure motive.

With a final look up at the thick branch that had brought about Stephanie's untimely nemesis, he threw a leg over his saddle and headed down through Deadwoods, finally hitting the road that would take him to Septon.

He was out of practice. The sixteen point seven miles took him the best part of an hour.

In Septon, he went into the reference room of the Public Library and ensconced himself out of the way of prying eyes. He selected a book that he thought would give him more than enough insight into what he needed to know. After only a few minutes, he had replaced it. Being too precise with what it had told him was unnecessary. He was trying to put himself in the frame of mind Stephanie Star must have been in when she learned her child had survived and lived. He remembered most of what she had said on the tape in her excited state that night to Major Wendy Clarke. Putting pen to paper soon after, she wouldn't have been any calmer. That's how he should approach this himself. Confused and from the heart.

Reaching into his shoulder bag, he pulled out a pad and a pencil and began to compose a final testament in the name of Stephanie Star: a Will that would unequivocally bequeath her entire estate to her abandoned daughter, Gloria Shaw, born 6th May 1967 at St. Stephen's clinic, Sheffield. He had scribbled that down when listening to the tape, so he was sure that part was accurate. Others too, that stood out, such as Abalone. He wrote that it was an offshore shell company created by her husband into which some, but not all, of her overseas earnings had been placed. Her husband would know where her other wealth lay, including where the bank accounts he had frozen were located. Zurich, she had known, was one of the places.

He wanted the draft to sound loose, but detailed enough for Ludlow to believe it could be genuine; something that he would in no way want aired in public. A document believable enough for him to prefer settling a life-changing trust in Sharon's favour rather than having the *Will* challenged publicly.

A fraction of what Stephanie's total estate must have been worth was all Peter would be suggesting, not *demanding*, put to Ludlow in conciliatory terms. Peanuts in the circumstances.

When he thought he had got the wording just about right, Peter packed up his things and left in search of a second-hand junk shop. There were a couple in Septon, and the first one he came across had a good choice of what he wanted in its window: a cassette recorder.

He chose a Sony Walkman.

First making sure the thing worked properly, he paid the asking price and took it away, blank cassette included.

That done, he headed back to see how his mother and Gwen were getting on with all the building work that had been going on. The damp-proofing and double-glazing had been completed, which made all the difference to the comfort of the place. Because of that, there had been no real thought given to the idea of moving closer to a town just yet. Come winter, that might change.

It was still more convenient to sleep at Compton Stud. More pleasant than home, too, with all its adjacent activities to indulge in. Tyler's Initiative Mark I was in production at various factories, already guaranteed marketing success. Some parts were now being produced at the new Marlsbury Pumps plant in Manchester, Ludlow took great pleasure in pointing out.

In the studio workshop at the Stud, Peter had been toying with the idea of a four-prop version of the Initiative designed for more heavyweight duties. This was *fun* now, having done all the hard work. Amazing what success could do for a person's self-belief.

But his interest was being overtaken by considerations of Sharon's future. Guaranteeing a happy result to this end needed Ludlow's blessing.

The idea of a fake Will had struck Peter as a possible way of achieving this. Just the *idea* of a Will being in existence would make Ludlow sit up. If he believed it was genuine, his compliance should be ensured.

Tyler made a clandestine midnight run to Hollom's Attic where once again he played back the telephone conversation between Stephanie and the major. This time through a speaker. Selecting relevant passages, he recorded them onto the Sony Walkman making sure only Stephanie's voice was ever heard. Then into one of the portable typewriters he knew to be sitting on dusty shelves, he slipped one of the sheets of paper he had taken from Compton Stud and tentatively typed out his first attempt at a fake draft Will.

It took him more than one attempt to get it how he wanted. There were typing errors, but he let them stay. It was more than conceivable that Stephanie would have made mistakes in her frame of mind at the time.

The trickiest part of the job he left till last; the laying on of Stephanie Star's signature. As one of the most celebrated signatures that the world of cosmetics had ever known, having graced so many products in its time, Peter could have traced it from any of a dozen labels or magazines a few years back. But not so these days. However, he could go one better.

Out of his bag he took an old, but remarkably well-preserved, autograph book of multi-coloured pages. There were only six entries, two of which belonged to the hand of Stephanie Star, gathered one year apart when she had opened Marlsbury's annual Christmas Fayre.

He studied both specimens, tearing out the one that appeared to make the boldest impression. Applying the technique of tracing, he transferred her signature as close to the last typed word of the Will as he could get it, surveying the complete counterfeit with a sense of achievement.

'Perfect!' he congratulated himself with a bite of excitement. 'Buggering-well prefect!'

In fact, it wasn't even close to being perfect, but as good as it needed to be for his purposes. He knew it wouldn't pass as an original on close inspection, but by the time it had been photocopied a couple of generations, it would take a brave man to call it a fake at first glance.

'Once he sees the polaroid snaps of Sharon and listens to the Walkman, Ludlow'll have few doubts it could be genuine,' he prided himself.

He would leave it a few days before approaching Ludlow. No immediate hurry. Spend a couple of days with the girls, think it through again before going for it.

When he got to the Septon flat, those girls were not there. They rolled merrily back in a while later, telling him they had been to the pictures. But he didn't believe it. 'What film was it?' he asked, playing them along. He could tell they had been out drinking. Their smell gave them away.

'Red Horn and Space Sluts,' Sharon lied. It was the only film showing at the independent cinema everyone called the Fleapit. She had already seen it back in Manchester, so she could have answered his questions, should he have asked any. But he didn't, so she volunteered a bit of evidence herself. 'All about sex in space. Weightless humping! That let you out, Kim, didn't it?'

'Ha! Ha! Very funny! I don't think!' Kim grizzled.

The girls wanted another drink and didn't deny themselves.

'It's my birthday tomorrow, don't forget,' Sharon reminded Peter. '21! Blinking heck! Really over the hill. I fancy getting legless tonight!'

And she did. Kim, too.

Chapter Thirty Three

Peter was up early the next morning. After a few token exercises, he made a pot of tea and took it through to the bedroom with a birthday gift for Sharon; a brilliant red mini-skirted dress with its back cut so low bikini bottoms would be in danger of showing. He'd had it made especially, copied from a dress Stephanie Star had worn once on a famous poster, one that had helped make her a cult figure.

Sharon unwrapped it as excitedly as a child, but when she held it in her hands there was nothing but disappointment. 'What am I supposed to do with this?' she asked. 'Blow my nose?'

'You know exactly what it is! You must have worn stuff just like it at Tony's place.'

Sharon grunted. 'Not a lot of it, is there?' She held it up against her. 'You can look at my arse anytime Peter, if that's why you bought it!'

Kim burst out from the covers to make her own judgement, breasts a-wobble, 'It's nice, Sharon. For your shape. It's coming in again all this stuff. Lovely material, in't it?' She felt it against her face and then rubbed it over her breasts. 'Cor! I wish I could get into something like this.'

The idea was hysterical, Peter thought.

'Bit bright, though, in't it?' Sharon suggested. 'Too bright.' That was the worst thing about it, she decided. If it had been black, she could have made it look punky wearing it on the outside. But post office red!

'You don't have to wear it in public,' Peter reassured her. 'Just for our little game.'

'I was afraid you were going to say that.' Sharon said, subdued. The penny had dropped. So, it wasn't a *real* present.

'You play games, do you, when I'm not around?' Kim joked. 'Ain't gymslips better for all that?'

While they drank their tea listening to the radio, a DJ made an announcement about a local village fete.

'That's today,' Sharon shouted. 'I want to go! It's my birthday and I ain't never been to a village fete!'

'Nor've I!' Kim added to endorse Sharon's case.

'Are you serious? You wouldn't enjoy it, you know.' Peter said patronisingly, trying to put them off. 'It's a church do, with bell-ringing

331

and home-made cakes. That sort of thing, not a fairground with dodgems and candy floss. It'd be a fate worse than death for you two. Get it? Fete?' They didn't. Perhaps he was really thinking of sparing the fete a visitation from this unholy pair of punks more than worrying about their own preferences. 'You might get dragged in to take your vows.'

'What's them?' Sharon asked. 'Not what them stone-mason blokes make you do is it? You're not one of them, are you, Peter? On the sly?''

'That's why he walks so funny!' Kim suggested, demonstrating by making her legs go bandy.

A few minutes later, another plug for the Fayre came on, this time promising 'yard of ale' drinking competitions and gun dog displays.

'Sounds like a bloody good laugh to me!' Sharon decided. 'Fancy it Kim?' Kim did.

'Come on Peter! We can all go. Better than sitting around all day watching videos.'

'All right.' Peter finally assented. 'As long as you promise me one thing.'

'I'm not wearing that bleeding dress!' Sharon told him straight out.

'No, not that.'

'What then?'

'Neither of you try to pull the vicar!'

Kim wobbled all over at the thought. 'Only if he's that one who used to come to Tony's!'

Eastcombe was a proper, living village, as clean as a clinic, unlike damp and dismal Newton Stoat which seemed to be dying off slowly along with its inhabitants. Everything centred around the 15th century church and village green.

Peter decided he could make use of this outing. He knew the Salvation Army Band would be playing there. It would be perhaps a good opportunity to give Major Wendy Clarke an inkling of what had been going on since their last contact. It had been weeks, if not months, and he had started to feel guilty about it, so he prepared a note to slip into her box to explain things.

Peter rode by bike to the fayre, happy that the girls wanted to take the local bus by themselves for the hell of it. He knew he would get there well before them. The bus took a circuitous route, and he guessed they'd be wanting to stop off at a pub or two on the way to get themselves in the mood.

There was so much on Peter's mind as he biked into Eastcombe, he failed to notice the gentle purr of the Jaguar bringing up his rear with Karl at the wheel having been instructed not to take his eye off the ball since letting Tyler slip off on his own the day before.

Karl was not alone in the car. Beside him sat a new face belonging to Dmitri, a young man looking every bit a student. In his jeans and loose-fitting sweater, he passed unnoticed as he walked the last few hundred yards into the village to merge with the growing crowds.

The band were already playing as Peter chained his bike to the church railings, so he had no problem locating Major Wendy Clarke. She was shining in her Sunday best, collection box as ever in her hand. She spotted him, and as soon as 'Come All You Faithful' finished, she made a beeline for him.

Giving her box a shake, her greeting was more like an accusation: 'Hello, Mr. Tyler. It is some time since you made a donation.'

He knew this was a gentle reprimand for not keeping in touch with her. But how much could he have told her till now? That he had been having fun screwing Stephanie Star's daughter, and that the little scamp might be arriving at the Fayre soon? He didn't think so.

'Sorry, Major,' he said, confident that in her punk gear, the Major was unlikely to recognize Sharon as Stephanie Star's unknowing daughter. 'Everything's been going just fine,' he said, fishing in his pocket for his prepared message and threading it into the hole in her box. 'I'll be able to give you more soon, I hope.'

Peter was saved from possible questions. An eager young man with amazingly rosy cheeks was impatiently trying to attract the Major's attention.

'Please Major, could you give me a hand to put this up, I wonder?' It was a Salvation Army cadet, rolled-up poster in hand, beckoning her into the church. 'Brass rubbings,' Was the explanation.

Peter brushed past a young man in jeans and sweater who had come over to make a donation while the pair had been talking. Peter was anxious to make himself scarce because he could see the Septon bus trundling into view through the exhaust fumes of slow-moving traffic.

As soon as his spiky-haired protege and her giggling friend stepped off the bus in their full punk regalia of black, with holes and chains, the pastoral scene of rural idyll was defaced. They didn't have to do anything. Their presence was enough. Added to that, he could tell they were drunk! What else might he have expected?

Being so close to consecrated ground, Peter felt his own spiritual stirrings rising in communion with these rascals. They were outcasts, as he sometimes felt himself to be. He loved their apparent ability to transcend disapproval. They didn't give a damn about what people thought of them.

The moment the Salvation Army band struck up a stirring march, Sharon and Kim slipped solemnly into the church as though drawn to the altar like penitent sinners.

In no time the irreverent pair re-emerged in fits of laughter, only to start soft-shoe-shuffling in time to the music, shimmying rump to rump like nobody's business as though trying to polish the balloons of flesh sticking through their tattered black jeans. Peter soon saw what was causing their giggles. Someone had torn the letters BR from the sign that should have read 'BRASS RUBBINGS £10. Please see the Vicar'. No need to wonder, who?

Next day Peter told them they were all going to London. It was a Bank Holiday. They could take in the sights at the same time as he prepared Sharon for her 'coming out', as he liked to call it.

It was a matter of mischievous judgement when and how to introduce her to Ludlow. Peter was now fairly sure his recent preparations were secure enough to introduce the new 'situation' to him. His thought was to get on with it sooner rather than later. The steady publicity he had received as a successful associate of Wilson Hughes had shored up his confidence. He was now part of the furniture. Trust was complete, so it seemed.

He kept reminding himself how it had all started; a chance meeting and a cry of 'no-one must know!'

Things had changed a little.

Kim was going back up North in a couple of days, but not before enjoying some of the sights of London on her way through. 'The Kings Cross area is all I've ever seen,' she laughed. 'And that, only in the dark! I wouldn't leave home for it, I'll tell you that much for bugger-all!'

Sharon didn't want her to go back to Manchester. 'Come and stay with me. Don't forget that fucker Jimbo!'

'No worries. According to the girls, he's not been seen thereabouts since you know when. I'll check that out while I'm there. I'll be back when I've sorted a few things out. Since letting our place go and having to stay with me mum I've had to behave meself! That's been wearing a bit thin, for both of us. She'll be glad to get rid of me.'

'Not hard to understand!' Sharon dived in. 'Whatcha told her you've been getting up to since Tony's closed?'

'Ain't told her yet.'

'You'll get a right bollocking, then, when she finds out. She must have seen all that stuff in the papers .when Tony died?'

'Didn't put two and two together. Wouldn't have made no difference. I usually get a bollocking anyway, just being there. I'll buy her a fridge magnet or something to remind her of Carnaby Street. She used to talk about going there in the sixties. Soften her up a bit. Will the shops be open on a bank holiday, Peter?'

'Course they will, won't they, Peter?' Sharon answered for him.

Peter confirmed it. 'The place'll be teeming with nosy tourists just like you two!'

'Geroff?' Kim barked, giving him a V-sign. 'Will there be other punks to eyeball?'

If it was more punks they wanted to see, Peter knew just the place; The Kings Road, Chelsea, which was exactly where he would be taking Sharon to have her hair done. 'I'll show you punks you'd never believe,' he told them.

Sharon and Kim were to get an earlier train than him. He would meet them later at the Norfolk Square hotel, which had been paid for a month in advance.

Peter wanted to make sure Karl didn't follow him and discover where Sharon was staying. Just in case. Things had eased up considerably, but he couldn't be too sure. Karl might want to see what he and the girls were getting up to having been very much an interested party in Manchester.

Arriving at Paddington Station, Peter took a devious route through the back of the station to get to Norfolk Square. No-one had followed him.

For once, the girls were ready and waiting, raring to go.

They took in Covent Garden, Carnaby Street, the Kings Road then finally down to the New Kings Road.

It was a Bank Holiday Monday. Everywhere the streets were packed. There were plenty of weird outfits on parade. The trio soon melted into the throng of activity.

The Kings Road seemed to impress the girls most, not so much the dozen or so designer punks lounging about a square, each dressed and groomed so elegantly they might have stepped straight from a film set.

'They ain't real, are they?' Kim gaped. 'They're just posing wannabees!'

'Never mind them,' Sharon responded, the evening sun putting colour into the white of her made-up face. The atmosphere of the trendy street was doing things for her. 'What it would be like to have a boutique here, eh, Kim?'

Kim didn't answer. Her attention was taken by a fleet of custom-built hot-rods cruising towards them at walking pace; dozens of them, of all shapes and sizes, some beautiful and purring, others ugly and rasping, but all immaculate.

The girls were speechless for a few moments, then Sharon nudged Peter and said: 'That's the sort of car I'd like, Pete.' She pointed at a vehicle that seemed to have most of its engine sticking out of the bonnet. 'A lot more fun than that hearse of yours.'

'Buy her one, moneybags!' Kim cracked.

'I'll have a boutique first, Peter darling, if that's all right with you?' Sharon joked, fluttering her eyelids flirtatiously, 'You can keep your catwalk and modelling nonsense. I can live without all that posing crap. Give me one of these little boutiques any day.'

'Gawd, Sharon! It'd only cost the odd 'undred grand,' Kim pointed out. 'Please let Pete buy himself some decent clothes first, will you?'

'If he bought me a shop, he could get everything there, couldn't he? I'd give you discount, wouldn't I, Peter?' Sharon finished by shouting since Peter had started off down the road. 'I fancy a unisex shop.'

Peter had unisex of a different order in his sights. About a hundred yards down the road, he stopped outside a hairdresser's called 'Strands'. It had been established for years. Since the early sixties. The original unisex parlour, a monument to flower-power and the first-generation swinging set. Inside, the walls were covered from ceiling to floor with signed photographs of the famous who had been *styled* there over the years. Taking pride of place among these was a large black and white blow-up of Stephanie Star herself. From day one of her association with trend-setting Edward Ludlow,
Stephanie's hair had been styled at Strands.

Where else to have Sharon pampered?

It was the sort of detail that appealed to Peter.

'Remember that new wig I promised you, Sharon?' he remarked jokingly when the girls had caught him up. 'This is where you'll be getting it. I've booked you in first thing Wednesday morning.'

Jenny Grant's Bank Holiday weekend was not such a bundle of fun. She had spent most of her time moping around her flat either waiting for Edward to ring as he had promised or frustrating herself even more by picking up the phone and trying to reach *him* on his brick mobile. But all she ever got was Victor, who gave her nothing but excuses about Ludlow not wanting to be disturbed by anybody.

'I've told him you called,' Victor had fobbed her off twice now, and she was pissed off. 'More than once! What is it with you, Jenny? Are you trying to lay claims, or something? You're just a secretary, remember? He'll get through to you in his own good time! What do you think we're running here, a fucking lonely-hearts club?'

That was all Jenny could take. Edward deliberately avoiding her was one thing, but to have Victor ridiculing her was unbearable. That last gibe of his was the limit. It was still ringing in her ear as she jumped into her Jeep and headed up New King's Road in the interminable snake of slow-moving traffic going into the West End.

More often than not she would cut down to the Embankment, but this morning she was planning to do something she'd never dared think about doing before; drop by Edward's Knightsbridge flat just in case he was holding up there. He hadn't responded to her calls for days.

The traffic lights were out at Beaufort Street, and consequently she sat for ages by The World's End pub without moving, inwardly brooding, outwardly steaming.

Paradoxically, that part of Chelsea had been the start of everything for Jenny. Just along from where she was sitting in the traffic jam was the first shop she had leased and turned into her temping agency: 'Jenny's Girls'. Before Edward bought her out, she had opened five more places in fertile West London. Maybe she should have fought off his job offer for a bit longer, stood her ground then, as perhaps she should have done more recently. She couldn't help feeling he would have more respect for her now if she had.

Drivers were becoming impatient and started sounding their horns. Jenny cursed them at first, but had soon joined in. It did no good, of course, except to aggravate an already intolerable situation for everyone but the smug pedestrians who glared back at the irate motorists as though they were in need of therapy.

Jenny perhaps was, because she was becoming uncontrollably tense inside with her personal frustrations on top of all this. She felt stifled. About to explode.

She wasn't the first to crack. A brief gap had appeared in the approaching traffic, and with a screech of tyres, the car behind her pulled out and sped down the wrong side of the road. For a second, she was furious with the driver for overtaking her, but if he could cheat then so could she and she was off scuttling through the chaotic gaps the reckless car in front was creating. Unexpectedly, it suddenly dived off to the right leaving her stranded facing the oncoming traffic as red-faced as the double-decker bus that wouldn't let her back into line. Shaking from all the aggressive looks coming her way, embarrassment overpowered her frustration until someone finally gave way to her.

She was just beginning to calm down when she saw something that sent her emotions flying again. She didn't understand how or why he should be there, but she couldn't possibly be mistaken about the figure of

Tyler, dressed, she could have sworn, in exactly the same clothes he had been wearing when he had arrived in Kenya!

A crowd had gathered outside 'Strands', where even Jenny still had her hair done sometimes. It wasn't just that Peter Tyler seemed somehow to be at the centre of it, it was who he was with and what he was doing that shook her. He was taking photographs of a girl in Strands' doorway. Not just any girl! Jenny looked and looked, and then looked again. She had plenty of time in the static traffic. She couldn't believe her eyes. for a moment she actually thought she was seeing a cardboard cut-out of a young Stephanie Star dressed as a punk, but then the girl moved, and a feeling of dread shot through her.

As she shunted slowly by, some of the hairdressers came out to look at the pictures Tyler had taken, gawking at them, obviously amused by the results. Instant Polaroids.

Jenny couldn't get her head round it. Tyler took the girl's arm and began to lead her up the street. Another girl joined in, grabbing his free arm. The traffic came to a complete stop again behind the bus that had trapped Jenny, allowing Tyler and the girls to get ahead of her. Even from behind in her punkish clothes, it was easy to see the girl was playacting as though on a catwalk.

Sharon had been displaying some of the strutting styles she had been learning at modelling school! Her scruffy punk gear did little to disguise her uncanny likeness to Stephanie.

For one desperate moment Jenny suspected the worst. 'Edward was in on it!' His so-called partnership with Tyler went further than making model aircraft! She began to seethe again as she let her imagination run riot.

The three on the pavement appeared to be in discussion, which ended when they jumped on the slow-moving bus.

Jenny followed as though hypnotized, somewhat calmer, but when the bus turned into Sloane Street towards Knightsbridge panic now really struck her. What if they were going to Edward's apartment? She could not have countenanced that. She'd kill Edward if he was playing that sort of trick on her.

She was almost snapping with tension as the bus stopped at the nearest point to Ludlow's flat. If they got off there, she would pass out!

But they didn't, and the relief unwound inside her. They stayed on until they got to Hyde Park Corner, where she immediately felt ill the moment she saw the girl again. The likeliness to Stephanie was frightening.

She pulled up a little way ahead of the bus and kept an eye on them in her mirror. At first it looked as though they were about to go into the park, but Tyler hailed a cab. Seconds later, it passed her and headed up Park Lane. The bus had taken off towards Piccadilly.

She nearly lost the taxi among all the others crisscrossing the wide thoroughfare, so was forced to stay as close as possible to it hoping the driver didn't move into the bus lane.

At Marble Arch, it led her towards Lancaster Gate. Just as she thought it was making for Paddington Station, it pulled off into Sussex Gardens, a narrow square, stopping about halfway down. She drove past, coming inconspicuously to a halt on the other side of its fenced off central garden in time to see Tyler and the girls disappear into one of the boarding houses calling itself a hotel.

She was certain Tyler could have no idea the trio had been followed, but before going in, he glanced round at the top of the steps with an urgent look of a man who thought they might have been.

Chapter Thirty Four

Sir Edward Ludlow was not looking forward to the day. 'I'm beginning to wish I never agreed to continuing with this damn documentary,' he complained to Rose as the chauffeur driven Rolls-Royce purred out of Compton Stud. 'Today'll be the end of it, whatever Dixon thinks!'

'Well, at least we seem to have lost that other prick from the Daily Scan,' Rose remarked. He was referring of course to the persistent Dick Baker, who had been camping outside Compton Stud's gates like the women at Greenham Common but was now gone.

'Small mercies,' Edward replied casually. His mind was on other things. 'The past few months have been quite a strain. I think another sabbatical might be in order once through this next engagement. With all connections to Bolichem now severed, there are more reasons to be cheerful. I'm not intending to spend much more time in England from now on, none at all at Compton. There's no reason why Tyler shouldn't take it over. Best to indulge his interests *there* as anywhere. It seems to work for him, and what better place for the hounds to keep an eye on him? I hear you've brought in a new guy to help with that?'

'Yeah. Karl and Johann are too easy for Tyler to spot these days,' Rose grunted a reply. 'I still don't trust Tyler. He's a scheming little bastard.'

That gave Ludlow some thought. 'I wonder what this new project he's dreamed up all of a sudden is about?' Another grunt from Rose. 'But first things first.'

Ludlow was about to make his first official public commitment in months, a visit to S.O.D.A.'s main sorting centre in Slough. As expected, a whole tribe of pressmen were kicking their heels outside the gates awaiting his arrival, cameras and microphones at the ready to mark the occasion.

Any hopes of grabbing a quick snap of him as they drove by were scuppered. The tinted windows of the Rolls-Royce were kept well and truly closed as the car rattled and scraped its way through the over-eager mob of flashing cameras.

'My god!' Ludlow retorted, looking out at the relentless mob. 'If they could see themselves!'

There were several police officers and security men on duty to keep people back. Once safely through the gates, Ludlow could still not completely escape the cameras as he disembarked. He was now in full view of the bank of lenses poking through the railings firing off shots like cannons from a galleon. He gave a perfunctory wave and smile, disappearing into the building before anyone had time to finish shouting unwanted questions.

The reception area was flood-lit by television lights with the management staff linked up like a football team to welcome S.O.D.A.'s esteemed founder.

Aware that Simon Dickson's camera would be rolling the instant he set foot through the door, Sir Edward smiled broadly, holding his arms out in readiness to embrace the top echelons of the Centre.

'Mr. Williamson, how lovely to see you again.' He expostulated in his usual grand manner for such occasions, turning his chief executive to face the accredited press party more squarely, taking care to look directly into Simon Dickson's camera himself. 'These BBC chaps have been following me everywhere. Let's take advantage of their presence today to tell the good people not to let up with their donations.'

He leant nearer to the lens, looking right into the iris. 'We still need all your help, you know. Keep it up!'

Everyone was delighted to see Sir Edward was on good form. There had been doubts. All the recent pressures might still be affecting him. 'Let me take this opportunity to announce the good news to you and the public alike, Mr. Williamson,' he went on after shaking hands with the rest of the welcoming party. 'Two more pumps will soon be ready for delivery. Keep the funds rolling in and this could be our best year yet!'

Simon Dickson conducted brief interviews with Sir Edward and Mr. Williamson which prompted Ludlow to have a quick word in Victor Rose's ear. 'Well done. Whatever you did to tame our BBC man, it certainly worked. He's falling over himself to be polite today. I hope you haven't caused him any permanent damage.'

'I merely hinted he might be invited to witness the delivery of those two pumps if the filming went well today. I've seen through him. He prefers the expense account freedom of the *African* bush to the canteen at *Shepherds* Bush! Everyone has his price.'

342

As they moved off on their walkabout, a folded note was handed to Ludlow by a staff member. Before he opened it, Victor's portable telephone rang. Victor covered the mouthpiece with muted irritation. 'Jenny,' he mouthed silently as if the word had a bad taste. Ludlow handed him the note. The written message was short. It read: 'Sir Edward, please could you ring Jenny Grant. Urgent.'

'Deal with it, Victor. I can't face her histrionics today.' At that, he turned to Mr. Williamson and said ebulliently: 'Shall we get on?'

The TV lights went out. Victor was left alone but for a security man and the receptionist, both of whom did their best to pretend they were not listening to his telephone conversation.

'What is it, Jenny?' he asked, his impatience burning through. 'How many fucking times do you have to be told? It's impossible for him to talk to you right now, we're in the middle of filming.'

'Oh! So, you're in Slough already?' she complained. 'I only discovered by chance just now that he was going there! No-one tells me anything! Didn't Edward get my message?'

'It's in my hand.' Victor said curtly.

'Then why hasn't he answered? Don't I mean anything anymore?'

'Got it in one!' Victor said cruelly, looking forward to the day when Jenny had been moved so far sideways, she'd have fallen off the edge. 'What's your problem? And be quick about it!' he asked rudely.

'Where's Edward?'

'I told you. Filming! He can't come to the phone. Won't! You'll have to talk to me. But make it snappy. I've got things to do.'

'It's Edward I want to talk to, not you!'

'Too bad. You're out of luck.'

'Fuck you!' She screamed. It had to be Edward. With that she hung up.

She's getting as bad as his darling wife! Victor was thinking as he caught up with the others. Has Edward been dipping his wick, he wondered?

Ludlow had not told Victor of his sexual entanglement with Jenny in Kenya. He had been hoping she would eventually see the affair as he himself did; animal lust in the dust. Emotional pestering was not wanted as part of the fall-out.

343

'Just another one of her tantrums,' Victor told his boss. 'Now she's refusing to speak to me at all. It has to be you. Isn't it about time she went out temping again?'

Ludlow grinned, or was it a grimace? Her uses were becoming more and more wasted on him as he saw things these days.

But Jenny had not been wasting her *own* time. When the filming was over and drinks had been taken, the visiting party prepared to leave. Victor looked out of a window hoping that the battalions of press people might have retreated only to see Jenny in her Jeep, looking hot, flustered and on a mission. She had come to a halt inside the gate and was now flaunting herself under full attack from the cameras.

'I don't believe it!' Victor exclaimed under his breath, watching Jenny pose for the over-zealous press pack, now all glowing smiles. 'I just do not believe it!'

But he had to. For there it was, and little could be done about it. He couldn't get to Edward to forewarn him as he said his final goodbyes. In the event, as soon as he was led outside, he came face to face with Jenny, in full view of the cameras.

Given this sudden shock, he handled the situation well. 'Ah! Miss Grant.' he said, businesslike, before she had chance to speak. 'Excellent! Perfect timing! Mr. Dickson and his crew are inside anxious for details of my next trip to Africa. Perhaps you would like to go through and see to their needs?'

'No! I *wouldn't* like to go through and see to his needs!' she hissed like a ventriloquist with toothache. 'Stop passing me off! I have got to speak to you!'

'Not now, Jenny!' Ludlow replied, trying desperately to maintain his poise. 'No scenes, please!'

'When then?' Jenny persisted, standing her ground, knowing he must concede soon because the cameras were sensing something was not right between them. 'When?' She repeated more loudly, the motor-drives whirring.

'Ring the car-phone in 15 minutes.' Ludlow said through a forced smile. 'But go inside now, do you hear? Or believe me you're out for good!'

Jenny was taken aback. He was seething. This was no idle threat. She could tell he meant exactly what he had just said. There had been enough hints about cooling things off between them, but that look he had just given her was like a guillotine.

As the chauffeur opened the car door, Victor put himself neatly between Ludlow and Jenny just in case she dared to leap in after him. 'Mr. Dickson awaits you,' he said. Taking a firm hold on her arm that would leave bruises, he pointed her in the direction of the S.O.D.A. building entrance.

'Don't ever do that again, Jenny!' Edward voiced with cold precision into his car-phone fifteen minutes later. 'Never! What the hell got into you behaving like that in front of the press rat-pack?'

'If only you'd answered my calls. I wouldn't have been there!' she squealed, trying to control her anger. 'You won't even let me speak to you anymore, let alone see you! What am I supposed to do? Disappear? Are you trying to pretend nothing happened between us? The least you can do is listen to what I've got to tell you, Edward!'

'What's so important, Jenny?' Ludlow asked impatiently, not wanting this conversation.

'Peter Tyler's in London! I saw him this morning.'

Ludlow was silent for a second as the car went under a bridge and the line crackled. 'Are you being serious, Jenny?' He asked when the reception got better.

'Deadly serious! I think he's planning something. He was at 'Strands', in the King's Road. With a girl!'

'Is that it? Tyler's in London with a girl? Christ, Jenny!'

Jenny fell silent. It was the tone of his voice.

'So, Tyler's in London,' he said again, giving Victor a look of exasperation. 'Gone to have fun with his punk playmate, no doubt. Yes, we do know he has a playmate. Two, in fact, I believe. Good luck to him. He's a free man. Is that really what's worrying you, Jenny? Really why you're pestering me?'

He was ridiculing her! She couldn't stand that. Maybe she should say nothing more. But she found herself trying to justify herself. 'Edward! The girl is the spitting image of your beloved wife!'

Ludlow did the worst thing he could possibly have done with Jenny in her present state; he burst out laughing.

'Really, Jenny! Your imagination!' He made a half attempt to cover the handset and turned to Victor. 'The silly cow thinks Stephanie's come back to life!' he said with a smirk, knowing Jenny must have heard him.

'Edward!' she screamed, incensed. 'I didn't say that! Something's going on! Are you too pig-headed to listen? They were taking photographs outside 'Strands'!'

Ludlow laughed again. 'If the girl looks anything like my dearly departed wife, it must be through plastic surgery. According to Karl, Tyler played the hero and rescued the 'damsel' after she had been beaten up. She's a hooker, Jenny. Why don't you take *your* hooks out of me and try to rescue this situation by taking a break,' he said condescendingly. 'Go to Cornwall for a few weeks. See your parents. You broke your last trip. They must be longing to see you. Go and get your head back together. I don't want to see or hear from you again until you've regained your senses. Is that clear? Jumping in like you just did with the Fleet Street pack around my neck was the last straw!'

'Please, Edward!' she implored. 'Don't do this to me!'

But she was pleading to herself. he had hung up on her.

'So, Tyler's in London, eh?' Victor mused. 'I wonder if Karl bothered to send anyone with him.'

'Is that necessary anymore?' Ludlow remarked. 'Let's face it. He's well on side now, surely?'

'Well, he's got something up his sleeve, hasn't he, so you say? Some new con, no doubt!'

'Ah, yes. For my ears only. Another invention? The man's got a brain on him. That Initiative of his is a groundbreaker. Can't argue with that. Not so sure about his taste in women, though. Hookers! You'd think he'd be able to do better than that now he's got money in his pocket.'

'Yeah. But he's not God's gift to women, is he, the way he dresses? Let me check something.'

Victor punched out a number on the car telephone.
Karl answered immediately.

'Where are you, Karl?' Victor asked without announcing himself.

'Stud,' Karl replied flatly.

'We've just heard Tyler's in London. Is that so?'

'He left 11.40 yesterday.'

'Did anyone go with him?'

'The punk kids left before him. They harmless enough.' No need to mention his own brief dalliance with Kim.

'I meant did you send anyone to watch him, dick head!'

'No point. Boss says ease up.'

Rose bit the bullet on that information.

'Everything else quiet?'

'Much. One chance contact Sunday.'

'So?' Victor said, frowning. 'Who with?'

'Salvation Army woman. Spoke long time with him at church funfair. Dmitri saw.'

'Salvation Army?' Victor queried.

'Major Wendy Clarke, her badge say. Dmitri thinks she knew Tyler,' Karl continued. 'He put note in her box.'

Ludlow's ears perked up. 'Did I just hear 'major' being mentioned?' he asked, exchanging a quizzical look with Rose.

'You did,' Rose responded, making the same connection. 'Precisely what I was thinking. Major!'

Stephanie's taunts came back to Ludlow about her *safe hands*. It couldn't be, could it? Stephanie would never run to the Salvation Army, would she? Surely not? But, Tyler? Worth investigating?

Could this be anything to do with this new *initiative* of his he wants to talk about, Ludlow wondered.

'Find out who this Major Wendy Clarke is, Victor, and where she's coming from. But no violence, please. It could be nothing. We don't want the sally-army chasing us, do we?'

With that instruction going in one ear and straight out the other, Victor said; 'Of course we don't.'

***

On the inside pages of the tabloids the next day, Ludlow's return to 'public' duty was displayed as eye-catchingly as possible with photographs of his seemingly irate Girl-Friday in confrontation with him outside the SODA building. Adding melodrama to the copy were two separate mug shots; one of
Jenny Grant with the caption, 'Out?'; the other of Peter Tyler, with, 'In!'

Although Jimbo had only one good eye as he sat in outpatients at Manchester General Hospital awaiting his final check-up before being given the all-clear, it homed in on Tyler like an eagle onto bait. He was still trying to get his head around the idea that weirdo Tyler was mixed up with Sir Edward-fucking-Ludlow of all people. That was something he had been looking into further. The prick had money! No wonder that cow Sharon had latched onto him. So where were they hiding out? Jimbo would like to know and he now had a few ideas.

Payback time was one step closer.

Chapter Thirty Five

Peter put Kim in a taxi to take her to King's Cross station the day after their jaunt around the punk hot spots of the west end. He had given her enough money for her journey home to Manchester with a warning to steer clear of the red-light district in case Jimbo had re-emerged.

'Huh! I wasn't born yesterday, but, point taken. Keep her away from 'em down here, too,' Kim chortled. 'There's plenty like Jimbo around. Do you hear that, Sharon? Behave yourself and don't forget to keep in touch. I want a full report of everything you get up to. You've got me ma's phone number, so use it! And you!' she flung her arms around Peter giving him the full benefit of her boobs. 'Look after her. You know what a tearaway she is. Lock her up at night till I get back.'

'You don't have to go,' Sharon pointed out. 'You could stay and have modelling lessons with me, couldn't she, Pete? I'll make him pay for it, or he gets no nooky!'

'Well…' was all Peter could get out before Sharon dived in again.

'They do accept all shapes and sizes, don't they, Peter?'

'Cheeky cow!' Kim scowled. 'I'd be a lot better at doing bras than you would with your little pinpricks, that's for sure!'

The girls hugged and kissed. There was even the threat of tears as Kim slumped into the awaiting taxi.

As she started on her journey heading North, Jimbo was working out how and when to start heading South on his payback mission. The tabloids were all over Ludlow with stories of his 'secret' dalliance with Jenny Grant which was seemingly falling apart. The broadsheets were still nibbling at how his assets had beaten the bell at Lloyds.

With Kim gone, Peter was keen to get on with taking Polaroid pictures of Sharon in Stephanie's lookalike clothes.

Stripping off her punk gear, she stood naked for a moment holding the delicate red velvet dress as though it were the Turin Shroud. 'Here goes,' she said stepping into it like an actress setting foot on stage for the first time. 'I haven't done this sort of thing for a while.'

With her hair now matching Stephanie's to perfection, the dress put the final seal on the transformation as Sharon spun herself around aping her mother's famous expression of childlike wonder in search of approval.

Peter melted. The months since Manchester had slowly drawn him closer to Sharon. Looking at her now, he realized things had gone further than that. This did not displease him. She was gorgeous. A gorgeous rascal!

He made her pose in the light of the window, placing a mirror against the wall behind her.

'What's that for?' she joked. 'You must have seen my cellulite-free arse enough times by now!'

'It's to get me in the same shot, big head!'

'Eh? What for? It'll make you look even more like a perve?'

'I tell you, Sharon, you look so much like Stephanie, I need something to prove these pictures weren't taken ten years ago.'

'Daft fucker! You're kidding me?'

'I kid you not!'

The photo-session over, Peter studied the results. She looked so feminine, so seductive, so Stephanie Star.

'Blimey!' she yelped, looking at them. 'I could be her!'

'Too right, you could. And do you know what? I think I'm falling for you, in case you hadn't guessed,' he said boyishly.

'Course I bloody did! Months ago. Daft fucker,' she grinned. 'It's only because you used to fancy Stephanie Star rotten! You're just using me to play out your wet dreams! That's what this is all about, really, ain't it?'

'Not true. But what is, though, is that I'm not too sure I like the idea of making a model out of you. All the blokes'll be dreaming of getting their evil way with you.'

'Bit late for that, ain't it? Most of Manchester's been there already!' She laughed at the thought, then added more seriously, wagging aa accusatory finger, 'I hope it's the real me you're after, Peter Tyler, not my bloody doppelganger. I don't mind playing her as a joke. But that's it. I don't want to be a phoney all me bleedin' life.'

The words seemed not too deeply meant. But not too shallow either.

'Don't worry. It's the real you I want.' he told her. But it made him wonder if he needed to reassess things. The last thing he wanted was

350

for Sharon to be hurt by any of this. She was beginning to mean more to him than hoping to tear the lining from Ludlow's wallet, as Stephanie had wished. His own fortunes had changed so much, he could probably provide Sharon with more than she would ever want himself, perhaps even including a 'classy little boutique' on the King's Road one day. But he felt it was morally more fitting that Ludlow should be the one to meet Stephanie's last wish. Such a closure would seem to be more just.

Next morning, Peter woke to the sound of Sharon vomiting in the sink. He jumped up, concerned.

'What's the matter?' he asked, putting his arm around her bare shoulder.

'Gawd. I feel like death,' she said, without lifting her face from the bowl. 'Don't worry, I ain't pregnant,' she joked. 'It's them bloody pills of Kim's. I'll be alright in a minute. You wouldn't make us a cup of tea, would you?'

He wrapped her in blankets first, lecturing her mildly about taking drugs, but not enough to upset her.

'You really like me, don't you?' she croaked pathetically, as if it was something she had just realized and was feeling guilty about. 'No-one's ever bothered about me this much before, never mind all the wild promises. Trouble is, you've got me half believing some of them.'

She looked up at him wondering whether the time was right to ask something she had been wanting to put to him for weeks. 'OK. Well, if you actually do like me that much, there is one thing you could do for me if you want to please me.' He gave her I neutral look, waiting for a wind-up. But it wasn't. 'You talk about setting me up as a model, yet you still insist on going around looking like a road sign yourself. If you've given up the idea of winning the Tour de France, you wouldn't mind buying yourself some jeans and a T-shirt or something, would you? Anything. But give your bike gear a rest. I mean, I put that dress on for you, didn't I?'

He had to smile. Here she was doubled up with gut-ache, vomiting, and she had chosen this moment to complain about the way he dressed! He just loved her.

The next day, she felt better, so he decided he could finally start putting his plan into motion.

Leaving Sharon with enough money to last her a week, he bade her goodbye with, 'And don't go playing hooky from your modelling lessons now Kim's gone.'

'I won't, if you don't forget to do something about your velcro-gear!'

'It's on my list. See you soon.'

Before going into Paddington Station for a train back to Septon, he grabbed a cab and asked to be dropped at a huge glass bunker of a building on Euston Road. Clasping an envelope marked 'Private and Confidential addressed to Sir Edward Ludlow CEO, he passed through the self-opening sliding doors of Wilson-Hughes main UK offices into a reception area reminiscent of a hot-house at Kew Gardens where tropical plants and fountains out-numbered people in the vast glass dome of a lobby.

One of the security men eyed Tyler with suspicion as if he had seen the man before and not enjoyed the experience. But when he noticed the name on the envelope, he responded suitably, pointing to the porter's desk. 'Deliveries over there, cock. They'll see he gets it.'

Peter wasn't particularly worried when or even if the envelope reached Ludlow. There was nothing in it. He was using it as an excuse to get into the Wilson-Hughes building without creating too much of a fuss.

Once he had handed it over, he went to a rack displaying the groups' publications and helped himself to a copy of the most recent Corporation Accounts Report before breezing out into the swirling wind and dust of Euston Road.

He was about to wave a taxi down, when just along Hampstead Road at the first corner, he noticed a shop boasting a large range of second-hand military paraphernalia. 'Lawrence Corner' it declared itself like a battle flag. Remembering Sharon's request to change his wardrobe, he delayed getting a cab and went to investigate.

Fifteen minutes later, he walked out wearing a camouflaged beret, but not the cotton combat suit he had also bought to go with it. That he carried in the provided bag since he didn't feel up to changing his image completely in one foul swoop.

On the train journey back to Septon, he studied the Wilson-Hughes annual report for 1987/88 he had purloined. And what good reading it made. He couldn't quite work out how the group had come through the recent stock-market crash with such flying colours, but somehow it appeared it had.

Peter had been thinking along the lines of suggesting 20% of Ludlow's personal stake in the group as compensation for Sharon. Stephanie's combined wealth as Lady Ludlow must have been far, far greater. At first, 20% had sounded the right sort of compromise, enough of a bounty, but not too greedy, modest enough for Ludlow to swallow.

As Peter looked closer at the group's various bottom lines, he realised 20% went far and away beyond what anyone could possibly need in life. Ludlow was infinitely richer than expected, even without Stephanie Star's personal estate thrown in!

5% worked out at millions! More than enough to see Sharon in clover, Peter concluded, and a stingy enough cut for Ludlow to stomach, especially since not a penny would necessarily need to come from his own pocket.

Once Ludlow got over the shock of seeing the polaroid photos of Sharon and the fake Will, Peter thought it might be as well to let the man come up with a figure himself. It could even result in a more fruitful outcome. Passing the problem to Ludlow would also seem a more friendly way of approaching this. Peter was just an innocent courier, after all.

As he collected his bike from left luggage at Septon station, Dmitri, who had been on duty awaiting his return rang through to Karl.

'Is he alone?' Karl asked.

'Yes,' came the reply.

'OK. Stay at the station in case the girl comes.'

'Will do.'

Karl settled himself in an armchair at the Septon flat still raging at being accused by Victor Rose of giving Tyler too much of a free hand. Karl didn't like being called a dickhead in any language.

As Peter cycled up to the flat, his carrier bag full of army clothes slung across the handlebars, he was shaken to see Karl's motorbike parked outside. How the hell did Karl know about the place? For a moment his heart sank. Were there any tell-tale signs of his Will-making lying about anywhere? Surely not. All evidence had been meticulously removed to keep Sharon's nose out of it. She would have freaked out if she knew exactly what he was up to.

'What are you doing here and how did you get in?' Peter roared, seeing Karl lounging as if he belonged there. 'I could get you deported for breaking and entering!'

'No break-in,' Karl said lazily through his dark smile. 'Back door open.'

'Bloody cheek!' Peter said, guessing he must have been followed at some point. 'Have you been sniffing around hoping Kim might be here? Too late, lover boy. She's gone back to Manchester.'

'You get me in trouble going to London on your own.' Karl explained, his normal inscrutability flaking at the edges. Was it a hint of smugness in his voice, or irritability? It was sometimes difficult to tell with Karl. 'You come, Peter. Boss wants to see,' he added.

'What brings this on?' Peter asked.

'Maybe give you kiss for Initiative success?'

Peter wouldn't be getting a kiss when he presented Ludlow with his latest initiative. And, out of the blue, this summons offered the perfect opportunity to do just that.

When the Major returned home late on Wednesday night after making her rounds and found her house ransacked, she was too shocked to react immediately. She stood in the doorway looking at it in horror, as though on the threshold of Hell. Why should her house be picked on? She had few possessions. Everybody knew that. Her life was devoted to helping others, as the bare walls and empty shelves bore evidence. Those 'decorations' she had allowed, all reflected her calling to God.

Walking into the debris, it seemed to her that the burglar must have thought she had a hidden cache of donations somewhere. Every place that might possibly have concealed something had been torn apart, armchairs, settees, pillows, cushions. Soot hung in the air from pulled out fireplaces. Covered alcoves she never knew existed had been ripped open.

She reached for the telephone several times to call 999, but in her dazed horror she kept forgetting the wire was hanging bare. There was little the police could have done anyway. Nothing was missing. She had nothing to *go* missing, not even a television set.

For a few minutes, she bowed her head in prayer, forgiving the desperate person who had done this terrible thing to her. After this brief entreaty, she felt more at peace and soon began to wonder if anyone else in the neighbourhood had suffered the same indignity.

But no-one else had been, nor had anyone seen anything suspicious. The old couple across the road who often sat at the window till dark had noticed a motorcyclist riding up and down twice: 'One of those messenger types, you know'. Nothing else had caught their eye.

Laying restlessly on her shredded mattress that night, a terrible thought seized her. She leapt up and went downstairs to where her papers and letters were still strewn across the floor. She feverishly rummaged through them.

It wasn't there!

Something *had* been taken!

The note that Tyler had slipped into her box at the fayre. But why all this ransacking? The note had been sitting in plain view on the dresser.

The disc!

Thank the Lord she had thrown it away. The two halves of it into different street bins.

Chapter Thirty Six

'It's got to be a hoax!' Victor exclaimed, holding the note Tyler had slipped into the major's collection box. 'The pair of them are in on it together. Trying to con you!'

Edward was grey faced, unable to be so readily optimistic as his friend. He couldn't credit Tyler with enough imagination to dream up something like this. The Salvation Army? But it was their involvement that gave it a possible ring of truth. Major?

'I wish you could be right Victor,' he said, his mouth dry. 'A hoax? If so, why?'

'Give me two minutes alone with either of them, and I'll soon find out!'

'No. Victor. Not that way. Not yet,' Edward responded. At the back of his mind was the disturbing possibility that what was on the note was genuine.

He slumped into an armchair holding it at arms' length. Why would Tyler go to such lengths to lie about the existence of a Will, no matter how roughly put together? If the signature was genuine there could be no disputing it.

What was in it for Tyler to come up with such a con. Nothing! Nor the Salvation Army, come to that. Could it be just to piss me off, he asked himself. Why would Tyler bother? Surely he had everything he needed these days? Money was coming out of his ears!

Ludlow had read Tyler's note to the major over and over:

Don't know how I missed it. But I found what looks like the last-minute Will I believe
Stephanie told you she would make. In it she leaves everything to her long-lost daughter and points to where evidence of her wealth was hidden, some of it on the disc I gave you. The Will is badly expressed in places so I'm not sure how it would stand up in a court of law, but I feel Ludlow will have to be told about it if the child is to benefit as Stephanie had wished. I see it as being in no-one's interest for the Will to be made public, and I'm certain Sir Edward Ludlow would agree. It could ruin him if any of what his wife says on it regarding shell companies and his SODA charity should

be investigated. I am sure he'll honour her wishes rather than take that risk. Of course, all this needs to be done anonymously, as we also both wish. Let me know your thoughts in the usual manner before I approach Ludlow. Regards, Peter. p.s. I have the Will in a safe place. I'll get a copy to you in due course, should you need to see it. Peter.

There had been things about his wife that Ludlow had never understood. But he had not expected anything like this. She had a child! When? Who's? This scrap of paper had shocked him to the core. If what Tyler was saying was genuine, its significance would be shattering on top of all his other worries.

A bitter memory rose in him.

That first conjugal night with Stephanie floated up from somewhere in his psyche only to have his right-hand man shake it away.

'Believe me, Ted, Tyler's rigged this to fuck with your head!' Victor cut into Edward's thoughts. 'I had a feeling the vengeful prick had something up his sleeve. He's got to be stopped now, or it'll go on forever!'

Edward looked up heavy-eyed. Victor was forgetting one thing. Tyler had started nothing. If they hadn't gone rummaging at the Major's house, he would have known nothing about this until Tyler had come out with it himself, as it seemed he had been preparing to do.

'He's dreamed the whole idea up!' Victor persisted.

'Some dream!' Ludlow responded, eyes fixed on …'if the *child* is to benefit…'

'It's a con, Ted. I'll stake my life on it!'

'I wouldn't like you to do that, Victor,' Edward said dryly, reaching for the Brandy decanter. 'Not just yet. Let me talk to Tyler first. It seems he was already planning to tell me about this without your 'big-ears' being involved, if you remember. Set something up. But go easy.'

The reference to 'big-ears' increased Rose's urge to cross swords with Tyler, not take it easy!

Peter was out of training, sweating-up noticeably as he pedalled behind Karl's trials-bike through the overgrown paddock into the empty stable yard. The lone horse had long since been given to a local riding school. The stables were active no longer.

Rose was waiting stiffly at the back entrance of the Stud like a totem pole, his face up to the sun. His wooden expression turned to aggression the moment he saw Tyler.

No words were spoken. He made a sign to Karl to stay on post outside, directing a fierce glare at Tyler.

Peter took note, feeling suddenly alert as he entered the house with Rose breathing down his neck. Something must have happened to bring this on.

'You sly piece of shit,' Rose hissed, spitting like boiling water. 'I've seen through your game! In!'

A sudden pain stiffened Peter as Rose grabbed the back of his neck and pushed him into the music room where Ludlow sat in wait.

'Well, Peter, we seem to have a new development,' Ludlow said through a thin smile which was neither pleasant nor ironic. 'I imagine you know what I'm talking about?' He paused, perhaps awaiting a response. Peter remained mute, nursing his neck, awaiting a clearer indication of this sudden new development. Eyebrows raised, he looked at Ludlow as if to say: 'Here we go again. *You* summoned *me*. So, *your* move."

'You have been playing with me, Peter,' Ludlow eventually obliged. 'Congratulations. Your initiative runs deeper than one might have realised. I believe you had a proposition to put to me? Please, take a seat.'

'I'll stand if you don't mind,' Peter said pertly, not because he thought he might have to make a run for it, but because he wasn't in the mood for a cosy chat while Rose was hovering over him like a rusty dumbbell. 'I'm saying nothing until *he's* out of the room.' A quick nod in Victor's direction, but no eye contact. 'His attitude does you no favours.'

Ludlow was coming round to believing there might be some truth in that. With an imperceptible tip of the head Rose went scowling from the room.

Peter now sat down.

The so-called music room they were in was expansive, one of the loveliest rooms in the house, blessed with glorious aspects over the lawns and gardens seen through several elegant tall windows along two of its walls. As Peter waited for Ludlow to clarify the reason for bringing him there, his attention was drawn to a grand piano, with its lid up ready for action. At its side stood a rather ornate candelabra, fully loaded as if in preparation for the arrival of Liberace. Around the walls hung elegant tapestries interspersed with paintings, mainly portraits, perhaps of past occupants. Two glittering cut-glass chandeliers decorated the ceiling, which was covered with molded patterns of star signs. What could be seen of the floor around the edges of an enormous Persian rug revealed dark oak boards.

A shiver went through Peter. On a similarly dark oak coffee table between the two men, he noticed the note he had slipped into the major's box at Eastcombe fayre.

Ludlow had been watching him closely. 'Yes, indeed, Peter,' he explained without malice. 'Your correspondence with the major. You seem surprised? But really, should you be? Still, I must say you did extremely well in keeping her to yourself for so long. We slipped up there, I'll be the first to admit. But then you were so plausible.'

Had the major sent Ludlow the note, or what? It had to be 'or what', surely? Either way, it was bad news. But no sign of the fake disc he'd cut in two. Good news?

Ludlow got to his feet. 'Let's take a stroll round the estate, Peter. We shouldn't be cooped up inside on such a beautiful day as this. It's almost as nice as it was for our walks in Kenya.' This pally-pally-ness seemed fairly genuine, which is what Peter was hoping for. 'I see you've been out already doing a bit of training. You've been getting on fine with Karl, haven't you? He keeps himself fit, doesn't he?'

'Yes, he does,' Peter agreed readily. 'Very fit. Did he tell you what he did for me in Manchester? Saved my ear from being cut off, if not my life.'

'Yes, he told me. He's very good like that, tells me everything. Talking of which, that episode under the arch with your punk friend perhaps helps make a little more sense of this,' Ludlow said, picking up the note and waving it. There was a slight stammer in his voice. Uncertainty? 'I shouldn't have thought punks were your style.' He regarded Tyler's newly acquired army fatigues jacket, which, along with the Lycra cycling shorts, were not exactly mainstream attire. 'I see you've taken to camouflage these days. What else have you been hiding from me?' The smile he gave Tyler was almost friendly.

'Give me two tics and I'll show you,' Peter obliged. 'I need to collect a couple of things to help with that.'

As they left the house, he ran across to his flat in the converted barn.

Whilst gone, Rose came out from the house to express his unease about the situation while the culprit was absent. 'It's got to be a hoax, Ted! A cheap lie and a trick! Don't fall for it!' Big-ears had somehow been listening in.

'Leave this to me!' Edward snapped, 'I know what I'm doing. Lose yourself until I've heard him out. I mean it!'

Inside the barn, Peter bumped into Karl who was on his way to the gym. The look he got from the Austrian was a silent 'what's going on?'

'Big showdown,' Peter told him as he clicked a pouch around his waist containing three polaroid snaps and a photocopy of the 'Will' he had composed. The original copy, he had destroyed. There was no further use for it. Even Clouzot on a bad day could have seen how Stephanie's signature had been traced onto it. With the photocopy, it was less obvious.

Rejoining Ludlow, they walked across the sunken garden and through to that part of the grounds called 'The Wilderness' until they eventually met up with the trout stream. Few words were spoken. There was something deep in Ludlow's thoughts as he checked a line of four eel traps; a certain philosophical submission, as though he had already accepted there could be some truth in Tyler's version of affairs.

The first three traps were empty, but as he lifted the fourth and found two eels twisted into a writhing ball, he remarked: 'Ah! Two slippery creatures tying each other in knots rather than seeking a way out!' Amused by his irony, a wan smile compressed his lips.

He lifted a flap and tipped the fish back into the water, throwing the trap in after them.

'We must stop wrestling with each other, Peter,' Ludlow said sincerely. 'When is all this going to stop? What more do you want? I thought I had provided you with everything you needed in life. And now you come up with this?' He waved the note again. 'Stephanie had a child?' Ludlow had been trying to picture it and it was beginning to focus. No-one could invent the existence of a child and expect to get away with it. 'How long have you known this and why hit me with it now? Especially this thing about a *Will*? Haven't you got enough on me with that disc, for God's sake? We are now meant to be partners, Peter. So, enlighten me, please.'

Peter was pleased the phantom floppy disc was still playing its part. But he was hoping the Sharon revelation could run on its own substance.

Ludlow was troubled, but his tone was of appeasement, not aggression, in consideration of which, Peter was happy to be conciliatory. Up to a point, of course. He, too, wanted a quiet life without the constant need to look over his shoulder. Exposing the real reason behind Stephanie's behaviour now seemed the way to go.

The sparring couple moved in silence toward an old wooden boathouse, sitting themselves on the covered balcony above the water's edge.

'If you want my honest opinion,' Peter ventured, 'whatever shit was going on between the pair of you, all Stephanie really wanted was for you to release some of her frozen funds so she could help her child, essentially without you and the world knowing it existed. Well, now you *do* know, but the world doesn't have to. She hadn't known for sure herself until the Salvation Army confirmed it while you were off on your dodgy dealings in Kenya waving your Knighthood. You know the rest; slaughtering her nurse to keep the child's existence under wraps, then enlisting me to see things through for her.' He took the fake Will photocopy from his pouch and handed it to Ludlow. 'Before I say anymore, you should read this. For your eyes only, I'm sure you'll agree.'

Ludlow took his time, reading dispassionately. The transferred signature seemed to interest him most. He said nothing, so Tyler went on to explain that the child was alive and well and currently living courtesy of him in temporary accommodation. 'Karl knows this, should you need confirmation,' he said, then added: 'By the way, along with 'big-ears' and your other watchers, Karl should not be made party to any of what we are discussing here.'

Ludlow nodded slowly.

'I'm sorry if it seemed I was instrumental in playing you along in Africa,' Peter confessed, 'but you were plucking your own strings. I was a mere listener. Perhaps not quite an innocent one. But I am only human. Even jet lagged in all that heat out there I could see an opportunity.'

Ludlow was still eyeing the 'Will'.

'What flying me to Kenya suggested was that everything Stephanie revealed about you and your dodgy dealings in that telephone conversation you bugged must have been true. And it's pretty damning stuff. Stuff I'm sure you'd rather the world didn't know about, along with the Will and what's on that note you keep waving about. So, what do I really care about your *skeletons* now you've set me up for life? Not at all, really. Someone else's problem. I've broken a few rules in my time myself. Anyway, if it's any reassurance to you, all Stephanie got from me was an obligation to do right by her daughter anonymously. From the start, the Salvation Army wanted me to do nothing to upset the status quo. Then, with Stephanie gone, they closed shop on the matter until, by chance, Stephanie's 'Will' slipped out from between the pages of an old War Cry that didn't go up in smoke with all my other stuff.'

Ludlow had been listening as still as a post, and just as silent, with the same hang-dog look Tyler had witnessed in Kenya.

It was as clear as daylight to Peter that Ludlow had used every trick in the book to get where he was in life, and probably a few more unwritten ones! That was business, he supposed. Then came drugs? Shell companies? Tax dodging charity. Trafficking. All activities Ludlow would fight to keep the world from knowing about. But what did Peter really care about all that now he'd been set up himself? Not much at all, was the honest answer. He wouldn't mind betting that somewhere in the small print of his 'partnership' with Ludlow, his own name would be up there in rogues' gallery shining brightly. *Sir* Edward would not be where he was in life without being cute enough to cover his back! Peter was just trying to do the same. So gently does it to get Ludlow on his side.

Taking the Sony Walkman from his pouch., he said like an insurance broker providing evidence of a company's recent bad performance, 'If it's not too painful, listen to this. It cost Bahnlich her life.' Next came the three Polaroids. 'Take a close look at these, too,' he added.

With Stephanie's voice in his ear as he looked at Sharon posing, his reaction was apocalyptic.

'I would write a cheque, now, if I could,' Stephanie was saying in faltering words as the cassette played, 'but my account's been frozen thanks to my bastard husband! I'm deemed irresponsible. He's a control freak! God forbid he gets to know about the child. Nothing would stop him trying to get rid of me if he did. I'll make a Will in case, and try to find some cash in the meantime for you to get to her somehow without her knowing where it came from. There are things about my husband's dealings to make him think twice if he won't release any of my funds. Tax dodging, offshore companies, you name it. And I'm not worth a penny in this country, apparently. Something called Abalone is where he keeps most of my money. Make a note of that in case anything happens to me. It's a shell company wherever the fuck he's hidden it. Sorry for the language. Compton Stud, that palace of a place is owned by one of his overseas companies. He rents it out to another company, which he also owns. I don't know how it all works, but enough to make him think twice if he won't release my assets. And that's not all. Drugs. His SODA charity shifts drugs all over the place. It's all on a floppy disc....'

Ludlow removed the earphones, devastated. Peter had stopped recording at that precise point because Stephanie had been about to reveal she had thrown the said floppy disc into one of the bins at Compton Stud. Best Ludlow did not know about that.

'The girl, Gloria Shaw, prefers to be called Sharon,' Tyler explained. 'She is blissfully ignorant of her true origins, which is something we should protect at all costs whatever settlement can be arranged for her.'

Ludlow held the pictures like playing cards, utterly convinced the girl was of Stephanie's flesh and blood. The voice in his ear had been the shattering confirmation.

'On whose behalf are you seeking this, er, settlement? Hers or yours?' he asked provocatively.

'Financially, of course, on hers. Morally, perhaps, on mine. And, I put it to you, dutifully, on yours,' Peter proposed, looking at the gently rippling stream.

Ludlow was suffering. His expression said everything. But there was something Peter could not see. An unexpected surge of emotion was shaking Ludlow to his roots. He was thrown back to the day Sheila Braithewaite had walked into his life, strangling himself with nostalgia.

'It goes without saying that you are not her natural father.' Peter advanced, as if to reassure the man. 'She was born on 6th May, 21 years ago, long before you met her mother. Sheila as she was called then, was raped at age 13, and it seems had blanked out the whole incident until, who knows, the mother in her suddenly emerged. Why she killed that Swiss woman can only be put down to that bugged telephone call you've just listened to. *No-one must know,* had been Stephanie's mantra. Had I not come across Stephanie's Will, we probably wouldn't be sitting here now like partners in crime trying to clean up our act. But here we are!'

Eyes still glued to the stream, Ludlow was being dragged backwards through the emotional barbed wire of his failed marriage.

There was a deep pool in the stream by the bank just below the balcony of the boathouse. For a few seconds, he was distracted by a water-spider desperately battling to avoid being sucked into a vortex. With a frantic flaying of its legs, it finally managed to break away from the deadly swirl only seconds later to be snatched by a flash of silver.

'What happens to the fake Will in all this?' Ludlow asked with hardly a flicker of interest. Something had told him it was fake, but that did nothing to alter the jeopardy of it ever becoming made public.

'What do you mean, *fake* Will?'

'Exactly what I said. Don't fuck with me, Peter. *Fake* Will! You are more transparent than you think. It's so obvious you've coddled that scrap together yourself. Even knowing that my dear wife couldn't possibly have put that together herself in the time frame of New Year's morning, you should have had the sense to use an electric Olivetti. They are the only ones available at the Stud. In the middle of the night, where would Stephanie have found the manual type you obviously used? Her signature? Well, that could have been copied from a thousand magazines or perfume bottles!'

Shit! That was quick. Peter had been sussed. However, it didn't change things too much. *Ludlow* had seen it was a fake, but other interested parties might seek to prove otherwise. That could only mean trouble for Ludlow and he knew it 'Tell me, what are you suggesting?' he asked, his eyes on the Polaroids.

'I've given a lot of thought to this as you might imagine. What I've come up with shouldn't be too demanding of you. If at all, personally.'

'Go on,'

Tyler stood up and leaned on the balcony railing with his back to the stream. He looked down at Ludlow's thinning pate. Grey tufts curled behind the ears making him look older than his mid-forties. Businessman's stress? 'You can see from the snaps, the girl is close to being the spitting image of her mother. Believe it or not, until it closed down a few months ago, she was working in a night-club flaunting herself as her own mother without the foggiest notion of knowing it. She's unfazed by attention. A natural. With you pulling the strings and me watching her back, she'd waltz it as a model. Not to the same heights you lifted Stephanie, perhaps, but high enough to satisfy Sharon. How does that sound to you?'

Ludlow got to his feet and leaned on the railing beside Tyler. 'Tell me more,' he said.

'Talk one of your fashion houses into taken her on. Do it through me if you wish, anonymously or not. Up to you. I'm not trying to teach you to suck eggs. Whether or not her likeness to Stephanie is used as a gimmick to give her lift off you decide. The main thing is to make her think she's making it off her own back, with a little help from me perhaps, pulling the contractual strings.'

Ludlow nodded thoughtfully. 'Almost unbelievable to think she is your punk playmate in disguise?'

'Amazing, isn't it?'

'I would have to see her in person to seal this proposal.'

'In the fullness of time. I've rattled her cage enough already putting this idea together without her catching on. She has to keep believing she's a fake. Meeting you would be pushing it. Can you imagine what would happen if the press caught the two of you together? Everything would come out. Not good.'

Ludlow gave thought to this. What if this was a double bluff on the girl's part to get money out of him? Leading Tyler on to act as go between? It sounded like the sort of scam a daughter of Sheila Braithewaite might try to pull. Was Tyler being duped?

Ludlow was experiencing something new. Something unexpected. Sympathy. Sympathy for the devil his wife had become in later years. Had she told him about the child - even after marriage - would things have changed between them? He spoke again as if addressing the stream. 'I was besotted with that woman, you know. Would have done anything for her.'

This unexpected confession made Peter recognize similar feelings in himself. He would do anything for Sharon. *Was* doing.

'Tell me more about the girl,' Ludlow beckoned softly, as if to not disturb the tranquility surrounding them.

Peter was happy to catch his mood.

'Apart from her looks, I imagine the girl is pretty similar in character to how Stephanie was before you 'discovered' her. She's fun, and streetwise of course, but lacking in a few morals, God bless her. She really could use a leg-up. She's a darling, really. Just getting her off the streets and giving her a better purpose in life would be enough. But I would like to do more for her. So should you, all things considered. Nothing to break the bank. Setting her up wouldn't need to touch the sides of that pot of Stephanie's you've got tucked away somewhere. Abalone? I won't presume to ask for complete disclosure.'

'I thank you for that consideration,' Edward said without a hint of sarcasm. If ever Tyler had made an understatement, that was it. Most of Stephanie's wealth was in hidden assets. Ludlow's, too, of course. Their joint pots could probably go close to buying out any number of struggling third world countries.

There was passion in Tyler's voice, almost a yearning. A drive that Ludlow had once seen in himself. The same animal infatuation had drawn him to Sheila Braithewaite. If ever he felt the pangs of lost youth, it was now. He was in full envy of Tyler, lost in a 'rose-bud' moment, longing for those carefree days beneath the dreaming spires of Oxford.

He turned and gave Tyler a disarming smile that seemed to say: 'Know exactly where you're coming from, you bastard!'

Chapter Thirty Seven

'I'm going riding for a couple of hours.' Peter told Karl, donning his newly purchased army hat to go with his fatigue jacket in favour of his full 'go-faster' lycra cycling outfit. 'I need the exercise. I'll be at the airstrip workshop later putting the final touches to the Sopwith Pup. Come down in a couple of hours if you fancy a burn-up.'

'Have fun, soldier,' Karl joked, showing no inclination to move.

Peter was buzzing at the outcome of his crucial meeting with Ludlow. The man still had a heart sleeping in the recesses of his beleaguered soul. With his backing, everything would fall into place. Stephanie would have a just closure and Sharon would be in the fast lane to dreamland!

Using the back exit through the stables, Peter headed up towards Beacon Ridge until he was out of sight of Compton Stud, then cut away towards the Marlsbury-Septon road. About three miles along, he stopped at the telephone box he had been heading for. He was pretty sure this one was still working. It was.

A man answered through a yawn.

'Queen's House Hotel, Good morning.'

'Room 27, please.' Peter said.

'It's ringing for you.'

It was some time before Sharon answered.

'Hello,' she said, suspicion in her voice.

'It's me, Peter,' He answered, relieved she was there. 'Just ringing to see how you are.'

'Oh, I'm all right, I s'pose, stuck in this dump!' she replied lazily, 'What about you? How did my audition go?'

'With flying colours! You want to be a model? You've got it! You want a boutique? That, too, all in good time. One in Paris as well, maybe. Rome!'

'Leave off, Peter. Stop kidding around.'

'Would I ever kid you about a thing like that? OK, forget Paris for the time being, but I knew he would see your potential when I showed him the snaps. He's going to help us, sure as Hell! I knew it.'

367

He was bubbling with school-boyish enthusiasm to convince her. Almost too much. 'You're on
your way! But you're going to have to knuckle down. No pissing it up too much. And ease up with those pills. I'll be keeping my eye on you, just so you know.'

'Daft fucker,' she said.

'I knew Ludlow would go for you,' he burbled on with relish. 'For nostalgia's sake, if nothing else. The man could see nothing but Stephanie Star in you. You blew his mind. More than anything that ever happened at Tony's, I bet. He couldn't believe you were that black-eyed punk I brought back from Manchester. He'll get us a good deal, believe me, with all his connections. You'll have money in the bank you wouldn't believe before you know what's hit you – minus my percentage of course! Just kidding.'

'Daft fucker! she gawked again. 'Give over! Stop winding me up!'

'You'll see,' Peter promised jubilantly. 'He really is sold on you! He almost cried when he saw your Polaroids.'

He bounced back into the saddle as happy as Larry. He could visualize the grin on Sharon's face. As big as a melon!

Before realising it, he was cycling across Beacon Ridge in the direction of Newton Stoat. His bike seemed to have forgotten he didn't live there much anymore. For a moment, he let it take him, but at the marker pylon he took control and turned off. He couldn't have faced Gwen if she was in one of her nosy moods with the inevitable bombardment of awkward questions. There wasn't usually any relevant mail to collect these days, just a non-stop flow of begging letters.

However, he was mistaken. There *did* happen to be one letter sitting in the pile that he would live to regret not having collected.

His new route took him through the dank terrain of Deadwoods travelling in the general direction of the airstrip. Today, with the Sopwith Pup back on the itinerary soon to be ready for a test flight, he was feeling jaunty. Tyler's Initiative Mark I was now in production at various factories, sales in the hands of professionals. Mark II, aimed at the heavier duties of surveillance and sports' coverage was taking shape. All was looking good. Next project? Setting Sharon up. He could still see that melon of a grin on her face!

He had not been long back at the airstrip workshop, when a car came screeching to a halt outside.

There was no time to wonder what was happening before the door flew open and Rose charged in wielding a revolver. With one vicious lunge, he swung it against Tyler's head then grabbed and twisted the neck of his T-shirt like a tourniquet. He was dragged out to the awaiting Range Rover struggling for breath and shoved into the back seat. His head was pushed down between his knees, arms bent up behind him by Dmitri. 'Just give me one reason, you conning prick!' Rose snarled, with another swipe of the gun.

Johann was at the wheel. Before reaching the entrance to Compton Stud, Tyler's head had been covered with a blanket should any journalists have turned up while they'd been away. None had.

Seconds after the car hit shingle and came to a halt, Rose pulled Tyler out, digging the barrel of the gun hard into his ribs to make him move faster. Peter wasn't so much winded by the pain as concerned the thing might go off. Once clear of the car, he was bundled into the house.

On the threshold of the music room, Rose threatened: 'One wrong move, Tyler, and you're dead! Make no mistake about that!' Giving him a final slap across the back of the head, he pushed him through the door.

Ludlow was standing by one of the windows with his back to the room. He spoke in level tones, but with an underlying tremor in his voice. 'You have fucked with me once too often, Tyler!' He turned ashen faced and produced a letter. 'This arrived at your house yesterday. No charge for collecting it for you!'

He moved forward and gave it to Tyler, then struck him full-bloodedly around the face with the back of his hand.

'You and I are finished!' he growled, trembling with rage.

Peters heart sank as he looked at the letter. It was written on Salvation Army paper! Reading it, he grew weaker by the second, the blood draining visibly from his face. He suddenly felt ill.

Dear Peter Tyler,

I've been burgled! Ferociously! I had to let you know. The only thing taken was your note to me! What can this mean? I should have destroyed it! Someone now knows about Stephanie's child. Thank the Lord I threw away the disc you gave me. That you were possibly thinking of using it to blackmail Sir Ludlow was despicable, even though it had been cut in two. Whatever happens now, I blame myself for creating this situation by listening to you. May God forgive us.

I pray for you with shame and humility, Major Wendy Clarke.

Peter now had some praying to do himself. Rose could barely contain his urge to do him grievous bodily harm. At a sign from Ludlow, he swung the revolver into Tyler's tender groin. Peter howled like a wolf. 'You don't understand! It was the wrong disc! I tricked her!'

That was too much of a red flag to Rose. He swung all his weight behind a blow to Peter's stomach. 'Arsehole!' he roared. 'Pull the other one! And was it the wrong tape we found in the back room of that model shop you used to work on the quiet, you conning prick!'

Peter's eyes rolled. He was silenced to the point of collapse. Why hadn't he destroyed the tape? Idiot!

'Take him downstairs and dose him up,' Ludlow ordered. 'But no more scars, Victor,' he added, with regard to the bleeding gash across Peter's temple. 'You know the form, but don't overdo it. We don't want him dead all of a sudden. Dose him slowly. Let him mull over things down there for a few days while I deal with something else. Then, I am done here. This place is history.'

Peter was manhandled out of the room and taken down a narrow staircase where he was thrown semi-conscious through a door into what had once served as a wine cellar.

'Get his legs!' Rose snarled.

Peter felt a knee go into his ribs as his limbs were twisted into an excruciating lock.

With all Rose's weight pinning him down, Peter could do nothing as a hypodermic needle was stabbed like a bayonet into a bulging vein in his arm. He pleaded pathetically as the syringe emptied and his head erupted. A few seconds later nothing seemed to hurt any more, even less, matter. Any fight that might have been left in him had gone.

As Rose got up, he raised Tyler's head by as much of its short hair as he could grab, and in one last fling of insubordination, let it go so his face slammed into the cold stone floor.

The door closed and a key turned in the lock.

Within seconds, Peter was throwing up, as sick as a dog.

Ludlow's thoughts had turned to the girl, Sharon. Did she really not know who she was? With those looks? He had to satisfy himself beyond doubt. Fake Will or not, if that scrap of paper were ever made public… Well, he didn't want to go there! It would open up another nightmarish scenario.

'That matter of bricks and mortar in South America, Gerald?' Ludlow was on a call Silver. 'Can the necessary be jacked up at short notice?'

'Relatively instantly. No problem.'

'Via Africa as usual?' The 'as usual' was a euphemism for 'to muddy my movements'.

'Of course. Any particular reason?' If something new had happened to cause this sudden exit, Silver would like to be in the loop.

'Just foresight. We'll see.'

'Fair enough,' Silver accepted. 'I'll get onto it.'

The next person Ludlow needed a word with was Karl.

'Where exactly has Tyler got his punk friend staying?' he wanted to know.

'He has place in Septon for her. Small apartment. A room somewhere in London while she does modelling school.'

'You know where?'

'Septon, is all. London, no.'

'OK. Jenny Grant thinks she knows the London address. Get it from her. Tell her it's important and I'm too busy at the moment to talk to her myself. Tell her you're dealing with that business in the King's Road she told me about. Be nice to her. Tell her 'well done' and all that. Then I want you to go find the girl and bring her to Compton Stud. Convince her it's Tyler who wants her to come here. Did you know Tyler was hoping to turn her into a model?'

'Yeah. He told me.'

'And that he wants me to fix it for him?'

'Yeah. Tell me that, too.'

'Tell you anything else?'

'He likes her. I, too. She good fun. Make good model, I think.'

'Has he told you anything else about her?'

'She *die nutte*. How you say? Hooker. No need tell me. I seen it. They fucking together, you know?'

Ludlow had wondered about that. 'OK. As soon as Grant tells you the address, let me know. Then get yourself down there and bring the girl to me. Understand? *Verstehen*? Ring me when you're on your way to the Stud.'

There was someone else looking to be on his own way to Compton Stud, for that's where the newspapers seemed to think Ludlow's 'in-crowd' hung out. Jimbo had no luck finding the place on a map, but he knew it couldn't be far from a town called Marlsbury. That seemed to be mentioned whenever Ludlow's antics featured. Weirdo Tyler's name generally cropped up somewhere in the piece as well. It was a bit of a guess, but Jimbo reckoned if Tyler was there, that cow Sharon wouldn't be too far behind. Finding either of them would do for starters. It wouldn't matter who came first. If he could get to both at the same time, so much the better. If he found his way to Marlsbury, that would be a start. It shouldn't prove too difficult to work out the next move from there.

***

Jenny parked her Jeep across Norfolk Square from the Queens House Hotel.

On the seat beside her was a pile of slightly crumpled newspapers she'd kept as a reminder. The 'Daily Scan' took pride of place on top. She glanced down at the front-page pictures of herself, one before and one after her confrontation with Edward at the S.O.D.A. Centre. The caption was in the form of a question: 'Girl Friday Left Marooned?' More pictures and the full story were promised inside.

She turned to the centre pages. The headlines ran from side to side across both: 'Second Lady of Compton Stud in SODA Shocker'. Underneath was: 'He won't speak to me anymore. Former *Jenny's Girls* Boss Reveals'.

372

There were three more photographs, the largest of which had surprised Jenny upon seeing it. Its caption read: 'Better Times?' The picture showed Ludlow with his arm around her at the Compton airstrip after their circuitous return from Africa. The second was taken at the S.O.D.A. Centre. The roof of a car obstructed most of their bodies, but the telling expressions on their faces were highlighted. They seemed to be arguing furiously. 'The Showdown?' was the caption. The third was the inevitable portrait of Stephanie looking young and innocent with, 'The 1st Lady Before Her Fall', in italics underneath.

'Serves him right!' Jenny said to herself without conviction. She was feeling self-conscious about her sudden new-found notoriety to the extent of hiding herself behind dark glasses and a headscarf.

She looked at her watch. 4.35pm. Having made a bet with herself that she wouldn't be kept waiting long, she was proved right. At just after 4.50 the Jaguar turned into the square, double-parking outside the hotel.

She was livid with Edward for not calling her himself. Why was he now so interested in the girl she'd seen with Tyler in London? Because she looked like Stephanie Star? Had someone else told him about her and he believed *them*, more than her? If that was the case, then fuck him for not taking her seriously! Fuck him, anyway. Whatever it was.

She had driven from Fulham to Norfolk Square in good time. It was about half two when she relented and told Karl the address. She estimated it would take about two hours for him to get there and had got it just about right.

Karl was alone in the Jaguar. Peaked cap in hand, he went up the front steps into the hotel. He was back within seconds, setting up post leaning against the car with his back to Jenny.

It wasn't until after six o'clock that he moved. The girl had entered the square at the far end, alone.

Sharon was laden with carrier bags after a shopping spree in Carnaby Street. She had splashed out on a new pair of knee-length boots with rounded toes like upscale Doc Martin's but covered in buckles and chains. Also in the bags were several printed T-shirts all with the word 'Suck' on them somewhere. Kim would love one of those if she could get into it. But her choice purchase was a spectacular pair of black jeans made to look as though they were being worn inside out by the addition of an

373

exaggerated suspender belt around the waistband with its studded straps hanging freely like a depleted grass skirt. Sharon wanted to show those punks in Chelsea a thing or two!

Jenny noticed the girl's hair was violently different from the other day. Sharon had thought of restyling it herself by shaving weird patterns into it like some of the Kings Road punks had done. But while she was experimenting with it, she had hit upon quite a different dramatic look without having to cut or shave anything off. Molding it with gel, she had managed to get it to stand out horizontally to one side of her head as though permanently caught in a wind tunnel. She liked it. It looked like her scalp had slipped ninety degrees.

Sharon saw Karl lolloping against the Jaguar before she got as far as the hotel and was moderately surprised, but no more than that. Karl was usually in the background somewhere. She hadn't seen him in London before, though.

'What the fuck are you doing here?' she blurted. 'Something happened to Peter?' It was the first thought that had come into her head. She hoped he was alright.

'Hi Sharon,' Karl said pleasantly, meeting her at the steps. 'No. He OK. He sent me to pick you up. Wants you to see big house. He ring you.'

'I've been out.' Sharon said, stating the obvious. She was slightly confused now. Peter hadn't said anything about being picked up when he had called that morning. 'Where is he now, then?' she asked.

'Big house. You know, with big boss.'

She supposed that tallied. 'He wants me to go down *there?* What, now?'

'Ja. I take you. Get things. I wait.'

Bemused, she went into the hotel. Through the reception hatch, she could see a slip of paper in her pigeonhole. She rang the bell and a tired looking man appeared from the room beyond.

'Is that a message for me?' she asked.

The man nodded and handed her the note. 'Same message came twice,' he explained. 'I only wrote it once.'

Sharon read it. It didn't sound like Peter, but she supposed that could have been the way the message had been taken down. It just said: 'Karl is coming to pick you up. Go with him. Peter'.

She went back outside and shouted across to Karl, loudly enough for Jenny to hear. 'Am I supposed to check out? If so, you'll have to pay the bill. I just spent all my money.' It was a lie, but Peter had said he was covering the hotel costs. Karl could get it back off him.

Karl came closer. 'No. Think you come back for Modelling school.'

'Oh, yeah. I was hoping I might have been spared more of that crap. It's just for kids, that place. A waste of money. It took five minutes to learn that poncy stuff at Tony's in Manchester. I'd rather be in me new flat in Septon than this shitty place.'

'Tell lover boy. His call.'

Jenny watched guardedly as Sharon came out of the hotel in some of her new clothes, minus the suspender belted black jeans. Karl came directly behind her carrying her bag. Was she checking out? Probably not. She had gone in with more than she came out with. But where was Tyler while all this was going on?

Slightly confused, she started the Jeep and pulled away after them as the Jaguar started to move, but she hadn't reached the end of the square before stopping again. There was no point trying to follow them. She wouldn't be able to keep up with that car. There was only one place they could be going: Compton Stud. Where else? And the idea made her feel sick. Things were getting worse. She needed to take her time and *think*! Drive carefully and think.

Chapter Thirty Eight

Once on the open road, Sharon asked: 'What's Peter up to today, then?' beginning to feel happier now she was going to see the 'big house' she had heard so much about. She didn't like the Paddington area a lot. It wasn't so bad when Kim was around. But on her own, shit.

'Touching up his models,' Karl said, playfully testing her.

She bit.

'Eh? You mean he's got others?' Peter had kept that quiet.

'With wings. Aircraft.'

'Oh, them? I was going to say. New one on me.'

A while later she surprised Karl with a question: 'Is he a good businessman? Peter? I mean, do you think he would make a good manager? You see more of him at work than I do. I can't tell. I think that's what he's at. Turning me into the next Stephanie Star and getting rich on it, the daft fucker.'

'Ludlow maybe thinks so, too,' Karl answered idly, eyes on the road. He had a shrewd idea about what was going on. 'Not make him partner, else.'

'S'pose not. But I've got my doubts. I can't really see him in the fashion business the way he dresses, can you? Toy airplanes, yeah. And I think that Ludlow geezer needs some tips himself. Maybe not about fashion, but have you seen the papers today? They're full of him! He's got no idea how to handle women, that's for sure. Do you have that expression in Germany, unlucky in love, lucky in money? Something like that?'

'If I have Ludlow's money, no chance unlucky in love, nicht?'

'Nest, not *nish*, yer daft fucker,' she said, pulling a face. 'Love *nest!* When are you going to learn some proper English?'

It was approaching dusk when Karl steered the Jaguar off the country road near some woods a few miles from Compton Stud. 'Must piss,' he explained.

He had left the motorway earlier than expected, but Sharon hadn't wondered why. She hadn't a clue *where* she was. She fully trusted Karl after what he'd done in Manchester. What a tough fucker!

As Karl drained his bladder, Sharon got out of the car and went to the other side of the bush he was using as cover. Through the sparse foliage, he saw her drop her knickers and squat like a squaw. 'Might as well go while I've got the chance,' she said. 'How much further is it?' She looked up and noticed he was watching her. 'Had yer eyeful!' she yelped, unabashed. 'Don't tell me a bloke like you hasn't seen a girl pissing before!'

As she was putting herself back together, she sensed something was going on, because he seemed in no hurry to go back to the car. Perhaps he was fantasizing about her arse? To add weight to that theory, he said: 'Sorry, Sharon, want you do something for me.'

'Fucking hell, Karl! What out here? Do me a favour!'

'Not fuck, Sharon. You have one track mind.'

'What then? I was going to say. Kim not good enough for yer? If I told her you fancied me, she'd give you such a clout next time she sees you, you wouldn't know what hit yer.' Sharon knew Kim wouldn't actually have given a toss about it.

'What is, *clout*?' Karl was interested to know. 'Proper English?'

'Clip round the ear, or more like a kick in the bollocks, knowing Kim.'

'Usch! Kim big girl. Good laugh. But, like you, big trouble too.'

'Eh? What d'ya mean?'

'You forget Manchester?'

Sharon had no answer to that.

'Boss say must hide you on floor in back of car. Else, lock you in trunk.'

'Eh? Why? Well, I ain't going in the fucking boot, chuck!'

'Paparazzi maybe at gate. Boss say no pictures of you, else more big trouble.'

'That's nice of him. No pictures. Ashamed of punks, is he?' Actually, she could see the point of there being no pictures. She hadn't forgotten about Jimbo just yet. 'Anyway, it's Peter I'm going to see, in't it? Or is this some trick being played on me?'

'Big boss wants to see you first. Orders. You want to be model? He can fix it, all I know. You get in back. I put blanket over. Best your friend Jimbo not see picture in papers, *nicht*?'

That reminder sealed her compliance.

'What the fuck have I got myself into?' She moaned beneath the blanket. 'Wait till I see that Peter. You'd better put some earplugs in unless you want to hear some choice new words when I see him.'

'I have pen ready,' Karl joked. 'Daft fucker.'

She had to smile at that.

He was alright, Karl. Good to have around. And could he handle himself? Wow! Good to remember, given his mention of Jimbo.

She spread herself out on the floor behind the front seats, thinking about the message left for her at the hotel. Something didn't sit quite right about all this.

'Cover head for sure,' said Karl. She did as she was told. The smell of fresh leather from the seats filled her nostrils mixed with the fragrance of freshly laundered blanket. She wished Kim could have been huddled there with her. That would have made her feel a bit better about things.

She was only left like that for about ten minutes. Then, after a couple of stops and starts, the sound of shingle beneath the wheels replaced Tarmac and the car stopped. The journey had ended.

Karl opened the rear door and helped Sharon out. 'Was for your own sake. Not want picture on front page. People get wrong idea.'

What *was* the idea, Sharon was thinking as she took in the surroundings?

As it happened, there had been no press lurking at the gates, which was something that cheered Ludlow up when he was told.

He had watched the car pull up from an upstairs window. The effect on him was chilling. Despite the strange hair, he could have been looking at a young Sheila Braithewaite down there. More similarity was to come when she spoke, almost syllable for syllable.

'What a place!' She couldn't believe the size of the frontage. It was like a town hall to her. 'Not a fucking courthouse, is it?' she joked.

Karl smiled. 'Welcome to Compton Stud.'

'Very nice! Where's Peter?'

She was asking Karl, but it was Ludlow who answered as he appeared through the portico. 'He'll be along later, Sharon,' he lied. 'Let me introduce myself.'

She turned and was gob-smacked at being confronted by the famous man Peter had been talking about so much. So, he hadn't been bull-shitting her after all? 'I know who you are. Peter told me. And if it's true what he's told me, pleased to meet you. But why isn't he here? Not a good start if he wants to be my manager.' She thought she'd throw that in for good measure to pretend she was up to speed with things.

'Let's not get ahead of ourselves, Sharon,' Ludlow said levelly, deja-vu seeping into him. 'Or should I call you Gloria?' A first test of her credibility. How would she respond?

'What is this?' she asked petulantly before reacting to his outstretched hand that indicated they should go inside. She had never bothered to ask Peter how he'd known her real name. But what did he want to go telling it to Ludlow for? Another mouthful coming his way.

Ludlow found it difficult to judge if she was faking ignorance. That quality was also in Stephanie's repertoire. '...to my daughter Gloria …'

Not quite so obvious in the outlandish clothes she was wearing now as she looked in the red dress of the Polaroids. But even with her hair jarring like a migraine after its stint under the blanket, her face spoke multitudes to Ludlow.

At that moment, Jimbo's battered face was also speaking multitudes to the clientele of The Turks Anchor, Marlsbury, as he shuffled into the saloon bar. In fact, it was more like shouting 'avoid me!' with the black eye-patch the first thing to turn heads. But then it was the scars, particularly the terrible one across the nose, begging the question; 'Shouldn't this brute be joining that lot in The King's Head?'

Luckily for Jimbo, there was one person in The Turks Anchor who was always nosy enough to volunteer his conversational services to newcomers; Old Pikey, who happened to be short sighted. He could see the eye-patch well enough, but the scars were in soft focus and didn't intimidate him at all until he approached close enough to spot them. Luckily for Jimbo, this didn't inhibit Pikey from being egged on to tell all about Compton Stud for the price of a couple of pints of five X. But once Jimbo had milked all he felt he needed to know from Pikey, he was on his way without so much of a thank you, leaving those interested to await Pikey's voluntary take on why this monster was in Marlsbury.

'Where's Peter?' Sharon asked again as Ludlow took her by the arm and guided her through a marbled hallway into a large sitting room.

'First, we need to have a quiet chat, Sharon,' was the answer she was given. 'Sorry about the dramatic way we brought you here. Karl would have told you about the newspaper hacks pestering the place?' Ludlow offered her a choice of soft-furnished settees and armchairs. 'Take your pick,' he said, heading for a drinks' cabinet. With his back to her, he asked: 'What's your tipple?'

She could not make head nor tail of this. What was going on? Maybe she was right about the messages at the hotel. Not from Peter? Nice place but why had she been dragged here? Another private audition?

'Large Negroni,' she replied, thinking the choice would show Ludlow she had some class herself. She could probably recite the full list of cocktails after two years at Tony's.

'Coming up. Ice?'

'Just poured over.' That was classier than shaken not stirred! 'What's going on? Why've you brought me here pretending Peter asked me?' No point being shy. 'I can scream pretty loud, you know.'

Ludlow believed she probably could without asking for a demonstration. 'No doubt, but please don't. It's not necessary, and no-one would hear you anyway, as I suspect you can guess. We're miles from anywhere. Joking apart, you're here because I've been asked to invest in you. So why would I want to damage the goods?'

The goods. So that was what she was? Peter had called her that once, she remembered. It sounded a bit different here, though, in such luxurious surroundings.

Ludlow presented her with a substantial negroni. Was he trying to get her pissed? She wouldn't mind too much, as it happened.

'Anything else I can get you? You must be hungry?' Ludlow asked. A butler could not have been more subservient.

'Got any crisps?' She asked. Not so classy.

'Afraid not. There's a selection of sandwiches. Or nuts if you're watching your figure?'

'Nuts'll do. But I in't too worried about my figure. I see you 're not so worried about yours, neither.'

'Thanks for pointing that out.' He slapped his paunch a few times. 'I call it my businessman's wallet.'

Sharon smiled at that. 'So. What's going on? You going to tell my why I'm here and Peter in't?'

'You obviously know what he wants me to do for you,' he said. 'I want to hear your side of it, because I think the two of you should have given more thought to the methods you're using to get money out of me.'

Sharon didn't know where this conversation was heading.

'What methods? I'm just *the goods* as you so kindly put it. It's Peter's idea. He said let's play a game with you 'cos I look a bit like Stephanie Star. I like games, so, yeah, I went along with him. I've been dressing up like her for years, so that was no problem. He said I had *potential*. That the right word? So, if you don't think I have it and you ain't interested, no skin off my nose. Keep your fucking money. Thanks for the drink.' She got up. 'Tara! Now where's that Peter?'

'Take it easy. Sit down. Finish your drink. Don't jump to conclusions. We're not done yet.'

'Sounds like it to me.'

'I need to know more about this game of yours.'

'You've got the wrong person. Talk to Peter. He dreamed it up. I'm just the *goods* again. Remember?' Sharon protested. Her indignation seemed real.

'I can't help it if I look a bit like Stephanie Star, can I, if that's what's upsetting you. No harm in it. Since you know all about the modelling game, he said you could easily get me a job in it. Like you'd done for your wife. You can't blame me for wanting that.'

Ludlow had a niggling suspicion that she was being completely open with him. That she had no sense of knowing who she really was, but purely masquerading as a Stephanie Star *lookalike,* plain and simple! Her way into a modelling career? Perhaps not with absolute purity, but at least it would seem she was being up front about it.

His next words might settle the question.

'Tell me what you know about the Will.' he said, eyes fixed firmly on hers.

'What Will?' She jumped to her feet awkwardly, plainly alarmed. 'Is Peter dead? Why he's not here …?' She fell back into her seat.

It looked like she was about to burst into tears.

'No! No. Peter's not dead. He's alive and well.' At least Ludlow hoped he was. For the time being, at least. There was no telling, with Victor being let loose on him. 'I'm talking of a Will my dear wife is supposed to have made.'

Sharon just sat staring. What would she have done if Peter *was* dead? Bloody 'eck. He must mean more to her than she had thought.

'Do you honestly not know what your friend Peter Tyler has been trying to make me believe?'

'All he ever told me was that you were partners or something, because of that doodle-bug thing he invented,' she replied innocently enough, gulping her Negroni like water. 'And that he thought he could talk you into setting me up as a model, like I just said. I didn't really believe him, but I wasn't going to stop him trying, was I? He told me it's who you know not what you know that gets you anywhere. Doesn't seem like it's working for me though, does it?' She raised her empty glass and added flippantly: 'Empty promises! Pleased to know you, I don't think!'

Edward smiled in recognition. It could have been Sheila Braithewaite sitting there. Sharon had that same cocky defiance.

'You're obviously narked about something, but don't drag me into it,' she said.

'He moved you down from Manchester, didn't he? Now why would he do a thing like that, do you think?'

That thought often came back to her. 'Because I begged him to! I had to get out quick. Ask your mate Karl, if you don't believe me. Look, I've told you all I know. I can't see anything wrong in what I've done, so why this guessing game? Just trying to get on the best I can, that's all. How did you get on to start with? Silver spoon up your arse, I expect!'

Close to the truth, Ludlow had to admit.

'I can't help it if I look like your bloody wife!' Sharon persisted. 'Listen, I don't know what Peter's done to piss you off. Where is he, the little bleeder? I want words with him!'

382

It was astounding; that anger in her voice, the way she animated herself. She was Stephanie's daughter, through and through.

Although he had immediately seen that the Will was fake, he believed it probably did contain the truth of Stephanie's wishes.

He produced the copy Tyler had given him and handed it to Sharon. One final test. 'This, dear girl,' he said gravely. 'Would get you both twenty years for fraud!'

She was horrified by what she read.

'Fucking O'Reilly!' she exclaimed, leaving no doubt as to the strength of her objection. 'Is that what he's been doing? Why he was so keen to get me down here? This has nothing to do with me, chuck! Forget it! Catch me trying on anything like this! What? You must be joking!' She blanched. 'He's bloody bonkers. Out of his tiny mind!'

Sharon was shaking with fury. To think she had been set up like this. So much for all Peter's sweet talk and lovey-dovey nonsense! He had been using her all this time! And she had fallen for it.

'Where is he?' she asked again, fired up for confrontation. 'Just give me five minutes with him! I'll kill the little snot! I'm not letting him get away with this.'

Jimbo was having similar feelings about getting his hands on Sharon. She was the cause of all his troubles, as he saw it. Every one of them! From the first day she had first started working for Tony, she had never stopped rubbing him up the wrong way. Always giving him grief! Always answering him back, sticking two fingers up at him. That scene under the arches had settled it! As long as he had air in his lungs, she would pay for it. All through his hospital treatment and the long recovery period it was the only thing that had been on his mind. An eye for an eye never had a clearer definition. Her nose, too, would be severely put out of joint, as his had been. Permanently. He would like to see how far her looks took her after he had finished with her!

Chapter Thirty Nine

'You must be easily fooled to let Tyler lead you on this far without sniffing out something was not as it should be,' Ludlow suggested. 'Dim's not the word.'

'Apparently, it is! OK, maybe I should have sussed he was up to something when he paid me four times over the odds for a shag in Manchester!'

Ludlow swirled his brandy around in the glass and breathed in the rising fumes. 'Whatever Tyler's trying to do to get at me,' he expounded, withdrawing his nose from the brandy glass with a sense his burdens might be evaporating. 'You, Gloria, or Sharon, are at the root of it. Don't you agree?'

'No, I don't fucking agree! I'm just like a bleeding ping-pong ball being bashed about in the middle. The *goods!* For fuck's sake!'

She felt better with having got a few 'fucks' off her chest.

Ludlow went silent momentarily. He felt the skin on both sides of his face and then in one movement smoothed his greying hair, looking to one side to catch his reflection in the window nearest him. It was dark outside, and he could see himself perfectly. Sharon watched him. 'He fancies himself on the quiet, does this bloke,' she thought. She had to admit he was in fairly good shape for his age. What was he, getting on for fifty?

He turned to face her again. He had enjoyed her outburst. Yet more confirmation. There was no more antagonism in him, quite the opposite.

She knew that look he was now giving her. She'd seen it often enough in older men. She called it an old-fashioned 'come-on'. Of all the fucking cheek! After all the crap he's been coming out with, he's gonna try it on with me!

Edward was slipping into a role that had deserted him for a long time, that of the charmer. Perhaps it wasn't the fairest test of his magnetism since she was in his captive company. Nevertheless, her youth represented a rare challenge to his libido. He laughed at himself. Challenge? He was forgetting she was a hooker!

'You will be staying with us this evening.' A statement not an invitation, yet, delivered in the tones of the perfect host. 'Perhaps even longer, we shall see. At least until this untidy business has been settled.'

'It won't be settled until I've had a chance to bollock Peter-bloody-Tyler for trying to pass me off as Stephanie's daughter! The stupid fucker!'

He was enjoying her growing distaste for Tyler.

Sharon wasn't ready for what came next. 'First, I want you to do something for me. Something I can't see you refusing in your position.'

Here we go again, she was thinking.

'You ain't having sex for nothing, if that's what you're after,' she said straight out.

'Give the hooker in you a rest' he said. 'I just want to show you something.'

Jenny had done her thinking, but it hadn't left her any closer to making a decision about what she was going to do once she reached Compton Stud. It all depended on what was going on there. Hopefully there was some simple explanation. But from the way she had been quizzed to find out where the girl was staying, she couldn't see it being that simple. And where was Tyler? Why send Karl to pick the girl up? What was going on? Who was this girl?

Jenny was winding herself up again. It was the long blast of a car's horn and its flashing headlights that told her she was driving like a maniac in the middle of the road. The shock made her pull over and cut the engine. But it didn't ease the tension that had gripped her again, fingernails biting into the steering wheel. It took her a minute or two to regain enough poise to start driving again, trying to keep the worst scenario she might walk into out of her mind. What would she do then?

Ludlow had lead Sharon upstairs where the corridor split in two. It was like a warren up there. Turning left, then further along right and left again, he pushed open a door and ushered Sharon into a large bedroom. It took her breath away. It was the most beautiful boudoir she had ever seen,

385

straight out of Vogue, all pinks and gold with mirrors galore and a carpet she could have lost herself in. In pride of place, an enormous four-poster bed surrounded by hanging lace.

She considered the situation for about half a second. It didn't take much to guess what was coming next.

But she was wildly wrong. It wasn't sex he was after, although she thought it must be somewhere at the back of his mind. Was this just part of the build-up?

Ludlow shook his head contemplatively as if guessing what she was thinking. 'No, that is not why I've brought you here,' he clarified. 'What I want you to do is to try on some of Stephanie's clothes. Select anything you like. The wardrobes are full of stuff. All clean and untouched for months. Feel free. Pretend you're about to go onto the catwalk. Let me see some of that *potential* you're supposed to have in the flesh, not in cheap snaps.'

He faced her briefly, and in that instant, she thought she saw pain in his eyes. The room had bad memories for him. Or was it the pain of desire? Good old animal lust? All men possessed it somewhere inside them in her experience, no matter what class or creed. But some didn't like it slipping out in case their vulnerability was revealed. It was a body language Sharon had come to understand and could handle. It neither intimidated nor excited her anymore. She was too old a hand.

'Is it the dressing up or the taking off you want to see?' she asked. It'll cost you if you want to watch. Premium rates in a gaff like this of yours!'

'Again, Sharon, show a little decorum, please. If you want to be a fashion model, you'll need to start losing some of your old habits,' he advised her, tut-tutting. 'I want to see what you've got hiding behind that punk make-up. You'll find plenty of wigs scattered about. And help yourself to any jewelry you find. It's all imitation stuff. The real gems are locked up safely. Just like *you* came very close to being!'

'Ha ha!' Was all that remark got.

She couldn't get her head around this. Being half-pissed didn't help. First threats, now lame jokes. Another strip-down audition. Jewelry! She was no fool. He must be after *something*. Porn?

'OK, moneybags,' she said decisively. 'You can take snaps, but no touching, even with gifts of fake jewelry. That's extra.'

Oh, how he wished *she* was a fake. He brushed her remark aside. 'I won't even embarrass you by staying to watch,' he said, making a move to leave the room.

'Suit yourself,' she told him. 'Stay if you want. I don't blush that easily.'

Ludlow had taken note of that familiar quality already.

As he left the room, she noticed a swarthy young guy was now sitting outside. There to stop her making a run for it? Some chance of that! Although the idea had been at the back of her mind earlier. Less of an issue, now. She was ready to go with the flow.

Where would she have gone, anyway? She had no real idea where she was. Besides, she had a feeling options were still there for the taking. Despite the palaver of dick head Peter trying to pass her off as Stephanie Star's actual daughter, it seemed there was still a good chance of something being in it for her.

Peter's pain was desperate, making any sane thought impossible in the timeless darkness. He couldn't remember where he was, which added to his mental torment. Pain was all over him, in his head, his limbs, his spine, especially in his guts. One second a blowtorch was melting his brain. The next, ice was in his veins.

Between spasms, visions flew at him. He was in a forest, then dark city streets. There was rain, deluges, then the sun was bright, burning his eyes. He was back at school flying airplanes, hundreds of them crashing into one another like blind starlings; the police were cuffing him, his mother was screaming at a burning window. He was cycling through trees shouting for help while guns went off behind him. Two women kept reappearing - the same woman, twice? Stephanie and Sharon, Sheila and Gloria. He didn't know which was which. They both accused him, lashing him with sticks. He seemed to be sinking in quicksand, only his outstretched arms keeping him afloat. Now he was in a warm sea and his buoyancy was going. He was being sucked under. The deeper he went, the weaker the pain became until, miraculously, it went away.

He came round gasping for breath.

Wherever he was, it stank. Stale vomit. *His*. He was face down on a cold floor. It was dark. What day was it?

It was growing into a *big* day for Sharon. Left alone in Stephanie Star's bedroom, she was like a kid in a toy shop helping herself to anything she wanted. It was a strange sensation to be in the room belonging to the woman she'd been impersonating for years. Like she was poking her tongue out at Stephanie.

Standing there surrounded by reflections of herself in her street clothes with the opulence of an unknown world of luxury spread around her like a panoramic stage set, she began to sense a real chance had come.

She would have to be up to it.

She went into a huge walk-in wardrobe and looked at herself critically in its full-length mirror as she stripped away her past. Her crooked hair appeared incongruous against her naked body. She caught herself smiling elusively. 'You're a right cheeky fucker, Sharon' she told herself. 'Mind yer manners!'

Her present hair configuration was the only thing that gave her character away. Without it, she would be ready to be molded.

Ten minutes later, that last remaining vestige of identity had been removed as she faced the mirror once more with the hair flat against her head still wet from washing.

Back in the walk-in wardrobe, her senses were bombarded with nostalgia. Inside were no ordinary racks of clothes. They were laden with the fashion of the seventies, an archive of Stephanie Star memorabilia. For an instant, Sharon was a little girl again, unsafe and unwanted. She felt so close to these clothes as she touched them and remembered how she had yearned for such fine things as a child, knowing that she could never have them. But there was something else taking her back, something deeper, something intangible. She sensed it through her nose, but it wasn't the smell of the clothes themselves nor the musky bouquet of a thousand stale perfumes clinging to them. She wasn't even sure it was a smell at all. It was a *feeling* in her nose, an animal scent of deja vu.

She gingerly fingered her way through the historic collection. Parting the garments one by one until she slipped back a hanger, and there it was, the red minidress that Peter had had copied. But the real one was different, softer than anything she had ever touched. She couldn't describe the sensation she felt to hold that immortal slip of clothing close to her naked body.

As she slid herself into it, a sensuous flutter went through her. It felt perfect, and its effect was dramatic. She had been taken over. In that setting, she didn't feel it was *her* standing there.

She selected a perfume from the dressing table and dabbed it in all her favourite places. Then, to boost her confidence, she popped a small blue pill into her mouth. 'Last one,' she lamented, slipping into a pair of Stephanie's shoes with the ease of Cinderella. 'Jesus, Kim! If you could see me now!'

At the dressing table, there was a drawer full of jewelry. Paste. But she couldn't tell the difference. What must the locked-up stuff be like? She slipped on two rings, both with single stones, classy ones that went with a bracelet she'd have sworn she'd seen Stephanie wearing in some advert. There was also a necklace she really liked. It had a big fake topaz surrounded by little ones on a gold chain. She would love to keep that. Top of her list.

She still felt half-pissed as she opened the door to leave. The pill was taking its time to liven her up. Dmitri was sitting outside. He got up, announced himself, then whistled.

'Been eyeballing me arse through the keyhole, have ya?' She quipped sarcastically, trying to remember which way the stairs were.

'Nice one,' he responded, leaving Sharon wondering how he meant it.

'It sounds like she's on her way down,' Ludlow said, breaking from his telephone conversation with Victor Rose. 'You're sure Tyler's safe?'

Rose let the suggestion that he couldn't handle Tyler pass without comment. 'Out like a light,' he responded. Almost too much *out*, it had first appeared. Fortunately, that wasn't the case. But only just. As a precaution, Rose had wiped the syringe and pressed Tyler's fingerprints onto it, just in case. What Ludlow had in mind was that small doses should be applied to start with and slowly built up. The calamitous overdose of one who had succumbed to the trappings of sudden fame and fortune should only come when Ludlow was appropriately 5.000 miles away.

Compton Stud's dining room was splendidly lit for the occasion, with lights dimmed the length of the oak-panelled walls, candles burning on the table.

Tears were in danger of bristling in Ludlow's eyes at the sight of Sharon as she paraded into the room like a queen of Paris fashion. The face, the hair, the body, the dress, the movement; it was all Stephanie Star! He was destroyed by belief. Speechless. Even the way she was wearing the tear-drop earrings that matched the necklace reminded him of how Stephanie would sometimes joke about. The left one was in the conventional earlobe position, the right in the uppermost of six or seven pierced holes, the weight of it pulling the top of the ear down making it look like it belonged to an elf. It was classic Stephanie fooling around.

The effect was working big-time on Ludlow.

Sharon played the part to her advantage, prolonging his stupefaction by strutting around the table twice before sitting down at her place.

Without bothering to ask which piece of cutlery she should use, she set about attacking the pasta he'd prepared with relish, which could only mean the blue pill was still taking its time to get going. She usually couldn't eat a thing with those racing around inside her.

Ludlow barely nibbled at his portion.

'Would you like coffee?' he asked when she had finished eating.

'No thanks, it might keep me awake,' she replied with a girlish giggle 'I'll have a go at that brandy, though.'

'Decorum again, Sharon. *Might I have a glass of brandy, please?* would have been a better way of expressing it,' Ludlow explained. He was delighted she wanted more of something, at least. It allowed the evening to continue. He was old enough not to lie to himself. Sharon intrigued and aroused him. As he gazed at her through the flickering candlelight, an obsession was threatening to reawaken in him.

Sharon thought she could see the doppelganger in her was getting to him, and she was happy to play on it. 'He really fancies himself does this dude,' she was thinking, guessing where he might be trying to lead things. Blokes usually came round to it in the end!

Ludlow was old enough to be her father, but so what? When had that ever made any difference to her at Tony's?

While getting up to go to the drinks trolley, Ludlow checked himself for imperfections again in the window. What he saw did not displease him. He was still a presentable figure of a man, particularly as seen in this flattering soft light, still charismatic enough to attract younger women. Perhaps not quite as much as he might have thought, though, were it not for his millions.

Had he been able to see beyond his self-congratulatory reflection into the darkness outside the window, his supposed magnetism would have been pole-axed.

Jenny Grant was glaring in at him, frozen to the spot not ten yards away! She nearly died when he came to the window, certain he must see her! He was looking straight at her! But when he turned his face to one side and touched his eyebrows, she realised his vanity had saved her. He only had eyes for his reflection. But she still dared not move, standing as rigid as a garden statue until he turned away.

Sharon had been watching him through glass as well as she drained the last dregs of her brandy. 'Big head!' she thought harmlessly. 'At least he takes a bit of pride in himself, unlike someone else I know.'

Accepting another brandy from Edward, she asked aloud: 'How come someone of your ilk went into business with a weirdo like Peter?' Her head was like a balloon from all the booze and now the growing effects of the pill. 'That's something I never could savvy.'

'Has Tyler told you everything?'

'Only about this initiative thing of his. Is it really as good as he says?'

'Yes, amazingly as you might think, it is. He should have stuck to *that* instead of criminal ideas of getting rich by using you.' Ludlow was happy to use the opportunity to increase her antagonism of Tyler.

'We're not going through all that again, are we?' she protested. 'I'll tell you something for nothing though, if you promise not to bite me 'ead off.'

Edward remained outwardly unmoved, although his pulse picked up a beat.

'It's all right. I ain't gonna ask for squatting rights!'

'As you wish. I promise not to bite your head off.'

'Good, 'cos I don't want you getting any wrong ideas. Well, I didn't realise what it meant at the time. I came home to the flat with Kim one night and Peter had a look on his face as if we'd caught him with his trousers down. He had an autograph book with Stephanie Star's signature in it. Right proud of it, he was. I had no idea what he was planning to do with it, promise, 'cos I'm dim, in't I, as you've told me. I never saw that Will, God's honour! I would have told the daft fucker where to get off if I had. I've had enough trouble with the Law as it is.' She took a swig at her brandy as if rewarding herself. 'I thought it a bit strange. But then he is a bit strange, the way he carries on. There. That's all I know about it.'

If ever Ludlow had needed confirmation, that was it.

'Fair enough,' he conceded, finally convinced Sharon was as innocent of her true identity as the day she was born! 'Time to call it a day.'

Jenny watched them get up from the table and leave the room together. They hadn't touched, but by the way they moved she sensed they were going to. Jealously was strangling her. She didn't know which way to turn. She felt sick with rejection.

She backed away from the house and looked up, waiting. A light went on. Stephanie's old room! Jenny held her breath. She couldn't bear it. She began to feel afraid. Afraid of herself. Of what she was thinking of doing!

Then it went on, the light in Edward's room next door.

Now alone, Sharon slipped out of Stephanie's dress humming 'Let It Be'. She rarely wore anything in bed but went into the walk-in wardrobe to nose around for something that might take her fancy for the occasion.

This could be her last chance to 'lord and lady' it up. There was almost too much to choose from a long rack of nightgowns. She closed her eyes and counted her way
along them, selecting the twenty-first in line to go with her age. This happened to be a lightly embroidered knee-length chiffon in light blue. Slipping into it, she went into the ensuite bathroom
for a goodnight pee.

When she came out, she noticed there was a door that she guessed connected to an adjacent room. His room? A key was in it. 'Not tonight, Josephine,' she said to herself, making sure it was locked in case Ludlow was thinking of trying something on. Neglecting to do the same to the main door, she climbed into the four-poster and snuggled down into its lush softness.

She hardly ever had first night principles in her life, but something was telling her she shouldn't rush into anything with Ludlow. This was no normal gig. OK, Peter was in for a right bollocking when she next saw him, that was for sure, but she didn't want him catching her at it with Ludlow all over her. Gawd knows what he would do. There was a guard outside the door. That was something at least. But to keep her in, or Peter out? Something still wasn't sitting quite right about all this. But she'd been in worse situations.

In his room, Ludlow tried to make sense of his feelings. He had not expected this reaction to meeting the girl. She was a replica! All evening it had been like sitting with Stephanie herself. So weird. Disturbing.

He must stand back. Take stock. Be sensible.

First, what to do with Tyler?

Chapter Forty

Jenny Grant had approached Compton Stud via the service road. Her mind was in bits. She had hidden her jeep behind the stables out of sight and crept to the house using the sunken garden as cover. She knew no-one manned the video monitors these days even if the cameras still worked. They had never been that efficient at night, anyway.

After the near miss of being seen while Edward was preening himself at the window, she had stationed herself close to the wall by the sunken garden steps. It was an overcast night with no moon to speak of. All her senses had then been focused as she stared up at the two lit bedroom windows. Which light would go out first? Did it make a difference?

She couldn't bear think about what might be happening in those two adjoining rooms. He had
even dressed the girl in Stephanie's clothes!
She waited, growing more edgy by the minute.

One light went out. Edward's room. Minutes later, the other.

She moved toward the house, trembling. Just the idea of setting foot in the place again mortified her, without dwelling on what she might do if she found them in bed together!

The safest way in was through the domestic quarters. Rose and the other two henchmen were staying in the barn accommodation. She had spotted them going over to it earlier.

As she turned the key to the back door and pushed, nothing happened. The door didn't budge. Shit! Bolted from the inside? She pushed again, harder this time, using her shoulder. To her relief, it gave. Shit! Again. She should have taken the key out first! The bunch it sat in was the size of a hand grenade. It rattled like maracas! Every key to the house was in it.

She stepped into a service room which had cupboards and pantries off it. Racks of boots and wet-weather gear on hooks ran along one wall, industrial sized washing and drying machines along another. She avoided buckets and brooms as she crept through the door leading to the kitchen area. A safety light glowed above the huge stove by which she could just make out the poky servants' stairwell at the far end of another corridor.

That was the way up for staff in days of old. But the main stairway was better for what she intended to do.

She felt as clammy as a spent poultice. She took deep breaths to calm herself before cagily going through to the central hall of the main house and listening. She thought she could hear muffled noises. Groans of ecstasy! Was she imagining it? Tormenting herself? No. All was silent.

She groped her way carefully up the marble staircase, taking great pains in the darkness to avoid any unseen obstacles that might be cluttering her way. She breathed a sigh of relief when she found the door to the office wing was not locked.

Going in, she closed the door behind her quietly. Inside, she felt it safe to turn on a light. There were no windows in the corridor and the office she wanted was at the back of the house, not seen from the converted barn. She eased past the fatal computer room. It had been sealed off, but the memory of what she had seen in it still sickened her. Once passed, she made for Edward's private office. This she knew would be double locked. The keys to it were somewhere in the bunch.

As she went in, she had a sudden thought. The house alarm! It was too late to do anything about it. She stood petrified for five seconds, expecting the worst. But nothing happened. It wasn't switched off. The thought had left her shaking even more. Her target was a tall slim cabinet. As she opened it, cold steel and oil hit her nostrils like smelling salts. Four shotguns stood in a row, glistening in the light from the corridor. She lifted out the first that came to hand. It didn't matter which. They all had two barrels!

From the drawer below them, she took out two cartridges and loaded them deftly; something she had done many times for Edward during the many hunting parties he threw. She pocketed two more, just in case. The gun felt heavier than she remembered. Tiredness, she imagined. She sometimes wished she would allow herself to take uppers. One or two might have helped her concentration tonight. She was going to need it. She was already feeling exhausted despite the adrenaline rushing through her arteries.

By the time she came out of the office wing, her heart was in her throat. After another precautionary listen, she made for the living quarters on the other side of the split stairway.

A light was coming from the corridor further along. All she wanted was to give Edward the shock of his life. The girl too. But her nerves were killing her. If they were actually in full throw together, God help her!

As she peered around the corner leading to the master suite, she froze! Someone was sitting in the corridor. A young guy she hadn't seen before. A sentry? Protection? Had they got wind of her being in the house? No way, surely?

The guy was either dozing or reading. He hadn't heard her. But she couldn't risk going further.

She backed away as quietly as possible and crept downstairs like a wrung sponge.

There was another possibility of getting to the suite by using the servants' stairway. It rose at the far end of the T-shaped corridor behind a door out of sight of the guard. If he stayed facing the way he had been, she might be able to get to Edward's bedroom before the guard knew what was happening,

But what then? What if the bedroom door was locked? Blast her way in? She would most likely be dead before then. The guy could possibly have a handgun. Edward kept several.

She needed to think. Sit down and think this through.

Peter Tyler had been having another horrifying dream. In it, someone had pulled his intestines out and tied his legs up with them.

He woke to his own screams, raging with pain in his stomach.

He sat up and arched his back, panting and perspiring, his heart pounding like a steam-hammer. His brain was trying to burst out. He gripped his hair in an effort to relieve the pressure inside his head, taking long deep breaths then emptying his lungs to the point of collapse. It worked to some extent. The devil inside him slowly began to let go, fraction by fraction control was coming back.

He lay flat on the floor again and tried to do press-ups. But he was like jelly. His co-ordination gone. He forced himself to keep trying. Small ones first, leaving his hips on the floor. One, then a rest; two, another rest; three, four, resting between each. Then starting again, now lifting the hips as well, punishing his body like old times until, cell by cell, his muscles began to respond and his brain to wake up.

Rose had done this! The needle. He had been drugged!

A vision of Sharon broke through to him. Had they got to her? No. What was he thinking? She was in London. They didn't know the address. She was safe.

His head was clanging like a tin drum, his stomach, a gas chamber. Worse was the anxiety grabbing him. He tried to stand in the darkness, but his knees wouldn't allow it. He had to get out! Get to Sharon.

Somehow, Jenny had dozed off. Shit! For how long? It was still dark, but by now it could be too late to change anything. It wouldn't matter which bed they were in. Both rooms would get it. A double barrel whammy!

She waited until first light before making her move. Darkness would give her more cover should anyone look out of a window, but she needed a bit of light to see where she was going. It would only take her seconds to get back inside and lock the door. That way no one would think the danger had come from inside the house. If all went well, she would be able to watch the panic unfold outside as dawn came.

With the shotgun securely tucked under her left arm and the breech open for safety, she unlocked the back door, leaving it ajar for a quick re-entry with the key in the lock.

Aware that her steps might be heard on the shingle path, she kept to the narrow grass verge at the side of it.

She had to be extra careful of her step. The grass hadn't been cut for weeks. She didn't want her feet getting snagged. To steel herself for what she was about to do, Jenny thought back to the lodge on the shores of Lake Naivasha, remembering what they had done and said to each other. They had been in raptures! It had been so long since something like that had happened for both of them. How could he suddenly change like he had? Mockingly! The pig! She was needed no more!

He had totally abused her! Fuck him!

Positioning herself directly under his bedroom window, she moved back a few paces from the building to give herself an easier target. In one sweeping movement she snapped the breech closed, raised the barrel and let loose in quick succession. First one then the other Grade I listed stone-framed windows shattered. The blasts and splintering glass created a premature dawn chorus as jackdaws and crows rose into the skies to the accompaniment of shrill screams from within one of the demolished windows.

These had come from Sharon as she leapt awake to the crashing sounds. 'What the fuck!' she yelled louder than the squawking flock rising outside, taking a moment to remember where she was.

Before bed last night, she had lowered the drapes around the huge four-poster to make it cozy, wishing Kim could have been there with her. The bed was more than big enough for the pair of them. What she hadn't been able to do was draw the heavy curtains over the windows. They hadn't budged with any of the tugging she'd been giving them, having not worked out that pull chords did that job. 'I will give that maid of mine a right mouthful in the morning!' she had fantasized gleefully. There had been no real reason to close them since the house was miles from anywhere. In consequence, there had been no buffer to the lead shot once through the glass.

Due to the upward angle Jenny Grant had let loose, most of the blast had ended up peppering the ceilings. There had been no danger of either occupant being hit unless they had been standing close to the window. Plaster had fallen everywhere; dust was choking both rooms. The initial impact had sent glass flying. But for the drapes around Sharon's four-poster, the covers might have suffered.

Ludlow, too, had not drawn his curtains, but he had not been so lucky. There were no fancy drapes around his bed. A fragment of flying glass had grazed him on the scalp. It was bleeding quite badly, but the wound was superficial. He pressed a wad of tissues on it to stem the flow. There were more urgent things to worry about.

Sharon had jumped out of bed on the side away from the gaping hole in the window. She made straight for the walk-in wardrobe, quickly shutting the door after her.

Seconds later, Ludlow was banging on the connecting door to the rooms shouting: 'Sharon! Are you OK? Sharon. Open the door!'

'I'm in the fucking cupboard and I ain't coming out until you tell me what the fuck's going on!' She shouted back, but the wall to wall hanging clothes soaked up the sound and he didn't hear her.

The next thing she knew, he was in her room, shouting. He must have come in by the main door. In passing, he had told Dmitri to check all the outside doors to the house were locked. 'Have the gun at the ready in case!'

'Sharon! Where are you?' He shouted again. Dust was thick in the air. Switching on the light didn't help. Where was she? Under the bed? She had to be in the room somewhere. Dmitri hadn't seen her leave.

Confirmation came.

'I'm in the wardrobe! What the fuck's going on?' She screamed again. 'It's that Peter, isn't it?' She had cast off the chiffon nightgown and started pulling clothes off the rails to find something easy to throw on case she had to make a run for it.

'I'm coming in,' he warned her at the same time as opening the door. She had just managed to get knickers on and one of her T-shirts. If Ludlow hadn't been in such a flustered state, he would have smiled at the irony. On the T-shirt in big letters was written *Life Sucks!*

The other thing that he found utterly incongruous in the dire circumstances was that, not only was Sharon still wearing the tear-drop necklace around her neck and the lop-sided earring, she had also filled all the remaining holes in her ears with a selection of Stephanie's studs and rings. It was a sight to behold. To complete the ludicrous picture was the accusing look she was giving him, a look he had often seen in that room in the distant past. An unabashed glare saying, 'So what, dick head?' She had plainly been sleeping with it all aboard.

He wasn't going to tell her it could not possibly be Tyler doing the shooting because he was locked up in the cellar. Rose would not have failed with that task. He'd been itching to get at Tyler since day one! Nevertheless, it needed checking pronto, just in case. A job for Karl.

'Peter's gone ape shit 'cos he thinks I've been screwing you?' Sharon screamed. That could only be what this was about, to her way of thinking.

Ludlow was saying nothing. It didn't seem to be the best time.

'How'd he get a fucking gun?' she yelped.

'I don't know,' Ludlow said, happy to ride with her misconception. 'I'm as mystified as you.' But not *too* mystified. The culprit could only be one other person. 'Stay here in the closet with the door shut until I can sort this out. We'll be away from here as soon as possible. Get dressed and be ready. You won't suffocate. It's well ventilated.'

'Not as much as it is out there with that fucking great hole in the window!' Sharon pointed out sarcastically, like the smart-arse she was.

'Don't worry. Tyler won't get to you.'

'Well, I *am* fucking worried! What the hell's going on between you two?'

Ludlow had not completely decided about that just yet. But whichever way it was done, it would be terminal!

Having heard the shots, Rose, Karl and Johann had come over from the barn. They'd seen the shattered windows. With hardly any glass in evidence on the ground, it seemed apparent the shots had come from outside the house.

Dmitri was in the entry hall having completed his check. 'Back door locked. Bolted now, also.' he reported. 'No-one get in from there. Front door double locked, too. See.'

As if to confirm this, Rose was just turning his key to get in.

Ludlow's first words were to Karl. 'Go check Tyler's still in the wine cellar.'

Then to Rose. 'You sure you took care of him?'

This was a blatant affront to Rose. He steamed up inside, answering sharply with his own question.

'What makes you think it could possibly have been Tyler out there?'

'Jealousy.'

'Oh Yeah? Even if the conning bastard could get to his feet, how would he have known the punk was here?' Rose pointed out, his umbrage glowing red. If jealousy was behind this, there was only one suspect! 'It can only be that prick teaser of yours!' he scoffed, not holding back with his sense of offence. 'Jenny fucking Grant!'

Karl came back in time to stop further bickering. Tyler was safe if not sound.

'OK,' Ludlow pronounced, already suspecting it had to be Jenny blasting the windows in. Still, he had got *jealousy* right. She must have guessed the girl had been brought here after he'd battled to get the address out of her. She would never have driven all the way out here on a whim having vowed never to set foot in the place again. Insult had changed that. 'Of course, you're right, Victor,' he admitted. But his decision was the same whoever the gunner. 'Listen up! We're out of here as soon as possible. Karl, keep watch in case Jenny shows herself. Johann, Dmitri, come with me.'

He took them up to the shotgun cabinet. As expected, one of the guns was missing. How the hell had Jenny managed to get in and out of the house without anyone hearing her? He gave it some thought and the conclusion he arrived at gave him some reassurance. She had been in the house with the gun, but had not come blasting her way into his room! That told him she hadn't completely lost it. She was pissed off, but she'd gone outside to announce her grievance, and it had a big 'Fuck you!' written all over it.

Jenny had retraced her steps quickly after letting loose. She didn't expect Ludlow or the girl would have been interested in looking out of the windows to see who the perpetrator had been, just in case another volley came. But the guys in the barn might well have been, so she hadn't hung about.

All in all, she was quite pleased with her little shock-horror show. She had surprised herself by not faltering. Her shoulder hurt a bit. But that was to be expected. It had been months since last using a shotgun. On that occasion she had missed everything! But then, flying clay targets were tiny by comparison to a brace of Grade One listed leaded windows!

She had entered the open back door and locked it at speed. Her idea was to hide herself until things settled. But first, she had the forethought to reload the shotgun to be ready for more shooting practice if needed. Right now, everyone would be running around like headless chickens outside. She was safe inside.

But was she? As she finished loading the cartridges, she heard footsteps charging through the kitchen.

With moments to spare, she dived into the pantry, pulling the door closed behind her. Shit! She should have remembered what that particular pantry was always used for. It stank! Too late. Shit again! She hadn't picked up the spent shells!

The footsteps pounded into the room. The back door was rattled and the bolts pulled across. Within seconds, whoever owned the feet had quickly gone.

Jenny breathed again.

If he could fight off one more spasm, he would survive. One more! That was all he asked.

Peter was still lying on the floor. He had tried to get to his feet several times but had to give up. Something was wrong with his balance. It was a terrifying feeling. The floor wouldn't keep still. It was like being on a conveyor belt that kept changing direction.

He tried again, this time stretching his arms out in the darkness, feeling for support. A wall came to his assistance. The drug had sent his mind tripping out of control, but sense was beginning to come back. Anxiety kept hitting him, and his concern about Sharon.

He kept forgetting she would be OK. She was in London. Safe.

Jenny had been standing in the pantry as rigid as a corpse. Only when the footsteps had gone, which to her relief meant the spent shells she hadn't picked up had not been spotted, did the vile smell in the pantry hit her with a vengeance. As she groped around for the door handle, something fell into her hair and started wriggling. She shrieked with horror, shaking her head in a frenzy only to set a thousand blue bottles buzzing and bombarding her. She lurched forward in a faint, banging her head on the door, certain she must have been heard.

A warm trickle ran down between her legs. She finally found the handle and threw the door open, not caring if she was discovered or not. But all was clear. She looked back with revulsion into the pantry. A row of pheasants, devoid of feathers, hung there running with maggots. The blue bottles had risen in a cloud and were breaking free. She quickly shut the door to keep as many of them in as possible, swatting ineffectually at the escapees. But it was too late for the stink, not helped now by the smell of her own urine. It was all too much. She couldn't stop the sobs.

'I won't go into detail,' Ludlow was telling Gerald Silver from his brick Motorola, 'but another trip to Africa has become necessary. How soon can the helicopter be at Compton Stud?'

Silver was answering the call from his bedside telephone. It took him a moment to put two and two together. One look at his watch told him things must be *very* urgent. It had just gone six. He gave the question some thought. 'Couple of hours at the earliest. It's parked at Battersea heliport. Depends how long it takes to raise the pilot.'

'OK. Give me an update on probable ETA when you've spoken to him. It might work better to take the Cessna to Elstree and pick the chopper up from there instead. Book me a seat on the first possible flight to Nairobi. It doesn't necessarily have to be BA from Heathrow. Any connection through Europe will do.'

'What's happened, Edward?' Silver asked, he thought he had heard the last of this sort of panic from Ludlow. 'How bad is it?'

'All in hand. Ring me when the chopper's ready to take off. By then I should know where best to send it.' That was all Silver needed to know for now.

Ludlow ended his call to Gerald Silver and brought everyone together at the front of the house. 'OK, keep alert, but I don't think there'll be any further need for guns.' At least, he hoped not. 'Rose got it in one. It has to be Jenny Grant who's done this.' He waved briefly at the shattered windows. 'Her grievance is against me and *only* me, and I don't think she'll cause any more trouble. It seems she's already hot-footed it. There's no sign of her jeep which is good news.' Good news for now but not forever, he suspected. That aggravation needed sorting out permanently. Something to be done from a distance, preferably.

Rose was about to say something, but Ludlow held up a hand to stop him and snapped: 'Shut it, Rose!' This caused a few smothered grins from the other three. They had often wanted to say exactly that to the *die Fotze*.

'Get the cars ready, but no fingers on triggers. If Grant should suddenly reappear, don't confront her. I'll deal with her. But let's hope that doesn't happen. She's made her point. OK. I'll be with the girl until all's ready to leave. We'll be going to the airstrip in convoy,' he explained.

'Victor, Karl and the girl will be flying with me. Where to I'm not exactly sure just yet. Probably Elstree. I'm waiting on Silver about that.' Addressing Johann and Dmitri, he went on, 'Once we're away, you two come back here and sort those windows out. Don't talk to the press if any turn up at the gates. Karl, you'll be taking the girl onward to her place in London or Septon, wherever she wants. Sit tight with her until you hear from Silver. I'll get him to find a better place for her. Don't let her out of your sight and keep her happy. Butter her up.' Ludlow turned to Rose. 'You'll fly directly back, Victor, to continue dealing with Tyler.' Ludlow wanted to be five thousand miles away when that endgame finally took place, reading such headlines as: 'Death by Drug Overdose. British Inventor suffers The Trappings of Sudden Fame and Fortune'. Something like that would put a smile back on his face.

Chapter Forty One

Despite the ventilation in the walk-in wardrobe, Sharon was getting hot and sweaty. It didn't help that she was now laden with enough of Stephanie's clothes for winter on the ski slopes, not mid-summer. She was wearing tights under a pair of leather slacks that had the sheen and feel of velvet. She bent her legs a few times, making sure she could run in them if she had to. They fitted perfectly. Over her *Life Sucks* T-shirt, she had on a loose silk bodice. Next, a Laura Ashley floral blouse, something she would never before have thought of wearing. Then came the softest woollen cardigan she had ever touched, purple in colour. On top of all this was a leopard skin jacket. A real one!

None of the clothes matched, which didn't bother her at all. She was just trying to pile on as much good stuff as possible. She looked a sight, but it was the sort of eye-catching miss-match of a sight she liked. This could be all the rage in Bond Street before long, she told herself. Posh punk!

She had stuffed a trendy carpet bag with as much paste jewelry as it would carry. Fake or not, some of it looked to be worth a fortune. There was loads more, but it would have needed a wheelbarrow to shift it all!

Coming out into the bedroom, she could hear Ludlow ordering people about as though he had an army out there! Just as well with Peter running wild with a shotgun!

As she was considering this, Ludlow came into the room and took the wind from her sails.

'You can relax now. It wasn't your lover-boy going gun crazy. It was my secretary getting the wrong end of the stick.'

Taken aback but relieved that Peter hadn't been the culprit, she imagined things wouldn't have been much different if Ludlow's lover-girl had caught them at it. How glad she was to have locked the adjoining door last night in case he had chanced coming in and jumping on her.

'It didn't much sound like it!' Sharon said. Then pointed out, cockily. 'And I'd say she wasn't too far off from the truth.'

He ignored the suggestive look she was giving him.

'OK. We're almost set to get away from here. Get yourself ready. You're coming with us.'

'Too right, I am. I in't staying here with a jealous woman gunning for me! I'll tell you that for nothing! I'd rather be having Peter to deal with! Anyway, where the fuck is he while all this is going on?'

'You're going to have to forget about him, Sharon. It's OK. You'll be taken care of. I'll see you get everything he promised you. And more. All in good time. First, we'll be making a short flight.

'What! Where we going?'

'Just away from here as quickly as possible. Then we'll see what's what. We'll get you set up in a new place. Better than Septon. Karl will be looking after you for a while until things are sorted. You get on with him OK, don't you?'

Not as much as Kim, she was thinking. It was all a bit too much to take in. Getting away from this place sounded about right, though! But in a plane?

Ludlow hadn't stopped: 'What I'll be asking you to do in return is to keep your mouth shut about all that's been going on here. Everything! You understand? That's the way it's got to be. Otherwise no-can-do. Come good with that, and I'll have you prancing about on catwalks before you know it, if that's what you really want. Or posing in that shop on the Kings Road you've been dreaming about.'

She looked at him blankly. What the fuck was going on?

The fight had gone from Jenny Grant. She was sitting in a corner of the kitchen, with her back to the outside wall, the shotgun propped up beside her. If anyone had barged in through the door, she wouldn't have moved. She was at her lowest ebb, her feelings all over the place. The whole episode had sucked her dry. No regrets, though. Being used and abused as she had been, would do that to anyone. Yes, she was feeling sorry for herself, but not suicidal. No-one could push her that far. She was worth more than that. There was still plenty going for her. That was a given. But she wouldn't simply disappear quietly from his life without recompense. Oh no! It wouldn't be that easy for him. She knew a thing or two about Sir Edward Ludlow! No curling up and going quietly!

Hurt was rising in her again.

When Karl had been sent down to the cellar to check on Tyler, he had feared the worst, knowing what Rose had been aching to do to him for so long. But Tyler was conscious. His eyes screwed up as the bright light went on. He covered them with a hand. The other he flayed about, as if trying to ward off impending attack. 'Peter,' Karl said, grabbing the free hand to put a bottle of water into it. 'Drink water. Stay cool. Sharon OK.' He couldn't tell if he was getting through. Peter didn't open his eyes. 'Hear me. I come back soon with something to help. Don't sleep. Try exercise.' Karl grabbed one of Peter's legs and bent it in demonstration.

The one thing Peter took note of was that Sharon was OK. Of course she was OK. She was in London. Away from any of this.

All areas immediately around the Stud where Jenny could possibly have been hiding were given the all-clear. The long driveway from the house to the main gate had been thoroughly checked out by Johann and Dmitri. There was no sign of Jenny or her car. But no-one had thought of going beyond the gates of the perimeter wall to search around the stable area, so Jenny's pink jeep had not been spotted.

That was, it hadn't been spotted by any of Ludlow's men.

But the man with a patch over his left eye had.

It had taken Jimbo the cost of those two pints of 5X and twenty minutes of idle chatter to glean the necessary information from Old Pikey about how to get to Compton Stud. The obvious choice was via the service road that led to the stables complex with access through perimeter wall gates to the main house a hundred or so yards beyond. Jimbo couldn't see there being a problem getting into the property from there over a wall or gates. But as it happened, Jenny had entered by the gates the night before using keys from her hefty bunch and had felt it unnecessary to lock them after her.

Jimbo had reached the stables but had not gone as far as the perimeter gates yet to discover this fillip of good fortune. He had chanced upon another unexpected bonus: the jeep. Pink or not, it was impossible to miss the way it was parked just off the service road behind one of the stable buildings. Having a handy set of wheels might prove to be very useful should a quick getaway be needed. Instinctively, he felt the bonnet. Cold. It was locked and there were no keys in it, but he knew he could get it to start if the battery wasn't dead. The bodywork was as clean as a whistle, so it couldn't have been there too long even though it seemed to have been dumped rather than parked.

Without a second thought, he set about getting into it.

Ludlow was on the phone, at the same time smiling at Sharon in her not quite *a la mode* garb. Somehow, Stephanie's silk-lined leopard skin jacket suited her.

He had mentioned Africa several times, but she knew that couldn't involve her. She had no passport, so she couldn't be flying any further than this Elstree place he was talking about, wherever that was. All she was concerned about right now was keeping the carpet bag glued to her. That was hers now. She wasn't going anywhere without it. If nothing else came out of all the promises and bullshit these two fuckers had been coming out with, she wouldn't have done too badly. The jewelry alone would go a long way to sorting herself out if the plug was about to be pulled from under her. Who could she really trust? Just herself and Kim. Always had been. What had that dope Peter been thinking, trying to pull that stunt of his? She'd forgive him. She knew that. In time she would get to see the funny side of it. But trying to pass her off as Stephanie's actual daughter! What a plonker! What had really shocked her last night, though, was the way she had felt when she'd suddenly thought he was dead. That had certainly slapped her round the face. He obviously meant more to her than she had realised. It had been good, the weeks together after Manchester. And no question, he had saved her by bringing her south and looking after her. Even if, so it seemed, he had done it as a way of getting at Ludlow's millions. Who'd have thought it? Devious little snot! 'Listen to me, pointing fingers!' she sniggered. 'I've been cashing in on Stephanie's looks for years. A bit different, though, I suppose, what he's been up to.' So where in hell *was* Peter bloody Tyler, anyway, while all this stuff had been going on? Why had he not shown his face? At least it was good to know it wasn't him taking pop shots at her. But this game of his she'd gone along with had left one very pissed-off woman out there somewhere who might still be gunning for her.

Rose signalled that the cars were at the ready, lined up bumper to bumper. Sharon was itching to get into the Roller. As she made a move toward it, Rose grabbed her. 'Not you, filth!' he said, pushing her back into the lobby. 'Wait till you're told to move.'

'Fuck you, too, pig-brain!' was what he got in return.

Ludlow was in the hallway on his Motorola to Gerald Silver. The helicopter was not yet ready to leave Battersea, so it would be going to Elstree and would be there by the time the Cessna arrived. A decision of where to proceed from there was still pending. Heathrow, most likely for Ludlow. Paddington for Sharon and Karl, or Septon? Victor would be heading straight back to Compton Stud.

With the final 'all clear', the group started to get into the cars. Sharon had so much bounty stashed in the carpet bag she could hardly lift it. Another first to gee up Kim, she was thinking as she climbed into the back of the Rolls Royce. The fact that she going to spend the journey on the floor with her head covered as she had done in the Jaguar, wouldn't necessarily be mentioned when the time came.

Visions of Sharon kept breaking through to Peter. His concerns for her would not leave him. Time and again he reminded himself she would be all right. She was in London. Safe.

His spasms of anxiety would not go away. His head was clanging like a tin drum again. But he would get through this.

Staring into the darkness, he was suddenly blinded by the light of the bulb in his dank cell.

Karl had come back. This time with more to offer. 'Take one with water now,' he urged, giving Tyler three pills. 'About Four hours, take another. If not feel better after four hours more, take last one. Is enough. Keep key to the door. Lock from inside. Soon as you feeling better go to Septon. Rose coming back to drug you more. They want kill you. Take motorbike. Is all ready by the barn. Turn key and starts. Easy rider! Go Septon, OK? Understand? Septon? I bring Sharon when I can. Ludlow flying away.'

Before Peter could take all this in and ask for clarification, Karl had gone.

Jenny came to life. She could hear vehicles starting up. She ran through to the kitchen window looking out onto the turning circle. Doors were slamming! And there was the girl! Sliding into the back of the Rolls Royce, looking more and more like Stephanie Star now dressed in her famous leopard skin coat! The mismatch of clothes beneath it were hidden. Anger rose in her again as the three cars sent gravel flying in their haste to depart. This was too much. Rage overtook anger. She couldn't let Ludlow get away with this.

She made her move.

Peter downed one of the pills with water, trying to unravel all that Karl had been telling him. Don't go to sleep. Rose was going to kill him! As if by second nature to help make him think, Peter started doing press-ups. Proper ones. His muscles were slowly coming to life, before long dragging his brain to life with them. Whatever was in that pill, it was doing a good job. Karl had said something about bringing Sharon to Septon. She was safe in Paddington. So why move her? Perhaps because he could get to Septon on the motorbike more safely? That made sense. But Septon must wait. More important right now was to stop Ludlow flying off, stop him getting away with this. That must not be allowed to happen. Things had to be settled once and for all. No more hiding the truth. Ludlow was not going to run away from any of this! Even if it meant Sharon's true identity would be outed.

Jenny had charged out of the building, shotgun at the ready to send a final blast at the convoy as it sped off, but she was too late. By the time she had managed to get to the front of the house, the cars had gone. But all was not lost. She knew the only place they could be heading; the airstrip! Her mind was set. She still had a chance to get at him there. And both barrels were loaded! No time to lose. She made for her jeep, rage bubbling up inside her.

She was so breathless by the time she got through to the back of the stables, she thought she was seeing things. Had she left the jeep's doors open like that? Both of them? She had no time to consider the answer. An arm went round her throat, the shotgun snatched from her grasp.

'Drive!' an intimidating voice breathed into her ear. There was no arguing. The barrels were pressing into her throat.

Jenny was shaking so much, she kept stalling the jeep. It was sitting on muddy ground and the tyres wouldn't bite. When she eventually got it out onto the track, her ears pricked up to the sound of a motorbike speeding off.

'Go!' Jimbo commanded.

Sharon's first experience in the back of a Rolls-Royce fell short of her dreams, having spent the short trip from Compton Stud flat down out of sight as she had been in the Jaguar with Karl. This had been a shorter trip, but frantic by comparison. As before, there had been no paparazzi in evidence at the gates, and to Ludlow's relief, no Jenny Grant either!

As soon as the cars had screeched to a halt alongside the only hangar still in use, Rose leapt out like a wildcat and started waving urgently at the others to get a move on.

Between them, Dmitri and Johann opened the hangar doors while Karl set about preparing the Cessna to be rolled out.

Still in the Rolls Royce, Ludlow was ordering people about on the car-phone as if his life depended on it. 'God, you're a bossy fucker!' Sharon muttered, not knowing if he heard her or not.

At the edge of the airfield, not leaving the cover of the trees, Peter had made it to his workshop. There was only one way he could think of stopping Ludlow without being gunned down first: the Sopwith Pup. There was a slight hump on the runway that partially hindered the view of the workshop from where Ludlow's convoy had parked by the hangars at the far end. This gave Peter some useful cover.

While final preparations for departure were going on at that end of the airstrip, Peter kept his head low taking full advantage of the gentle rise in the middle of the runway as he wheeled out his secret weapon. The heeby-jeebies that had been strangling his mind had gone thanks to Karl once again coming to his rescue in his hour of need, this time with the magic pills.

Peter knew if he kept his head down and stayed low, he would be hard to see him. Creeping out to the runway, he lined up the Sopwith Pup and primed the engine.

At the far end, Rose was signalling to his boss that the Cessna was ready for him.

'Stay put for now. I've got some technical stuff to see to first.' Ludlow told Sharon, getting out of the Roller with a sign to Rose to be sure she did just that.

When Rose got to the car, Sharon had the cellphone in her hands. 'Put that down, you conning bitch!' Rose barked.

'Fuck off, pig-brain!' Sharon spat back. 'I wasn't going to use it.' Not yet anyway, she was thinking, She would love to tell Kim what was going on when she got a chance.

Peter's nerves were hanging in shreds. He had to get the timing dead right! Too soon and the Pup's bulky double wings might be seen. Too late, and the Cessna might have lifted off. The idea was to put it out of action on the tarmac. Hitting the undercarriage would be enough. If the props got entangled in the air, it would be more like wipe-out. But so be it!

Ludlow had checked all was in order for takeoff. He waved to Rose who cocked a thumb at Sharon. 'OK, filth, move that worn-out arse of yours!'

'More life in my arse than your *tongue*!' she snapped back, always one to have the last word. 'With all the *arse-licking* you do!'

She slid through the gap behind Rose's seat, putting the collar of the fur coat up around her neck. Ludlow gave her a strange look. Nothing like last night's come-on. More like suggesting he was now lumbered with her. Serves him right. His own fault. She was lumbered, too. Still, it wasn't all bad, was it? She had the carpet bag well stuffed with jewellery. Kim wouldn't believe it. This was life in the fast lane, she bragged to herself, now feeling a whole lot safer to be getting away from gun-toting Annie Oakley! A flutter went through her at the thought of the shattered windows.

Karl had not got aboard yet. He was running round the plane checking the flaps were operating properly.

Peter couldn't see exactly what was going on with the Cessna. There still seemed to be a lot of activity going on around it, but he sensed the time was right to get the Pup up and running on its maiden flight. If all went to plan, it would be its final one as well.

There were a few seconds of panic, but then, on the third attempt, the propeller span to life with an angry buzz sending the Pup lurching forward before suddenly stalling. 'Shit!' he hissed. He tried to start it again. Nothing! Shit! Shit! Then at last, it fired. His relief was electric, but short-lived. There was an unanticipated weakness in the controls that was about to be cruelly demonstrated. The Pup refused to sit as if waiting for a take-off slot! Even with the throttle pulled right back the Pup began to move forward, defiantly gathering momentum. There was no way of stopping it short of cutting the engine, and the risk of doing that was too great given the trouble he'd had firing it up.

But it was getting so far ahead he might have to. Over the rise, the Cessna had not moved. Bodies were still busying around it. The Pup was bound to be seen if it went much further.

Another 50 yards perhaps could be risked. After that it would be in plain view. It stood off the ground like a jumbo with those double wings.

In desperation, he ran to catch it up ready to stop and start it again if he had to. He knew by then he would himself be in full view and all his efforts could have been in vain!

But it didn't come to that. Before he had caught up with the Pup, Jenny Grant's pink jeep had suddenly come skidding to a halt by the Cessna. Peter was stopped in his tracks. Whatever was happening down there, he could now let the Pup keep to its course? All eyes had turned to the jeep!

He was about to wind up the Pup's engine to send it more urgently on its Kamakase mission, when a gun shot rang out across the field and he threw himself flat on the ground. Had he been spotted? Then came two more shots. But not for him. Crashing sounds resounded across the airfield, accompanied by yelling and screaming. Mayhem was breaking out around the Cessna.

He didn't know it, but the most terrifying screams had come from Sharon. The pink jeep had appeared from nowhere, but it wasn't Jenny Grant leaping out. Unbelievably, it was Jimbo! There could be no mistaking that evil prick, even with a black patch over his left eye! She was in absolute horror. He was holding a shotgun!

In an instant, all hell broke loose. Jimbo had the shotgun to his shoulder, his one eye looking along the barrels seeking Sharon. She let out another terrifying scream, tearing at the fur of her coat in a desperate effort to undo the seat belt and throw herself down. But it wouldn't release. Instead, she lent sideways hiding as much of herself as possible behind Rose.

The blast shattered the windscreen throwing Rose backward like a dummy with one leg hanging out of the door he had been trying to escape through. The side of his head had taken the full blast, sending a shower of blood into the fur of Sharon's coat as she ducked behind him.

She continued to struggle with the seat belt, not daring to look up for fear Jimbo had not given up getting at her. She was right, but he could only see her wriggling shoulder under the bloodied fur coat. He needed to move round the Cessna to get a clearer view of his target. However, the delay in doing so was his downfall. Ludlow had finally been shocked into action. For a few seconds, his mind had gone into lockdown. He had seen Peter Tyler in the distance, chasing his Sopwith Pup! Impossible? Far, far, worse, the pink jeep had suddenly come skidding to a halt not yards away and a gun-wielding one-eyed monster had emerged letting rip through the windscreen! All within seconds.

Finally freeing the seatbelt, Sharon threw herself to the floor of the cabin. As Jimbo came round to the side of the Cessna to get a better view of her, Ludlow had come to life. He drew his revolver, leaned over Rose's body and fired through the open door. Jimbo had seen the shot coming and reacted simultaneously, sending shotgun pellets sinking into Ludlow's neck and shoulder. But he was milliseconds too late. Ludlow had already pulled the trigger and his single shot was even more on target. Jimbo dropped like a stone with a bullet-hole in the centre of his forehead, dead before hitting the ground. Sharon was whimpering. Something had hit her on the head. She went berserk, thinking she had been shot. But the flying lead had gone over her head. The hefty brick cell phone had not.

The smell of smoke was burning her nostrils. Without thought of what might be waiting for her, she cast off the bloodied fur coat and squeezed out from behind Rose's seat to freedom to the sickening sounds coming from Ludlow's throat. Smoke meant fire and no-way was she going to be cremated! She ran and ran without looking back until she was under cover of the woods. With no idea where she was heading or what she was going to do, her only thought was to get as far away as possible from the madness.

Jenny Grant hadn't moved. She had witnessed the whole debacle sitting in a state of shock, screaming non-stop, sobbing hysterically.

Karl, Johann and Dmitri had not been able to do anything to stop the raging madman who had jumped from the pink jeep. It had all happened in seconds. Their weapons were where they had been told to leave them in the cars. Only when the gunning had stopped did Karl spot the charging Sopwith Pup coming up the runway with its obvious target. This could only be Tyler's doing! What on earth was the man thinking? Hadn't he understood that Sharon was about to fly off with Ludlow and right now was strapped in the Cessna? Karl had been too occupied with the carnage to notice Sharon had cut loose and done a runner.

He leapt into the Range Rover intent on preventing even more destruction. Any sort of collision might send both aircraft up in flames! The chunky four-wheeler could take on a model biplane any day. As it swerved onto the runway, Peter's heart sank. He knew his plan had failed. Seconds later, his flying bomb disintegrated as the Range Rover's heavy metal caught it side-on, sending up a flash of flames. As he ran closer, only then did Peter see the Cessna's shattered windscreen and a bloodied Ludlow being lifted from its cockpit by Johann and Dmitri. His plan might have failed, but someone else's had not! Closer still and he was dumb struck! What in hell's name was going on? Realisation hit Peter like a mallet. He would have recognized that man from a mile off! There on the tarmac lay Jimbo, eye-patch all a-squish, revealing a gaping eye socket, dead as dead could be.

Karl had seen Peter but first he had to get Sharon out of the Cessna. Smoke was billowing from it and that was not good.

He pulled the Range Rover up alongside Johann and Dmitri who had carefully lifted Ludlow clear.

'How bad is he?' Karl asked briefly in passing, anxious to get to Sharon.

'Bad!' one of them declared.

'Rose?'

'Dead. Very.'

Only then did he sense something was wrong. Sharon was never this quiet! He couldn't see her. Did she still have her head down?

'Schiesen!' he breathed, seeing the empty seat, 'Wo geht Sharon?'

The other men shrugged blamelessly. Neither had the slightest idea.

There was a whoosh as the Cessna's engine threw out flames! Karl jumped back smartly. No smoke without fire.

'Call Gerald Silver,' he yelled to Johann. 'Tell him to send chopper with medics. Quicker than Septon hospital.' He nodded toward Jenny, who was still in a heap of rigid hysteria in her pink jeep. 'Keep eye on her. Tell Silver what happened. He can deal with it. If polis come, shake head, say no understand. Say suddenly happened. Point to Jenny girl. I go get Tyler and look for girl. I see you maybe three, four days. See you when all calm down.'

With that, he jumped in the Jaguar and drove across the runway to where Peter was standing stock-still, looking wide-eyed at the smoldering Sopwith Pup.

No words were needed. Peter slid into the passenger seat while the Jaguar was still moving.

'You see where Sharon go?' Karl asked.

'Sharon?' Peter replied, confused. 'What do you mean? She's in London.'

'Not London. She was in Cessna with Ludlow. Is why I crashed Sop plane. Sorry. She gone somewhere.'

Peter had no answer.

'We find her.'

Chapter Forty Two

Dick Baker of the Daily Scan was fuming. 'Bloody typical, isn't it,' he complained to the photographer at the wheel of their press car as they raced along the M4. 'As soon as they say ease off and we stop doorstepping Compton Stud, I get a call from my tame air traffic controller telling me Ludlow is on a four-minute warning to leave his airstrip!' That hadn't been the worst of it for Baker. They had almost reached the motorway turn-off point to Marlsbury when another call came. 'Destination Elstree', was all it said. So, they had been told to turn round and head back towards London. 'We could have copped the whole bloody story!' Baker complained. 'What's the betting he's gone by the time we get to Elstree?' As a helicopter passed overhead going in the opposite direction, little did Baker know things had changed yet again for the worse; for him, as well as for Ludlow.

Sharon sat in the bushes by the roadside not daring to show herself just yet. A police car had gone flying past at the speed of sound. Then another. Minutes later an ambulance went by in the opposite direction with similar urgency. She guessed the news must be out. It had been like a war zone back there. Who could have believed it. Jimbo! Dead! Fucking good riddance!

She just *had* to tell Kim. And about everything else that had happened since Karl had collected her from the hotel in Paddington only yesterday!

Having got her breath back from escaping the madness at the airstrip, she felt ready to make use of her other bit of good fortune. Given the whack on the head it had given her, she felt she had a right to keep the cell phone, so she did. There was no room for it in the carpet bag and it was a pig to carry, but no matter. She wanted it. It could be a lifesaver.

She had watched moneybags Ludlow making calls with it, so she'd got the hang of it. More questionable was expecting Kim to be awake. It wasn't yet ten o'clock. Kim was staying with her parents, who would have gone to work by now, she reckoned. So, it was potluck if Kim was up and heard the phone. Sharon would love to see Kim's face when

417

she told her she was calling from a cell phone, let alone everything that had been going on. Wow! It would take some believing.

Despite the weak signal, Sharon's luck was in. Kim was still half asleep but sprang to life when she heard Sharon bellow out her standard wake-up call of; 'Hands off cocks, on with socks! Guess who's calling and where from?'

'Phoney!' Kim screamed with delight. The nickname quite appropriate whenever getting a phone call from Sharon. 'What's up?'

'You wouldn't believe it if I told you!' Sharon teased.

'Nor will you when I…' Kim couldn't get the rest out before Sharon charged on with her news, adopting what she thought was a posh voice for the occasion: 'I ham speaking to yoo on may Motoroller roving telephone having hesscaped an explodin' hairplane.'

'Leave off!' Kim yelped. She had her own news. 'Listen up….' But that was as far as she got before Sharon breathlessly went on with her story from the moment she had been picked up by Karl at the hotel Paddington to having not a few minutes ago sat down exhausted in the bushes.

Kim had felt it best to let Sharon rant on. She was obviously in an excited state and needed to get it off her chest.

'I could have killed that Peter for trying to pass me off as Stephanie's long-lost kid! The daft fucker! Faking a Will, for fuck's sake! I could have got twenty years for that, according to Mr. Moneybags. And I can tell you, that fucker would have had his hands all over me last night if I'd given him half a chance!'

'Have you done?' Kim asked, spotting her chance. 'If so, give that mouth of yours a rest for a minute, will yer? My turn.'

It worked. Sharon stopped yapping, but not before a final, 'Go on then. Tell me how exciting it's been in Manchester, and then pack your bags and get your arse back down here! I need you with me.'

'Already planned! But shut yer gob for minute and listen to me, alright? When did you last speak to your mum?' No answer came. 'Thought as much. You haven't for ages, have you? Well, your mum told my mum she's been trying to get hold of you about something important ever since your birthday. I didn't believe it could be true at first, but from all this stuff you've just been going on about, I think it bloody-well must be.'

Kim stopped, waiting for a reaction. Silence was all that came down the line.

'Well, according to my mum, your mum had something she'd been waiting for you to be twenty one before telling you.' Kim paused again, but Sharon said nothing. 'That's shut you up good and proper, hasn't it?'

Sharon finally broke her silence. She'd had enough of Kim's teasing.

'Come on, out with it, Burly. Knock me sideways.'

'Well, I will, since your mum can't, 'cos she doesn't where you are. So, anyway, you'd better hold on to your hat!'

'Stop the waffle!'

'Well, old lycra-pants Peter hasn't been trying to pass you off as Stephanie's *phoney* lookalike daughter as he wanted *you* to think he was. Wait for it! You are not a phoney, Sharon. You are the real thing! Stephanie Star's actual flesh and blood! Your mum was going to tell you she adopted you, that's she's not your real mum. Well, she is your real mum *really,* isn't she? But not *really really.* D'yer know what I'm saying? That Peter has known all along, s'why he's been looking after you on the quiet. Never mind all his kidding and pretending, he's been trying to get what you deserve out of Ludlow. You know, with that will you just told me about Ludlow showed you. That's exactly what your money-bags blood mum Stephanie had wanted for you.'

Kim was waiting for sparks to fly at the other end, but Sharon hardly managed to get 'You daft fucker' out before the battery died on them.

The Jaguar with Karl at the wheel and Peter in the passenger seat had driven up and down the stretch of road where they figured Sharon must eventually show herself. The woods were the only place she could logically emerge from, and she could not have made it through them to the road in the timeframe that had lapsed. She could be holding up somewhere getting her breath back; traumatized by her lucky escape?

There was a long straight stretch of road where they thought she was most likely to appear, so Karl pulled off the road with a good view along it. There was no point searching for her. Sooner or later, she would have to show herself.

Sharon was trying to get her head around what Kim had told her. Was she having her on, the silly cow, because of the fake Will? Would Kim pull a stunt like that? Then saying her mum wasn't her real mum. No. She wouldn't joke about something like that. But it was unreal to think any of that stuff was possible. All a bit too much to take in without that fuck Jimbo having suddenly turned up trying to top her!

She stood a little way back from the road. Quite a few cars had passed, so she hoped she would get lucky. It didn't matter where a lift took her once a car stopped. Just away from here for starters. If she hung about much longer, someone might come looking for her.

She stood at the edge of the trees ready to put her thumb out. Fast cars wouldn't be able to see her until the last second, but so be it. She didn't want to be too obvious in case another police car came along. Eventually, she got lucky. What first looked to be a public service bus appeared, coming belching to a stop in response to her outstretched thumb. But it was no ordinary bus on a regular route. It was about thirty years too late for that looking ready for the knackers' yard. Yet someone had taken great pains to paint a magnificent picture of Stonehenge all round its bodywork, filling its back end with a glorious sunrise over the Heel Stone. Every inch of the bus was covered by this extraordinary canvas including the windows, apart from those the Christ-like figure at the wheel was needed to drive by.

Before fully coming to a stop, the passenger door slid open. Without a word passing, she stepped aboard into a dark cave of smoke and incense, immediately falling somewhere soft between two friendly bodies. Within seconds she felt safe and comfortable. The only light she was aware of came twinkling through in ever changing patterns from a small stained-glass kaleidoscope fixed in the roof where perhaps an air vent had once been. 'Nice,' she thought.

When her eyes began to pick things out, she realised there must be at least a dozen other travellers aboard, but no fixed seats. Instead, were cushions and armchairs. These people really know how to travel, she was thinking.

A quarter of a mile back down the road, Karl saw what was happening. 'There's Sharon,' he said, nudging Peter, who had fallen asleep not long after they had parked up. 'She got on bus,' he said, pointing. 'We follow for a while until away from here. Obvious where is going.' Karl was astute enough to work out as they glid at a gentle pace behind the painted sunrise.

'Staying all summer, sister?' a male voice asked. Sharon guessed the question was intended for her, although she couldn't quite see who it came from.

'Maybe,' she answered, neither here nor there.

'Come far?'

'You could say that.'

'Ah, from up north?' someone else with a keen ear for dialect suggested.

'Dreamland, more like,' Sharon muttered.

Everyone seemed to like that notion. The laughter was genuine.

'I'm Daz.' The first voice said. 'What do people call you?'

Something about the dark reassuring atmosphere made Sharon reply: 'Glori...' before stopping herself.

'Well, brothers and sisters, let us welcome Glory of Dreamland to join us this coming mid-summer solstice.'

'Welcome, Glory of Dreamland!' echoed in the darkness.

'Thanks.' Sharon said awkwardly, thinking Glory wasn't such a bad name to have in the circumstances. She bet Daz was really called something like Denis. Still, what was in a name? It was who you really were that mattered.

For her right now, that needed some working out.

Karl and Peter were happy to purr along behind the hippie bus as it trundled toward Stonehenge. Best to leave things until it stopped before giving Sharon another shock, albeit more pleasant than the others she had recently suffered. The further from the airstrip for that the better.

The closer they got to their destination, the heavier the traffic became.

The old bus seemed to struggle with the slow pace, smoke belching from its exhaust at every gear change, so *Jesus* at the wheel pulled into a lay-by noticing it had the convenience of portable toilets. All aboard seemed to need their use but most preferred to pee in the adjoining field.

The woods had provided that purpose for Sharon, so she stayed on the bus, having purloined one of the armchairs. When Peter and Karl looked in at her through the open door, she was so relaxed that their sudden appearance merited no more than a restrained; 'Well, I'm fucked!'

Peter looked all-in. She thought she could see tears in his eyes. It was Karl who spoke, however, holding his hand out to her. 'Come, Sharon. Is safe now. We go to Septon. Peter has 'present' for you.'

Sharon rose willingly, changing her grip on the carpet bag that had never left her hands, heavier now. By regaling herself with two of the bulkier necklaces, she had finally made room for the Motorola to be squeezed into it,

Her temporary brothers and sisters were agog to see her climb into the gleaming Jaguar. 'My other lifesavers,' she explained, with a friendly wave goodbye.

In the Jaguar, Peter gave Sharon the Walkman with the cassette of Stephanie's conversation with the major loaded. No need for him to say anything. The tears in her eyes said it all as she listened. So, what Kim had been saying was all true.

'Have another present,' Karl announced when Sharon had finished listening to the cassette. 'Peter keep it for you. In glove box.'

'Not a bloody gun, is it?' Peter joked half-heartedly.

He would have been less gob-smacked if it *had* been a gun. It was a floppy-disc! *The floppy-disc!*

'You look after, Peter. Sharon might lose it. Like mother did. Useful in case Gerald Silver, how you say, try to pull fast one!'

'You sly foreign person, Karl!' Peter gaped, getting a sly foreign smile in return.

Sharon was in wonderland. She could be rich! She felt rich already. Very rich! But how rich did you have to be, for fuck's sake, to be happy? She had to get back to Kim right away.

'Have you got a spare battery for this thing, Karl,' she asked, catching his eye in the driving mirror, waving the dead Motorola. Karl was slightly bemused to see she had one. He passed his own to her instead,

'Don't kill battery. No spare,' he told her. 'Two minutes. Not life history.'

A familiar grunt came from Sharon.

'Get your arse to London!' she yelped as soon as Kim picked up. 'I know now, that stuff you were talking about. All true! I need you to keep me feet on the ground till I get used to this rich-bitch business. You can be my lady in waiting,' she joked. 'All legit! Two weeks 'oliday a year! Your first job is to find where my mum is so I can tell she's the one I love. My real mum. And you, Kim, have I got a present for you!? It keeps glaring at me in the driving mirror 'cos I'm using his phone. Come to think of it, I think it's my phone now, all-of-a-sudden.'

'Two minutes up, Sharon.'

'Just concentrate on the road, Karl, or I'll set Kim on you when she gets down here.'

'Where's Peter?' Kim asked.

'Sitting hup front in my limooosine with his bollocks in all of a twist, as usual, in those Lycra shorts of his!'

'Will you ever change, Phoney? You daft fucker.'

'You *rich* daft fucker, hif you do not mind, Burly!'

Printed in Great Britain
by Amazon